a novel

Freefall

a novel

Freefall

by
Linda Howell Betz

Editors: Donna Melillo, Kayte Middleton, Adam Tillinghast
Cover Design: Randy Hamilton / Hamilton Art Agency / hamiltonartagency.com
Interior Design: Rick Soldin / book-comp.com
Interior Layout: Michael Covington
Cover Photograph: Ted Haub / Haub Photographic Studio & Gallery
Cover Concept: Bruce Jonas
Cover Model: Jessica Betz

Indigo River Publishing
3 West Garden Street Ste. 352
Pensacola, FL 32502
www.indigoriverpublishing.com

Ordering Information:
Quantity sales: Special discounts are available on quantity purchases by corporations, associations, and others. For details, contact the publisher at the address above.

Orders by U.S. trade bookstores and wholesalers: Please contact the publisher at the address above.

Printed in the United States of America

Library of Congress Control Number: 2013930406

ISBN 978-0-9856033-6-6

First Edition

*With Indigo River Publishing, you can always expect great books,
strong voices, and meaningful messages.
Most importantly, you'll always find … words worth reading.*

This book is dedicated to those of you who have given your all, trusted, and loved, only to find disappointment, pain, and betrayal. Release the strength that only survivors possess. Pick yourself up, hold your head high, and take life back. You haven't gone too far—there is hope for the future.

Kansas City, Kansas
1947

part one

1

Laundry billowed and swayed gently on backyard clotheslines as a soft breeze whispered through the streets of Strawberry Hill. It was the perfect Indian summer day. Elizabeth Molech pulled bed linens from the line, stopping for a moment to smile and wave at her neighbor.

In an instant, the tranquility of the afternoon was shattered by shouting and the sound of a small mob invading the quiet neighborhood. Elizabeth stumbled, scattering clothespins in every direction. Her heart raced as those wretched boys thundered down her street. She rushed to the front of the house, waved her arms, and shrieked. "Don't you dare run through my flowers again! Go home—you don't belong here!"

The teenage boys bolted across the street to avoid another tongue-lashing. Without giving Elizabeth a second look, they continued to cut through yards, jump over flowerbeds, and race down the block.

"Hoodlums," Elizabeth muttered and stomped back to the clothesline.

As the boys ran, their open shirts trailed behind them like wings; they barely broke a sweat. It was 71 degrees, and the humidity was low. Laughing, stumbling, and feigning punches at one another, the boys reached their favorite corner. Each one casually leaned against the building and waited for a certain girl to walk by.

Moments later, a group of girls rounded the corner at the other end of the block. Estelle Prebilica and Kate Molech were in the lead.

Ricky Shannon smiled. God, she was beautiful. Every time he skipped school, he crept as close to her classroom as possible just to watch her. She always sat in the third desk by the window. Her dark brown eyes sparkled, and her lips parted when she smiled. He longed to see that thick chestnut hair tumble down her back. Even the uniform couldn't hide her tempting curves. After a little checking around, he knew her name: Estelle. It wouldn't be long before he met her, talked to her, held her. He almost groaned with anticipation.

Estelle noticed the boys and fixed her gaze straight ahead, pretending to ignore the long, slow whistle. With a hint of a smile, she sneaked a glance at Ricky Shannon and found herself staring into his sky-blue eyes. She blushed, and a rush of excitement coursed through her.

Passing by the boys, Estelle made sure her ponytail bounced and her hips swayed. The other girls in the group giggled and whispered—all except one, Kate Molech, Estelle's best friend.

"Estelle, stop it! That's Ricky Shannon. He's nothing but a hoodlum, and his family has a really bad reputation—so don't say a word." Kate couldn't imagine what her best friend was thinking, flirting with the likes of Ricky Shannon.

"Kate, he can't be *that* bad." She laughed as Kate fretted. When Ricky smiled at her, Estelle could barely think straight.

"You have no idea. Now let's go." Kate took Estelle by the arm and headed toward home.

The two girls were like night and day, yet they were practically inseparable. Estelle was beautiful and carefree. Kate, serious and opinionated, was a bit plain with straight brown hair and thick glasses.

Kate and Estelle grew up together in the quiet Croatian community known as Strawberry Hill. Nikola and Mary Prebilica moved to the neighborhood when Estelle was barely eighteen months old. The couple developed a quick and lasting friendship with their next door neighbors, Anton and Elizabeth Molech.

Kate was the responsible one; and from the time the girls were small, she felt it was her responsibility to watch over Estelle. In spite of Kate's efforts, Estelle was determined to meet Ricky Shannon. It would have been simpler had they all gone to the same school, but Estelle and her friends went to Bishop Ward; the group of boys went to public school at Wyandotte High School.

Estelle's thoughts raced as she headed down the walk to the back door of her house. If she could make up an excuse to stay after school and ditch Kate, then maybe Ricky would talk to her. "Kristina—that's it!" Kristina, one of Estelle's friends, always needed help with one subject or another. She was a bit awkward and not extremely popular—she would love a little attention. Estelle knew it would be easy to convince her to keep a secret.

Pleased with her neat little scheme, she couldn't imagine why she hadn't thought of it sooner. Estelle smiled as she opened the kitchen door.

"*Ako sa mas*?" Mary Prebilica bustled around the kitchen.

Estelle loved her mother's warm, cozy kitchen. The walls were the color of soft yellow wildflowers, and hand-embroidered curtains hung at each window. A matching curtain hid the shelves under the sink, and the countertops were wiped sparkling clean. The bowl of fresh fruit on the kitchen table made Estelle's mouth water.

"Momma, I thought we were supposed to speak English in this house." Estelle grabbed an apple and pretended to scold her mother.

Mary smiled. "How are you, dear, and how was your day?"

"School was okay, considering Sister Elizabeth was as grumpy as usual, but I enjoyed the walk home. How was your day?"

Mary shrugged. "Cooking, cleaning, a little visiting with the ladies." Estelle kissed her mother on the cheek. Mary's flawless skin and thick black hair certainly didn't reveal her age.

"Mmmm, what are you cooking?"

"We are having *sarma* tonight. Oh, please forgive me. We are having cabbage rolls and potato salad, and I made a wonderful wine cake," Mary bragged.

Estelle glanced at her mother and smiled. "Momma, you have flour on your face. Oh, I almost forgot—I'll be a little late tomorrow afternoon. I need to help Kristina with an assignment after school."

Her mother smiled. "Do you know how late you will be? I can meet you and walk home with you."

Estelle sighed. "I won't be long. I'll be fine Momma. I'm almost 15!"

The next day after school, Estelle had to convince Kate to walk home without her. "Why do you need to help Kristina with an assignment? She can get help from Sister Elizabeth." Kate squinted and looked directly into Estelle's eyes.

"Kate, there are just of couple of things she doesn't understand, and you know she's scared to death of Sister Elizabeth. Go on home. I'll stop by and see you later."

Estelle breathed a sigh of relief when Kate started home without her. She turned to Kristina, "Please don't tell anyone about this."

A few minutes later, Kristina took a different route home to avoid running into Kate. Estelle walked a block out of her way before going back to her normal route. Finally, she saw Ricky and his friends. "Oh, sweet Mother of God," she whispered. Her hands trembled. "What was I thinking?"

Estelle kept walking. Tiny beads of perspiration formed on her forehead. Her heart pounded as she forced herself to breathe slowly. Ricky Shannon smiled and walked toward her. She smiled back as the warmth of a deep blush spread from her throat to her face.

"Hi, Estelle." He knew her name! She felt giddy and lightheaded. Her mouth refused to work. "Cat got your tongue?" His easy laughter made her knees weak.

"Hi, Ricky," Estelle giggled and looked at her feet.

"Hey, you're blushing, little girl." She blushed even more. "Can I walk with you?"

"Yes, that would be nice," Estelle answered.

The two walked together for several blocks. Just when Estelle started to relax, she realized they were only a short distance from her house. "Thank you for walking with me, Ricky, but I need to go home now."

"I can walk you home."

"Um, my parents are pretty old-fashioned, and I'm not allowed to date. I would be in a lot of trouble if they saw me with a boy, so I should go on from here alone." Estelle fidgeted and looked at the ground.

Ricky stepped in front of her. "When can I see you again—tomorrow?"

Embarrassed and fumbling for words, she rambled, "I, I don't know. My friend Kate and I usually walk to and from school together, except in bad weather, and then her father takes us and picks us up. She's my best friend, but she tells her parents everything."

Ricky's sweet, lazy smile made her tingle. "I'll watch for you. When she's not with you, I'll walk with you. See you later." Ricky sauntered back to meet his buddies.

Estelle Prebilica was everything Ricky Shannon had ever wanted. She was beautiful, innocent, from a nice family, and she liked him— Ricky Shannon. She didn't make him feel like trash. He wanted her more than he'd ever wanted *anything*.

Estelle's feet barely touched the ground the rest of the way home. "How was your day, darling?"

"Wonderful, Momma, it was wonderful!" She kissed her mother on the cheek and danced across the kitchen.

"Aha, so you do like to Polka after all."

"Oh Momma, Polka is for old people."

"Were you able to help Kristina with her studies?"

"Yes, Momma." Estelle glided down the hall to her bedroom as Mary laughed.

After that first encounter with Ricky, Estelle frequently made excuses to walk to and from school alone. One morning Kate voiced her suspicion. "What is going on, Estelle? You've stayed after school three times in the last two weeks. You've gone to Kristina's house twice and left late for school two mornings this week. Are you mad at me?"

"No, Kate, I'm not mad at you. That is so childish." For a moment, Estelle felt guilty and looked away. "I do have other friends, you know. For heaven's sake, we're almost 15 years old. You need to spend time with other people now and then too."

Each time Estelle managed to get away from Kate, she and Ricky walked together, and every stolen moment left them wanting more. Estelle agonized over not inviting Ricky to celebrate her birthday, but there was simply no way she could bring him home to meet her parents. She spent as much time with him as possible, but the sporadic after-school walks just weren't enough.

"Hey, baby, can I see you tonight? I only get to be with you for a few minutes before and after school. And that doesn't happen every day."

Estelle didn't know what to say; her parents would never accept a boy who came from a family like Ricky's. "You know my parents won't let me go on a date. They think I'm too young."

Ricky's husky laughter made her blush. "Have they looked at you lately?"

"Ricky, stop it, you're embarrassing me." Her face was crimson. "I can't tonight, but I'll think of something. I have to get home now."

The next week at school, Estelle overheard a conversation that provided the perfect opportunity to spend more time with Ricky. She stopped Kristina in the hallway. "Kristina, I heard your sister Anna and her husband are taking you to Fairyland Park this weekend."

"Yes, we're going Saturday."

"Do you think they'd mind if I tag along? You and I could have a great time. I'll pay my own way. Please, talk to them and let me know."

Kristina enjoyed all the new attention. "Sure, Estelle, they're coming over for dinner tonight."

The next day at school, Kristina met Estelle in the hallway. "My sister said it would be fine for you to come with us on Saturday. She knows I'll have more fun if someone my own age is there."

"Thank you. Oh, Kristina, I'm so excited!"

"My sister has taken me twice," Kristina bragged.

"Well, my parents would never go to an amusement park. You know they'll want to talk to your mom."

"Sure, that's okay. See you tomorrow." Kristina headed home.

Mary wasn't in the kitchen when Estelle came home that afternoon. "Momma, where are you?" Estelle walked through the house to the living room. Mary was sleeping on the couch with her feet resting on the footstool. Estelle had never seen her mother sleeping in the afternoon. Mary's face was pale. "Momma, are you all right?"

Mary sat up with a start. "Oh Estelle, what time is it? I only meant to sit down for a few minutes." She stood up and then sat back down quickly; her lips turned almost white. "Goodness, I stood up too fast. Let me sit here for just a moment." Mary patted her hair and then stood up slowly. "There. I am fine. I didn't sleep well last night, and I'm a little tired today. Don't worry; dinner will be ready on time." Mary headed for the kitchen.

"I'm not worried about dinner, Momma. I'm worried about you. It scared me when I saw you so still and pale."

"Estelle, I was just tired. You can help me. Please go take the laundry off the line. I'll be in the kitchen. Go on."

Estelle ran out the back door to the clothesline. A strong breeze whipped the sheets against her legs as she pulled them from the line. She nuzzled her face against the sheets, breathing in the fresh, clean scent of laundry that had dried in the sun.

Later, Estelle waited for the right moment to talk to her mother. "Momma, Kristina Harvey is going to Fairyland Park on Saturday with her sister Anna and her brother-in-law John, and their two little girls. She's invited me to go. It will be so much fun, and there is a roller coaster there. I really want to go. Please, talk to Poppa," Estelle begged.

"It is Thursday already. There is not much time to plan. I don't know …" Mary answered.

"Momma, I can use my allowance, so there is nothing to plan. We're going to have a picnic lunch and stay until a little after dark. You can call Mrs. Harvey. Please?" Estelle pouted.

"All right, all right, I will speak with Mrs. Harvey and then talk to Poppa tonight."

Estelle hugged her mother and kissed her on the cheek. "Thank you, Momma."

Mary pointed her finger at her daughter. "Poppa has not said yes yet."

That evening, Nick walked home from the tailor shop tired as usual. Estelle met her father in the yard. "Poppa, did you have a good day?"

"Yes, my princess, did you?" Nick put his arm around Estelle's shoulder as they walked toward the house.

"I did," Estelle paused, "but I'm worried about Momma. When I came home today, she was sleeping on the couch, and she was dizzy when she stood up."

A worried look crossed Nick's face. "I'll talk to her tonight. She works very hard taking care of us. Sometimes she doesn't sleep well, so I'm sure she was just tired. Don't you worry, Momma is fine. Let's go see what wonderful things she has prepared for our dinner tonight."

Later that night, Mary approached Nick about the trip to Fairyland.

"What is this Fairyland? Is it a decent place for a young lady? And it is over in Missouri?" Nick worried.

"It is in Kansas City, dear." Mary patted Nick's arm. "Mr. and Mrs. Harvey's oldest daughter Anna and her husband are taking Kristina and their little ones. There are rides there—roller coasters for heaven's sake. We would never do such things. Estelle will have fun, and Anna will watch over her. We should let her go, Nick."

Nick sighed. "I suppose you're right. She is growing up, isn't she? I just want her to be safe. Now, my sweet Mary, what is this about you sleeping in the afternoon and looking pale?"

"Oh, Nick, Estelle told you. I was tired and sat down for a few minutes. I drifted off to sleep. When Estelle came in, I stood up too fast and had to sit back down for a minute. It was nothing."

"Mary, I know better than that. You have been tired many times lately. You have pain that keeps you awake at night. Why can't we just make an appointment with the doctor?"

"I am not going to the doctor. You can't trust them!"

"Mary, that is foolish. They helped me when I had a heart attack."

"They didn't help my friend Anna. She went to the doctor, and then to the hospital," Mary's voice grew louder, and she pointed her finger at Nick, "and then to the cemetery!"

"She was sick for a long time—and like you, she was stubborn and wouldn't go to the doctor until it was too late." Nick was practically shouting.

"I am not going. Now don't talk to me about this again!" Mary stomped to their bedroom and slammed the door.

Estelle didn't want to eavesdrop, but her parents' conversation made her nervous. Her mother had always been strong and healthy, and Estelle couldn't stand for her to be sick. Her eyes grew heavy, and her thoughts drifted in another direction—Ricky. On Saturday she would go to Fairyland to meet him. Sleep finally overtook her, and that night, she dreamed of laughing with Ricky and holding hands.

The next morning, Estelle wasn't ready when Kate stopped by to walk to school. "Late again? My word, Estelle, I think you are getting lazy."

"Oh hush, Kate. I'll be there on time. Now go on," Estelle shooed her friend out the door.

Estelle met Ricky as she walked to school alone. "Your little friend stomped by a few minutes ago."

Estelle was breathless with excitement. "Oh, don't worry about her; she'll be okay. Guess what? I have the most wonderful plan! I'm going to Fairyland Park tomorrow with Kristina Harvey and her sister. Our parents aren't going. Can you find a way to get there?"

A big grin spread across Ricky's face. "Sure, baby. Dominic's got a car, and I can get him to take me. Meet me at the roller coaster at 6:00—alone."

On Friday night, Estelle lay awake for hours. The next morning, it seemed as if she'd only slept a few moments. She did all of her chores without being asked and made sure her room was spotless.

It took forever to decide what to wear. Estelle wasn't allowed to wear trousers or the cute little above-the-knee outfits. Finally she chose a yellow floral dress, tailored to accentuate her tiny waist. The skirt fell just below her knees. Pleased with the way she looked, she pulled her long, wavy hair back with a pale yellow ribbon. It was useless to apply the rouge that was hidden in her drawer; her mother would just make her wash it off.

At last, it was time to go. "Yes, Momma, I have my money. I promise I won't go to the lady's room alone, and I won't ride the roller coaster right after I eat. Kristina will be with me. I'll be fine. Momma and Poppa, they're here. I love you. " She hugged her parents and ran out the door.

Estelle trembled with excitement as the car pulled into Fairyland's crowded parking lot. There were so many people, and somewhere Ricky watched and waited for her.

"Oh, Kristina, this is wonderful! Let's eat and get started."

After a picnic lunch, the girls were ready to have some fun. "Kristina, Estelle, I know you don't want to tag along with the old folks and the little ones. So, if you promise to stay together, you can go on. Just meet us at the gate at 7:30." Anna was busy washing her daughters' hands and faces. "Don't talk to any strangers."

"Great. We'll stay together and meet you on time. I promise," Kristina answered.

Estelle smelled hot buttery popcorn as they entered the gate. Children carried fluffy pink cotton candy on white paper cones. Music floated through the air from every direction. She heard laughter and squeals of delight as the roller coaster cars dipped down steep tracks.

That evening after riding the roller coaster three times, Kristina was sick to her stomach. "Estelle, I can't ride the roller coaster again. I'm dizzy, and my stomach hurts." Her face was pasty.

"You shouldn't have gobbled down all those cookies and cotton candy." Estelle pretended to be irritated.

"You bought it for me, and I told you I wasn't hungry."

"Why don't you wait for me on that bench? I can ride the roller coaster and a couple of other rides again while you let your stomach settle. Then, we can meet Anna and John on time."

"But Estelle, I told my sister we would stay together."

"Kristina, Anna will never know."

Kristina was miserable and easily convinced. "Okay, I'll wait here." Estelle hurried toward the roller coaster.

"Baby, over here." Ricky was waiting at the roller coaster, just as he promised. "You look gorgeous tonight."

"Thank you." Estelle's face was flushed with excitement. "I can't believe we did it. We have about an hour. Kristina is sick and resting on a bench, but we have to meet her sister at the gate at 7:30."

Ricky smiled. "Okay, let's go."

He took her hand and led her to a deserted area behind the rides. They sat on a wooden crate covered with Ricky's jacket. Estelle smiled. "So, what do we do now? I thought you might want to ride the roller coaster."

Ricky laughed out loud. "I want to be alone with you."

She blushed. "That's sweet, Ricky. I love being with you." Ricky was a perfect gentleman. He held her hand and put his arm around her shoulder as they talked and laughed together. After joking about Kate and making idle chit-chat for a while, Estelle turned the conversation in another direction.

"Ricky, you've never told me anything about your family."

"There's not much to tell." He looked away. "You first. Tell me about your family."

"Well, I told you my parents are pretty old-fashioned. They try to be strict, but they really hate to say *no* to me. I'm an only child you know.

Momma and Poppa came here from Croatia before I was born and thought they'd never have a child."

"How old are they?"

"Momma is 57. She was 42 when I was born. Poppa is 60."

"Jeez, they *are* old."

"Ricky! That's not very nice."

"I'm sorry. I didn't mean it that way."

"You're forgiven," Estelle laughed.

"So, tell me more."

"Well, I was born in Chicago. We moved to Kansas City before I was two and have lived in the same house ever since. We don't have any other family here. They're all in the *old country*, as my parents call it. I guess that's about it," Estelle shrugged.

Estelle suddenly jumped up. "Oh, Ricky it's ten minutes after seven. I have to head back and get Kristina. I am so glad we …"

In the middle of her sentence, Ricky leaned toward her. He brushed her lips with his, and then lingered for just a moment. "Me too, I love being with you," his husky whisper made her tingle.

Estelle was breathless. She trembled as Ricky pulled her close and kissed her. Feelings she'd never experienced awakened. She closed her eyes and leaned against him. Heat spread through her entire body; her knees felt weak. His lips were soft and warm, exploring hers. Her heart raced, and she wasn't ready when he released her. Her breath came in short gasps, and a soft moan escaped her lips. No fantasy she'd ever conjured up was as tantalizing as this first kiss.

Ricky smiled and took her hand. "Come on, I'll take you back."

She was still shaking when she found Kristina sitting on the bench waiting for her. "Estelle, what's wrong with you? You look worse than I do. Are you going to faint?"

Estelle was in a daze. "I'm just tired. Let's find Anna. I'm ready to go home."

2

Week after week, Ricky and Estelle grabbed a few moments together before and after school. Occasionally, Estelle sneaked out her bedroom window at night to meet Ricky. By slipping down an alley and behind a building, they found a little privacy. It became more and more difficult to control themselves when they were together. Estelle struggled not to go too far, but she was completely smitten with Ricky Shannon and wanted to spend every waking moment with him.

On the other hand, Ricky's refusal to answer questions about his family bothered Estelle. One afternoon as they walked together, she decided that she would no longer allow him to put her off. "Ricky, I want to meet your family."

"You don't understand, Estelle. We live in an apartment. It's crowded, and there are a lot of things going on right now. My family isn't like yours. Besides, you won't let me meet your parents."

"You know that's not the same. I told you what they are like. And, yes your family *is* different. You told me they don't care if you have a girlfriend, so why can't I meet them? Is there someone else? Is that it?" Estelle demanded.

Ricky's face turned red with anger. "Okay, you want to meet my family? Come on." He grabbed her by the arm and started down the street.

"Ricky, you're hurting my arm. Stop it!" Estelle cried.

"I'm sorry." He let go of her arm. "Come on. It's a few blocks, so keep up."

Finally he led her down a walk and into a three-story apartment building. The hallway was dirty and dimly lit. She heard children fussing. The smell of meat frying in lard and onions, mingled with a musty odor, was unpleasant. She tried to hide her reaction.

Ricky took a deep breath, grabbed Estelle's hand, and started up the stairs. As they stepped onto the second floor landing, Estelle heard shouting and cursing. Ricky stopped dead in his tracks as a man ran past them, pulling on his shirt.

Meanwhile, from an apartment upstairs, they heard a woman's voice. "Get away from me, you lousy drunk. What was I supposed to do? How did you think these kids were going to eat? We can't live on the street!" The woman screamed at the top of her lungs.

"Whore, you're nothing but a whore! These brats probably ain't even mine." Glass shattered as something hit the wall with a thud.

"Why'd you marry me then?"

"You're a witch. I was under your spell. My sweet mother told me you were no good."

"You're not a man, Momma's boy. Look at you, you're disgusting!" The woman laughed. Estelle heard children whimpering in the background. "Get out! You spend more time in the bar than you do here, you lazy bum! You can't even hold a job. I said get out!"

"Before the war, I had a good job and took fine care of you. You don't know the horrors I saw!"

"I'm sick of your hero stories. You're a coward. You probably stole those medals."

There were sounds of a struggle, and someone fell against the door.

The woman screamed, and Estelle heard a stream of curses. "I'll kill you if you ever hit me again."

Frightened by the commotion, Estelle grabbed Ricky's arm. "Who is that? Are they your neighbors?" she asked innocently.

"Come on, Estelle. Let's get out of here." Ricky reached for her hand.

Estelle jerked her hand back and stood her ground. She was not going to be deterred by these horrible neighbors. "But, Ricky, I thought I was going to meet your family."

"You just did. Let's get out of here—now!" He started down the stairs without her.

For a moment, Estelle's feet wouldn't move. Then she ran down the stairs after Ricky. She was out of breath when she came out of the apartment building.

While Estelle tried to make sense of what just happened, a scraggly, ruddy-faced man with red hair came crashing out the door. He tripped and fell on the sidewalk. Cursing and spitting, he struggled to get up. Estelle was close enough to smell his unwashed body, filthy clothes, and sour breath. He stood up, staggered a few feet, and found himself face to face with Ricky. "Get out of my way, boy."

"Go around me, old man."

"I said get out of my way. You're your mother's son, you son of a whore."

"Don't call my mother a whore, you stinkin' drunk." Ricky raised his fist.

"Ricky, stop!" Estelle was white with horror. "My God, don't hit your father."

"He's no father. He's a drunk. The only thing he knows how to do is knock women and kids around. He ain't beatin' on me anymore."

Mr. Shannon turned and staggered away, cursing as he went.

Just then Estelle saw Kate across the street. "Oh God, Ricky, it's Kate! She'll tell my parents!"

"Tell your parents what, Estelle? Why don't you tell them yourself? Tell them whatever you want. Just don't tell them you were with that low life, Ricky Shannon, right?" Ricky whirled and walked away.

"Ricky!" She started after him. "Ricky, you know that's not true. Come back!" Estelle cried, but he didn't answer. She watched Ricky stomp off in one direction and Kate in the other.

Kate hurried home and told her parents, and Anton and Elizabeth Molech immediately headed next door to talk to Nick and Mary.

Estelle waited, hoping Ricky would come back. When he didn't return, she realized she had no choice; she walked home alone to face her parents. As she opened the screen door to the kitchen, she heard her parents talking in hushed tones, and they were upset. The screen door creaked as she gently pulled it shut.

"Estelle, please come in and talk to us." Estelle walked into the living room and sat down on the sofa. "Kate says that she saw you with a boy today—a boy named Ricky Shannon. Is this true?" Nick waited for his daughter to answer.

"Momma, Poppa. He said hello to me on the street, and I stopped to talk with him. I can't be rude," Estelle lied.

Nick and Mary looked at each other. Nick spoke up, "We don't like to judge people, but we have heard talk about this young man's family. He is older than you, Estelle. He is wild and undisciplined, and his family doesn't go to church."

"Poppa, it's nothing. I promise. Kate is making a big deal about nothing. She's just jealous because I've been spending time with other friends. Please don't worry."

"Are you sure?" Mary asked.

"Yes, I'm sure. Have I ever lied to you? I love you," she replied.

Nick and Mary wanted to believe her. "We just want you to understand that when the time is right, you will meet a young man who will respect you and treat you like a lady, a young man who has things in common with you and our family. You are too young for these things right now. We want to protect you." Mary's stern look melted as she looked at her daughter.

"I know, Momma. I'm sorry if I worried you. May I go to my room now?"

"Yes, dear, I'll call you when dinner is ready."

Estelle was fuming as she pressed her ear against her bedroom door and tried to listen to her parents' conversation. Their voices were muffled, but she understood a few words. "What are they talking about—'something happening again'?" she whispered. "I've never been in this kind of trouble before. That Kate!" Maybe they suspected she was seeing Ricky but just didn't have any proof until today. She hoped that they believed her and not that nosey Kate Molech.

The next day, Estelle refused to speak to Kate.

"Estelle, you have to talk to me sometime. We see each other every day."

Estelle looked straight ahead and didn't say a word.

"I only told my parents because I care about you. You have no business messing around with Ricky Shannon." Kate's voice grew louder.

"I am not messing around with Ricky. He said hello; I was being courteous."

"It looked like you came out of his apartment building. Then he and his father almost had a fist fight."

"Oh for heaven's sake, you are imagining things. And I know you've been running to my parents and talking behind my back. I thought you were my friend." Estelle walked faster trying to leave her friend behind.

"I *am* your friend! What are you talking about?"

"Friends don't spy on friends and tattle like children. You've been spying on me and telling my parents lies."

"That's not true!" Kate didn't know what to say. She had never spied on Estelle.

Estelle didn't talk to Ricky for a week or so. Day after day, she saw him sulking and watching her from the alley as she walked to and from school. Things had to settle down before she could meet him again. Otherwise, her parents would never let her leave the house unattended. She hoped Ricky understood.

Finally one morning, an opportunity presented itself; Kate was sick. Estelle started for school alone and saw the group of boys on the corner. She headed toward Ricky. When he saw her, he turned and walked away. She ran after him.

"Ricky, wait. Please talk to me! I promise this has nothing to do with you." She lied, knowing it had everything to do with who he was. Her parents might have approved of a friendship with a *nice* boy from one of the right families in their tight-knit community. "I told you my parents were old-fashioned." Ricky pouted and pretended to ignore her. "Remember when you asked about my family? I told you what they were like." Ricky continued to ignore her. "They are very religious, and they can't face the fact that I'm growing up."

"So, tell them you're tired of being treated like a baby," Ricky replied.

"Ricky, I love them. It's not that simple. I told you they're old. They aren't in the best of health. Poppa had a heart attack a few years ago and still works too many hours in the tailor shop. Momma isn't well either."

"That's a bunch of bull," Ricky said.

"Ricky, she won't go to the doctor, and I heard Poppa almost shouting at her. I have never heard my parents fight, and I can't cause them more worry."

"How nice," Ricky preened as he mocked her. "You've never heard Momma and Poppa argue; welcome to the real world, little girl."

"Ricky, I promise, I'll work something out. Just give me a little time," Estelle begged.

Over the next few weeks, Estelle made sure that she did nothing to make her parents suspicious. She went to school and stuck close to home. Occasionally, she sneaked out late at night to meet Ricky.

One Saturday morning, as Estelle watched her mother prepare breakfast, she asked cautiously, "Momma, I'm worried about you. Are you sick?" She truly was worried, and she also wanted permission to get out of the house without Kate.

"Estelle, I am fine." Mary continued with her work.

Estelle ventured further. "But, Momma, you're tired so much."

Mary whirled around, glaring at her daughter. "The house is clean and the laundry is always done. Have you gone hungry, Estelle? I told you I am not sick."

Estelle realized she had broached the wrong subject. "I'm sorry, Momma."

Estelle fidgeted and stayed at the table. "Estelle, what is it? Do you have other questions for me?" Mary snapped.

"No. Well, yes. May I walk to the movie theater with some of the girls tonight? I haven't been anywhere for so long." Estelle's voice was barely audible.

"Who will be going?"

"Beth and Kristina asked me to go." She hated lying to her mother, but her parents weren't being fair. To make matters worse, Ricky had quit school to help his mom and take care of his sisters. Ricky's dad never came back after the fight she'd overheard.

"Is Kate going?"

"No, Momma, she isn't."

"Why not?"

"I don't know. This time, she isn't going. I do have other friends."

Mary continued to stare at her daughter. Estelle tried to look at Mary's forehead and not straight into her eyes. "Please, Momma?"

"You may go, but come home as soon as the movie is over."

That evening, Kristina knocked on the Prebilicas' door and asked for Estelle. The two girls left together. After walking a few blocks, Kristina headed home, and Estelle met Ricky a few blocks away. The young couple walked to a theater outside Estelle's neighborhood. Just as they settled in their seats to share hot buttered popcorn and a soda, Kate Molech walked in and sat down in the row right behind them. Estelle was horrified. Kate leaned forward and hissed, "Estelle, come to the ladies' room with me, now!"

"Ricky, I'll be right back," Estelle whispered.

Beth and Kristina stood in the lobby. "Kristina, what are you doing here?" Estelle was furious.

Kate lit into her best friend. "What are *you* doing here, Estelle? You know you aren't allowed to be with him! Your parents would *die* if they knew you were here with that hoodlum!"

"You *are* spying on me!"

"No, I'm not. Beth and I saw you with Kristina, and then she headed home. You kept walking and met Ricky."

"Kate, please don't tell my parents. I love Ricky. We're not doing anything wrong," Estelle begged.

"Not doing anything *wrong*! For heaven's sake, Estelle, you are lying to your parents!" Kate couldn't believe what she heard. "He is no good, Estelle. You are asking for trouble. What do you have in common? His father is a drunk, and his mom is, well she is … I can't even say what she is."

Estelle bristled with anger. "I don't care. I don't care what you think or what my parents think. No one can keep us apart." She stormed out of the restroom. Beth and Kristina were right outside the door, trying to hear every word.

"What are you two looking at? Kristina, I will never forgive you for this!" Estelle fumed as she went back to her seat.

"So, do we have to leave?" Ricky asked.

"No, we're staying."

"Are you sure?"

"Yes, I'm sure." She snuggled next to him and watched the movie. She was already in trouble, so what difference did it make?

Kate didn't know what to do. If she didn't tell someone, she was afraid of what might happen to Estelle. Her stomach churned. Ricky Shannon was nothing but trouble.

That night, Kate talked to her parents about Ricky and Estelle. Anton and Elizabeth Molech went to speak to Nick and Mary the very next morning. Nick and Mary were shocked. Estelle had come home on time the night before, went to her room, and acted as if nothing was out of the ordinary.

"Oh my God, Nikola, something must be done." Mary cried as she spoke. "She looked in my eyes and lied to me—her mother! How could she lie to me? What have we done to deserve such treatment?"

Nick Prebilica stormed through the house. "Estelle!" He pounded on his daughter's door. "Come out this very minute and speak to us!"

Estelle was terrified as she heard her father walking back to the living room. She had never heard her parents so upset. Her father had never raised his voice or his hand to her.

Her bedroom door creaked as she opened it slowly. Tiptoeing down the hall, Estelle could hear her own heart pounding. "Momma? Poppa?"

"Estelle," slumped in his chair, her father sounded so tired. The pain in his voice frightened her even more than his shouting.

"Yes, Poppa?"

"You have lied to your momma. You have disobeyed us." As Nick stood up, he loomed over his daughter. "You will not leave this house except to go to school and to Mass. You will walk to and from school only with Katherine Molech. You are not to speak to Ricky Shannon. We forbid you to see him again, ever!" Mary sat on the sofa and cried as Estelle glared at both of them.

Estelle pleaded with her father. "Poppa, you don't understand. I love him! Ricky is not what you think."

"Estelle!" Nick shouted, "You will not see him again!"

She grabbed her father's arm and pleaded. "But, Poppa, please. I love him!" Estelle turned to her mother, begging. "Momma, I'm sorry. Please don't do this. Please let me see Ricky."

Mary stood up and wiped her eyes. "You know nothing about this kind of love. You are just a child. Young men do not treat girls with respect, who sneak around and lie to their parents. I never want to hear of this young man again. Go to your room now."

Estelle spent the day in her room. When she finally went to bed, she cried for what seemed like hours. It was over. Her parents would never change their minds about Ricky. They were so stubborn. How could they understand? They were old and had forgotten what love was about.

Three nights after being caught with Ricky, Estelle sneaked out her bedroom window. She crossed the street to avoid a barking dog, then cut through yards and made her way toward Ricky's apartment building.

She was frightened when she saw a patrol car down the street and ducked into an alley until it passed. How on earth would she explain being out on the street alone at such a late hour? A cat hissed at her as she rounded the last corner. She jumped and almost fell, but quickly recovered her footing, realizing she had reached her destination.

She climbed the fire escape, holding her breath as the ladder creaked. Finally, she stood outside Ricky's bedroom window. She pecked on the window softly. He didn't answer. Again and again, she tapped, but he didn't come to the window.

Suddenly, the door to the landing opened and slammed against the brick wall. Lucille Shannon's voice was gruff and angry. "Who's there?" Estelle was terrified. "I see you. Come over here." Trembling, Estelle climbed across to the landing. Lucille Shannon laughed, "Estelle Prebilica. My, my, do Momma and Poppa know you are out so late at night?"

"No ma'am, they don't. I, I came to see Ricky," she stuttered. "I didn't mean to wake you. I'm so sorry."

Lucille laughed so loud Estelle thought the entire neighborhood would hear her. "Oh my dear, you didn't wake me. I have company this evening."

In the moonlight, Lucille looked almost pretty, with her long blonde hair gently blowing across her face. The older woman's flimsy robe was open, revealing voluptuous curves under a light filmy gown.

Like a bird of prey, she slowly circled the frightened young girl, thoroughly enjoying the game of intimidation. "Ricky talks about you, and I've seen you from afar, but I had no idea you were *this* lovely. My

Ricky has good taste. You know, if you tire of the old folks someday, you can come and stay with me."

Estelle's face turned bright red. "Is Ricky here?" Lucille's scrutiny made her skin crawl.

"No, he's down at the park, with some friends. Why don't you surprise him?"

"Thank you Mrs. Shannon." Under her breath Estelle whispered, "*Veela!*" Mary Prebilica told stories many times of the birdlike creature who changed into a woman with long flowing hair, and was so beautiful she lured gullible young men to do her bidding. Estelle heard Lucille's husky laughter as she climbed down the fire escape and hurried toward the park. Chills ran down her spine.

As Estelle approached the far end of the park, she heard boys and girls teasing and laughing. She kept walking. Her heart pounded at the thought of Ricky with another girl. Suddenly, she heard his voice. The streetlight provided a clear view of Ricky leaning against a car with a girl. Estelle froze in her tracks. Should she call his name or run away?

It was too late; Ricky saw her. He threw down a bottle of beer, pushed the young girl away, and cursed. "Get out of here." With a few long strides, he crossed the street. Before Estelle could react, he spit angry words at her. "What are you doing here?"

"I came to see you, Ricky," she answered quietly.

"Where were you last night and the night before? I saw your daddy on the street today; he told me to stay away from you."

"Ricky, I'm sorry. They don't understand. I love you."

Ricky screamed in her face; his breath was sickening. "Don't understand! No, they don't think I'm good enough for their little girl. Am I good enough for you, Estelle?" He grabbed her by the arm and shoved her against a tree. "Answer me! Am I good enough for you?" He hated her for making him feel inferior, yet he still wanted her.

"Yes, Ricky, you know I love you," she cried.

He leaned against her, rubbed his hand down her side and whispered. "Prove it, Estelle."

"I'm here. I've disobeyed my parents and sneaked out of the house to see you. Isn't that proof enough?"

"No, baby, it isn't. You know what I want," he snarled.

She panicked and pushed him away. "I am not that kind of girl and you know it."

Ricky grabbed her by the hair and pushed her against the tree again. "No kidding. If you're not that kind of girl, what are you doing out here with me, in the middle of the night?"

Estelle struggled against his weight. "Ricky, you're hurting me. What's wrong with you? You know we have to wait until we get married."

Ricky spit on the ground. "That's just all that religious crap your parents shove down your throat. If you want to act like a baby, go home! Mind your mommy and daddy and stay away from me. There are plenty of girls who would be happy to have me."

Hot, salty tears streamed down Estelle's face. "Please, Ricky, you know I love you. I can't live without you." She leaned against him.

"Good, come on." He led her across the street and into a small wooded area at the end of the park. Ricky's jacket didn't completely cover the ground where Estelle lay. In the darkness, he held her close, "I'm sorry, baby. I didn't mean to hurt you. Your dad made me so crazy. I'll never leave you. Please, just let me love you." He was sorry, and he couldn't stand to lose her. She was the only decent thing he'd ever had.

Estelle closed her eyes as bitter tears streamed down her cheeks. Dreams of a beautiful wedding and the perfect white dress gave way to shame. She lost her virginity in the grass and dirt, behind a stand of bushes in the park. It wasn't romantic or beautiful. It hurt; and when it was over, she felt dirty inside.

3

Nothing was ever the same for Ricky or Estelle. Ricky's fantasy came crashing down. He wasn't good enough for Estelle's family and friends. Humiliation turned to anger as he realized he'd been foolish to believe that anyone could look past his family or his circumstances. He was Ricky Shannon; his dad was a drunk, and his mother was a prostitute. He wasn't ready to let Estelle go, but he no longer cared about trying to be different.

As the weeks passed, lying became second nature for Estelle. She felt a little guilty, but her budding romance with Ricky overshadowed everything else. Estelle was very careful, acting as if nothing had changed. She continued to walk to school with Kate, and she never complained about going to Mass with her parents.

When school was out for the summer, Estelle spent her afternoons with Kate. Each morning she finished her chores without being reminded. Nick and Mary relaxed, believing their daughter had listened to reason and was over her crush on Ricky Shannon. Once again, Estelle appeared to be the model daughter and Kate's best friend. Almost every other night, she sneaked out her window to meet Ricky.

Estelle was still fifteen and in the ninth grade when she realized she was pregnant. It took weeks to gather the courage to tell Ricky.

"Ricky, I have to tell you something." She hesitated and looked down. "I, uh, I didn't have a period last month, and I'm late this month. I've been sick to my stomach for days. I'm terrified."

"What? Are you sure?" Ricky paced back and forth in the alley.

"Yes, I've never been late before. What will we do?" Estelle started to cry.

"Why didn't you tell me last month?"

"I thought I was just sick. I didn't know what to do."

"Quit whining and let me think." Ricky ran his hand through his hair. "So, you've never missed before?"

"No. Last month was the first time. I'm over a week late this time." Estelle's lower lip quivered as she spoke.

"Go home and let me talk to a couple of people. I'll figure something out. Meet me here tomorrow night at the same time." Ricky turned and walked away without saying goodbye.

The next night, Ricky sauntered up to Estelle as she waited for him in the alley. "Don't worry, baby; it's all taken care of. Dominic knows about a lady on the Missouri side who can help us. We're going tomorrow, so I have to get some dough tonight."

"Ricky, what are you talking about? A lady who can help us? Help us do what? We need to tell our parents and get married." Estelle was confused and frightened.

"We can't get married right now. Your parents would go through the ceiling!" Ricky shouted. "My mom would kick my butt. I work and help keep the girls out of her hair."

"What are you saying?" Estelle asked.

"Well, this lady is kind of a doctor. She can take care of it for us." Ricky wouldn't look at her.

"Take care of it? Are you talking about an abortion?" The color drained from Estelle's face, and her voice grew louder with every word. "I can't have an abortion. It's evil; it's a sin!"

Ricky grabbed her by the hair and screamed in her face. "You'll do what I tell you to do. Do you hear me?"

Terrified, Estelle whispered, "Yes, Ricky, I hear you."

"Good. Now make some excuse to your little buddy about being sick tomorrow. Then make sure you're late so you have to walk to school alone. Dominic's older sister will call the school and tell them you're sick. Meet me in the alley. See you tomorrow morning." Ricky left Estelle standing in the alley, alone.

The next morning, Estelle met Kate at the door and told her that she was sick and wouldn't be at school that day. She told her mother she was running late so Kate went on without her. Carefully watching the clock, she allowed enough time for Kate to be far ahead. "Goodbye, Momma, I'm running late."

"Do you want me to call the school and let them know you may be late?"

"No. If I hurry, I can get there before the bell rings. I love you." With that, she ran out the door and hurried up the street.

When she reached the alley, Ricky and Dominic were waiting in the car. Estelle climbed in the backseat without saying a word. She was quiet during the entire trip.

"When we get there, I'll handle everything. You just do what the lady tells you. You don't need to say anything." Ricky's nerves showed as the words tumbled out much too fast.

"There it is," Dominic said as he pulled the car over to the curb in front of a two-story house. "I'll wait for you around the corner on that side street."

For a minute, Estelle couldn't move. "Come on. We need to get going." Ricky pushed the seat forward, took her hand, and helped her out of the car.

Estelle shook, and her knees started to buckle as she walked toward the house on Linwood Boulevard. Ricky knocked on the door. A moment later, a woman who looked to be in her sixties opened the door and smiled at them. Surely they were at the wrong house. The woman looked like someone's grandmother. When she smiled, there were dimples in her plump cheeks; her blue eyes twinkled. Her manners were impeccable as she invited them in.

Ricky showed the woman that he had the money. She stuffed the bills in her apron pocket.

Estelle looked around the living room. It was lovely. The overstuffed chairs were soft and inviting. A hand-crocheted throw was draped over the floral couch. Beautiful lace curtains hung at the windows, and light streamed in. House plants flourished. There were fresh-cut flowers in a crystal vase.

"Dear, please come with me." Estelle felt a gentle hand at her elbow, nudging her forward.

Obediently, Estelle followed the woman through a door into the treatment room. It was as if she had entered another world. The windows were covered with shades and heavy, dark drapes. She saw a sink in the corner. On the counter, there was an assortment of steel instruments. A simple desk and wooden chair sat in another corner. One leather, straight-back chair was positioned near the desk. The examining table was in the middle of the room. Estelle's knees felt weak when she saw the metal stirrups. A gown and a clean white sheet were placed neatly on the table.

"Now, dear, this won't take long. Remove your clothes from the waist down and put on this gown." Estelle didn't move.

"I know this is frightening, but everything will be fine. Now come on. Put the gown on." Estelle's feet felt glued to the floor, and she barely moved. "Now, now, just don't think about it. It will be over quickly. Then you can forget all about it. You have plenty of time to have other children."

Estelle couldn't speak. She stopped and wouldn't take another step.

The woman lost patience, grabbed Estelle's arm, and pulled her toward the table. "I've had enough of this foolishness; don't just stand there, take the gown. I want you to climb up on the table, lie down, and put your feet in the stirrups."

Estelle shook so hard, her teeth chattered. She was finally able to speak as she jerked her arm away and backed toward the door. "I—I don't think I want to do this right now."

The woman's voice was cold and harsh. "Get on the table now! I don't have *time* for this. This is what you get for acting like a whore!"

Estelle's face burned with shame as she ran from the treatment room and out the front door. Ricky stood frozen until the woman came out of the treatment room yelling at the top of her lungs. "Get out of here, and don't ever come back. You have wasted my time. You said your girlfriend was as anxious to get rid of this kid as you were. She better not say anything to anyone. Now get out, and don't come back!"

"Give me my money back. You didn't do anything."

"As I said, you wasted my time. It is my money now."

Ricky shoved the lady against the wall, ripping her apron as he grabbed the wad of bills from her pocket.

"Give me back my money!"

"Whatcha gonna do lady, call the cops?"

Ricky darted out the door and ran down the street after Estelle. He easily caught up with her. Grabbing her by the arm, he pulled her behind a building and pinned her against a wall. "What do you think you're doing? If we don't take care of this now, it'll be too late."

Estelle smelled fresh-baked bread from the bakery down the street. Blended with the smoke and alcohol from the tavern on the corner, the odors were sickening. Her stomach churned and she gagged. Ricky let her go as she started to vomit. "Jeez, that is so disgusting."

She straightened up and wiped her mouth with a hankie. "Ricky, I can't do this. I can't kill our baby!"

"Yeah, well, according to your fanatic parents, having sex before marriage is a sin. So what!? We can have kids later. The last thing we need right now is a kid! Now I have to find someone else to take care of this. You ruined everything, and the old hag won't let us come back."

"I'm not going to do it, Ricky. It's a mortal sin!" Had she seen it coming, she might have braced herself, but she didn't. Ricky pushed her so hard she fell against the brick wall and smacked the back of her head. Pain shot through her head, and for a few seconds, she saw stars.

As soon as Estelle hit the wall, Ricky panicked. "Oh, baby, I'm sorry. I didn't mean to hurt you. You just keep pushing me, and you make me so mad. Why do you do that?" He held her close and kissed her face. "It's okay. Dominic's waitin' in the car. Let's go home, and I'll figure out something else."

Estelle had never been so frightened in her entire life, but she knew she had to tell her parents she was pregnant. That night she dreamed of purgatory and the horrors of hell. There was no end to the flames. She heard agonizing screams. The terror of Ricky forcing her to have an abortion far outweighed the fear of telling her parents.

She waited until Saturday morning when she and her mother were alone. "Momma, I need to talk to you."

Mary had finished the breakfast dishes and was ironing in the kitchen. Nick was already at the tailor shop. "Estelle, you have been so quiet. You hardly touched your breakfast. Are you sick? What is it?"

Just then, Estelle's stomach churned, and she ran to the bathroom. Her mother followed her down the hall. "Do you have a fever?" Mary heard Estelle vomiting before she got to the bathroom door. Her heart pounded as she stood in the doorway.

"Here, wipe your face with this cool cloth. Do you have a fever?"

"Momma, I don't have a fever. Please, I feel dizzy. Let me sit down." Estelle sat on the edge of the tub.

"You're not getting enough rest." Mary's thoughts raced; she was frantic.

"I'm getting plenty of rest. Momma, I'm not sick."

The color drained from Mary's face. She knew before Estelle spoke the words.

"Momma, I'm sorry. I've lied to you and Poppa. I've been seeing Ricky. I'm so sorry. Momma, I didn't mean for this to happen." Sobbing, Estelle finally said the words. "I'm pregnant."

Mary collapsed against the bathroom wall. She felt as though she'd been punched in the stomach. She couldn't breathe. "Oh God, how will I tell Nikola?" As Mary stared into her daughter's eyes, she knew it was true. There were dark circles under Estelle's eyes. She had been picking at her food for weeks and had lost weight.

"We believed you. Estelle, we trusted you. Oh my God, you're just like …" Mary slapped Estelle across the face.

"You hit me!" Estelle screamed, "I can't believe you hit me!" Estelle sobbed and rubbed her face. "Wait—who were you talking about? Just like who, Momma?"

Mary's struggled for an answer. "I don't know."

"Who am I like? Why did you say that?"

"You're, you're no better than Ricky's mother."

"Ricky's mother is a prostitute. Men pay her. I love Ricky. I'm not a prostitute!"

"How could you do this to us? Oh my God, are you trying to kill your father?" Mary ran to her room, collapsed on the bed, and dissolved in tears.

Slowly, Estelle turned and studied her reflection in the bathroom mirror. The red handprint on her face throbbed. She walked into her room, shut the door, and lay down on her bed. All she wanted to do was sleep and wake to find this nightmare over.

Hours later, Estelle awakened to the sound of her father's sobs, coming from the living room. She had never heard her father cry.

"What did we do wrong? Should we have locked her in a monastery until we found a husband for her? I should have worked harder and sent her away to school—away from here."

"It is too late to know what we did wrong, Nikola. There are decisions to be made."

The thought of Estelle being married to Ricky sickened them. But, there was no other choice. Estelle was pregnant, and Ricky had to marry her.

Estelle heard her father pace back and forth in the living room. "That boy is going to do the right thing by our daughter. He is going to marry her, or I'll—I'll…"

"Nikola, please calm down, your heart. You can't do this," Mary pleaded. "We will go and talk to Mrs. Shannon tomorrow. From there, we can make plans. Please darling, calm down. I love you."

Nick rested his head on Mary's shoulder and wept again.

Estelle went to the bathroom and then back to her room. The thought of food made her sick, and she was completely exhausted; she only wanted to sleep.

The next evening, Nick, Mary, and Estelle walked to the Shannons' apartment building. It wasn't too far, but it seemed like a death march. No one spoke a word as they walked together.

"Who is it?" Lucille Shannon's voice was anything but friendly when Nick knocked on the door.

"It is Nikola, Mary, and Estelle Prebilica. We need to talk with you about our daughter and your son," Nick answered. "It is very important. May we come in, please?"

Lucille cursed under her breath as she opened the door. "This really isn't a good time. I'm expecting company a little later this evening. Can we make it fast?"

Nick looked her straight in the eye. "Is Ricky home?" Lucille nodded, and Nick continued. "He needs to be here."

"Ricky, get up and come in here. Your girlfriend and her parents are here!" Lucille bellowed. She took a puff of her cigarette. "He just started a new job, and he's pretty tired. Come on in."

Ricky staggered into the room, rubbing the sleep from his eyes. He glared at Estelle when he saw her mom and dad.

"Well, son, is there something you need to tell me before they do? Are you two breaking the rules?" Lucille's sarcasm did not amuse Nick and Mary.

Ricky crossed his arms and pouted. He refused to say anything.

"Mrs. Shannon," Nick started, "Estelle is pregnant. Ricky is the baby's father."

Lucille threw her cigarette on the floor and started toward Estelle. "You lying, sneaking brat, trying to trap my Ricky. You know I need him here at home." She turned to Nick and Mary. "She's been chasing him, coming over here in the middle of the night."

Mary bristled and moved between Lucille and Estelle. "Do not talk to my daughter that way. I'll slap your painted face."

"Mary!" Nick shouted. "Stop! Both of you stop! Ricky and Estelle have been seeing each other against our wishes. They are going to have a baby, and they are going to get married immediately!"

"Married?" Ricky shouted. "I'm not getting married! How do I know the kid is mine anyway?"

At that, Estelle burst into tears and screamed, "You know I have never been with anyone else. I thought you *loved* me. How could you *say* such a thing?"

In two strides, Nick crossed the room and backed Ricky against the wall. His face was almost purple. "You are going to marry my daughter, Ricky Shannon. You have shamed her, and you are going to marry her and give this child your name!"

Subdued, Ricky answered quietly. "Okay, okay. I'm sorry, Estelle. I know the baby is mine."

Suddenly, Nick grabbed his chest and stumbled. His face was drained of color.

Lucille whispered profanities as she cleared a pile of clothes from a chair, and Nick sat down.

"Please, get him a glass of water." Mary fell to her knees near her husband. "Nikola, calm down, please, please."

"I am fine. Just let me sit here for a moment." As Lucille shoved a glass of water at Nick, he said, "Thank you."

"Ricky, go get Dominic. Ask him to drive them home." Lucille didn't want the old man to drop dead in her apartment.

"Sure. I'll be right back." Ricky ran out the door.

Estelle was too terrified to cry or speak. She stood motionless in the corner until Ricky came back for them.

After they were home, Mary fussed over her husband and made him go straight to bed. The following morning, Nick's doctor came to the house and insisted Nick rest at home for the next few days.

4

Estelle had dreamed of a fairytale wedding since she was a little girl, but her circumstances overshadowed what should have been the happiest time of her life. Money wasn't the issue; her parents had been saving for the occasion for years. It was the fact that she was pregnant and Ricky was being forced to marry her.

Mary and Estelle's conversations were strained and awkward. Mary poured over magazine pictures of wedding cakes, and Elizabeth Molech worked on the design of the bride's bouquet.

Nick and Mrs. Purdy, a seamstress at the tailor shop, created a beautiful gown for Estelle. The cream-colored satin was fashioned to fit her perfectly. She couldn't wear white, but her father made sure the gown was exquisite. Mrs. Purdy designed the veil herself and spent hours attaching a multitude of pearls and sequins to the dress and veil, by hand.

Lucille couldn't have cared less about the wedding, and she made her opinion quite clear to her son. "I really don't care if you marry her or not. I just don't want her ma and pa on my doorstep every day." Her dark lipstick left a red print on the end of her cigarette. "The old man almost dropped dead in the apartment, for Christ's sake. Just do whatever makes them happy and get it over with. I don't have time for all this crap."

"They want me to become a Catholic." Ricky flipped ashes in the ashtray on the table. "I don't go to church now, and I'm not gonna go for them."

"Your worthless father is a Catholic, and he hasn't gone to church for years. Be smart; compromise. There's a little Protestant church not far from here. See if they'll agree to have the wedding there and just get it over with."

"I think we should just go to the courthouse," Ricky complained.

"Wise up, kid. Those fanatics aren't like your father. They will never agree to that. Just get this over with." She took a swig of whiskey straight from the bottle. "And you'd better make sure you get your butt to work every day. I'm not taking care of another whining kid. You wanted to play house and weren't smart enough to protect yourself, so you better find a place to live."

"You're kicking me out?"

"If you think that whimpering brat is going to hang around my place, you've got another thing coming. She thinks she's Miss High and Mighty. She ain't livin' here. You know how to make extra money."

That night, Ricky met Estelle at a neighborhood diner. "I've been thinking about us getting married, and I'm not going to your church." He laughed, "What would I convert from? I don't go to any church now."

Estelle pleaded with him. "Ricky, you don't have to go to church after it's over. Please just do this. We've hurt my parents so much."

Ricky leaned forward and yelled, "No!" Ricky didn't notice the two men at a corner table taking in the whole scene. He quieted down to a whisper when the waitress walked by and glared at him. "You can tell your parents to forget it. I don't go to church, and I ain't gonna start now. If you want to get married, you're gonna have to do it my way."

"I don't want to fight with you."

"Good. There's a little Protestant church that's not too far away. Tell your parents to talk to the preacher and see if he'll marry us. If he won't, we're going to the courthouse."

"Oh, Ricky, we won't be married in the eyes of the Church."

"I don't care about the Church. I've been trying to get that through your head. It's the little church or the courthouse. That's it."

"I know the church you're talking about. I'll tell Momma," Estelle sighed. "Ricky, where are we going to live?"

"I don't know. My mom's apartment is too crowded. And she wouldn't like having a crying baby around," Ricky answered.

"Fine, I don't want our baby living in a whorehouse," Estelle said defiantly. He reached across the table and grabbed her arm. "Ricky, you're hurting me."

"Don't call my mother a whore. She doesn't do anything you haven't done. She's just smarter."

The younger of the two men who had been watching saw Ricky grab her arm. He got up, straightened his suit jacket, and walked over to them. "Young lady, is everything okay here?"

"Oh, yes. We're fine." Estelle was embarrassed and hardly looked at the man.

"Are you sure?"

Recognition and terror registered on Ricky's face as he looked up. He let go of Estelle's arm. "I was just playing with her, mister. She's fine."

"Don't play so rough, young man." The man smiled and held out his hand to Ricky, but he looked at Estelle. Red faced, she looked down at the table. "My name is Jerry." Ricky grasped the man's hand. It felt as if he'd been caught in a vise grip. Finally, the man released Ricky's hand and turned to go.

"Ricky, do you know him?" Ricky's reaction to Estelle's rescuer had not escaped her.

Rubbing his bruised hand as the man walked away, Ricky mumbled, "No, I've never seen the guy before." He tried to keep his face calm and spoke softly. "Let me tell you something, I'm not living with your fanatic parents. They'd drive me nuts with all that God crap."

"Don't worry; they've already offered, and I said no." She knew her parents couldn't tolerate Ricky's drinking and their frequent fights. "You have a job. We'll just have to find a place. I can go apartment hunting."

"Oh great, I get to work and pay the bills while you lounge around the house and play mommy. I love this already." Ricky stomped out of the diner. When Estelle stopped at the cash register, the waitress told her the bill had already been paid. Estelle knew Ricky hadn't paid the bill. She looked around, but the man who had come to her defense was gone.

Estelle dreaded telling her parents there would be no wedding in their church, but it had to be done. The next morning at breakfast, she took the opportunity to talk to them. "Momma, Poppa, last night Ricky and I made a decision," Estelle stopped and tried to swallow the lump in her throat. "There's a small Protestant church in the neighborhood. We would like to get married there." She couldn't look at her parents.

Nick sighed, pushed himself away from the kitchen table, and went to the bedroom.

"Fine, we will arrange everything." Mary stood up and followed her husband.

Closing the door softly, Mary sat down on the bed and put her arm around Nick's shoulder. "Nikola, nothing about this wedding is what we want for Estelle, but we cannot change it now. They must get married, and it needs to be soon—before everyone knows her condition."

That afternoon, Mary took a taxi to the Protestant church. She explained the situation to the pastor, and he agreed to perform the ceremony for the young couple.

It was an October wedding; only family and the Molechs attended the simple ceremony and small reception. No one was surprised when Lucille Shannon made her entrance in a tight red dress that revealed ample cleavage and left little to the imagination.

Estelle looked like a princess as she walked down the aisle at her father's arm. Her thick chestnut hair was swept up in a chic twist with soft curls at the crown of her head. A delicate cloud of lace and tulle enveloped her face and rested on her shoulders. Pearls and sequins, sprinkled on the exquisite gown and veil, sparkled like diamonds in the candlelight.

Nick made Ricky's suit himself, and the fit was perfect. His black bow tie was straight, and Mary made sure his shoes were shined. Ricky was quite handsome, but his good looks were ruined by his smug attitude. He even frowned when he saw his bride. Each of his responses to the minister was no more than a mumble.

There was no romantic honeymoon; Ricky and Estelle spent their first night as husband and wife in the tiny apartment that would be their home. Estelle was sick to her stomach, and Ricky drank whiskey until he passed out on the couch.

The marriage was a disaster from the very beginning. Estelle tried to take care of her duties as a wife, but she was nauseated and sick practically every day. Ricky was no longer interested in romance, at least not with her.

Estelle was bored and missed her friends and school. Ricky worked all day and stayed out drinking with his buddies practically every night. Since the apartment was so small, it didn't take long to clean and tidy up. Estelle washed and rinsed laundry by hand and hung it to dry on the lines strung across the landing at the back of the apartment. She starched and ironed their clothes, just as her mother had taught her.

The neighbors were nice enough, but most of them had children and were at least ten years older than Estelle and Ricky. Mrs. Pratt, who lived a few doors down the hall, was older than Estelle's parents. Her grown son lived with her, and he worked during the daytime. Estelle didn't see much of him, but every time Ricky came home late, and the young couple argued, Mrs. Pratt peeked out her door or found an excuse to walk down the hallway. She was sweet and friendly, but she was definitely nosey.

Estelle looked forward to Tuesdays and Fridays when her mother brought a sewing basket and fabric. The two women made curtains and tea towels for Estelle's apartment, and they spent hours making gowns, bibs, and receiving blankets for the baby. Soft cloth diapers were folded and placed in the small chest of drawers. One afternoon, Nick and Mary even dropped by and surprised Estelle with a crib. Everything was ready long before the baby was due to arrive.

One afternoon, about an hour after Nick and Mary left for home, there was a soft knock at Estelle's door. "Who's there?"

"It's Kate. Please tell me you're not still mad at me."

Estelle opened the door and quickly pulled Kate inside. "Kate, what are you doing here?" she whispered.

"I knew Ricky wouldn't be here, so I thought I would stop by. Why are you whispering?" Kate laughed.

Estelle smiled. "Oh Kate, I'm not mad at you. I know you were just trying to protect me. Your parents don't know you're here, do they?"

"No. They aren't being fair, Estelle!"

"That may be true; but if they catch you here, I'll never get to see you again."

"I was really careful. School's boring. I miss you so much, and nothing's the same without you." Kate hesitated, but she had to ask, "Are you happy?"

Estelle answered slowly, her smile not quite reaching her eyes. "Of course, I'm happy. I'm married to the boy I love, and we're going to have a beautiful baby!" Careful not to look in her best friend's eyes, Estelle fidgeted and looked at her own hands. "It is a little difficult. Ricky works so many hours, and I'm sick a lot. It's also hard not seeing Momma and Poppa every day." Tears streamed down her face.

Kate didn't know what to say. Finally, she put her arms around her friend and cried with her. "I'm sorry, Estelle. I thought your mom and dad visited often."

"They do, but not every day. I know they don't want to see Ricky, so they only come over in the daytime. I get so lonely at night."

"You like to read. The next time I come over, I'll bring some magazines and one of those mystery stories you like."

"Kate, that's sweet. You know, it's strange not to have homework at night."

"I'd be happy to let you do mine." Both girls laughed.

"Come on, Kate. Let's have some tea. Momma made the most delicious cookies."

It was a wonderful afternoon. Kate and Estelle drank hot tea, ate cookies, and laughed together. "I guess I'd better go. I don't want my mom to get suspicious."

"Kate, I loved our visit, but you shouldn't disobey your parents. We can see each other when I'm at Momma and Poppa's."

"No. We've been best friends our whole lives. I can't come every day, but I'll drop by sometimes."

"Bye." Estelle held back tears. "Kate—." She wanted to tell Kate how miserable life was with Ricky.

Kate turned and smiled. "What?"

"Nothing, I'll see you soon."

Estelle's pregnancy became more real to her as her belly grew larger. Time seemed to crawl by. The leaves on the tree outside her kitchen window changed from blazing orange to brown. The family of cardinals she'd watched for weeks took flight for their warmer winter home, and finally, the tree was stripped of its leaves as the air turned cold.

One evening, as she sat in her living room, alone as usual, she felt a twinge of regret for having turned down her parents' invitation to see the Plaza Christmas lights. Memories of piling into the Molechs' car and heading for the Plaza flooded her mind. It had always been such a treat to drive up and down the Plaza streets as darkness fell. Each elegant building was outlined in lights, and a blanket of snow made the scene more beautiful as snowflakes floated out of darkness and danced under streetlights. It was enchanting. Estelle had always dreamed of strolling through the exclusive Plaza shops wearing mink and diamonds. Now she only longed for life to be as it had been before.

Estelle closed her eyes and drifted back in time. Christmas had always been her favorite time of year. Preserving old country traditions was important to her parents and made the season all the more fun for Estelle. As a child, on the Eve of Saint Nikola (*Sveti Mikula*), weeks before Christmas, she would place her oldest pair of shoes on the front porch. The next morning, she peeked out the door and held her breath, hoping she had received a sweet gift, not coal and onions.

Memories of Mary planting wheat in a dish for good luck brought a smile to Estelle's face. She now treasured the times when she and her mother spent days making holiday goodies—eggnog, povitica, and cookies of all kinds. The povitica dough was rolled so thin it practically covered the entire kitchen table. Estelle hated chopping walnuts, but she loved to sneak bits of filling. The thought of layer after layer of sweet dough and heavenly walnut filling made her mouth water.

Lost in her daydream, Estelle's thoughts drifted to memories of walking to Midnight Mass with her parents on Christmas Eve. She could almost feel the frigid air nipping at her cheeks and pulled a quilt tight around her shoulders. The beauty of the candlelit sanctuary never ceased to take her breath away. Many times she saw tears streaming down the faces of older members as they sang Christmas carols from the old country. She loved to hear neighbors greet one another in their native tongue: "*Sretan Bozic*" (Merry Christmas).

Each Christmas morning had been filled with excitement and anticipation. The gifts were never expensive or extravagant, but they were special.

For years, Mary invited the Molechs and the old widow from across the street for Christmas dinner. Fine china and wine-filled crystal glasses sat at each place. All the guests ate until they could hold no more. After dinner, as they sat in front of a warm, cozy fire, the adults told stories about Christmas in the old country. Estelle had heard these stories for as long as she could remember, but she never tired of them. There was no other time like Christmas.

Estelle's daydream ended abruptly when a gust of wind toppled a trash can in the alley. As reality overwhelmed her, she shivered and pulled the quilt tighter. Christmas would never be the same again. Ricky's family didn't care about the holidays. He and Lucille only saw another excuse for a drunken party.

As the holidays drew closer, Nick and Mary made sure Estelle spent time at their house in preparation for the big day. They bought a small tree and decorations for their daughter's apartment, but it seemed nothing could make her smile. Mary worried and didn't know what to say to Estelle. Their time together was often strained and awkward.

"Estelle, please come home on Christmas Eve. We can spend time together and then go to Midnight Mass." Mary paused, "Ricky is welcome too. I don't know what his mother has planned for Christmas Day, but we would love to have you here with us." Estelle promised her parents that she and Ricky would come over on Christmas Eve.

The morning of Christmas Eve, as Ricky left for work, Estelle reminded him of their evening plans. "Ricky, please come home on time tonight. My parents have invited us for Christmas Eve. Later, I'd like to go to Midnight Mass." Ricky ignored her as he walked toward the door. "Ricky, did you hear me?"

Without turning to look at her, he mumbled, "Yeah, I heard you."

Trying to control her anger, Estelle spoke quietly, "You ignored me. I talk to you, and you act like I'm not here. Why don't you listen to me?"

Ricky turned slowly and deliberately. He looked directly into her eyes. "Because I'm sick of listening to you; and if you don't shut up, I'm going to shut you up." He walked out the door. Estelle slid onto a kitchen chair, laid her head on the table, and sobbed until she made her herself sick.

Ricky didn't come home on Christmas Eve, but Estelle went to her parents' house as planned. The family trekked to church through powdery snow that blanketed streets and sidewalks. Estelle was unaffected by the clear night sky and brilliant twinkling stars. Not even the beauty of the candlelit sanctuary moved her. Everything in her life had changed. She didn't go home that night, and she knew Ricky wouldn't care. It was nice to sleep in her old room, knowing she would wake up to share Christmas morning with her parents.

On Christmas day, the morning sickness wasn't too bad, so she managed to eat a few of her favorite things. They even managed to get through dinner with no one asking about Ricky. "Estelle, why don't you go rest for a bit; and if Kate will clear the table, Elizabeth and I will do the dishes.

A short time later, Mary and Elizabeth were alone in the kitchen. "Mary, I don't mean to pry, but how is Estelle doing?" Elizabeth Molech wiped the last dish and put it in the china cabinet.

Mary sighed. "She's fine. She's tired, but she's fine."

"Mary, she doesn't smile. She's so quiet."

Mary stopped wiping down the counters and covered her face with her hands. "Oh, Elizabeth, we don't know what to do. She is so sad. She tells us nothing about how the marriage is going. We can only guess."

"Mary, I'm so sorry." Elizabeth wrung her hands. "We love Estelle, but we have not let Kate visit with her unless she is here. I hate it that she is so lonely and unhappy."

"We can only pray, Elizabeth. I understand your fears for Kate. We can only pray." Elizabeth put her arms around her friend as she cried.

At last, the holidays were over, and late winter gave way to the promise of spring. Estelle found herself adjusting to her solitary existence. She actually preferred being alone over being ignored when Ricky was home and arguing when he was drunk.

The young couple's relationship had not improved, but their income had. Ricky came home with more money every week. In fact, he told Estelle he got a raise, and he had the extra cash to prove it. Though he left for work every day and brought home cash each Friday, Estelle had no idea where the money went. She simply trusted Ricky to take care of all of the finances. Ricky rarely gave Estelle money; the money her parents gave her over the months was hidden in a sock in her dresser drawer.

One Friday night, Ricky came home completely elated. He grabbed Estelle and danced around the kitchen. "Look, baby, I made more this week than ever before. Let's celebrate! I can get some booze."

Estelle smelled whiskey on his breath. "Ricky, you know I can't drink. The smell alone makes me sick." Immediately, she knew she had ruined the moment and wished she could take the words back.

Ricky was furious. "Can we forget about you being pregnant for one damned minute? Jeez, you're boring. You make me sick." With that, he staggered back out the door. Estelle sat down at the table, too numb to cry.

One night, a little over a week before the baby was due, Estelle grew tired of waiting up for Ricky. Completely exhausted, she went to bed and fell into a deep sleep. Suddenly, a loud noise startled her; she sat straight up in bed. It was 4:00 a.m., and Ricky came crashing through the door. He ranted as he stuffed clothes and cash in a pillowcase. "I gotta get out of here. They'll kill me if they find me!"

Estelle, half asleep and confused, followed him from the bedroom. "You're leaving me?" She cried and grabbed his arm.

Profanities spewed out of his mouth as he pushed her away. "Get off me; I can't stay here!"

She pleaded with him and grabbed his arm again. "Ricky, please, what are you doing? What about the baby? Don't leave me!"

"I said get off me!" Ricky backhanded her and sent her reeling across the small kitchen. She fell against the sink and slid to the floor. As Ricky ran out the door, Estelle's water broke. It was the one time she was thankful for nosey old Mrs. Pratt.

The old widow couldn't sleep. When she heard all the commotion, she slipped out her door and down the hallway to see what was going on. Stopping just across from Ricky and Estelle's open door, Mrs. Pratt saw the whole thing. Ricky didn't even notice the old lady standing right across the hall.

"Estelle? Honey, are you all right?" Mrs. Pratt hurried through the open door of Ricky and Estelle's apartment and saw Estelle sitting on the floor in a puddle of fluid. "Oh my God, the baby's coming! Let me wake my

Jimmy and send him to get your parents. Just sit still; don't get up. I'll be right back." Mrs. Pratt screamed her son's name as she ran down the hall.

A short time later, Nick and Mary hurried into their daughter's apartment. "Nick, please get her bag—it's in the bedroom." Mary helped Estelle to her feet. "It's going to be okay. We're here now. A taxi is waiting for us. Can you walk?"

"Yes." Estelle was frightened, and her voice was barely a whisper.

Nick came out of the bedroom with a small suitcase and a blanket. "Mary, this is light. Why don't you carry the bag, and I'll help her out?" Mary grabbed the bag. Nick wrapped the blanket around Estelle and helped her out of the building and into the waiting taxi.

"General Hospital, please." Nick climbed in the front seat.

The driver made the trip in record time, afraid he might have to deliver a baby in the back of his taxi.

Once they were inside the hospital, a nurse brought out a wheelchair for Estelle, and they headed for labor and delivery. Nick tried to follow his daughter, but he was directed to a waiting room. Mary completed the paperwork, and then she joined her husband.

"Has anyone come out yet?" Mary hurried to Nick's side in the waiting room.

"No one has told me anything." Nick tried to be calm.

Just then, a nurse walked in. "Are you Mrs. Shannon's parents?"

"Yes." Mary stood up.

"It's going to be a while. Her water broke, but there are no contractions yet. You can see her if you'd like. Once her labor starts though, you'll need to wait here."

"Yes, we want to see her. Thank you so much." Mary's nerves were frazzled.

"Come with me."

Nick and Mary followed the nurse and walked into the room to find Estelle crying. Mary rushed to her daughter's side. "Sweetheart, are you in pain?"

"No, I want Ricky. He came home, got his things, and left. He didn't make any sense! He said someone was after him. Where is he?" Estelle wailed.

"He hit you and knocked you down, Estelle! Mrs. Pratt told us." Nick tried to control his anger.

"He was terrified; he didn't know what he was doing."

Nick was furious. There were bruises on Estelle's face, but he knew it wasn't the time to argue.

"Estelle, try to relax and rest. The baby will be coming soon, and you will need your strength. Please don't worry right now. We will contact Mrs. Shannon, and I'm sure Ricky will be here." Mary spoke softly as she stroked Estelle's hair.

Estelle cried incessantly, hoping Ricky had returned home to find that she had gone to the hospital. For hours, she watched the door, but he never came. Nick and Mary stayed with her until the contractions started.

Estelle's labor was worse than anything she had imagined—hour after hour of excruciating pain. The pain weakened her resolve to be brave, and she panicked when a nurse placed the mask over her face to administer gas. She lost all awareness of her body and wondered if she was dying as she sank into unconsciousness.

Nick and Mary rushed to Estelle's side as soon as she was out of recovery. "Have you seen him yet?" she asked her parents.

"Not yet. How are you feeling, sweetheart?" Mary hovered over her daughter.

"I was sick to my stomach when I woke up."

"That will pass, dear."

When she was finally allowed to hold her son, he seemed to recognize her voice. Estelle whispered, "I love you," and kissed him. She had never touched anything so soft. He was absolutely perfect. At that moment, she truly understood love at first sight. "I will take care of you and never let anyone hurt you. Your daddy will come back to us; I know he will." The baby's perfectly shaped head was covered with black hair. She hoped his eyes would turn to sky blue, but they looked so dark. She named her baby Jacob Richard Shannon and called him Jake.

Later that day, Nick and Mary beamed as they watched their grandson through the nursery window.

The next morning, Estelle and her parents were shocked when a detective walked into Estelle's hospital room.

"Mrs. Shannon, I'm Detective Patterson, and I need to ask you some questions about your husband."

"I don't understand. Why do you have questions about Ricky?" Estelle answered.

"Where is your husband, and why isn't he here with you?

"Um, I don't know where he is right now."

"I don't want to frighten you, but your husband is in a lot of trouble, and turning himself in is the safest thing he can do right now. He has far less to fear from us than he does from the men who are after him."

Estelle's heart pounded, and she sat straight up in the bed. "Trouble? Who is after him? What are you talking about?" She remembered Ricky's ramblings as he fled the apartment, but she didn't want to believe it was true.

Mary hurried to comfort her daughter. Nick stepped between Estelle and the detective. "Sir, our daughter has just had a baby, and she is exhausted. It may not be your intent, but you are frightening her. Whatever this is about, I assure you, she knows nothing that can be of help."

"I apologize for the bad timing, but it's urgent that we find your son-in-law. He is working for some men who run a crime ring—burglary, narcotics, and prostitution—and they are very dangerous men. Ricky was picked up for questioning last week and agreed to cooperate and provide information about these men—now he's disappeared. I need any information that your daughter may have."

Nick turned to Estelle. "Sweetheart, do you know anything that can help Detective Patterson?"

Estelle was afraid to tell the detective about Ricky's behavior the night before. She had no idea where Ricky was, and she didn't want the detective to think she was involved in any way—she had a child now. Surely there was some sort of mistake. "I don't know where he is, and I don't know why he's not here." She burst into tears. "This can't be true. Ricky has a job, and he brings money home every week." Mary handed her a hankie. "I don't believe it; you must be mistaken. I'm sure he'll be here soon to see our son. He will!" Estelle cried.

"I'm sorry to have bothered you at a time like this." Detective Patterson realized he was wasting his time; the girl didn't know anything about her husband's *real* job. "Thank you, Mrs. Shannon. I will contact you if I need further information, or if there is any news about your husband." With that, he left the hospital.

5

Detective Patterson never called, and Ricky never came back. It was as if he had disappeared from the face of the earth.

Estelle was heartbroken. She couldn't believe Ricky had abandoned her and their son. One minute she despised him, but the next she cried and thought she would die if he didn't come back. She was sure that everyone hated him, so she kept her feelings to herself.

To make matters worse, it appeared Ricky had not handled the finances well, and Estelle had no money. He had even taken the money she'd hidden in her drawer. She was shocked when her parents told her they had found a note on the door of the apartment demanding two month's rent that hadn't been paid.

Nick and Mary paid Estelle's hospital bill, the back rent, and the grocery bill at the neighborhood market. They welcomed their daughter back home and lavished their new grandson with love and attention.

Estelle was glad to be back, but she would not allow her parents to support her and her son indefinitely. When Jake was barely two months old, she went to work as a waitress.

Nick and Mary cared for little Jake while Estelle worked in the afternoons and evenings. Nick had retired just a few months after Ricky and Estelle were married, and he was so much help with the baby and the housework. Mary was often weak and tired and couldn't have done it alone.

In spite of the circumstances, Nick and Mary had hopes and dreams for a better life for Estelle and Jake. One afternoon, Mary approached the subject. "Estelle, maybe you could take one of those correspondence courses or night classes and finish high school. Then you could do something besides stand on your feet all day. If you take typing classes and shorthand, you could get a nice job as a secretary."

"Momma, I have a baby. I would love to finish school, but I can't let you and Poppa care for us for that long."

"Estelle, it wouldn't take too long. You could still work a little if it makes you feel better. Please think about it."

The frustration that had built up for months boiled over, and Estelle's voice grew louder. "I work in the afternoons and evenings so that Jake will sleep part of the time when you watch him. If I have to study too, when will I have time for him? I have to sleep!" Estelle saw the hurt in Mary's eyes and was flooded with guilt. She put her arms around her mother. "Momma, I'm sorry. None of this is your fault. I promise I'll think about getting my diploma. I love you."

That night, Nick and Mary talked for hours and prayed for their daughter. "Nick, I just want her to finish school and get a decent job. I am afraid for her. You know Katherine and Estelle talk about everything." Mary hesitated, "Katherine tells her mother that some of the men at the diner make comments to Estelle that are not so nice."

Nick sighed, "Mary, we can't make her do anything. She is no longer a little girl—she has a child of her own. Praying for her will do far more good than pushing her. We must trust God to take care of her and little Jacob."

Mary felt increasingly desperate about Estelle and her grandson. Her illness had progressed steadily, and she was exhausted much of the time.

One cool fall morning, when Jake was barely six months old, Mary was sleeping late. She had been weak and tired the night before, yet still refused to go to the hospital. Estelle prepared breakfast for her dad and Jake. They were all very quiet in hopes that Mary would get some rest.

"Estelle, thank you for breakfast. You have Momma's touch. It was delicious. I think I will slip in and check on her." Nick excused himself from the table.

"You're welcome, Poppa. I'll keep some hotcakes and sausages warm for her. Hopefully, she can eat a little more today."

Moments later, Estelle heard her father's cry. "Mary, oh my God, Mary, wake up! My darling, please wake up!"

Cold chills shot through Estelle's body. Holding Jake on her hip, she ran to her parents' room. "Poppa, what's wrong? Does she need to go to the hospital?"

Nick sat silently on the edge of the bed, holding the lifeless hand of his beloved Mary. Estelle was on the verge of hysteria. "Poppa, answer me! What's wrong?"

"She is gone, Estelle. She is gone!" Nick cried. Mary had slipped away peacefully in her sleep.

Estelle fell to the floor. Jake was frightened and started to cry. Barely able to breathe, Estelle crawled on her hands and knees. She reached the other side of her father and rested her head on her mother's shoulder. "Momma," she sobbed. "Momma, I'm so sorry. Oh God, I broke your heart. Forgive me, Momma. Please forgive me. I love you so much." Sobs racked her body.

The next several days were a blur for Nick and Estelle. Anton and Elizabeth Molech helped with the funeral arrangements. Somehow, they all made it through the wake and the funeral Mass.

Standing beside the closed casket at the graveside was more than Estelle could bear. After the priest prayed, the casket was lowered into the ground. One by one, family and friends each took a handful of dirt and threw it on the casket. Nick and Estelle stood silent for what seemed like hours. Estelle threw a handful of dirt and roses into the dark grave. Jake dropped the daisy he was holding and put his head on his mother's shoulder. Estelle held him close. It was so final—her mother was gone.

As Nick approached his wife's grave, he collapsed and fell to his knees, sobbing, "Mary, Mary, my darling." Then Estelle heard him whisper as he cried. "Rosalie, Rosalie. Oh my God, Mary, what have we done?" Anton and some of the other men helped Nick to his feet and supported him, as he walked back to the family limo that was parked directly behind the hearse.

The house seemed empty. It had been so alive with Mary's sweet voice, just days before. There was food everywhere. People kept coming by and bringing food, but Estelle had no appetite. Anton practically forced Nick to eat, and Kate was at Estelle's side day and night.

One afternoon as Jake wiggled and whined on his mother's lap, Kate offered to take him for a bit. "Estelle, let me hold him. You're tired."

"No, it's okay. He's been so fussy. I know he misses Momma. He just needs me to hold him. I think he's about to fall asleep," Estelle answered.

"I'm worried about your dad, Estelle," Kate continued.

"I'm worried about him too. He loves us so much, but he's lost without Momma. I think Jake is the only thing that keeps him going. He drifts away and daydreams. Sometimes, he doesn't make a lot of sense." When Jake fell asleep, Estelle handed him to Kate and started folding laundry.

"What do you mean, he doesn't make sense?"

"Well, the other day Poppa woke up when I walked in the room, and he seemed confused. He looked up and called me Rosalie."

"Who's Rosalie?"

"How would I know? We don't know anyone named Rosalie."

"That's weird."

"Yeah, it's creepier than you know. I hope he isn't losing his mind."

"Losing his mind?" Kate leaned forward.

"Well, when he fell on the ground at the Momma's grave, he cried Momma's name; but he also called her Rosalie."

"Is Rosalie your mother's middle name? Maybe that's it."

"Kate, you know my mother's middle name is Elizabeth,"

"Oh yeah, that's right. Well, I am going to ask Momma if she knows anything about this Rosalie."

Kate put Jake in his crib and marched straight home.

"Momma, I was talking to Estelle today, and we're both worried about Estelle's father."

"Your father and I are worried too. He doesn't eat right. He just sits and stares out the window most of the time."

"There's more than that. He is saying very strange things."

"Oh, Kate, what on earth are you talking about?"

"Estelle is worried that he might be going crazy."

"Crazy? What a horrible thing to say!"

"Well, she didn't exactly say *crazy*. She said she hoped that he wasn't losing his mind."

"Why would she say such a thing about her father?"

"Remember when he fell down next to the grave? Well, Estelle heard him call her mom by another name. And, the other day, he called Estelle by the same name. Isn't that weird?"

Elizabeth had turned her back to Kate and was chopping onions for a recipe. "What did he call them, Kate?"

"Rosalie."

Elizabeth gasped and dropped the knife in the sink. "Oh my God, I cut my hand. Kate, get a clean cloth from the drawer. Please hurry!"

"Are you all right?" Kate stood as if frozen for a moment.

"Yes. I'm fine, but I need something to stop the bleeding."

Kate grabbed a clean cloth and quickly handed it to her mother.

"Thank you, dear."

After a moment, Kate probed her mother for information. "So do you know this Rosalie?"

"No, Kate, I don't."

Kate squinted; her mother would never lie to her. But something wasn't right.

One night when Estelle came home from work, Jake was sleeping on the couch, and her father sat in his chair, barely awake. "Poppa, why don't you get some sleep? You look tired." Nick didn't answer. He sat in the chair and stared straight ahead. "Poppa," Estelle spoke louder. Nick look startled. Then he got up, walked to his room, and closed the door.

"Come on, little guy, let's get you to bed." Estelle scooped Jake up in her arms and carried him to his room. After tucking him in, she kissed his cheek, walked back to the living room, and turned on the radio. It felt good to lie on the sofa and listen to the soft music. She drifted off to sleep.

Suddenly she sat up, wide-awake. Someone was talking. She picked up a vase, walked to the kitchen, and checked the back door. Then she went to the front door and looked out. No one was in the yard. She listened closely and followed the voice to her father's room. Chills ran up and down her spine as she tiptoed to his door.

"Yes, yes. I'll calm down. I'm sorry Mary, but that good-for-nothing hoodlum will marry her! I'll find him, and he will marry her!" There was a moment of silence. Then Nick began to cry softly. "I shouldn't have said those things to her. But she can't raise a baby without a husband. Oh, Mary, she is so headstrong, so stubborn. What was I supposed to do?"

Estelle's eyes filled with tears as she listened. She tapped on the bedroom door. "Poppa, are you okay?" Nick didn't answer. "Poppa, are you okay?" Estelle slowly opened the door to her father's room.

Nick stood in the middle of the room and looked at Mary's picture. He seemed dazed. "Ro … ." He stopped and his expression changed. "Estelle. I'm fine. I should get ready for bed now. Good night, my dear." Her father kissed her on the cheek.

"He started to call me Rosalie again," she whispered as she headed for her and Jake's room.

The next day, Estelle told Kate about the incident. "Kate, it was so strange. It was like someone else was in the room with him, but when I opened the door, it was just Poppa."

"That is so creepy. I would have been scared to death."

"Kate, did you ever ask your mom if she knew who Rosalie was?"

"Yes, and it was a little weird."

"What do mean, weird?"

"Well, when I cornered her, she was chopping onions. I thought she was going to faint when I said the name Rosalie, and then she cut her hand."

"Well, what did she say?"

"Nothing, she said she didn't know who he could be talking about."

"Do you believe her?"

"Momma doesn't lie. But I have to admit, her reaction was really strange."

"It's more than strange."

Kate jumped up. "Estelle, do you think your father had an affair with someone named Rosalie?"

"An affair? I can't believe you would say something like that about my father! He loved my mother more than anything in this world!"

"But, Estelle, those things happen. Your father was a very handsome man when he was younger."

"You know as well as anyone how devout he is."

Kate thought she was on to something and didn't know when to stop. "Of course he's devout. But maybe he wasn't when he was younger. Maybe he had a little wild streak like you did. Maybe that's where you got yours."

"What?"

"Well, Momma says that these things sometimes run in families."

"Run in families? What on earth are you talking about? Does your mother talk about me?"

"No, Estelle. Kate hesitated, realizing she'd said too much. "My mother loves you, and you know she always loved your parents. I—I just got carried away. I'm sorry. Oh Estelle, you know I talk too much, and I don't always think about what I'm going to say."

"You can say that again. Please, just go for now. I need to get some rest."

Estelle often heard her father talking in his room. She knew he sometimes forgot Mary was gone. One evening, right before bedtime, she decided to talk to her father about his nightly conversations with Mary.

"Poppa, sit here with me for just a few minutes. I want to talk to you."

"What is it, Estelle? Are you and Jacob okay?"

"Yes, Poppa, we're fine. I'm worried about *you*."

"Why are you worried about me?"

"Poppa, sometimes I hear you, in your room, talking to Momma."

Nick's face turned red, and he looked down.

"Poppa, do you know Momma is gone?"

"Of course, I know Momma is gone! I go to our empty room each night. I think about her every day. Part of me is gone."

"But, Poppa, sometimes you talk to her. I hear you."

Nick began to cry. "I miss her so. I just talk to her picture sometimes. But I know she is gone."

Estelle went to her father and put her arm around his shoulder. "Poppa, I've heard some of your conversations. Who is Rosalie?"

Nick stiffened. "Who?"

"Rosalie."

"I don't know anyone named Rosalie." Nick stood up and turned his back to Estelle.

"But, Poppa, you called out the name Rosalie at Momma's grave. And you've called me Rosalie a couple of times."

"I said I don't know anyone named Rosalie!" Nick shouted in anger and started toward his room.

Shocked by his reaction, Estelle asked, "Poppa, did you have an affair? Did you cheat on my mother?" Her voice was shrill.

Nick whirled and faced his daughter. He crossed the room and put his finger in her face. "How dare you say such a thing to me? My Mary was the only woman I ever loved. She had never been with a man when I married her, and I had never touched another woman—never! Never did I even look at another woman in our entire marriage! I loved your mother with my whole heart. Don't cheapen her memory by saying such a thing." Nick walked into his room and slammed the door.

Estelle stood in the middle of the room, tears streaming down her face. "How could I have accused him of having an affair?"

She sat on the couch for what seemed like hours. She could hear her father walking back and forth in his room. She wanted to knock on his door and apologize, but she'd made him so angry. Finally, he quit pacing and she heard him climb into bed. All was quiet, and Estelle went to her room and drifted off into a fitful sleep.

The next morning, Nick was quiet. Estelle was miserable.

"Poppa, I'm sorry for what I said last night. I don't know what I was thinking. Please forgive me." Estelle started to cry.

"I forgive you, Estelle. We have been lost without Momma. Some-times, I think I am going crazy." Nick held his daughter as if she was a little girl again. "I love you, Estelle."

"I love you too, Poppa." Estelle hugged her father and kissed his cheek. "You know I have to work tonight, and you look so tired. Why don't I check with Kate and see if she can come over to help with Jake? You can get some rest."

Nick didn't answer. He sat in his chair and looked out the window.

"Poppa, it's been almost a year." Estelle's voice was soft and gentle. "We all worry about you. I think it would be good for you to get out of the house. Maybe you could rest this morning and then go walking with Mr. Molech."

"Yes, Estelle, that would be nice. Maybe tomorrow I will. For now, I just want to rest. Momma loved fall, you know. Aside from Christmas, it was her favorite season. The leaves are so beautiful this year." Nick stared out the window.

Estelle went next door to check with Kate about babysitting that evening. "Kate, would you mind coming to our house to sit with Jake tonight? I'll feel better if Poppa isn't alone. He seems to be going further and further away from us. He hardly talks anymore and eats like a bird. He just sits in his chair and looks out the window. I hear him talking to Momma more and more often."

Kate and her parents were worried about Nick too. Since Mary's death, they had watched their friend retreat further and further away. "Sure, Estelle, I'll come to the house. Maybe I can get Poppa Nick to work on a puzzle with me."

"Good luck. I can barely get him to *eat*. Jake seems to be the only one who can make him smile." She hesitated. "Poppa and I had a little argument last night when I asked him about his nightly conversations with Momma."

"Really, did he admit that he talks to her?"

"Yes. He said that he misses her and he talks to her picture. That's not what made him angry though. I asked him about Rosalie."

"You did?" Kate covered her mouth; her eyes were as big as saucers.

"He said he didn't know anyone named Rosalie. And then I asked him if he had an affair."

"Oh sweet Mother of God, what did he say?" Kate crossed herself and waited to hear more.

"He yelled at me. I can tell you one thing; he never cheated on my mother."

"So where does that leave us? We still don't know who this Rosalie is."

"Right now, I don't care. I'm going to take a nap when Jake takes his. I'll see you later."

Estelle was completely exhausted as she walked home from the diner that evening. Her feet throbbed, and her back ached. As she rounded the corner, she saw the flashing lights of an ambulance. Panic gripped her as she ran down the middle of the street toward home; the ambulance was in front of her house. She screamed as she reached the front yard, "Poppa! Jake! Kate!"

Anton Molech met her at the door. His face was ashen. "Estelle, please, calm down. There is nothing you can do."

She tried to push him out of her way. "Poppa! What is it? Is it Poppa? Has something happened to Jake? Tell me!" She screamed and fought as Anton tried to hold her back. She heard Jake crying as Kate tried to calm him. Estelle managed to push Anton aside and run into the living room.

Her father lay on the floor, and two young men knelt on either side of him. Nick's eyes were closed. She was unable to see if his chest was moving and fell to her knees beside him, "Poppa!"

"Ma'am, he still has a weak pulse, but he hasn't talked to us for a few minutes now."

"Poppa, I'm here. I love you!" Her tears dropped onto his cheeks. "We're going to get you to the hospital, and you'll be okay."

Nick's eyes fluttered and then slowly opened. He seemed to look past her. "Estelle. My sweet little Estelle, I love you. I won't let anyone hurt you." He closed his eyes again.

"Poppa!" Estelle screamed.

Again, Nick struggled to open his eyes. His voice was soft, just barely a whisper. "I've always loved you, Rosalie; please forgive me." He closed his eyes and didn't speak another word. His shallow breathing stopped, and Estelle knew her father was gone.

Estelle fell across her father's body and could hardly breathe. The walls seemed to close in on her. From far away, she heard screaming. "Poppa, don't leave me! Don't leave me all alone. Poppa, please come back!" Then everything went black.

For the second time in barely a year, the Molechs helped Estelle plan a funeral. Estelle moved through each day in a daze. Jake needed to be fed and bathed. Again, Kate stayed by her side day and night.

"Kate, do you think I caused Poppa's death?" The girls sat in the living room of what was now Estelle's house. Jake was sleeping with his head in Estelle's lap.

"Of course not. Everyone knows how much your father loved you."

"But Kate, I badgered him with questions and accused him of having an affair the night before he died. He was so upset. He didn't sleep well." Estelle covered her face with her hands and wept. Jake started to stir. "Shhhh, Momma's sorry. Shhhh."

Kate whispered, "Estelle, your father had heart trouble for years. When your mother died, he was never the same. I think the only reason he stayed as long as he did was because he loved you and Jake."

"It was my fault. Everyone knows it. I put my parents through hell. I defied them and humiliated them."

"You hurt them, that's true. But everyone makes mistakes. Your parents both had health problems long before you got involved with Ricky Shannon."

"I can't stand to think about it."

"Right now you need to rest and try not to think about it. Is there anything I can do before I leave?"

Kate, can you go down to the cellar and get a bottle of Poppa's wine for me? I'd like to have some wine with dinner tonight. If I get up, I'll wake Jake."

Kate came back from the cellar with a bottle of Nick's wine. "Estelle, you have plenty of wine down there. Let me take this to the kitchen for you."

"Thank you."

Kate straightened the kitchen a bit. As she tossed some garbage into the can, she noticed two empty wine bottles. "What on earth?" she whispered.

"For heaven's sake Estelle, are you drinking wine with every meal?"

"No. I've had a few nights that I couldn't sleep. I drink a little glass of wine, and it helps me go to sleep." Estelle fidgeted and didn't look at Kate.

"Well I think I am going to go home. Try drinking some warm milk before bed."

That night, after Jake went to sleep, Estelle listened to the radio and had a glass of wine. Then she had another and another until the bottle was empty. She got up, stumbled across the room, and glared out the window at the night sky. "God, why are you punishing me—why?" Only silence met her angry words. "Are you even there?"

6

With the funeral behind them, Anton, Elizabeth, and Kate did their best to help Estelle and little Jake. Elizabeth and Kate cared for Jake when Estelle went back to work. Kate tidied Estelle's kitchen during her daily visits and found far too many wine bottles in the trash. She suspected Estelle was drinking in the daytime as well as at night.

"Momma, I don't think Estelle is doing very well."

"I'm sure she isn't, dear. Her husband ran away, and she lost both her mother and father less than a year apart. It takes time to heal."

"I know, but I'm really worried about her. I think she's been hitting her father's wine cellar for more than just wine with dinner. I caught her drinking before lunch last week."

"How is she caring for little Jacob?"

"She seems to function, but she is drinking a lot. I think she's getting drunk after Jake is asleep."

"We need to talk to her. She has a child, and she must take care of him and herself."

"Momma, we need to do more than just talk to her. She is in that house with memories of her parents everywhere. We need to invite her to come live with us."

"Live with us? Well, I, I don't know. We will have to talk to your father."

"We have plenty of room."

"Room is not the only issue. Estelle has a home. I know she is your age, but she is more mature. She's been married and has a child. You're still in high school. I just don't know if it is a good idea."

"What? Estelle and I have been friends forever. Why would you worry about her living here with us?"

"Kate, you and Estelle are very different. You would never have done the things that she's done."

"Momma, I can't believe you're *talking* this way. Estelle is like my sister."

Elizabeth tried to keep the edge out of her voice. "But she is not your sister. People sometimes can't help the way they are. It is in their blood!"

Just then, Kate thought she heard someone run down the back steps and across the yard. "Great. I hope that wasn't Estelle. I hope she didn't hear you. Now, can she stay with us or not?" Kate headed for the back door.

"We need to talk to your father, and that is final. And you are not going anywhere. Get back here and help me with dinner."

After much pleading and cajoling, Anton agreed that Kate could ask Estelle to stay with them. Elizabeth was not happy about the decision, but Kate had appealed to her father's sense of duty to his friend, Nick Prebilica.

The next day Kate went to visit her friend after school. Estelle was very quiet and barely spoke unless Kate asked a direct question. Her face was pale and drawn. She slammed drawers and cabinet doors as she worked in the kitchen. Kate approached Estelle cautiously. "Estelle, my parents and I have been talking. We have an extra room, and it would be nice to have you and little Jake stay with us. I know you have the house, but there are so many things involved in taking care of it. There are bills to pay. It is just the two of you. We thought ..."

Estelle lashed out in anger. "I don't need your charity. I can take care of Jake and myself. If the house gets to be too much, I'll sell it. Thanks, but no thanks."

Kate pleaded. "Estelle, this isn't charity. We're best friends, and you're alone. Look at this place—it's a mess. Your mother would turn over in her grave. There are wine bottles everywhere. Why are you drinking so much?"

"What business is that of yours?" Estelle snarled.

"You and Jake are like family. Your parents would have done the same thing for me and you know it," Kate argued.

Estelle's voice cut through Kate like a knife. "But it isn't you! You are the good girl. I'm the tramp who got pregnant. I'm the one who was abandoned by my husband. It's my fault my parents are dead. It's in my blood! You have no idea how I feel, Miss Goody-Two-Shoes. I know you and your parents talk about me. I heard your mother yesterday. You just didn't have the guts to say it to my face."

Kate wept. "Estelle, that isn't true. We have always loved you. Momma didn't mean anything by what she said. I didn't say anything about you. I was just worried about you and Jake."

"Your mother doesn't want me around you. She thinks I'll lead you astray."

"We love you. We want to help you. We pray for you every day."

At the mention of prayer, Estelle exploded. "Keep your prayers to yourself. Don't pray for me anymore. If God is real, then He took my parents away to punish me for my sin. I don't want your prayers!"

Kate was horrified and pleaded with her friend. "Estelle, you know that isn't true. You're still grieving. You're frightened; you're not thinking straight. Please don't talk that way. God loves you. He didn't take your parents to punish you. They were just sick."

"Frightened? I'm not frightened. Get out of my house, and don't come back! Do I need to spell it out for you? Don't pray for me anymore. You'll be wasting your time. Go home and gossip with your mother. Now, get out!" Estelle slammed the door as Kate stumbled out crying.

Day after day, Anton and Kate came and knocked on the door. Sometimes Estelle shouted curses at them and told them to go away. Other times, she simply ignored them. Finally, Anton gave up, and Elizabeth refused to let Kate go near Estelle's house.

Without Kate and Elizabeth to sit with Jake, Estelle quit going to work and lost her job. A good portion of Nick and Mary's savings were gone. They had paid for Estelle's wedding, her hospital bill, and other bills Ricky had left unpaid. And then there had been the funeral expenses. Estelle was running out of money. She couldn't bear to ask the Molechs for help after hearing how they really felt about her. She couldn't go to any of her other friends' families. They all felt the same way about her as Elizabeth Molech. She knew they did. All of the mothers kept their precious daughters away from Estelle after she got pregnant. They treated her like she had the plague. She had no one to turn to.

The person she hated most became her only hope for survival. Late one afternoon, Estelle carried Jake up the stairs to the Shannon's third floor apartment and knocked on the door. "Who is it?" Lucille shouted.

"It's Estelle and Jake." Estelle trembled.

Lucille opened the door. "Well, to what do we owe this honor? I've only seen my grandson twice, you know. Come in."

"I didn't see you at either of my parents' funerals," Estelle snapped.

"Okay, cut the crap. You must want something, or you'd never darken my door." Lucille enjoyed making Estelle sweat.

"We need a place to stay because I can't afford to keep the house anymore. There are more bills to pay after I sell the house. I'll work and pay rent. Then when I save some money, I'll get an apartment." Estelle was completely humiliated.

"You're kidding. You'd stay here? I can't believe it. Queen Estelle and the little prince want to stay with me," Lucille laughed. "You'll pay rent all right."

"I promise it won't be for long. Please don't make me beg." Estelle choked back tears.

"Save the theatrics. Let's talk about an arrangement. With Ricky gone for now, I could use help keepin' the girls out of the way, and the extra dough won't hurt." Lucille turned and mumbled one last comment. "And maybe you can go to work for me."

Estelle shivered. "Lucille, have you ever heard anything from Ricky?"

"No. He'll come back when things cool off here. I know he will." Estelle thought she saw a glimpse of emotion pass over Lucille's face.

"I haven't heard anything either. You will tell me if he contacts you, won't you?"

"My son may not have done everything right according to your way of thinking, but he'll want to see his son, that much I'm sure of."

Having no one to advise her, Estelle practically gave the house away. She paid her past-due bills and moved in with Ricky's mother. Estelle paid her sister-in-law Dixie to care for Jake while she worked. Dixie loved Jake and was thrilled to have money of her own. The arrangement was tolerable only because Estelle avoided Lucille much of the time.

When Jake was almost three years old, Lucille purchased a three-story house on the Missouri side. Estelle made the move with her mother-in-law, hoping wages were better in Missouri.

Waiting tables was hard work and paid little. Estelle's looks drew regular customers—some left decent tips, others were a bit on the stingy side. In spite of the remarks and "accidental" touches, she was friendly, hoping for bigger tips.

There were exceptions. "Hey, baby, when are you going out with me?" Johnny Moran asked loudly.

"When hell freezes over, Johnny," Estelle replied. "I thought you liked my mother-in-law. I see you at the house occasionally."

Johnny laughed. "That Lucille, she knows what a man wants. But you, I could teach you a thing or two."

"No thanks. You dropped ketchup on your shirt." Estelle walked away. Johnny never gave up. He leered at her every time he was at the house. And he managed to have several meals a week at the diner. Johnny Moran made her skin crawl.

Estelle was shapely and more beautiful than ever. When her shift at the diner was over and she pulled off the hair net, her thick curls tumbled onto her shoulders and cascaded down the middle of her back. The soft graceful way she moved set her admirers aflame. Without trying, she had the attention of every man around her.

But she never let her guard down. Ricky Shannon used her and ran out on his own child. Many of the men who came to the diner flirted outrageously and asked her out—even the ones with wedding bands. She knew exactly what they wanted. Sometimes, she missed Ricky. And at other times, she hated him. Her father was the only decent man she had ever known, and even he had a secret.

Estelle wiped down her last table and prepared to go home for the night.

"Estelle, don't you ever go out?" Vivian had worked with Estelle for months and never heard her take any of the many offers to go out.

"Vivian, I don't have time. I take care of Jake all day and work here at night. I have to sleep sometime," Estelle answered.

"Well, it's a shame. A lovely young girl like you shouldn't act like an old maid. You need to get out," Vivian fussed.

"Thanks for caring, Vivian. I'm heading home. See you tomorrow." Estelle grabbed her bag and headed for the door.

As she walked home, she thought about her life. She worked, paid rent to her mother-in-law, and tried to save what she could. She had to buy Jake new clothes every month or so. She really didn't do much to have fun, other than take Jake to the park.

Estelle opened the door and tried to enter the house unnoticed. She heard laughter and a female voice she didn't recognize. "Thanks, Lucille. You won't regret this."

"Sandy, you can have a room on the second floor, just down the hall from my room," Lucille answered. "You'll pay room and board and a percentage of what you make. I have a lady who cleans, does laundry, and cooks all of our meals."

"It's a deal," Sandy replied.

Estelle and Jake had a room on the third floor. She was thankful she was on the floor above Lucille and her new business partner, not below them. Lucille's four daughters had the other large room on the third floor, keeping them out of the way of business.

And business picked up. Lucille and Sandy entertained men at all hours. A few weeks after Sandy joined the household, Connie moved in. She came with an entourage of her own male friends. And, last but not least, Rita and Monique moved into the last available room. They couldn't have been much older than Estelle. Monique said she was French. She did have some sort of accent, but Estelle didn't believe her. She'd overheard Rita and Monique talking in their room, and Monique didn't always speak with an accent. Estelle didn't really care. She hated being there more and more every day.

The second floor was full at last. Sleeping during the nightly drunken parties was next to impossible. The steady stream of male customers gave Estelle the creeps. They leered at her and Ricky's little sisters. Her face burned hot with shame each time she heard their lewd comments, but Lucille didn't seem to care. Estelle despised Lucille and the noisy, over-crowded house.

She wondered about the few customers who were given very special treatment. Their visits were shrouded with secrecy. That probably explained why Lucille's house was never raided. Estelle knew her mother-in-law must have someone very important in her back pocket—and in her bed.

One night, Estelle contemplated her situation. "You know what, Jake? We don't have to stay here anymore." Jake listened intently to his mother. "I've saved some money, and I think we can get a little place of our own." The thought actually terrified her, but she had to get out. There would be rent, utilities, and food to pay for. But, she was determined. The house had become a full-fledged brothel, and she had to get Jake out of there.

The very next day, Estelle started her search. The small, furnished apartment she found was perfect and would be ready in two weeks. It was close to the diner, and she could save streetcar money by walking to work. The landlord introduced Estelle to an older woman who was delighted to take care of Jake while Estelle worked. Pauline was so sweet. She was a little too religious, but Estelle would be comfortable leaving Jake with her.

Estelle bubbled over with excitement about the move. "Dixie, can you keep a secret?" Dixie was sixteen and loved secrets. "I found an apartment for Jake and me. It isn't too far from here. Things are getting much too crowded in this house."

Dixie's smile disappeared. "Estelle, when will we see you and Jake?" Since moving in, Estelle tried to watch over the girls. They were part of the reason she had stayed so long. She made sure they were out of the way when the men were coming and going and saved them from at least *some* of Lucille's tongue lashings.

"I'll visit and maybe you girls can spend the night with us sometimes. Please don't tell your mom. Not that Lucille will care. It's no secret that she can't stand me. I just don't want anything to spoil my plans. I promise we'll see each other often." Dixie didn't say another word before she stomped out of the room.

Minutes later, she was back. "You won't come back to see us, and you know it!"

Estelle fumbled for words. "Dixie, you know I love you girls." Dixie walked out and slammed the door behind her.

Two weeks seemed to fly by. It was apparent that Lucille was aware of Estelle's plans. And she was angry. It didn't make sense. The two had never cared for each other. Dixie sat on the bed as Estelle packed the last bag. "Mom is jealous of you."

"Jealous of what?" Estelle replied.

"She hates it because you're so pretty," Dixie said.

"Dixie, we both know your mom has more than her share of men. For heaven's sake, they pay to be with her!" Dixie's face turned bright red as she looked away. "Dixie, I'm sorry. What your mom does has nothing to do with you. You don't have to be like her. You're going to graduate next year. Get your diploma, get a job, and get out of here."

Dixie's eyes brimmed with tears. "Is it really that easy for you to leave us, Estelle? Do you think I just can walk out on Sally, Lynn, and Sarah? Do you expect me to leave them here with her and all the perverts? It's too late for me, but I have to protect them."

Chills ran down Estelle's spine.

Dixie's voice grew louder as she continued. "How can you leave us? You know Mom has always wanted you to work for her. She hates you because she knows her men want you, and she can't use you. What she hates most is that you stand up to her. What about us? Don't we matter to you?"

Estelle was torn. "I can't stay here any longer. I can't take care of everyone, Dixie. I have to do what's best for Jake and for me. Don't stay here. Come with me. If you and the girls left, your mom wouldn't care. Please, come with me." Estelle hesitated, her voice almost a whisper, "What do you mean it's too late for you?"

Dixie laughed. "You are blind, aren't you?" Tears streamed down her face. "You think you know what goes on around here. You work, and then at night you lock your door and go to bed. You have no idea." Dixie's voice grew louder. "I can't get out of here. I have no place to go. Are you stupid? Don't you know she's already put me to work? She just plans to be really careful until I'm older. Those old guys pay more to be with me than with her. They like young girls. She can't stop you from leaving, but she won't let us go. We're too valuable to her. We're her property!"

It was true. Lucille was using her own daughter as a prostitute. Estelle ran to the bathroom and gagged until she threw up. She rinsed her mouth and leaned against the door. "I have to get out of this house. It's not my fault. I can't save these kids." Estelle walked back into her room. Dixie glared at her and then stormed out. Estelle slammed the door and locked it. Jake was her responsibility. She had to do what was best for him.

Trying to control her emotions, she whispered. "It's my last night in Lucille's crazy house. I'm leaving it all behind." She hoped that somehow the girls would be okay. "It's not my fault." Finally, she managed to calm her nerves and went to bed. Jake was already sleeping, and Estelle's eyelids were heavy.

She didn't know how long she'd been sleeping, but suddenly, she was fully awake. Goosebumps covered her arms, and the hair stood up on the back of her neck. There was a creaking sound just outside her door and then silence. She was accustomed to hearing people on the floor below at night, but someone had come up the stairs and stopped at her door. She heard whispering; one voice was female, but it was so soft, she didn't recognize it.

The doorknob turned. Thank God, she had put the slide lock on the door. Some drunk had the wrong room. She heard cursing. It was more a hiss than a whisper. "Kick it in. We're not good enough for her? Who does she think she is?" Estelle recognized her mother-in-law's voice. Her heart pounded, and she was paralyzed with fear. Just then, wood splintered, and the lock gave way.

In two bounds, Johnny Moran was across the room and on her bed. Estelle's scream was silenced as Johnny's big, rough hand covered her mouth and bruised her lips. She prayed this was a nightmare; little Jake was right next to her. Lucille followed the burly attacker into the room. Estelle smelled whiskey as Lucille bent down and scooped Jake up in her arms. The older woman laughed as she left the room. "Have fun, Johnny. She thinks she's better than the rest of us? Show her what she really is!"

Fighting was useless, but she fought anyway. Estelle could barely move under Johnny's weight. Her stomach churned, and she felt as if she was drowning. His breath was putrid. She tried to stop him, but her arms were pinned over her head. Her legs were trapped beneath his weight. As he ripped away her gown and panties, Estelle wanted to die. "I been wantin' you for a long time, girl," Johnny mumbled.

"No, noooooo! Please stop. Oh, God, help me, God, please help me!" She struggled and screamed. Finally, Estelle managed to get one hand free; she scratched and gouged at Johnny's face. His fist glanced off the side of her face. Her head exploded into a million lights. Then

Estelle lay very still, closed her eyes, and drifted far away. She could hear a young girl screaming. She felt sorry for her, but she couldn't help her.

Pain shot through Estelle's temple as she opened her eyes to the morning sun streaming through the drapes. Her jaw ached; her whole body was racked with pain. Wrapping herself in a sheet, she barely made it to the bathroom down the hall before her stomach revolted. She threw up until she had dry heaves. The terror of the night before crept back into her mind. It wasn't a nightmare. She looked in the mirror at her bruised face. Salty tears ran down Estelle's face; she flinched and touched the deep cut on her lip. Her left eye was swollen and bruised, and her cheek hurt. There were bruises and scratches on her arms, breasts, and thighs.

Panic gripped her. "Jake!" Estelle sprinted down the stairs to Lucille's room. The door wasn't locked, and the Madame of the house was sleeping soundly. She wouldn't wake for hours.

Estelle gently picked up her son and slipped quietly from the room. It took only minutes to wash up, dress, and get Jake ready. She carried their few belongings to the front porch and then used Lucille's telephone to call a taxi. Safe in the cab, she didn't look back. It was over.

The taxi driver glanced at her in the rearview mirror. He finally asked, "Young lady, are you okay? Would you like to go to the police station? Do you need a doctor?"

Her voice was cold and calm. "No thank you. I'm fine. Please stop at that market on the corner, Polanski's. I need to get a few things. Then take me to the address I gave you." The driver nodded his head and asked no more questions.

Estelle had a key to her new apartment. Thankfully she didn't need to see the landlord since her rent and deposit were already paid and all of the utilities were on. Vivian had given her a few days off from the diner to get settled in. Thank God. She needed the time to heal and experiment with makeup to cover her bruises.

Once their belongings were inside the apartment, Estelle locked the door, put Jake down for a nap, and headed for the bathroom. The tiny room filled with steam as she filled the tub. No matter how much she soaked and scrubbed, the dirty feeling didn't go away. Her skin was red, and the water had cooled. A second tub of water didn't wash away the stench of the night before. Heaviness, threatening to crush her, lingered in the air. There were no more tears. She felt all dried up inside.

There was no way she could go back to the diner and face Johnny Moran. She had to find another job.

As the days passed, her bruised body healed, but her heart didn't. Ricky had abandoned her. Her parents were dead, and now she'd been raped by that monster, Johnny Moran. Estelle wondered if her decisions had really been bad enough to warrant this kind of punishment. What did it matter? Feeling nothing—just being emotionally numb—was much simpler than dealing with her pain. Another wound in her heart and soul was carefully buried and hidden away. Within days, she started a new job at another diner where Vivian worked a second job. The baby-sitting arrangement with Pauline Temple turned out to be perfect. She lived on the floor above Estelle, and Jake absolutely loved her.

7

stelle managed to pay her bills, but she rarely had extra money. Though it was difficult to put anything aside for emergencies, she managed to save a little.

She had been in the apartment for about six weeks when she started feeling queasy. Within a week, she was fatigued and could barely keep anything down.

She managed to get an appointment at General Hospital's clinic. "Mrs. Shannon, please open the door after you're dressed; I'll come back and talk with you." The doctor stepped out and closed the examination room door.

Slowly, Estelle pulled on her clothing, opened the door, and sat in the chair next to the examination table. She waited for Dr. Simpson to come back into the room.

Dr. Simpson cleared his throat as he walked in. "Well, I understand why you thought you had influenza. But there's no fever. Your only symptoms are vomiting and fatigue. The date of your last period was almost two months ago." Estelle's heart pounded. "Mrs. Shannon, congratulations, you're pregnant!"

"Pregnant?" Estelle whispered. "I can't be pregnant!" She stood up quickly and started for the door. The floor seemed to sway beneath her. She felt lightheaded, cold, and hot all at the same time. The room started to spin, and then everything went black.

"Nurse, get smelling salts and a cold compress, quickly please! She's fainted." Dr. Simpson's voice sounded very far away. Little by little, Estelle came out of the fog. "Just sit here for a few minutes. Fainting is perfectly normal during pregnancy."

"I'm so embarrassed. Please, I need to go now." Estelle started to stand up again.

"Young lady, you sit down until I tell you to get up. You'll be fine in a few minutes. I don't want you fainting again and hurting yourself or your baby."

Estelle barely remembered going home and getting Jake. She fed and bathed him, and then she put him to bed. Jake had been sleeping for hours, but sleep still escaped Estelle. She paced the floor of the small living room. "I can't take care of another baby. I just can't do it. It's hard enough to take care of Jake." Desperation gripped her, and she sobbed. "I won't have that animal's baby." She knew what she had to do.

The next week, she went to the house on Linwood Boulevard where she had gone with Ricky almost five years before. Estelle knocked, and the door creaked open. "A friend told me about your services, and I need them right away. Are you busy today?" Estelle asked.

"Do you have money?" the old woman asked.

"Is this enough?" Estelle pulled out a handful of bills, and the woman snatched them out of her hand.

"Come in. I can work you in right now." The woman's smile still made Estelle's skin crawl.

Estelle looked around as she walked toward the treatment room. Nothing had changed—lovely lace curtains, hand-crocheted throws, and flowers. The house was warm and inviting. There wasn't a speck of dust anywhere to be seen. She could smell fresh-baked bread from the kitchen.

The woman didn't recognize her, but Estelle hadn't forgotten one detail of the "treatment" room. It was cold, stark, and sterile.

She whispered to herself. "Don't think about Jake. I can get through this. I cannot have this baby." She undressed and put on the gown. "I must do this. I was raped. Who wouldn't do what I'm doing? I can get through this. I know I can." She climbed on the table and put her feet in the stirrups, just as she had been told. She closed her eyes and tried to think of the future. It would be okay. She and Jake would be okay.

"Now, this won't knock you out, but it will help with the discomfort."

There was no discomfort. There was pain—excruciating pain and humiliation. Estelle cried out, and the woman told her to shut up. It felt as though a knife pierced her abdomen and her insides were being ripped out.

When it was over, the old lady made a feeble attempt at sounding concerned. "Now, go on home and take it easy for a couple of days. You may cramp and bleed for a while, but that's normal. Take the pills I gave you for pain. Just go home and forget all about it."

Estelle climbed into the back seat of the waiting taxi, but she wasn't sure who called for it. She was cramping, and she just needed to get home and go to bed. Jake would be with Pauline until the next morning. She told Pauline she had to work a double shift and help close the diner.

At last, she was home. She dropped her clothes on the floor, slipped into a clean gown, and climbed into bed—the soft mattress felt wonderful. Her eyes were so heavy. Thankfully, sleep came quickly, and she slept for sixteen hours.

Estelle heard knocking and someone calling her name. She tried to climb out of the haze. "Estelle, are you in there? Estelle, answer the door!" Was it a nightmare? Sharp pain shot through her lower abdomen. Her teeth chattered. "Estelle, dear, are you in there?" Estelle's eyes opened slowly. She still heard knocking and the voice.

She stumbled to the door, turned the lock, and fell back on the couch. Pauline came in, holding Jake's hand. "Estelle? You're so pale." She felt Estelle's forehead. "You're burning up. Oh my God, you have blood all over your gown."

Estelle fainted and remembered nothing until she woke up in the hospital.

"Are you her mother?" The emergency room doctor asked angrily. Dr. Simpson couldn't believe this was the same young woman he had seen in the clinic, just days before.

"No, I'm a neighbor and friend. Her little one stays with me while she works. She lost both of her parents, and there is no other family, except little Jake," Pauline replied.

Shaking his head, the doctor continued. "She's lucky. The butcher who performed the abortion wasn't thorough. If you hadn't checked on her, she could have died. She won't tell us anything."

"Abortion?" The color drained from Pauline's face. "Her husband has been gone since before Jake was born. She doesn't have a boyfriend. I had no idea she was pregnant. She is such a sweet young girl."

"She was pregnant and had an abortion. I shouldn't be telling you this, but someone has to take care of her. Can you watch over her and her son when she is released? She may be weak for a few days."

"Why, of course. I'll look after both of them. Her son can stay with me until she comes home. Thank you, Doctor. May I see her now?"

Estelle looked like a little girl lying on the hospital bed. A dark halo of hair framed her face. Her long black lashes fluttered as she slowly opened her eyes. "Pauline? How did I get here? Where's Jake?"

Pauline's motherly instincts awakened as she rushed to Estelle's side. "Now, dear, it's okay. Jake is with my friend, Rose. She is completely trustworthy. We go to church together." Stroking Estelle's forehead, she continued. "The doctor told me about the baby. I know you were desperate. I wish you could have talked to me. Maybe I could have helped you." Estelle turned away.

"Well, it's a little late for that. What's done is done. I had no choice. You have no idea what happened to me, so don't judge me." Her voice was filled with bitterness and anger.

Softly, Pauline answered Estelle's angry outburst. "Estelle, I'm not judging you. I want to help you and Jake in any way I can."

"I was raped." Estelle's voice was flat and monotone. "My husband left us the night Jake was born. Before moving here, I lived with my mother-in-law. She's a prostitute, and she hates me. One of her perverts was paid to teach me a lesson."

"Oh, Estelle, I am so sorry. You've been through so much." Pauline stroked Estelle's forehead. "God will help you through this. He'll even help you forgive."

"Forgive? Do you honestly think God expects me to forgive the man who broke down my door and raped me? I prayed. I screamed and asked God to help me. But no one rescued me, and that animal raped me!" Estelle cried.

"Oh honey, I am so sorry for what's happened to you. I don't want to see you hurt any more than you already are. God can start to heal all of the wounds inside of you," Pauline answered softly.

Estelle's wounded heart grew colder. "I don't need Him to do anything—He's done enough. I'll be fine. I need to get some rest now."

Pauline sighed and left the room. She was more determined than ever to pray for this young woman and little boy that God had brought into her life.

Pauline made all of the arrangements to bring Estelle home from the hospital. She kept Jake for a few days, giving Estelle a chance to rest. She made sure the young mother and her son had three hot meals each day.

Estelle was back to work in a matter of days—pale and a little thinner, but working. She had no choice. The abortion and the hospital stay had just about wiped her out financially. What savings she had was almost gone. The rent was due in three days, and she didn't have it all.

Estelle was riddled with guilt and angry with God. She had defied her parents, and God took them away. It was her fault that Jake didn't have a father. She should have listened to her parents. Even the Molechs, who had loved her all of her life, didn't trust her. She'd lost her best friend. Then she had done the unthinkable—she had an abortion.

She was determined not to let anyone get close to her again. Jake was all she needed. That night, alone, afraid, and too stubborn to ask for help, Estelle cried herself to sleep.

Kansas City, Missouri
1955

part two

8

The air was thick and deadly still. A huge thunderstorm loomed on the horizon, drawing closer with each passing minute. Dark clouds churned and swirled across the strange green sky.

Each clap of thunder rattled the windows in the tiny apartment. Estelle hurried to get ready for work, hoping to beat the rain and avoid getting drenched. She cooked the last of the oatmeal for Jake. There was no bread and only one cup of milk. "Mommy, where's your oatmeal?"

"Well, I'm running a little behind this morning; I'll eat at the diner. Now finish your breakfast; we need to hurry." Her stomach growled.

"But, Mommy, you didn't eat supper last night."

"I ate after you went to bed," Estelle lied.

"Okay. I love you, Mommy." Jake's smile melted her heart.

"I love you too, sweetheart." Estelle held back tears as she hugged her son.

Estelle rushed into the diner mere seconds before the sky dumped a deluge of rain on the city. High winds swept through, bending trees and overturning garbage cans. Pea-sized hail tapped against the diner's front window. The temperature dropped 10 degrees in a matter of minutes. The newscaster on the radio reported that a small tornado had touched down in a rural area just outside the city.

As Estelle prepared for early customers, Vivian filled a plate with scrambled eggs, homemade biscuits, and sausage gravy. "Young lady, you eat every bite. We are going to put some meat on those bones."

Jerry Bradley came in late that morning. The first time Estelle saw him at the diner, she thought there was something familiar about him,

77

but she didn't remember having met him. He was one of her regulars and always left unusually large tips. "Thank God, I'll be able to get a few things at the market," Estelle whispered.

"Estelle, more coffee please," Jerry demanded in his gruff, joking manner. "That was quite a storm that blew through here this morning."

"Yes it was. I made it just before the rain started." Estelle hurried to Jerry's table and poured steaming coffee into his cup.

"Thank you. You look lovely this morning." Jerry was nothing like Johnny Moran. He was older than Estelle, probably in his thirties, clean-cut and well-dressed. No one was a stranger to Jerry. It was impossible to ignore his smile. In spite of her resolve to hate all men, Estelle enjoyed Jerry's attention.

"Thank you." She blushed and hurried to the next table. As she passed Jerry's table again, he reached out and gently touched her hand. "Estelle, why won't you go out with me? I've begged you for weeks."

"Jerry, I'm working. You're going to get me in trouble," Estelle snapped.

"Go out with me and I'll stop. You work too hard. Everyone needs to have a little fun." He flashed a dazzling smile.

"Okay, I'll go out with you. Now will you please be quiet?" Her face turned red.

"Tonight? I know where you live. When will you be ready?" Jerry smiled.

"I get off at four o'clock this afternoon. I have to ask the babysitter if she can watch my little boy tonight."

"Okay, so what time?" Jerry didn't give up.

"Seven o'clock, pick me up at seven o'clock." Estelle's smile faded. "How do you know where I live?"

"I was driving down the street and saw you go into your apartment building one night," Jerry answered as he went out the door.

It seemed seven o'clock would never come. Jake was at Pauline's. Estelle had changed clothes four times and finally decided to wear her hair down. She paced around the living room and checked her reflection in the mirror every few minutes. Was this a huge mistake? She should have said no, but she was so lonely and Jerry seemed nice enough. It was just a date for heaven's sake. She took a few deep breaths and tried to calm her nerves.

Jerry arrived promptly at seven o'clock. Taking her arm, he led her to his car and opened the car door for her. Estelle was quiet during the ride to the restaurant. They had almost finished their meal before she relaxed and said more than a few words.

"Thank you, Jerry. Dinner was nice. I haven't had a steak in a very long time." Estelle smiled at him.

"I'm glad you liked it. I'm a steak and potato man," Jerry answered.

"You know, you've been coming to the diner for months, and I don't even know what you do."

"I'm in sales. I sell jewelry, gold, diamonds, and I travel. That's why I'm here one week and gone the next," Jerry explained.

"You travel? I've never been out of Kansas City. Well, I was born in Chicago, but I was too young to remember when my parents moved. I grew up on the Kansas side. It must be fun to see different places." Estelle's eyes danced with excitement. "My parents came here from Croatia. They talked about going back and taking me to see relatives, but we never did."

"You've never been anywhere but here? Huh, I thought you took a trip that time you were gone from the diner for about a week. Seems like they said you took a vacation." Estelle froze and didn't reply. Jerry paid the bill, and they left the restaurant.

"Anyway, traveling is great. I've been to New York, Chicago, Dallas, Los Angeles. You name it, and I've been there," Jerry bragged. "Hey, let's go have a drink. It's too early to go home." He took her hand and started down the street.

"Ah, no, I can't. I—I ..." Estelle stuttered.

"What, you don't drink? Are you a teetotaler or something?" Jerry teased.

"No, I just don't want to." She fumbled for words. "I, ah, I have never been to a bar before." Estelle was embarrassed.

Jerry tried to look shocked and laughed. "You're not 21? How old are you? Am I robbing the cradle here?"

Estelle stamped her foot. "Yes I'm 21. Don't laugh at me. I just haven't made it a habit to go to bars."

He roared with laughter. "I like that little number. Stomp your foot again. That's cute."

"Jerry, stop it," Estelle pleaded half-heartedly.

"Okay, next time I'll get some wine, and we can go to your place and have a drink. Sound good?" His voice softened.

He stood too close, and Estelle stepped back. "Um, I don't know. I have to go home now, please." Her face turned red and she tingled with excitement.

"Okay," Jerry laughed. "But, you have to promise that we'll go out again."

"Okay, I promise. Will I see you at the diner next week?"

"Hmm, no, I have to go to Texas next week," Jerry replied. "When I get back, I'll come to the diner or stop by your place."

It was two weeks before Jerry came back to the diner. Estelle ignored him when he came in and sat down at the counter. "Hi, gorgeous, how have you been?"

Estelle continued to ignore him.

"Estelle, I know you can hear me." Jerry refused to be ignored. "I'm sorry. I got tied up with business and couldn't get back last week."

Estelle set a glass of water in front of Jerry and poured his coffee. "Sorry? What are you apologizing for? Why would I care if you came in last week? We barely know each other."

"You are good, aren't you? I know you're sizzling, but you're acting so cool," Jerry smiled.

"I don't know what you're talking about, Jerry Bradley. But, you are starting to annoy me." Estelle turned and walked to the counter.

Jerry laughed. "Okay. Then I'm not sorry. It's Friday, and you've worked all week. Will you have dinner with me tonight? Maybe we can see a movie first?"

"I don't know; it's been a long week and I'm tired. I'd have to check with my babysitter first. If you want to show up at six o'clock, I'll let you know if I can go." Estelle enjoyed his little game.

"I'll be there. Wear your dancing shoes. You never know what we may do." Jerry downed his coffee, put his money on the counter, and headed for the door.

Estelle knew Pauline would be thrilled to keep Jake for the evening. She had become more like Jake's grandmother than a babysitter. The biggest challenge was deciding what to wear. She chose a pink floral dress with a full skirt. Her white cardigan looked nice draped across her shoulders. A little rouge on her cheekbones and lips was all the makeup she needed. She liked the way it added a little pout to her full lips. "Well, maybe I'll use a little pencil to emphasis my eyes," she said to herself.

"Jake, what should Mommy do with her hair?" Estelle smiled down at her son as she brushed her hair.

"Wear a ponytail, Mommy," Jake answered.

"You are a little genius. I will wear it in a ponytail with my pink ribbon." Estelle laughed as she thought about Jerry's concern over robbing the cradle. "Come on, let's get you ready and go see Miss Pauline."

Once again, Jerry was right on time. Smiling as she opened the door, Estelle realized she couldn't stay mad at him. "Come in."

"Lord o' mercy, girl. You're going to get me arrested." Jerry whistled as he walked through the door.

"Jerry, what are you talking about?" Estelle tried to look serious.

"You know exactly what I'm talking about. You're all woman and innocence rolled into one tempting package." Jerry moved closer.

"Well, I guess we should go." Estelle stepped away to get her bag.

After the movie, the couple dined at a small restaurant that served what Jerry called "down-home cooking."

"If I ate like this every day, I'd be as big as a barn." Estelle was stuffed, but she left room for hot apple pie, topped with homemade vanilla ice cream.

"I doubt there's much danger of you ever being big as a barn, little girl," Jerry teased. "Did you enjoy the movie?"

"Yes. I love comedy." Estelle hadn't felt light-hearted in a very long time.

"I guess it's time to get you home. We don't want the spell to wear off." Jerry's tender, husky voice made her feel tingly all over.

Neither said much during the drive to Estelle's apartment.

"Do you need to get your boy?" Jerry asked as they climbed the stairs.

"I'll get him in a bit. I had a really nice time tonight." Estelle looked down and blushed. Her heart raced. She was reluctant to tell Jerry that Jake was spending the night with the sitter.

Jerry brushed his lips across her forehead and down the side of her face. "I have a present for you. I picked these up on my last trip."

Estelle trembled and her eyes grew wide as Jerry latched the lovely string of pearls around her neck. "There. Perfect. You deserve to wear nice things. These are beautiful, like you."

"Jerry, I can't accept a gift like this. These are real pearls." Estelle fumbled for the clasp.

"No, don't take them off. I want you to have them. So you know real pearls when you see them," Jerry smiled.

"Momma had a shorter string of pearls, just like these. Poppa worked hard to get them for her. The pearls and her wedding ring are about the only things I have left. Both my parents died, and I don't have any family, except for Jake." As her fingers touched the pearls around her neck, she remembered how lovely Poppa's gift had looked on her mother. "Their wedding date is inscribed on the inside of the clasp. Jerry, please, it isn't right for me to take these," Estelle insisted.

Jerry tenderly pulled her to him "There'll be more where these came from. You may as well get used to it. I want my girl to have the best." The sweater slid from her shoulder, and her eyes closed slightly as his lips trailed along her shoulder and neck and then found her lips. Estelle had never been kissed the way Jerry kissed her. She felt as if she was on fire.

Ricky was a fumbling boy, and Johnny Moran was a vicious beast. Jerry was tender, yet completely in control. Just when she thought she couldn't take anymore, Jerry gently released her. "Are you okay? You're breathing a little fast." His sweet, lazy smile made her knees weak.

"I—I'm fine," Estelle stammered. A deep, red blush spread from her throat all the way to her forehead. She pulled her sweater back around her shoulders and smoothed her hair. "I should go in now. Um, will you be at the diner next week?"

"Sure, I'll be here next week and then I'll be gone for a couple of days." Estelle hadn't realized just how handsome Jerry was. "See you for breakfast on Monday."

Estelle stood in the doorway while he walked down the hall toward the stairs. "Go on, so I know you got in safe and sound." He chuckled as he went down the stairs.

Over the next several weeks, Estelle was comfortable with the relationship that developed between her and Jerry. When he was in town, he came to the diner every morning and took her out every weekend. He never failed to bring gifts to her—jewelry, clothes—she felt a bit spoiled, and she missed him when he was gone. It sometimes bothered her that his trips were often longer than he anticipated, and a couple of times, he even left town without telling her.

When they were together, she managed to keep him at bay. Occasionally, she let him come in when he brought her home.

"Come on, Estelle," Jerry pleaded, "you're killing me."

"Jerry, you need to go now." Estelle pulled away and stood up.

"Go? What do you mean?" Jerry demanded. "How many times are you going to tease me like this?"

"I'm not teasing you!" Estelle cried.

"Then what do you call it? I'm not a kid, Estelle. This little game is getting old. We've been seeing each other for a while now. I get you gifts and take you to nice places," Jerry's voice grew louder.

"Is that what this is about?" Estelle was livid. "Gifts and money you spend on me? So, I'm supposed to sleep with you as payment?"

Estelle stomped into her bedroom and opened the small jewelry box her father had given her. "Here, take the pearls, and the earrings!" She flung them across the tiny room at Jerry. "You want the dress back too?" She rummaged through her closet. "I'm not a whore."

"For cryin' out loud, Estelle, I didn't call you a whore." Jerry stood in the doorway of the bedroom. "But I'm sick of making out like a couple of teenagers, then getting up and going home."

"Home? I don't even know where home is for you! It's a big secret."

"Secret—it sounds like you don't trust me. Maybe I do need to get out of here." Jerry turned to leave.

When Estelle started to cry, Jerry turned and pulled her into his arms. "Baby, you know I'm crazy about you. I just want to be with you all the time."

Estelle stiffened. "I can't just let you move in. We've talked about that. What would people think? What about Jake?"

"We can just tell people we got married. It's nobody's business anyway. Jake is too young to know the difference," Jerry answered.

"Why don't we just get married, Jerry? I can have my marriage to Ricky annulled. I don't understand."

"Baby, I told you, we will. We just want to make sure the time is right. Come on, baby," Jerry sweet-talked her.

"I don't know. I'm afraid someone will find out we're not married," Estelle argued.

"For God's sake, Estelle, grow up. What we do is our business. Besides, I know you barely make ends meet on your own." He moved closer and drew her into his arms again. "What do you say?"

"Jerry, I love you, and I don't know what I'd do if I lost you." Estelle's resolve crumbled.

He carefully guided her toward the bedroom. Estelle was trembling as Jerry playfully tumbled into bed with her in his arms. "I'm all yours, little girl."

Later that night, Jerry told Estelle his plan. "I'm going to St. Louis next weekend. It's a short trip, and you can come with me. We can tell the old lady, what's her name?"

"Pauline," Estelle answered.

"We can tell her and the people at the diner that we got married over the weekend. Then I'll move in."

"She is a nice lady and takes such good care of Jake. But, sometimes she is a bit nosey. She's hinted that we may be spending too much time alone."

"If she gets too nosey, find someone else to watch the kid."

"No! Jake loves her. And, she takes such good care of him. She's just very religious—she talks about God all the time. My parents were like that. I can handle it, but what about my name? People will think it's odd if I don't change my name."

"Don't worry about it. Who's going to know the difference anyway? You can use any name you want. When we do get married, I can adopt Jake and we can all have the same name." Jerry was tired of her questions.

"Adopt him? You would do that? Jake would have a real dad?" Estelle threw her arms around Jerry's neck.

"Sure, it may be a while, but we can work it out." Estelle didn't see the uncomfortable look on Jerry's face. "I'd better go now. I'll come by on Sunday afternoon, and we can go to the park or something. In the meantime, find out if Pauline will watch Jake next weekend."

9

Saturday morning, Estelle knocked on Pauline's apartment door. "Come in, dear. Did you and your young man have a nice time last night?"

"Yes—yes, we did." Estelle found it difficult to look the sweet, little lady in the eyes.

"Pauline," Estelle hesitated.

"Yes, dear?" Pauline answered. "Sit down, Estelle, and we can visit."

"Thank you. Can you watch Jake next weekend—for the entire weekend?" Estelle asked quietly.

"Estelle, you're not going to go on an overnight trip with your young man are you?" Pauline asked. "It's always important for a man to treat a woman with respect, you know."

"It's not what you think. I don't really want to make a big deal about this, but we're getting married," Estelle lied.

Pauline looked up from her embroidery work. "Married? Are you sure you know him well enough? Marriage is for a long time."

"Pauline, I appreciate your concern, but I know what I'm doing. Jerry and I love each other. He even wants to adopt Jake. Jake will finally have a dad." Estelle was excited about the possibility of a real marriage at some point. "It will be good for Jake and me. I barely get by with my wages and tips."

"Estelle, what about Jake's father? Aren't you still married?"

"No. When he didn't come back, my parents helped me get an annulment. We weren't married in the church." The lie came out of Estelle's mouth like the most natural thing in the world.

"I see. Well, darling, you don't want to make a decision like this because you feel that you can't make it on your own. God will always make a way, if we let Him. You know I'm willing to help you in any way I can."

"Thank you, Pauline. I appreciate everything you do for us. Jerry is coming by tomorrow to take us to the park, and I need to let him know if you can take care of Jake next weekend."

"Certainly, I'd love to. Jake can go to Sunday school at my church. He will enjoy it so much." Estelle saw the concern in Pauline's eyes.

Sunday afternoon was beautiful. It was sunny, and the temperature was perfect. Estelle made sure the apartment was spotless, and she baked brownies, which Jake and Jerry both loved. She looked at the clock; Jerry was late.

"Momma, where's Jerry? You said we could go to the park to play. You said Jerry was coming to take us to the park," Jake whined.

"Ouch!" Estelle cursed and dropped the knife she was washing. "Jake, we'll go in a minute, just leave me alone."

"Okay, Momma." Jake dropped his head and went to the living room.

Estelle dried her hands and followed him. She heard Jake sniffling. "I'm sorry, sugar. It's not your fault Momma is upset. Get your shoes on and let's go."

Jake had a great time at the park. Estelle was distracted and couldn't stop thinking about Jerry. She hated when he disappeared like this. There was a lump in her throat and a knot in the pit of her stomach. What had she done wrong? He had been happy when he left Friday night. Maybe she shouldn't have argued with him about living together.

"Come on, Jake, it's almost dinner time." Estelle felt like crying.

"Just a little longer, Momma, please?" Jake asked.

"I said come on. It's getting late," Estelle snapped.

Jake's smile faded, and tears formed in his big brown eyes. Estelle dropped to her knees. "Baby, don't cry. Momma's tired. I didn't mean to take it out on you. Come on."

Like clockwork, Jerry sauntered into the diner Monday morning. Estelle was livid and didn't trust herself to speak. "Vivian, can you wait on him? I'm going in the back for a minute."

"Looks like I'm in hot water." Estelle could hear Jerry as she stood behind the door in the kitchen. "Vivian, can you get her to come out and talk to me? Please?" Jerry begged.

"Jerry, she's pretty upset. You not only stood her up, but little Jake too!"

"It wasn't intentional. I had some spur-of-the-moment business, and I got in really late last night. Come on, Vivian, ask her to come out here," Jerry pleaded.

Estelle stepped out from behind the door. "I don't need anyone to coax me out, Jerry. This isn't the time to discuss your lack of consideration. Why don't you come by the apartment tonight and we'll talk."

"Sure, baby. I'm sorry. I really am," Jerry apologized.

That evening, after Jake was in bed, Jerry knocked on Estelle's door. "Who is it?" Estelle put her ear up to the door.

"It's the big bad wolf, baby," Jerry teased.

Estelle made sure that she didn't smile when she opened the door. "Come in."

"Oh, you are *mad*! Come on, baby. I didn't mean to stand you up. It was last-minute business. I would never hurt you on purpose." Jerry tried to get Estelle to look at him.

"It's not just about me; Jake doesn't understand. I was so upset that I took it out on him." Tears spilled down Estelle's cheeks. "None of it was his fault—all because you couldn't even stop by to let me know."

"Baby, I'm sorry. I'm not used to having little kids around. I've been on my own for so long, I don't always think about letting someone else know what I'm doing. Please forgive me." Jerry put his arms around her.

Estelle cried softly. "Jerry, I'm so afraid. Even before he left, Jake's dad wasn't around half the time. After he left, I found out he was in a lot of trouble. There were so many secrets. He never came back."

Jerry held her closer. "Come on, you know you're my world. You're the best thing that's ever happened to me. I'd be nuts to run out on you. You have to trust me—I trust you."

"I have a problem with trust. It wasn't just Ricky running out on us. After my parents died, and I ran out of money, I went to stay with Ricky's mother. It was horrible. She is a prostitute and has other girls working for her," Estelle sighed and continued. "Lucille and I hated each other. I don't know why she let me stay there. When I finally saved some money and decided to get an apartment, she was really angry. I should have been smarter and more careful." Estelle covered her face with her hands.

"What happened, baby?"

"The night before Jake and I moved out, she paid one of her flunkies to, to …" Estelle started to cry.

"She paid him to what?" Jerry was agitated.

"He kicked in my bedroom door and raped me."

"That no good…" Jerry let out a stream of curses.

"There's more." She trembled and could barely speak. "Later, I discovered I was pregnant. I couldn't take care of another child, and I couldn't have a baby by someone like Johnny Moran. I had an abortion. It didn't go well, and I wound up in the hospital. That's the week I was gone from the diner. I wasn't on vacation," Estelle sobbed. "Do you hate me? Do you think I'm horrible?"

"No, baby. You were afraid and alone. You had no choice." Jerry held her and stroked her hair. "You're not alone anymore. I'll take care of you now. Do you trust me?"

"I'm sorry, Jerry. I love you so much. I do trust you." Estelle clung to him.

"That's my girl." Jerry smiled as he held her. "Come on, let's make up."

"No. Jake is in the next room."

"Okay, I guess I'll just have to wait until my wedding night," Jerry laughed. Estelle pretended his lighthearted words hadn't hurt.

The week dragged by. Estelle packed and unpacked her bag at least six times. It was as if she really was getting married.

One evening after dinner, Jake wandered into his mother's room. "Mommy, are we going on a trip today?"

"No, Jake. Mommy is going on a little trip this weekend. You're going to stay with Miss Pauline. She's going to take you to the park and to Sunday school. Won't that be fun?" Estelle couldn't understand why she was so nervous talking to her six-year-old.

"Are you going by yourself, Mommy? Won't you be scared?"

"Uh, no Jake, Mommy won't be afraid. There's something I have to tell you." Estelle hesitated, then took Jake into her arms and sat him on her lap. "Mommy and Jerry are getting married this weekend. Jerry will live here with us. You're going to have a daddy." She felt guilty for not telling him sooner.

Jake's lower lip began to quiver. "No, Mommy. Please."

"Why would you say something like that?"

"I don't like him. He's a bad man, Mommy. He's a bad man!" Jake cried. "He lies!"

"Jake, don't ever say that again! Jerry is not a bad man. He loves me very much, and he'll love you too. Has Miss Pauline said bad things about Jerry?" Estelle demanded.

"No. Miss Pauline doesn't say bad things about anybody."

"Well, we are going to get married, and Jerry is going to live here. Mommy knows what's best for us. Now go play in the other room." Estelle was shaken by her son's reaction.

Jake glared at his mother and stomped out of the room.

Friday evening finally arrived, and Estelle took her sullen little boy to Pauline's apartment. "Pauline, he's a little upset over all of this. Please don't say anything that will make it worse. I know you don't approve of our getting married, but that's how it's going to be," Estelle announced defensively.

Pauline smiled and took Jake's hand. "Jake, go to the kitchen please. I baked chocolate chip cookies, and they are still warm from the oven. I'll come in and get some milk for you in just a minute." That seemed to do the trick, and Jake ran to the kitchen.

"Estelle, I am concerned that you're jumping into this marriage, but I would never say anything against you—and definitely nothing that would upset Jake. I love you both, like you're my own. I pray for you every day." Estelle saw tears in Pauline's eyes. "I wish you would wait and get to know Jerry a little better. I just want what is best for you and Jake."

Estelle felt a lump in her throat. "Thank you, Pauline. Since my parents died, Jake and I have been on our own. I guess I'm not used to having anyone worry about me." Jake ran back into the living room with a cookie in each hand.

"Mommy has to go now. Give me a kiss and promise you'll be a good boy for Miss Pauline." Estelle hugged him and kissed his face.

90

"I love you, Mommy. Be careful and come back fast." Jake hugged his mother's neck.

"I'll take good care of him. Be careful, and I'll see you on Sunday night." Pauline gave Estelle a quick hug.

Later that evening, Estelle paced the floor of her living room. Jerry was an hour late. That too-familiar knot in her stomach was back. "Did I make him mad last night? Why would he do this?"

Two hours later, there was a knock at the door. "Who's there?" Estelle asked.

"It's the boogeyman, now let me in."

Estelle flung the door open. "You're three hours late. We are going to be driving in the middle of the night."

"We're not going anywhere." Jerry was fidgety. "My trip was can-celled."

"What am I supposed to tell Pauline? She has Jake." Estelle slammed the door.

"Why do you have to tell her anything? We'll just spend the whole weekend here. All my clothes are in my car, and I'll move them in on Sunday." Jerry flopped down on the sofa.

"Stay here? Jerry, I took Saturday off at the diner. My bag is packed, and I shipped my son off with Pauline for the entire weekend. He's never been away from me for more than a few nights and that was because I was in the *hospital*," Estelle fumed. "Believe it or not, I was excited about this trip."

"Estelle, I'm tired, and it's not my fault. What do you want me to say? Our trip was cancelled." Jerry couldn't sit still.

"Do you think we can stay here all weekend and no one will know it?" Estelle felt trapped. Jerry was here, but it was as if she'd been stood up.

"No one will know the difference." Jerry laughed and growled, "My plan is to consummate our marriage."

Humiliated, Estelle finally gave in. She didn't want Pauline to know about the change of plans, but Jerry was right. It wasn't his fault, and Pauline would never understand.

Jerry and Estelle didn't leave the apartment all weekend. Their rendezvous wasn't quite as romantic as Jerry promised. After that first night, he slept a good part of the time. Estelle was amazed that anyone could sleep so many hours. She was sure he must be sick.

Sunday night, just after dark, Jerry told Estelle to go get Jake and he would bring the car around and carry in his clothes.

Estelle pasted on a smile as she knocked on Pauline's door. "It's me. We're back."

Pauline opened the door. "He's sleeping, dear. He tried to stay awake until you got here. We had such fun, but he missed his mommy. You know, we didn't even see you leave Friday night. So, how did everything go?"

Estelle smiled and looked down at the floor. "It was a very simple ceremony, and Jerry made all of the arrangements ahead of time. I guess I'll just carry Jake. I don't want to wake him."

"Estelle, is something wrong? You seem nervous." Pauline reached out and took the young girl's hand.

Estelle almost blurted out the whole truth. Instead, she jerked her hand back. "I'm fine, Pauline, really. It's just that this will be very new to Jake, so I am a little nervous. We have to go. Jerry is bringing our bags in from the car.

"Okay dear. Let me get his things together." Estelle gently picked Jake up from the couch. Pauline handed Jake's bag to Estelle. "Oh, I didn't get to see your ring."

Estelle panicked. She and Jerry had never discussed a ring. Her face turned red. She mumbled, "Well, Jerry picked out my ring and it didn't fit properly. It's at the jeweler's. Thank you so much, Pauline." Estelle rushed out the door.

She didn't see the worried look on Pauline's face as she hurried down the hall to the stairway.

Pauline put away clean dishes and tidied the kitchen. She walked to the window just as Jerry pulled into a parking spot in front of the building. He made a couple of trips into the building, dragging some bags and a couple of boxes from his car. Pauline couldn't put her finger on it, but she knew Jerry had something to hide. She didn't trust him and was afraid for Estelle and Jake.

Pauline walked to her chair, picked up her Bible, and began to pray. "Lord, I know you love Estelle and Jake even more than I do. I don't want to judge her, Lord, but I don't think she knows you. She needs you so desperately. I don't know how to break through the wall that she's built around her heart. I am afraid of what she may go through before she will let you help her. Protect little Jake and Estelle. I know you love Jerry too, Lord. Something is very wrong; please bring the truth out into the light. Father, I pray in Jesus' name, Amen."

Jake stirred as Estelle put him in bed and covered him with his favorite blanket. Jerry wasn't back yet, but he didn't say exactly where he parked the car. She decided to wash her face and get ready for bed. A few minutes later, Jerry knocked on the door.

"You know, baby, I need a key now that we're hitched," Jerry laughed.

"I'll get a key for you tomorrow." Estelle wasn't impressed with his humor.

"I'll get the rest of my stuff." He put the bags down and went back out the door. Minutes later, he was back with a couple of boxes.

Jerry walked over and put his arms around Estelle.

"I'm really tired. Can we go to bed now?" Estelle still felt uneasy.

"Sure, baby." Jerry pulled her toward the bedroom.

"Jerry, I'm tired. I just want to go to sleep," she snapped and pulled away. "Oh, by the way, Pauline asked to see my ring. I never even thought about a ring—did you?"

"Wear the ring I got you." Jerry yawned.

"It's not a wedding ring. It's my birthstone." Estelle's voice was tinged with anger.

"Well, you said you had your mother's ring. Has Pauline ever seen it?

"No, she hasn't. I lied and told her you bought a ring for me and it didn't fit, so we took it to the jewelers." Estelle was embarrassed.

"Hey, that was a good story. If she hasn't seen your mother's ring, wear it." Jerry headed for the bedroom. "Since you're so tired, I'm going to bed."

10

Over the weeks following their so-called wedding weekend, Jerry and Estelle fell into a pattern. His travel continued to be sporadic. As usual, his business was often spur-of-the-moment, and his trips were sometimes longer than expected. When he was home, he frequently had business meetings that kept him out late at night.

One night as he packed his bag, Estelle asked about his trip. "How long will you be gone this time?"

"I don't know, a few days, maybe the whole week."

"Jerry, this is ridiculous. Why don't you know how long you'll be gone?" Estelle tried unsuccessfully to keep the edge out of her voice. "I never know how to get in touch with you. What if something were to happen?"

"Like what? This crap is getting old. You act like you don't trust me." Jerry threw socks into his suitcase. "Don't I pay the bills around here? You don't even have to work full-time now. Do you and Jake go without anymore?"

"That's not the point. I need to know where you are. We have a telephone now, but you never call when you're traveling," Estelle replied.

"I'm a salesman. I travel." His voice grew louder with each word, and he pointed his finger at her face. "Sometimes I get to my hotel late, and I don't want to wake you and Jake by calling. You are not going to third-degree me, and I'm not going to check in with my mommy every day." Jerry went into the bathroom and slammed the door.

The next morning, Jerry kissed Estelle goodbye, picked up his bag, and headed for the door. "I should be home by the weekend. This time it's Chicago. Don't worry, okay? You have money?"

"Sure, we're fine." Estelle choked back tears.

Later that morning, Estelle finished getting ready for work and took Jake to Pauline's apartment.

"Estelle, don't you have Thursday off this week?" Pauline asked.

"Yes, I'm off on Thursday."

"Well, Jake is out of school on Thursday and Friday. I thought we could go downtown and do a little window shopping. Then, we could have lunch." Pauline smiled.

"I don't know, Pauline. I have a lot to do." Estelle struggled for a legitimate excuse.

Jake interrupted his mother. "Please, Momma? Please can we go?" He practically jumped up and down.

"Okay, Jake, we can go." Estelle gave in.

"Wonderful!" Pauline smiled.

With Jerry gone, time crawled by. Estelle was on edge, and she was often cranky with Jake. "Why did I ever agree to go downtown with Pauline?" She whispered to herself. "Jerry might call since I made such a big deal about it." She couldn't get out of it; she had promised Jake. She sat down in a chair, put her head back, and closed her eyes.

She jumped when the telephone rang. "Hello?" She heard a click, and the line was dead.

Wednesday night, long after Estelle had gone to sleep, she heard ringing. "Is it time to get up?" She managed to open her eyes and look at the clock. It was 3:00 a.m., and the ringing persisted. Fear gripped her heart when she realized it was the phone. "Hello?" There was no answer. "Hello, who is this?" Again, there was a click, and the line went dead.

Thursday was a beautiful day. Jake was so excited; he chattered until it was time to leave. Pauline, Estelle, and Jake walked to catch the streetcar. Jake pointed at buildings and trucks and asked a steady stream of questions during the ride downtown. Pauline chuckled and patiently answered every one, but Estelle was silent during the ride.

As they passed through an unfamiliar part of town, something caught Estelle's eye. It was a car that looked just like Jerry's. Trying not to draw Pauline's attention, she turned to take a closer look. Near the car, a man stood in the doorway of a building. She could only see part of his back, but he was Jerry's size. Two women were talking to him. Both women had tinted hair; one was blonde, the other a redhead. Their clothing left little to the imagination, and they reminded her of Lucille and her "business partners." Estelle felt sick to her stomach. "How foolish; it's not him," she whispered.

"What dear?" Pauline asked.

"Oh, nothing, I was just thinking out loud." Estelle felt the all-too-familiar knot in her stomach and lump in her throat.

Jerry was home by late Friday night. "Oh, baby, I had a great trip. I sold more than I have in a long time! Let's celebrate!" Jerry was practically wild with excitement.

"So, were all of your stops in Chicago?" Estelle asked.

"Yeah, Chicago. Hey, let's go to dinner, get some wine, and party!" Jerry slipped his arms around her and began to nibble on her neck.

"I already had dinner, and there are leftovers in the icebox. I'm going to bed."

"Well aren't we exciting? I've been gone all week, you're tired, and I have to eat leftovers?"

"Look, Jerry. I've had a long day. If you want to come to bed when I do, come on."

"No thanks. I think I'll just go out and get some dinner. Please don't let me interrupt your *schedule*."

Estelle turned and walked to the bedroom as Jerry walked out the door. About an hour after Jerry left, the phone rang. Estelle picked up the receiver, but no one was there.

One morning as Estelle glanced through the newspaper, a small front-page article caught her eye. She read further. A man and woman had been murdered in a house in Kansas City. Narcotics were found, and there was evidence that the house was being used as a brothel. Both victims were drug users and had been shot—the other residents of the house heard nothing until shots rang out. No one saw an intruder, but it looked like a botched robbery. The bedroom where the bodies were found had been ransacked. The victims were Lucille Shannon and Johnny Moran. "Oh, sweet Mother of God! Murdered?" Estelle whispered. She had no idea Lucille or Johnny used drugs.

She read on. Five other women in the house were arrested for prostitution, including an 18-year-old girl. Three minor children were taken into state custody.

"Dixie and the girls, what will happen to them?" Estelle sighed. She felt so sorry for the girls, but there was nothing she could do for them. She and Jerry certainly couldn't take care of three more kids, and Dixie was probably beyond help. Estelle planned to tell Jerry about Lucille and Johnny when he came back from his trip.

When Jerry came home, Estelle told him about Lucille and Johnny's deaths. "Sounds to me like they got what they deserved," he said.

"Jerry, I can't believe you said that! I hated both of them, but I didn't want them dead!"

"You're too sweet, baby. People like that, they always get what's coming to them sooner or later; it's life."

"I guess you're right, but it's still sad. I feel sorry for the girls." Estelle sighed, and dropped the entire subject.

The next morning, Estelle decided not to bring up Lucille or Johnny Moran again. "Jerry, we've been together for months now. Don't you think it's time we talked about really getting married?" Estelle asked carefully.

"Sure, baby, we can talk about getting married. I have a meeting in about an hour; I don't have time right now." Jerry headed for the bathroom to start getting ready. "Oh, by the way, I have a very important client coming to town this weekend. We need to wine and dine him. I want you to go with us."

"Really? You want me to go? What will I wear?" Estelle almost squealed with excitement.

"Don't worry; I'll take care of it. I know your size." Jerry answered as he closed the bathroom door. "Talk to Pauline about watching Jake."

"Okay. You take care of it." Estelle's excitement faded just a little.

Friday evening, Jerry rushed into the apartment with several boxes. "Here, get dressed. I want you to put your hair up tonight. Is Jake at Pauline's?"

"Yes, I took him up earlier. What on earth? Look at all of these boxes!"

"These are the only ones you need to open tonight. Your shoes and evening bag are in the smaller one. Here's the dress." Jerry opened the dress box. "Come on, we need to hurry."

Estelle pulled the little black cocktail dress out of the box. "Jerry, there isn't much to this. The straps are so tiny. It looks more like a slip than a dress."

"Estelle, put it on! You'll look elegant."

"I'm not used to bare shoulders. It looks a little low cut." Estelle grew more frustrated.

"Put the dress on, now! We have to leave in less than an hour. Oh, here is some perfume, too. Use some rouge and a little lipstick. And make those gorgeous eyes stand out." Jerry walked out and shut the bedroom door behind him.

Jerry peeked in one more time. "Wear your mother's pearls, the pearl earrings I got you, and this diamond cocktail ring." Once again, he shut the door.

Estelle stood for a moment looking at the tag on the dress. "Oh my God, this thing cost a fortune—and all of this other stuff?" she whispered.

"Estelle, hurry up!" Jerry shouted from the bathroom.

Finally Estelle emerged from the bedroom. She opened the door slowly and walked into the living room. Jerry whistled. "You look absolutely beautiful. Maybe we should just stay home."

"I've never worn anything quite so bare. I'm not really comfortable." She blushed and turned away from him.

In two strides, he was across the room. He gently stroked her arms from her shoulders down to her fingertips. Estelle shivered as Jerry's lips brushed across the back of her neck. "You look ravishing. Do you have any idea how beautiful you are? Tonight, I'm going to show you off."

"Thank you, Jerry. You make me feel beautiful," Estelle sighed.

"If it will make you feel better, you can wear this. Close your eyes." Estelle felt something silky as Jerry placed a stole over her shoulders.

"Oh my God, is this real?" Estelle stroked the soft mink.

"Don't worry, there's more where that came from. Let's go." Jerry straightened the lapel of his conservative black suit and checked his diamond cuff links.

"You look so handsome." Estelle kissed him on the cheek.

"Oh, and don't mention Jake tonight."

"Why?"

"Just don't. Our personal lives are our business."

In the wee hours of the morning, Jerry and Estelle climbed the stairs to the apartment. "I have never danced so much in my life."

"You are quite the little stepper. Mr. Lawrence was impressed." Jerry steadied her as they walked down the hallway.

"Why did we take a taxi instead of your car?"

"I told you. Mr. Lawrence is pretty well off, and my car is not quite what he's accustomed to," Jerry replied.

"Do you think I drank too much? Did I laugh too much?" Estelle giggled.

"You were perfect," Jerry answered.

"Why did Mr. Lawrence want to dance with me all the time? He is a little old, don't you think? I didn't want to be rude." Estelle gave Jerry an innocent look.

"That's my girl. He's been traveling, looking at pieces for his stores, and he needed to relax a little. You were just what the doctor ordered. Come on, let's get these clothes off and get you to bed." Jerry guided her to the bedroom.

Estelle was under the covers and sleeping within minutes. Jerry shut the bedroom door and went into the living room to smoke a cigarette. "Just what the doctor ordered, baby. Beautiful, innocent, classy—just what the doctor ordered. I've waited so long for you." He whispered as he blew smoke rings. "We are going places. It's time."

The next morning, Estelle slept late. Her head throbbed when she tried to get up. "I feel like I've been run over by a train." She pulled the blanket back over her head.

Jerry laughed as he walked into the bedroom. "You sure had a time last night. Here, drink this and take these."

"What is this?" Estelle squinted.

"It is a little tomato juice concoction and a couple of aspirin. Come on, drink up." He handed her the glass and aspirin tablets.

Estelle obediently took the aspirin and drank Jerry's concoction.

"Are you sure that we can't take Jake on the picnic this afternoon? It seems such a shame for him to miss out."

"Estelle, I told you this is an adult gathering. And Jake is none of Mark's business. Did you make sure Pauline could keep him? We'll pay her extra," Jerry replied.

"Yes, I did," Estelle pouted. "I'm going to get him right now. I want to have some time with him today."

"Don't be in such a hurry. I have plans for you first." Jerry pulled her into his arms. "You're my world, girl. You're the best thing that's ever happened to me."

Later, Estelle managed to pull herself together enough to go to Pauline's apartment and get Jake.

"Tell Momma how you helped me put some of the puzzle together, Jake," Pauline coaxed.

"I don't want to tell her. She's leaving me again," Jake pouted and refused to look at his mother.

"Sugar, Momma doesn't do this every weekend. This is special. Someone Jerry works with is in town for the weekend. He doesn't know anyone here, so we're spending some time with him." Estelle knelt down in front of Jake.

"Well, why can't I go too?" Jake crossed his arms.

"Jake, he's an old man. He doesn't have any little kids and would probably be grouchy and boring to you." Estelle put her arms around her son. "I love you."

"I love you too, Momma. I miss you so much." Jake put his arms around his mother's neck.

"Come on, let's go home and play until it's time for me to go." Estelle took his hand and headed for the door. "I'll bring him back in a couple of hours, Pauline. Thank you so much. We are going to pay you for the extra time."

"You're welcome, dear. Don't worry about the money; he's a joy." Estelle again didn't notice the worried look on Pauline's face.

"Thank you again, Pauline. I appreciate you so much." Estelle and Jake hurried out the door.

11

Jerry, what is this?" Estelle held up the little skirt, blouse, and sweater. "Shouldn't I wear trousers or a longer skirt to a picnic?"

"It's a tennis outfit," Jerry laughed. "We're going to hit a few balls and then have a picnic."

"I don't know *how* to play tennis. What on earth were you thinking?"

"Don't worry, baby. Mark is an excellent tennis player. He'll be happy to give you a few lessons. Put your hair in a ponytail with a ribbon. It makes you look like a little girl."

Estelle dressed and tied her hair up in a ponytail with a powder-blue ribbon. She had been excited about Jerry's attention, but suddenly she was uneasy.

Mr. Lawrence was a patient teacher. Estelle was nervous and uncomfortable as he moved close and put his arms around her to show her the proper way to hold the racket.

"Well, dear, that's probably enough for today." Mark Lawrence let his hand slide down Estelle's arm as she stepped away. "Jerry, let's have our picnic. I'm a bit tired, so would you mind if we improvise and dine in my hotel room? I have a lovely suite."

"Sure, Mark. That would be great. No ants or flies? Perfect," Jerry answered. "Come on, Estelle, here's your sweater."

Estelle was quiet during the ride to Mr. Lawrence's hotel. She and Jerry followed Mark into the hotel and to his luxurious suite. "Make yourselves comfortable while I change," Mark said as he walked into the bedroom.

"Jerry," Estelle hissed. "I thought we were going to have a picnic. Where is the food?"

"I'm sure Mark is going to order room service. It's okay," Jerry whispered.

A few minutes later, Mark was back, wearing a blue silk smoking jacket, silk pants, and leather slippers. "I took the liberty of ordering for all of us. I hope you don't mind."

"Of course not; that's great," Jerry piped up.

"Do you like champagne my dear?" Mark asked.

"Well, yes. I—I just don't drink often, Mr. Lawrence." Estelle stuttered and tried not to blush under Mark's penetrating stare.

Mark and Jerry made small talk until someone knocked on the door. "That should be our food," Mark said as he went to answer the door.

"Jerry, he is wearing his pajamas. Don't you think that is a little odd for this time of day? And, he keeps looking at me. I want to go home," Estelle whispered.

"Estelle, calm down. He's old, and he's rich. We'll have some food, a little wine, and then excuse ourselves. Shut up and don't ruin this for me."

"Thank you." Mark pressed several bills into the young man's hand.

"You're most welcome, sir. Shall I put out the 'Do not disturb' sign?" The young man smiled.

"No, that won't be necessary. I'll take care of it. Thank you." Mark closed the door.

"Jerry, won't you pour some champagne for us?" Mark asked.

Estelle was starving. There was fruit, a variety of cheeses and meats, crackers, and champagne. She didn't see Jerry drop something into her glass as he poured the champagne.

"That was wonderful. Thank you Mr. Lawrence," Estelle said as she finished her third glass of champagne.

"Please call me Mark, dear." Mark Lawrence's face looked a little distorted. She didn't want to be rude, but Estelle started to giggle.

"Jerry, I think you need to get me home. I feel really funny." Everything started spinning. She felt like she was in a dream, and Jerry's voice was so far away. Estelle slumped back on the sofa.

"You can leave now, Jerry. Come back around midnight to pick her up." Mark led the wobbly young woman toward the bedroom and placed her on the bed. "She isn't going to be completely out, is she?"

"No, she'll be fine. She just won't remember anything." Jerry hesitated, "Uh, I want half now and the rest when I come back for her."

"She is lovely, isn't she? My guess is that she is worth every penny. Here, now please leave us." Mark escorted Jerry to the door.

Jerry hadn't expected to be nervous and worried, but he was. He decided to wait at the apartment until it was time to go back for Estelle. A few minutes after he closed the apartment door, the phone rang. "Hello?"

"Jerry, I need Estelle. Jake has a fever," Pauline answered.

"She's sleeping. Can't you take care of it?" Jerry panicked and fumbled for words.

"Jerry, he wants his mother. He's sick."

"Well, she's sick too. It must be something she ate. She's sick as a dog. Can't you keep him for the rest of the night?" Jerry broke out in a sweat.

Pauline was silent for a moment. "Well, I suppose we have no choice. I'll try to comfort him and let him know that his mommy is sick too. Please tell her." Pauline sighed and hung up.

Jerry waited until he thought Pauline would be back in bed; then he sneaked out the door.

Unable to go back to sleep, Pauline turned off all of the lights and watched out her window. Moments later, she saw Jerry leave alone. She had never trusted that young man. Something just seemed wrong. She picked up her Bible and started to pray. "Lord, your Word says that things done in darkness will be brought to light. Something is going on, and Estelle is in danger." Tears trickled down Pauline's face as she prayed and read her Bible. It was some time before she went to bed.

At midnight, Jerry went back to the hotel for Estelle. He knocked for several minutes before Mark answered the door. He had worked for Mark for years and knew how dangerous the man was. Jerry could handle hoodlums and gangsters, but Mark was a different breed. The old guy was cold as ice and gave him the creeps. Finally the lock clicked and the door opened. "Come in, Jerry. Here is your money."

"Hey, this isn't what we agreed on. Where's the rest of my money?"

"You led me to believe that she was practically innocent. I am giving you most of your money because she is so lovely. She was definitely worthwhile. At one point, she thought I was you. My, my, you are a lucky man," Mark smiled.

"I never told you she was a virgin, and you know it!" Jerry shouted.

"Jerry, quiet down. I thought you were the only man who had been with her, but she talked about her husband and her baby. I couldn't quite make out her husband's name. Tell me, Jerry, she isn't the young woman you've been watching, is she?"

"What are you talking about?" Jerry panicked. How did Mark know that?

"You know exactly what I'm talking about. Is she the one?"

"No, no she's not. That ... she took off after, you know ..."

"Good, just a coincidence I suppose." Mark's expression turned ugly. "Now consider yourself lucky that I am paying you at all. I don't like being lied to."

"Where is she?" Jerry demanded.

"She is in the bedroom. I might like to see her again the next time I'm in town. I will pay you in full then." Mark clicked his tongue as if he were talking to a child. "You need to learn that lying isn't profitable in every situation, Jerry."

Jerry stormed into the bedroom. Estelle was still out, and her clothes lay in a heap on the floor. "How do you expect me to get her home? You ripped her clothes off."

"Here, wrap her in this old robe." Mark held out a silk robe.

"What did you do?" As Jerry covered Estelle, he saw red welts on her backside. He turned, grabbed Mark, and pushed him against the wall. "You didn't tell me you would do *this* to her."

"Jerry, take your hands off of me and I'll let this go. Remember who you are dealing with." Mark's stare was cold and steady. "Now get her covered and get out of here."

Jerry backed off. He wrapped Estelle in the silk robe, carried her down the stairway, and out a back entry to his car.

Back in their apartment, tears streamed down Jerry's face as he put a clean gown on Estelle and got her into bed. "Oh, baby, I'm so sorry. I didn't know he would do this to you." He kissed her cheeks and eyelids.

He walked into the bathroom, locked the door, and took a loose tile off the wall under the sink. A small package fell out, and Jerry removed the contents. He gently pulled out the syringe, spoon, and makeshift tourniquet, while reaching for the tiny bag in his pocket. Sweat began to bead on his forehead and his upper lip. He licked his lips as his hands shook. "Calm yourself, big boy." He could do this in his sleep. "I should have been a doctor." Minutes later he chuckled as he cleared all of the air out of the syringe and hit a vein on the very first try.

Releasing the tourniquet, he slowly pushed the plunger all the way in and emptied the contents of the syringe into his vein. Within seconds, the rush hit him like an explosion in his head. He barely pulled the needle from his arm as he smiled and slid to the floor next to the commode. "Oh yeah, that's good, so good." It felt like warm liquid spread through his body. His eyes closed. "Everything is going to be okay," he whispered as he nodded off.

The next morning, Pauline knocked on the door until Jerry answered. "Jerry, this child needs his mother. Where is she?"

"I told you she was sick. She's still sleeping." Jerry turned away to light a cigarette.

"She may be sick, but Jake still needs her. Now please wake her and ask her to come in here." Pauline trembled with anger.

"Man, you don't give up do you?" Jerry ran his hand through his hair and headed for the bedroom. "Estelle, wake up. The old lady is here with Jake, and she says he's sick." Jerry shook her. Estelle stirred just a little, but she didn't wake up.

"What is wrong with her, Jerry? What did you do to her?" Pauline put Jake on the sofa and walked into the bedroom behind Jerry.

"I didn't do *anything* to her. She had too much to drink. I tried to get her to slow down, but she was having too much fun," Jerry answered.

Pauline moved past Jerry to the bed. "Estelle, wake up. Jake is sick. You need to wake up." Pauline practically shouted. "Estelle, wake up!"

Slowly Estelle's eyes opened, then closed and opened again. "Where am I? What happened?" She tried to sit up and fell back on the bed.

"You had too much to drink last night and Sherlock Holmes here is trying to make a big deal out of it." Jerry moved toward the bed.

"Estelle, Jake is sick. He's had a fever all night. I came by last night, but Jerry wouldn't wake you. He said you were sick too."

"What?" Estelle sat up and then grabbed her head. "Oh God, I think I'm going to throw up." She stumbled to the bathroom.

"See, I told you. She has a hangover." Jerry puffed on his cigarette like a maniac.

Pauline ran to the bathroom when she heard Estelle scream. "Oh my God, what is this?"

"Estelle, unlock the door," Pauline demanded. Estelle unlocked the door and Pauline walked into the bathroom. "What's wrong?"

"I have welts and bruises all over my backside!" Estelle cried.

Jerry ran to the bathroom. "Look, you were a little out of control last night. When I was trying to get you home, you fought with me and fell over a chair. You broke the thing and fell on the legs. You must have landed harder than I thought."

Pauline's gaze pierced through Jerry. She didn't believe a word he said.

"I don't remember drinking *that* much," Estelle said.

"Of course you don't. You got drunk and passed out." Jerry wouldn't look at her.

Pauline took a deep breath and scowled at Jerry before turning to Estelle. "Jake is sick, and that's all that matters at this point. We have to take him to the doctor because he's had a fever all night. I've done everything I know to do, and I can't keep the fever down. Now wash your face and get some clothes on. We need to go."

Estelle washed her face and threw on some clothes. Jake was sleeping on the couch so she picked him up and headed for the door with Pauline. "He is burning up. Jerry, can you take us to General Hospital in the car?"

"Sure, I'll take you." Jerry grabbed his keys.

The ride to General Hospital was quiet. Jerry pulled up to the emergency entrance to let the two women and little Jake out. "I have some business to attend to, but I'll be back. I'm sure you'll be here for a little while."

An hour and half later, Pauline, Estelle, and Jake listened to the doctor's instructions. "Now make sure that he takes this until it's all gone. Put these drops in his ears and then put a little cotton in each ear. The shot we gave him should kick in and help to get a head start on the infection. As long as he has a fever, he'll need baby aspirin every four hours. A cool wet cloth on his forehead will be helpful too."

"Thank you, Doctor. Thank you so much." Estelle held Jake close.

The threesome waited for Jerry for another hour. Pauline knew Jerry wouldn't come back for them. "I'll call a taxi, dear. We need to get Jake home."

"Okay. Thank you, Pauline. I guess Jerry got held up and lost track of time." Estelle tried not to cry.

"I'm sure he did," Pauline said, trying not to take her frustration out on Estelle.

When they got home, Estelle kept Jake in the living room with her all day. At bedtime, she got her pillow and spent the night in Jake's room. Around midnight, she heard Jerry come in. Jake's fever had broken, and she felt safe leaving him for a few minutes to talk to Jerry.

"What on earth were you thinking?" Estelle paced back and forth across the small living room. "How could you just leave us there?"

"I got tied up on some business. What do you want me to say?" Jerry fidgeted and ran his hands through his hair. "You got home, didn't you?"

"Only because Pauline called a taxi; she knew you weren't coming back. God, she must think I am an idiot."

"Estelle, I would have come back sooner. I thought you would be there for hours." Jerry was desperate. "I did go back. Um, they said you were already gone."

"Really? I take that back, it's you who must think I'm an idiot. What time did you go back, Jerry? Who did you talk to?"

"You think I'm lying, don't you?" Jerry feigned indignation.

"Lying? I don't know what to think anymore! I don't even know what I *did* last night. There's an entire night that is a complete blank for me. And you tell me that I put these bruises on my butt myself? My son was sick, and you didn't even try to wake me." Estelle walked into Jake's room and shut the door.

Jerry grabbed his keys and cigarettes and left the apartment door wide open as he ran out.

"Estelle? Estelle, are you here?" Pauline heard the fighting from upstairs and saw Jerry drive away.

Estelle came out of Jake's room. "I was checking on Jake to make sure his fever is still down. Thank you so much for going with us and making sure that we got home. Jerry forgot to give me any money. I couldn't even have bought the baby aspirin if you hadn't been there. I'll pay you back when Jerry gets home."

"Estelle, I don't care if you pay me back. I'm just worried about you and Jake. It seems that things are not going very well with Jerry. I don't mean to pry, but I care about you and Jake."

"Things are fine." Estelle turned away. She couldn't stand for Pauline to know how upset she really was. "Jerry has never had children, and he's been on his own for so long. This is all new to him."

"I'm sorry—I know it isn't my business, but I think there is more going on here than adjusting to the responsibility of a family. I don't trust Jerry. Please Estelle, you must know something is wrong. Think of Jake!"

Estelle bristled. "How dare you imply that I am not thinking of my son! Jerry loves me, and he is learning to love Jake. It just takes time. Jake and I have a life now. I'm not scrimping and scraping or wondering how I will pay the rent and buy groceries. Jerry takes care of us!"

Pauline shook her head. "I can see that we are not going to agree here. Estelle, I love you and Jake. I'm here if you need me, and I'll continue to care for Jake anytime. I will do my best to stay out of your business because I don't want to destroy our friendship. But I have one more thing to say and then I'm finished." With tears in her eyes, Pauline continued. "Mark my words: if you let pride, bitterness, and fear from the past continue to affect your decisions, you may find yourself in circumstances that you cannot imagine. I don't want to see that happen to you." Pauline turned and let herself out of the apartment.

Estelle was speechless. For a moment, she wanted to run after Pauline and tell her everything, but she was too afraid. Pauline would never understand. Jerry loved her, and somehow everything would work out. He hadn't run out on her like Ricky did. He was gone a lot, but he always came home. Estelle realized her suspicions would only drive Jerry away, and she couldn't stand to lose him; she had to trust him.

After that first night with Mark, Jerry and Estelle acted as if nothing out of the ordinary had happened. They settled back into the old routine, but Jerry's business meetings and travel were more sporadic than ever. Estelle made excuses for him and even began to believe them herself.

12

Late one night, Jerry came home, climbed in bed, and drifted off to sleep. Estelle was already sleeping. Suddenly, a scream pierced the silence; Jerry jumped out of bed ready to confront an intruder. "Who's there?" His eyes adjusted to the dark bedroom. Estelle was flailing and moaning, still not completely awake. "Estelle, wake up!" He turned on the lamp next to the bed, grabbed her by the shoulders, and gently shook her until she stopped moaning and opened her eyes.

"What is wrong with you? You almost gave me a heart attack. I thought someone broke in and was killing you!"

Estelle's only answer was deep wrenching sobs. "Estelle, it's okay. No one is here but us. What is it?" Jerry held her against his chest and rocked back and forth.

"It was him again! He's trying to kill me!"

"Him? What are you talking about?"

Estelle wiped her eyes and blew her nose on the handkerchief Jerry handed her. "I don't know who he is. His face is in the shadow, but it's always the same. He takes my hand and leads me to a beautiful, fragrant garden. Then he asks me to lie down with him, but he doesn't join me. After I lie down, I realize the bed isn't a bed at all. It's like a box, and he tries to lower the lid on the box. It's really a coffin! That's always when I wake up." Estelle put her face in her hands and wept again.

"You've been reading too many mysteries or something. What did you eat last night before you went to bed?" Jerry tried to calm her.

"It has nothing to do with what I ate, and I don't read too many mysteries! I have been having the same dream for weeks," Estelle answered indignantly. "It just keeps getting worse. How would you know what I read? You're not home enough to know what goes on around here."

"Okay, forget it. I try to be nice and you complain. I'm going back to sleep. If the boogey man comes back, get someone else to protect you." Jerry climbed back in bed and turned away from her.

The next morning, Estelle prepared breakfast. Jerry sat at the table and stared into his mug of steaming coffee. "Well, are you okay this morning?"

"I'm fine." Estelle was embarrassed and didn't want to think about the night before. "I'm sorry I yelled at you last night. That dream is horrible."

"Well, don't think about it. Maybe you should drink warm milk before you go to bed." Jerry dug in to the ham, eggs, and biscuits on his plate. "Oh, I forgot to tell you. Mark Lawrence will be in town next month. He's planning a little get together and wants us to be there."

"I really would rather not go. I'm pretty embarrassed about drinking so much that night. I don't even remember what I did." Estelle wouldn't look at Jerry.

"Well, you were fine while we were with him. You just acted up a little bit on the way home. I'll make sure that you don't drink so much."

"Jerry, I don't want to go. There is something about Mark that gives me the creeps."

Jerry slammed his cup down, spilling coffee on the table. "Well that's too bad! He is a very important client, and we are going to entertain him when he's here."

"Why can't you just make it a guys' night out? There is no reason in the world why I should have to go!"

"You intrigue him and add a little class to my act. This guy buys a lot of jewelry, and I know you remember what pays the bills around here." Jerry grabbed a dishcloth and wiped up his mess. "I'm not talking about this anymore. You're a grown woman, not some stupid kid. This is business." With that, he grabbed his keys and headed out the door. "I'll be late tonight."

After the door closed, Estelle whispered. "You're always late."

Estelle's day was typical. She woke Jake, made his breakfast, and bathed him. After walking Jake to school, it didn't take long to tidy up and clean the kitchen and bathroom. The little bit of ironing was done in no time.

When she finished cleaning, she realized Jake wouldn't be out of school for another two hours. She walked to the bedroom closet and pulled her mother's hatbox from the shelf. Inside, under Mary's favorite hat, were a couple of writing tablets. One was completely full. She took the second one out, went back to the living room, and started to write.

She didn't remember exactly when she started her own little diary, but it had been a while. Sometimes it helped to put her feelings down on paper.

It seemed just minutes had passed, and it was time to get Jake from school. She carefully hid her journal in the hatbox and put it back on the closet shelf. There it was—right in front of her—the box with her parents' important documents, and she still wasn't ready to go through those papers.

After Jake took a nap, he and Estelle went to the park. She let him play until he was all played out. "I love you, Mommy." Jake looked up at his mother with a smile that melted her heart.

"I love you too, sweetheart. We had fun, didn't we? Let's go home and have dinner."

Once home, Estelle made dinner, and Jake cleaned his plate. When it was bedtime, Estelle read to him until his eyes were heavy. "Okay, young man, it's time for you to go to sleep. I love you. Give Mommy a kiss."

Estelle went to the living room, read for a while, and then started to get ready for bed since waiting up for Jerry was useless. She would be exhausted tomorrow if she stayed up any longer.

It was a little after midnight when Jerry sneaked in. He had just locked the door and was tiptoeing across the living room when Estelle started to scream. Startled, Jerry dropped his keys and then realized Estelle was in the middle of another nightmare. He sprinted to the bedroom. "Estelle, wake up! You're dreaming again. Estelle!"

This time, her screams awakened Jake. He ran to his mother's room, completely terrified. "Mommy, Mommy!"

"Jake, go back to bed. Your mom is having a bad dream."

"I want my mommy!" Jake cried.

"I said get back to bed *now*!" Jerry yelled.

"Don't yell at my son! He's terrified." Estelle grabbed her robe and carried Jake back to his bed. "Mommy is so sorry. I had a very bad dream. I didn't mean to frighten you."

Just then, there was a knock at the door. "Estelle! Jerry! What is going on in there? Estelle, answer me or I'm going to call the police!" Pauline shouted from the hallway.

Estelle hurried to the door with Jake in her arms. "Pauline, I'm okay. I had a terrible nightmare and woke up screaming."

Pauline rushed in when Estelle opened the door. She made sure that Jake and Estelle weren't hurt, and she glanced around the apartment for any signs of violence. "Are you sure?" Pauline wouldn't have been surprised had she found Jake and Estelle bruised and beaten.

"I promise, Pauline. We're fine. I'm so sorry I woke you, but I need to get Jake back to bed."

"You didn't wake me. I couldn't sleep. I heard screams and realized they were coming from your apartment. Are you sure everything is okay?"

"Yes, we're fine," Estelle reassured her one more time, "and I am so sorry for all the noise."

Pauline hugged Jake and Estelle and went back to her apartment. On her way, she reassured a couple of other tenants who had come out into the hallway.

Estelle put Jake back to bed. She stayed with him until he was sound asleep and then went into the kitchen. "Are you coming back to bed?" Jerry peeked out of the bedroom.

"In a minute. I'm wide awake, so maybe if I have some warm milk, I'll be able to get back to sleep."

"Oh come on, Estelle, warm milk isn't going to help. Get a glass of water, and come here. I have something that the doctor gave me to help me sleep because of how jittery I am sometimes." Jerry opened a dresser drawer and pulled out a bottle of pills. "Here, take one of these and you'll sleep like a baby."

"I'd rather not. The doctor gave those to you, not me."

"They're not going to hurt you. They're mild and will just help you go back to sleep. But if you want to stay up all night and be grumpy with Jake, suit yourself. Go drink your warm milk."

Afraid that Jerry would be angry with her, Estelle asked, "They really will help me sleep? And they're mild?"

"Yes. Here, just take one."

Estelle took the little red pill that Jerry handed her and downed it with water.

The next morning, Jerry had to wake Estelle; she slept right through the alarm. "Hey, sleepyhead, wake up. You need to have some coffee and get Jake up for school."

Estelle heard Jerry, but it was as though she was crawling out of a fog. "Come on—wake up!"

Slowly, she sat up on the side of the bed, but it took several minutes before she could make herself stand up and pull on her robe. "Oh my God, I have never slept so hard in my life. I feel like I could still sleep for hours." She yawned and headed for the coffee pot. Somehow Estelle managed to get Jake up. She didn't have the energy to cook breakfast, but Jake was happy with a bowl of cornflakes. After walking her son to school, she took a nap and woke up just in time to go back to school and get him.

That night, she was still awake when Jerry came in late. "What are you still doing up?"

"Well, I was so tired today that I took a nap. It was late afternoon before I felt completely awake. Now here I am, wide awake."

"Let Dr. Jerry take care of that. I'll get you one of my pills."

"No thanks. It took all day for the last one to wear off."

"Estelle, you were tired because you've been having nightmares and not sleeping through the night."

"That's okay. I'll go to bed when I'm sleepy, and I'll be fine."

"Suit yourself. I'm going to bed."

A few nights later, Estelle woke Jerry again, moaning and crying in her sleep. "Estelle, wake up. You're dreaming." Jerry grabbed her shoulder and shook her until she woke up.

Estelle clung to Jerry and cried. "I'm sorry," she sobbed.

"Look, I'm sorry that you're having this dream, but I can't take much more. We *all* need to sleep. At least you didn't wake Jake this time."

"I can't help it. You act like I'm doing this on purpose." Estelle turned away from Jerry.

"I know you can't help it, but you have to do something. We need to sleep around here, and I've told you over and over again that the pills I have will help you sleep."

"Jerry, I don't like to take something that makes me so groggy."

"Take it earlier and you'll just sleep through the night."

"Okay, I'll take one. You'll have to make sure that I get up in the morning. Tomorrow night, I'll take it earlier."

"That's my girl, here." Jerry handed Estelle a glass of water and the little red pill.

The next morning, it took Jerry a few minutes to get her out of bed. "Come on, coffee's on, and Jake needs breakfast."

Rubbing her eyes and stretching like a lazy, old cat, Estelle slowly climbed out of bed. "I don't like feeling like this. It's like being in a fog. I just want to sleep more."

"Once you get caught up on your sleep, you'll be fine. If you're so worried about it, take a couple of these and you'll be able to wake up." Jerry pulled out two tiny white tablets.

"What are those? I don't want to take anything else. I just want to wake up."

"Quit whining. These are nothing more than coffee in a pill—just a smaller package." Jerry handed her the pills and a glass of water. "Take them and get moving, or Jake is going to be late for school. I have to get out of here."

She didn't want to take the pills, but she didn't want to fight with Jerry either. She popped the pills in her mouth and washed them down with water.

On the walk back from Jake's school, Estelle felt energized. "*I have so many things to do*," she thought to herself as her steps quickened.

She opened the door to the apartment and noticed every speck of dust. "This place needs a thorough cleaning." Estelle dusted, mopped, and scrubbed every nook and cranny in the apartment. She wiped down the walls and all of the woodwork. She decided to strip and re-wax the kitchen and bathroom floors.

I should re-organize our closet and Jake's. They are really cluttered, she thought to herself.

Before she knew it, it was time to get Jake from school.

"Jake, let's go to the park. It's a beautiful day!"

"Okay, Mommy. Let's go!"

Jake and Estelle played on the swings, the teeter-totter, and the slide until Jake was exhausted. "Mommy, I want to go home. I'm hungry."

"Okay. Mommy will cook a wonderful meal!" Jake's shorter legs worked hard to keep up with his mother's fast pace all the way back to their apartment.

"I'm tired, Mommy." Jake flopped down on the couch.

"Okay, Sweetheart, you just sit there for a bit and I'll have dinner ready in no time at all." Estelle headed to the kitchen.

Estelle sailed around the kitchen opening cabinets. She began preparing meatloaf, mashed potatoes, gravy, peas, and carrots. In no time at all, she also started a wine cake that her mother would have been proud to serve. A couple of hours later the kitchen was a mess. The meatloaf was done, the potatoes were mashed, and the gravy was just about ready. The cake would be done by the time they finished their meal.

Estelle wiped her hands on her apron and walked into the living room to tell Jake that dinner was ready, but he was sound asleep. "Jake— Jake, dinner's ready." The little boy's chest rose and fell steadily. He didn't move. "Jake!" Estelle shook his shoulder. "Wake up, it's time to eat!"

Jake's eyes opened. "I'm tired. I don't want to eat." He whined and turned over.

"I've worked on your favorite dinner for hours. Get up and come to the table now. You are going to eat!" Estelle took her son by the arm and led him to the kitchen.

"Ouch! Mommy, why are you so grumpy?"

"I am *not* grumpy. You can't go without supper even if you're tired. Now eat. Dessert is in the oven." Estelle picked at the food on her plate.

Cooking had been so much fun, but she had no appetite. She forced herself to eat a little and made sure that Jake ate as well.

"It's dark outside. Is it the middle of the night?" Jake rubbed his eyes and leaned on one elbow as he ate.

"It is a little later than we usually eat, but it's not the middle of the night." Estelle looked at the clock and realized the cake should be done. She took it out of the oven, but she had no room for dessert. "We can eat cake tomorrow. It is too hot to eat right now anyway. Come on, let's get you ready for bed."

Later, Estelle cleaned the kitchen and read for a while. Finally, she went to Jerry's top drawer and got the bottle of pills that made her sleep. "I hope I can get back to normal at some point."

The apartment was dark and quiet when Jerry came home. He went into the bathroom and locked the door. Sometime later he staggered out and went to bed.

When Mark Lawrence came back to town, the get-together once again consisted of only Mark, Estelle, and Jerry. The morning after, Estelle was so angry with Jerry that she refused to speak to him.

"Come here and give me my good morning kiss, beautiful." Estelle turned to the stove and ignored him. "What? No kiss, not even a good morning? What's wrong now?"

When he moved behind her pulling her into his arms, she pushed him away and walked to the other side of the kitchen. "Stop it! Don't touch me!"

"Ooh. You must really have a hangover."

"It's *more* than a hangover."

"I'm not the one who can't stop drinking, baby."

"I don't remember drinking more than a couple glasses of wine, Jerry."

"I guess you just can't hold your liquor."

"I grew up drinking wine with meals, and I have never blacked out after two glasses of wine." Estelle glared at him.

"You had more than two glasses of wine, little lady."

"That's my *point*! You promised you wouldn't let this happen again."

Jerry turned away and stuck his hands in his pockets. "I tried to get you to stop, but oh no, you just kept it up."

"Why didn't you make an excuse and bring me home? The last time I came home with bruises because you supposedly had to subdue me to get me here."

"Yeah, that's right. You were a wildcat."

"What are you hiding, Jerry? What happened to me? I have bruises again!"

Jerry panicked. "What happened to you? What kind of question is that? You got drunk and I brought you home. Drunks stagger around and bump into things. That's it."

"I think you left me with him."

"Whoa, I think you're nuts. Why would I do something like that?" Jerry grabbed his jacket and headed for the door.

"Why? Because he's a big spender, isn't that what you said? What is he paying you for?" Estelle's voice got louder. "Answer me, Jerry! What is he paying you for?"

"He buys gold and diamonds from me. You know that." Jerry fidgeted and wouldn't look at her.

"You let him have sex with me, didn't you?"

"What?" Jerry laughed nervously and ran his hand through his hair. "Are you still drunk? How could you accuse me of something like that?"

"My nightmares started after our first weekend with Mark. And last night, I wasn't sure if I had a nightmare or if I remember you leaving me with him."

"You have nightmares all the time."

"Not until we started entertaining Mark."

"You need to see a doctor; maybe one of those shrinks. I think you're losing your mind."

"Last night was different. I felt like I was in a fog, but I knew it was real. I don't remember everything, but I know he hurt me, Jerry. Just like the last time. I didn't fight with you and fall down." She tried to grab his arm, but he kept moving away from her. "You left me with a disgusting pervert. Did you drug me? How could you do that to me? I thought you loved me!" Estelle's volume rose with every word. She moved directly in front of Jerry. "Look at me!"

"Get out of my way. I'm out of here. I'll come back when you're sane." With that he walked out and slammed the door.

Jerry didn't come home that night or the next. Estelle took the little red pills to sleep and the white ones to wake up. When Pauline mentioned that she hadn't seen Jerry in several days, Estelle told her that he was out of town on business.

A few days after Jerry left, the hang up calls started again. Estelle ran to the phone every time it rang. One minute she hated him, but the next minute she missed him and wanted him to come home.

13

Late one afternoon, over a week after Jerry walked out, there was a knock at the door. It wasn't Pauline's soft tap. Estelle ran to the door and threw it open, thinking Jerry had come crawling back to apologize.

"So you're the newest one." The woman at the door looked Estelle up and down. She was taller than Estelle and very shapely. Her brittle blonde hair was pulled back in a twist, and her clothes were skimpy and cheap. Despite the heavy makeup and dark circles under her cold blue eyes, the woman had pretty features. She reminded Estelle of Lucille and the women who worked at the brothel.

"I'm sorry, but I don't know you. You must have the wrong apartment." Estelle started to close the door.

"Why would you know me? You think Jerry's gonna introduce you to his wife and kid? Now are you gonna to ask me to come in or not?"

Estelle looked down, and for the first time she noticed the little girl clinging to the woman's leg, almost hiding behind her. "His wife? You must have the wrong Jerry."

"Jerry Bradley—and this here's our *kid*."

Estelle couldn't speak. She simply stepped aside as the woman and little girl walked in.

There was a long, uncomfortable silence as Estelle stared into the faces of the woman and child sitting on her couch. The little girl had long, curly strawberry-blonde hair. Her eyes were a deep blue, and there were freckles sprinkled across her nose and cheeks. The tiny face was sweet, but nothing about her resembled Jerry.

"What's your name?" Estelle spoke softly to the little girl.

"Geraldine. What's your name?"

"Geraldine, you hush while I talk to the lady." The little girl sat back and hid behind her mother.

"That's okay. My name is Estelle." Estelle was numb and wasn't sure what to say next.

Just then, Jake walked into the room. "Jake, please go back to your room. I'll come and get you later."

"Mommy, who's that?" Jake smiled and pointed at the little girl.

"Jake, I said go to your room, please."

After Jake sulked back to his room, the blonde woman started again. "Jerry ain't a bad man; he just likes to roam sometimes. He does his thing, and I do mine. We have an understandin'. You're so young and pretty, I can see why he's gone so much." For a moment, the woman looked sad.

The woman recovered her composure, and her lips twisted into a cruel smile as she continued, "He ain't leavin' me to marry you. We've been married for years, and she's not our only kid. The others are big enough to be on their own. They're not in my hair anymore. Jerry Junior's in jail, because he liked them drugs just like his daddy."

"Drugs? Do you think we should discuss this with your little girl in the room?" Estelle could see those big blue eyes peeking around the woman's arm. "And I'm sorry, but I don't even know your name."

"People just call me Bobbi. She don't know what we're talking about anyway."

Estelle sighed as she lost patience with the woman. "Bobbi, how can I be sure that what you're telling me is true? You could be chasing Jerry and are jealous that he's found someone else."

"Well, I don't have our marriage license with me, but I can probably find it somewhere. We're married, little lady; and when he's in trouble, he always comes home. Look, it don't matter to me what you believe. He watches out for me. You know, he checks out my clients. As long as he don't take too much of what I make, he can do what he wants. He's just never kept a thing goin' as long as he has with you, and I was curious. I followed him once and saw him looking out your window. It was easy to find you."

"Jerry loves me. You're lying."

"Believe what you want." Bobbi stood up and grabbed little Geraldine by the arm. "And by the way, when he comes home to me, he takes *full* advantage of his husbandly rights. Oh, and those hang up calls you get, they're from me. I found the number in his jacket—in my *bedroom*. I call you when he's with me." She smiled an evil smile at Estelle as she walked out and slammed the door.

Estelle sat in the chair like a statue. Her chest felt tight, and there was a knot in her stomach. It was hard to breathe. She was still sitting in the chair staring at the door when Jake came back into the room.

"Mommy, who were they?"

"They were looking for someone and had the wrong apartment."

"How come they came in?"

"Jake, please, I was trying to be nice. Now go play. I have to start dinner."

Estelle went to the kitchen, but nothing sounded good. She had to make something for Jake, so she opened the icebox door and grabbed eggs, milk, and sausage. Since she had plenty of flour, she made eggs, pancakes, and sausages for dinner.

"Jake, come on, dinner's ready."

Jake walked to the table slowly. "Mommy, are you mad at me?"

"No, I'm not mad at you."

"You said you didn't know that lady, and you looked mad at somebody."

"Oh Jake, I'm sorry. I'm tired and grumpy."

"Where's Jerry?"

"Well, he is on a business trip. You know, he goes on trips a lot."

"He's been gone a long time, Mommy." Jake hesitated and then asked. "Is he coming back?"

"Of course he's coming back. He just had a lot of work to do this time."

"Oh." Jake frowned and walked away.

Two days later, the phone rang around 4:00 in the morning. Estelle managed to pick up the receiver and say hello. "Baby, were you sleeping?"

"Jerry? Where are you?" Estelle sat up.

"Well, I'm back in town now. When we had our fight, I decided to make the rounds with my customers and give you some time to cool down."

"Are you coming home?" Estelle was almost afraid to ask.

"If you'll have me, I'm just a few minutes away."

"Come on. I'll get up and wait for you." Estelle heard a click as Jerry hung up.

Fifteen minutes later, there was a knock at the door. "Jerry, is that you?"

"It's me. I forgot my key when I left."

Estelle opened the door, but she quickly walked away and sat down in a chair.

"I thought I might get a little welcome kiss or at least a smile." Jerry sat on the sofa.

"Jerry, we have a lot to talk about. I'm very upset and confused right now. I don't even know where to start."

"Maybe we should start where we left off." He walked over to Estelle, got down on his knees, and put his hands on her shoulders. "Look at me, Estelle. I would never let anyone hurt you. I love you." He sighed and his eyes filled with tears. "I can't stand that you think I left you with another man. You were right about one thing. I should have hauled your butt out the minute your drinking got out of hand. I didn't, and I apologize for that."

"What about what I remembered that night?" Tears were streaming down Estelle's face.

"Baby, you didn't remember those things, you dreamed them. You've been having bad dreams for months now. I think everything you've been through is coming back to haunt you." Jerry pulled her into his arms, and she sobbed until she couldn't cry anymore.

"Oh, Jerry, I said such awful things to you. How could I accuse you of such a horrible thing?"

"It's okay, baby, I love you. We'll lick this drinking problem together. You know sometimes people black out and don't remember a thing. We'll make sure that you have a limit."

"Okay." Estelle leaned back in her chair and looked at him. "There is something else we need to talk about. I think you need to sit down."

Jerry laughed a little and went back to the couch. "Okay, shoot."

"For months now, whenever you're gone, I've received hang up calls at all hours of the day and night."

"Just kids playing pranks. Are you afraid to be here alone when I travel?"

"No, I'm not afraid." Estelle looked down at her hands and fidgeted before she could go on. "A couple of days ago, there was a knock at the door. When I answered it, a woman and a little girl were standing there." Estelle stopped and wasn't sure how to go on.

"Okay, so a woman with a little girl knocked at the door. Who were they?"

"She told me she was your wife, and the little girl was one of the children you have together."

Jerry came up off of the couch laughing. He turned away from her for a moment, and ran his hands through his hair. "My wife and kid? What the hell?"

"Her name is Bobbi, and the little girl is Geraldine. The little girl was adorable, but I stared and stared and I couldn't see any resemblance to you."

"Well, that's because I don't have any kids. And, I have never been married. Until you came along, I was a happy bachelor."

"Jerry, how did she know your name and where we lived?"

"Estelle, I travel all the time. I wine and dine customers when they come to town. I spend time in bars and restaurants. Women flirt with me—I'm not going to deny that. Some sleazy broad must have a thing for me and followed me around. I can't believe this!" Estelle had never seen Jerry so agitated. His jaw was clenched, and he paced around like a madman.

Estelle didn't say another word. She sat still until Jerry calmed down. Finally, he walked over and pulled Estelle into his arms. "No one is going to come between us. You are my world. How many times have I told you that you are the best thing that has ever happened to me?"

"I know, you tell me that all the time."

"Estelle, I don't have a wife and children hidden away. I didn't sell you to Mark. I love you, but if this is going to work, you have to trust me. Okay? Do you trust me?"

"I can't live without you. I love you so much." Estelle cried as Jerry held her close.

About a week later, Estelle noticed a disturbing piece in the morning paper. A prostitute named Roberta Smith was found dead in an alley. The article stated that she was a heroin addict and had overdosed. There was one sentence about a five-year-old child who had been found alone in the woman's apartment and was now in state custody. There was no mention of whether the child was a boy or a girl, and no other relatives could be found in the area. Roberta had grown children, but the authorities had failed to locate them, other than one son who was in prison. Estelle thought about showing the article to Jerry, to see if he knew Roberta Smith. Instead, she cut out the article and put it with the journals in her mother's hatbox. She didn't want to believe this woman was Bobbi, who had come to her door just days before. It *had* to be coincidence.

14

n no time at all, things were back to normal. As usual, Jerry had meetings and traveled. Estelle stayed home and worked one or two days a week. She cleaned, cooked, and spent time with Jake. And there were no more hang-up calls.

One evening, when Jerry was out and Jake was already in bed sleeping, there was a soft knock on the door. "Pauline, come in. I was just reading."

Pauline stepped into the small living room. She was quiet and looked a little downcast. "Pauline, are you okay? Here, sit down."

Pauline took a seat on the couch and sighed. A tear ran down her face. "Estelle, you know that I love you and Jake like you're my own. God has given you both to me to love." A sob escaped and Pauline worked to regain her composure.

"Pauline, are you ill?"

"No, I'm not. I'm as healthy as can be, but my sister isn't. She lives in California. Her children are grown, with jobs and families. One lives in the Midwest, and the other on the East coast. Anyway, they have just discovered tumors and her prognosis is not good. She lost her husband a few years ago; and with the children living so far away, there is no one to care for her. I need to go to California and care for her as long as she needs me. She's desperate, otherwise I would never leave."

"Oh Pauline, Jake will be lost without you." Estelle felt a lump in her throat. She would be lost without Pauline too, but she hardly knew how to say it. She looked down and spoke softly. "I'll miss you too."

"Estelle, I love you and Jake so much. You have no idea what you mean to me. This has been a horrible decision for me to make, but I must trust the Lord to look after you and hope that I can return." The two women hugged and cried in each other's arms.

"When do you have to leave?" Estelle wiped her eyes.

"In about a week. The landlord has agreed to let me sub-let my apartment to my friend Rose. She was looking for a new place, so this will work out well for her. You haven't met her, but she kept Jake when you were in the hospital. She is a good friend. We go to church together, and she is a lovely Christian woman. If I am able to come back soon, Rose and I will share the apartment and expenses. But, in the meantime, she can sit with Jake when you need someone. She has no family of her own, but she's wonderful with children. She teaches Jake's children's class at the church, so she won't be a complete stranger to him."

"Oh Pauline, how will we tell Jake? He was too young when my parents died to remember them, so he sees you like a grandmother."

"I'll come over tomorrow afternoon, and we can talk to him then. I really want to be here and tell him myself, if that's okay with you."

"Yes. I want you to be here. This won't be easy for him."

"Estelle, this hurts right now, but I will be in prayer and trust that God will take care of us." Pauline kissed Estelle on the forehead and let herself out of the apartment.

Pauline was leaving her. She and Jake would be alone again. Estelle sat quietly in her chair, until hurt and anger boiled up inside her. "God, here we go again! You just keep taking people away. Punishing me isn't enough, so now it's Jake who's going to hurt. What has he done to you?" Estelle threw her book across the floor.

It was midnight when Estelle took her nightly sleeping pill and went to bed. Jerry wasn't home yet, but right now, she didn't care. She could only think about Jake. How would he handle losing Pauline? Finally, the little red pill did its work and sleep overtook her.

The next morning, Jerry shook Estelle and managed to get her to wake up and take her little white pills. "I didn't even hear you come in last night. I was up until a little after midnight."

"Yeah, it was a late one. I didn't want to upset you, but Mark was in town. I told him you were sick and couldn't join us."

"Is he here for long?"

"No. This time he was just here for one night. He's leaving today."

"Jerry, thank you for telling him I was sick. I know I have been silly, but I just don't like being around him."

"I know, baby. It's okay. I'll protect you."

"There is something I need to talk to you about. Pauline is moving to California, hopefully for just a short time."

Jerry smiled as he turned his back to Estelle. "Really, why is she moving?"

"Her sister lives there and is very ill. There's no one else to care for her, and Pauline has no choice. It was a hard decision because she loves Jake and me so much and doesn't want to leave us." Estelle started to cry.

"Oh, baby, I know this will be hard, but I'm here. We'll get through this. Um, who is going to watch Jake when you need a babysitter?"

"Pauline's friend Rose. They go to church together, and Jake knows her. I haven't met her yet, but I trust Pauline's judgment. Rose is going to sub-let Pauline's apartment, so she'll be right upstairs."

"Sounds like a plan."

"Jake doesn't know yet. Pauline is coming over this afternoon, and we will tell him together. This isn't going to be easy for him."

"He's a kid, and kids always bounce back. He'll be fine. I gotta go now. See you tonight." Jerry kissed Estelle on the cheek and went out the door.

She was disappointed he hadn't shown a little more compassion for Jake. But, as always, she convinced herself that he wasn't uncaring; he was just not accustomed to having children around. Estelle headed for Jake's room to get him up and ready for school.

"Good morning! How's my favorite little boy?"

Jake sat up and rubbed his eyes. "Mommy, I'm your only little boy."

"Well that doesn't matter. You are still my favorite. What do you want for breakfast this morning? I'll make you anything you want."

"I want pancakes and sausages."

"Done. Get dressed and wash your hands; I'll get started in the kitchen."

"Mommy, I love you."

"I love you too." Estelle fought back tears. Why did Pauline have to leave?

That afternoon Pauline and Estelle walked together to get Jake from school. They stopped at the park for a short time on the way home.

"That was fun. Can we read books now?" Jake asked as they walked into the apartment.

"Jake, uh, Pauline and I need to talk to you about something." Estelle quickly turned away as tears spilled down her cheeks.

"Am I in trouble?"

Pauline sat down on the sofa and pulled Jake onto her lap. "Of course not, Jake, do you know that I love you and your mommy very much?"

Jake nodded.

"Sometimes we have to do things that don't really make us happy, but we do them to help other people."

Jake didn't say a word; he just looked at Pauline and waited for her to continue.

"Jake, I have a sister who lives in California. That's very far away. She is sick, and there is no one to take care of her. As much as I love you and your mommy, I need to go and live with her for a while and take care of her. I love her too."

"Is she going to die?"

"I hope not, but she's very sick."

"You mean you have to move away?"

"Yes Jake, I will have to move away. I don't know how long I'll be gone." A single tear slid down Pauline's cheek.

"You love her more! I hate you!" Jake jumped up and ran to his room.

"Jake, come back here this very minute, and don't ever talk to Miss Pauline like that." Estelle started after Jake.

"Estelle, please let me talk to him."

"Okay."

Pauline walked to Jake's room, knocked on the door, and went in. Jake was lying across his bed sobbing. "Jake, you don't hate me; you're just angry right now. My sister is so sick, and she has no one else to help her. I love you, Jake, and I always will. You are like my very own grandson. You'll have your mommy, even when I'm not here."

"She loves Jerry and does everything he says. He's a bad man. He doesn't like me."

"Jake, has Jerry ever hurt you?"

"No, but he doesn't like me. I think Mommy loves him more."

"That's not true, Jake. Your mother loves you very much. Have you talked to her about Jerry?"

"No, she won't listen anyway. One day, a lady and a little girl came to see her. Mommy made me stay in my room, but I opened my door and listened. The lady said she was married to Jerry, not Mommy. Mommy believes him, but I think he lies."

"Jake, maybe you misunderstood what your mother and the lady were talking about. I love you, sweetheart." Pauline planned to pray about this situation. "Now, I will write to you often and call you when I can. I leave next week, so we need to spend as much time together as possible. I bet your mommy will let you help me pack. What do you say?"

"I can help you pack?"

"Let's go ask her right now."

Pauline's last week with Jake and Estelle went by much too quickly. Jake spent every evening helping Pauline pack. Rose was there a good part of the time too, helping Pauline while getting acquainted with Jake and Estelle.

"Well Jake, tomorrow is the day. I'm happy that you and your mommy are going with me to the train station. Saying goodbye will be very hard; hopefully, I won't be gone too long. I believe we will see each other again."

"Yeah, maybe your sister will get better really fast and you can come back."

"That's my prayer—for her to get well and for me to come back to you." Pauline held Jake close.

The next morning, Estelle didn't know which was worse—Jake's tears one minute or his excitement over being in Union Station the next. Finally, Pauline's luggage was loaded, and it was time to say goodbye.

"Now, Jake, promise me you will mind your mother and say your prayers every night, just the way I taught you." Pauline wiped her eyes and tried to smile. "You will have fun with Rose. She will take good care of you when Mommy has to work."

"Do you *have* to go? Can't someone else take care of your sister? I don't want you to go." Jake's voice grew louder with each word; then he just sobbed.

"Jake, come here. Let me hold you." Jake walked into Pauline's arms. "I'm sad too. It breaks my heart to leave you. But, my sister is sick and alone. You have your mommy, Rose, and your friends at school. I'll call and write—I promise. Now hug me one more time before I board the train. I love you, Jake. I love you so very much."

Estelle could no longer control her emotions, and she started to cry. Pauline hugged Jake and kissed his cheek, and then went to Estelle. "You know I love you too. Just please be careful and take care of yourself and Jake, and let Rose know if you need help. Do you understand? If you need help of any kind, you let her know. I'll call to check on you, and I'll write," Pauline said. "I love you." With that, Pauline kissed Jake one more time, hugged Estelle and Rose, and boarded the train.

Rose, Estelle, and Jake stood close together and watched Pauline take a seat by a window. They all waved until the train pulled away and was out of sight. "Oh, what will we do? Pauline was like a mother to me and a grandmother to Jake. I took her so much for granted."

"Estelle, Pauline was thrilled to be a part of your lives and never felt taken for granted. She always told me how blessed she was because of the two of you." Rose put her hand on Estelle's shoulder.

"Thank you." Estelle sniffled and blew her nose on a hankie.

"Mommy, I want to go home." Jake was exhausted.

"Okay, sugar, let's get a taxi and head home." Estelle took his hand.

"I think we're all worn out. This has been quite an ordeal." Rose wiped her eyes and followed Estelle and Jake.

Rose seemed to be nice enough, but she wasn't Pauline. She was older than Estelle, but much younger than Pauline. She didn't look like a grandma. Actually, she was quite beautiful. Estelle couldn't begin to guess her age. Her skin was flawless. Sometimes, she wore her thick dark auburn hair up in a twist. Other times it was down and wavy, past her shoulders. She had brown eyes with long black lashes and perfectly arched brows. Her smile was beautiful with full, pouty lips and perfect white teeth, and she certainly had kept her figure and was quite shapely. However, she didn't flaunt herself. Her kind, loving nature made Rose even more beautiful.

The emotionally drained group arrived back at the apartment building. "Well Jake, we're home. Rose, thank you so much for going with us."

"I was happy to be there. I'll miss her too."

"Yes, she mentioned that you went to church together."

"You should visit our church sometime. Jake loves Sunday school. I'm sure you'd enjoy it too."

"Well, ah, thank you. But, I'm Catholic and I haven't been to church in a very long time anyway."

"I was raised Catholic too and am so thankful for that upbringing. It doesn't matter what denomination we are. I have wonderful friends who are Protestant and Catholic. We all love the same Lord. That's what counts."

"Thank you, Rose. Now, excuse me, Jake is exhausted, and I need to put him down for a nap. I'll talk to you later."

"Okay. Remember, I can watch Jake on Tuesdays and Thursdays, and I'm always available in the evenings and on weekends. Just let me know when you need my help."

Once inside the apartment, Estelle put Jake down for a nap. She decided to have a second cup of coffee and sit down for a while. She hoped Rose wouldn't constantly try to get her to go to church. That would get old really fast.

Jerry came home late that night to find Estelle still up, reading a book. "You're up late. How'd things go today? Did the old lady head for California?"

"Jerry, you know her name is Pauline. You don't have to call her the old lady. She's been like a grandmother to Jake, and—" Estelle sighed, "and like a mother to me. You could be a little nicer about all of this."

"Aren't we sensitive? Well, sorry, but I never liked her. She was nosey, and she didn't like me. I never did anything to her. She was a holier-than-thou Bible thumper, and I'm glad she's gone."

"How could you be happy about this? Jake's heart is broken, and I miss her too. She was always there when we needed her. It never bothered you to ask her to sit with Jake."

"Oh brother, I rushed home to this? Well, at least I'm honest. I didn't like her and that's that. From what I've seen of her, Rose will probably be a lot easier to deal with."

"Why would you say that? Rose goes to the same church, and she's already started inviting me there. She's no different than Pauline." Estelle paused for a moment. "Well, I take that back; she's a lot younger, and she's very beautiful. Does that have something to do with your attitude?"

"What the—? Are you nuts? I just think she's not as fanatic as the old lady. I could care less what she looks like. I'm going to bed." Jerry went into the bathroom and slammed the door.

The next morning, Jerry and Estelle didn't mention Pauline or Rose. "Mark is coming to town this weekend. I let you off the hook the last time he was here, but I want you to go with me this weekend."

"Jerry, you know I don't like being around him."

"Estelle, knock it off. You won't be the only woman there, so quit whining. He's hosting a cocktail party Saturday night, and there will be other important clients there. I've already bought a new black dress for you to wear, and you're going. Make sure you talk to Rose and see if she can keep Jake overnight on Saturday. He can go to Sunday school with her, so that'll make her happy." Jerry finished his coffee, grabbed his jacket, and went out the door.

15

On Saturday evening, Estelle took Jake to Rose's apartment and started getting ready for Mark's cocktail party. She didn't want to go, but reasoning with Jerry was useless. Estelle pouted as she went in to bathe. The steamy bubble bath was exactly what she needed to relax. She finally forced herself to climb out of the tub and headed to the bedroom to get dressed.

For a moment, she could only stare at the slinky black dress Jerry bought for her. She pulled it on and fastened the low-cut back. It was floor length with a thigh-high slit that revealed enough shapely leg to make any man's imagination run wild. It fit like a glove, accentuating every curve of her body. Estelle sighed and dabbed on perfume.

The delicate gold chain with a single diamond was perfect; it was simple, yet elegant. Estelle's long hair tumbled down her back; she refused to cut it in one of the new, shorter styles. Her makeup was simple: a touch of rouge on her cheeks, lipstick, and smoky eyeliner. She didn't need to do anything to her long black lashes or her brows. As she clipped on diamond earrings, her reflection in the mirror almost took her breath away. Hadn't she always wanted to wear diamonds and expensive clothes? "Why do I feel so nervous?" she whispered to herself.

Jerry walked in while she stood staring in the mirror. "Oh my God, I thought I was home, but I must be in a palace. Look at you, beautiful—you look like a princess. Come here." Jerry drew her into his arms and kissed her. "No one will outshine you tonight."

"Don't we have to leave pretty soon?" She pulled away.

"Yep, you're right. I got carried away. Did you lay out my clothes?"

"Yes. Your cuff links and tie tack are on the dresser."

"Good girl. I'll take a quick bath and be ready before you know it." Jerry danced around and practically ran to the bathroom.

There was nothing more to do than wait for Jerry. Estelle's open-toed stilettos clicked on the hardwood floor as she paced and tried not to chew her manicured nails. She became increasingly aggravated, realizing the high heels drew even more attention to her bare thigh.

"Okay, beautiful, here's your mink. Let's go." Jerry placed the mink stole around her shoulders and opened the door.

Estelle's smile was forced. She clutched the mink and her evening bag.

Neither Jerry nor Estelle spoke more than a few words during the taxi ride to Mark's hotel. Like a perfect gentleman, Jerry opened doors for Estelle and took her arm as they walked through the elegant hotel lobby. Heads turned as men openly admired Estelle's beauty, but she tried to ignore their looks and whispers. She blushed and her eyelids fluttered, which made her all the more desirable.

Finally, she and Jerry stepped off of the elevator and stood at the door of Mark's suite. Jerry barely had time to knock when a young man opened the door. Estelle gasped. "Jerry, this is unbelievable!" The huge suite was lush, yet tastefully decorated. A spacious living room opened to a dining area with a bar where a young man served drinks. Estelle saw two bedrooms at one end of the suite, and at least one bathroom and a powder room.

"May I take your wrap, please?" A maid slipped Estelle's mink from her shoulders.

"Yes, thank you."

Estelle felt a chill as Mark's hand caressed her bare shoulder. "Estelle, Jerry, I am so glad you could make it. Let's get you something to drink."

"Sure, thanks Mark. Come on Estelle."

Estelle walked to the bar with Mark and Jerry. "What would you like, dear? Champagne?"

"Um, no, actually, I really just want a soda right now." Estelle reached up and patted her hair, trying to calm her nerves.

"Soda? My dear, we have the best champagne and wines here tonight," Mark replied.

Jerry squeezed her elbow. "Okay, I'd love to have a glass of champagne." She winced and shot an angry look at Jerry.

"Here you go. Let me introduce you to the other guests."

Mark made the rounds, introducing Jerry and Estelle to the other guests. There were four other men and only three other women. Estelle couldn't tell who went together—they didn't really seem to be couples. Mark held Estelle's arm through the introductions as though she were a trophy.

The minute Estelle finished her first glass of champagne, a young man appeared with a tray offering a fresh glass. "Oh well, maybe this will help calm my nerves," she whispered to Jerry.

"What are you nervous about? You're the most beautiful woman in the room. Look at those gals. They're smiling, but they hate you." Jerry grinned from ear to ear.

"Great, that helps my nerves. Everyone here hates me."

"No baby, not everyone; just the other women. They don't really hate you; they just hate it because you put them all to shame." Jerry took a drink of his bourbon.

"Are we having dinner or just these fancy little snacks?"

"No, we're not having dinner. Believe me, this stuff is expensive."

"Fine. I plan to eat these expensive little snacks and not get drunk. I have no intention of a repeat of my other nights with Mark."

"Shut up, Estelle. You can eat what you like. Just smile and be friendly. These are some very important men, and I want you to make a good impression."

"Don't you mean *we* need to make a good impression?"

"Don't start anything. Just do what I tell you to do." Jerry smiled and walked away to talk to a man he seemed to already know.

Hours went by. Estelle's face hurt from smiling. Her plan to eat while she drank seemed to be working, since she'd had several glasses of champagne and was still quite in control of herself. After finishing a boring conversation with Mr. Anderson, who leaned far too close and touched her bare arm and shoulder much too often, Estelle excused herself and walked over to Jerry. "I'm ready to go. I've smiled and talked to everyone here, and I think the redhead and Mr. Smith disappeared into one of the bedrooms. The blonde and Mr. Jones are getting pretty friendly, and if

Mr. Anderson touches me one more time, I am going to slap him. He had the audacity to put his hand on my leg; and of course with this dress, he touched bare skin." Estelle smiled her sweetest smile at Jerry.

"Well, I'm not ready to go yet. I could get some pretty hefty accounts from this little deal, so calm down. He's just a lonely old guy. He probably thinks of you like he would his own daughter."

"If he treats his daughter that way, he should be arrested. I want to go home."

"Estelle, Jerry, what's going on?" Mark walked up and put his arm around Estelle's shoulder.

"Mark, I'm really tired, and I'm ready to go home. It's been a lovely party." Estelle tried to be gracious.

"Dear, the evening is young. Why don't you sit down for a bit?" Mark took Estelle by the arm and guided her to one of the plush sofas. "Jerry, may I have a word with you, please? Estelle, we'll be right back."

Estelle watched as Mark and Jerry walked to the other side of the suite. "One of the girls didn't show up. I was looking forward to an evening with Estelle, but there has been a change of plan. Mr. Anderson is quite taken with her. He has expressed that he would like to spend some time with her. Now, we've danced around and drugged her enough. You need to let her know who is boss and make sure that she entertains Mr. Anderson fully. He is a bit more timid than I am, but he has some business interests that will prove quite lucrative for us."

"For God's sake, Mark, she doesn't even know what she's done with you before. You think I can just tell her to go in the bedroom with Anderson and get it on?"

"I don't care what you tell her. I'll get the waiters to remove the food, and we can get a few more drinks down her. Just don't drug her. When she's drugged, it isn't nearly as much fun as it could be. Now go on. You know why you're here."

From where Estelle sat, it looked like Mark and Jerry were arguing. She grabbed another drink and gulped it down. Waiters started removing all of the trays, but the bar remained open.

Jerry walked over and sat down next to Estelle. "Well, can we go now?" Estelle hissed.

"No, we can't go yet. These are very important people, and we need to be friendly. Now smile and have another drink." Jerry grabbed another drink and handed it to Estelle. "Get that frown off your face. This is important to me."

"Yes, sir; what else do you want me to do, sir?"

Jerry took her by the hand, led her into the small powder room, and shut the door. "Smile and look beautiful—that's why you're here. Be nice to Mr. Anderson; he likes you."

"What? He likes me? Be nice to him? What's that supposed to mean?"

Jerry forced a smile as he looked straight into Estelle's eyes. "What do you think it means? I'm tired of playing games with you. This is about money—lots of money. So what if you have to be nice to an old man? Do it. Be friendly. Don't you understand? I don't want to live in that apartment building forever and neither do you."

"Jerry, you're hurting my wrist."

"We do whatever we have to do to make it—to get where we want to be. It isn't about us. It is about doing whatever it takes. Do you get it?"

It was out in the open. There were no more excuses—the truth hit Estelle like a ton of bricks. "You *did* leave me with Mark, didn't you? You've done it more than once. I hate you!"

"Shut up and do what you're told. I pay the bills and take care of you and your kid."

"Oh my God, I'm a whore. You've sold me like a whore!"

Before Estelle could get loud enough to be heard in the other room, Jerry pushed her against the wall and put his hand over her mouth. "You listen to me. I do what it takes to get what we want. Do you understand? You spend the money and wear the clothes and jewelry; I support your kid. You are *not* going to ruin this for me. It isn't just for me; it's for us. Things won't always be the way they are now. Someday we'll have everything we want and need; but for now, we are going to do whatever it takes to get there. Do you understand me?" He enunciated each word. Estelle smelled bourbon and nicotine on his breath. She could almost see Ricky's face as Jerry kept talking and squeezed her wrist. "Do you?"

Tears spilled down her cheeks. "Yes, I understand. I'm your whore. You're worse than Ricky. His mother may have been a whore, but he would never have sold me to other men." She jerked her wrist away. "I don't even have a job anymore. What am I going to do?"

"You're going to put cold water on your face, come out of here smiling, and entertain Mr. Anderson. That's what you're going to do. Here, you'll need this." He handed her a small case.

"My diaphragm—oh how thoughtful of you, Jerry. We certainly don't want a pregnancy, now do we?" Her voice dripped with sarcasm.

"Take half of one of these and you'll be relaxed." Jerry handed her half of one of his little red pills, straightened his tie, and walked out of the powder room.

Estelle looked in the mirror. Her eyes were puffy, and her face was a little blotchy. She popped the pill in her mouth and washed it down with water. She turned on the faucet and let the water run over a clean cloth until it was nice and cold. The cool cloth was soothing. "This is going to be as good as it gets." She opened the powder room door, walked out, and grabbed another glass of champagne.

By the time Mr. Anderson led Estelle into the master bedroom, she was giggling and hanging on to him. "So you've traveled to Africa to buy diamonds?"

"Yes, dear, I even had the opportunity to go on a safari while I was there. It was spectacular. Africa is a land that is both breathtakingly beautiful and quite untamed—a bit like you." Mr. Anderson closed and locked the bedroom door.

Later, in the wee hours of the morning, Mark and Jerry waited for Mr. Anderson and Estelle to emerge from the bedroom. "For cryin' out loud, when is he going to let her out of there?" Jerry was irritable and fidgety.

"Jerry, stop acting like a jealous schoolboy. You managed to talk some sense into her, and she's doing what you asked her to do. Now exercise some patience. Would you like a cigar?" Mark opened a wooden box containing expensive cigars.

"Sure. Thanks." Jerry lit his cigar and tried to relax. "This is just different, and I didn't know how she would react when it all came out in the open. She's a smart girl, but I'm just a little worried. It's the first time that she's known what is going on."

"You're right, Jerry, she is a smart girl. Once she realizes how important she is, it will be fine. You have to reassure her that she belongs to you, and this is temporary."

"I know. Somehow I have to make her realize that she's not some street whore. She has class. And we only deal with elite clientele."

"Remember that, Jerry, and don't get her hooked on narcotics. You can control her without them. I let you come back after the last episode, but, if I catch either of you using drugs, our business relationship will be over. And I'll make it final. Do you understand?"

"Yes, I understand. You know Bobbi was different—she had no class. I told you I didn't get her on drugs, and I'm *not* a junky. She was lying."

"She was rather difficult. I do not want any more messy situations."

"Mark, I took care of Bobbi. She was a pig, and it wasn't my fault that she threatened you. She was stupid."

"She was your wife. At some point, you must have thought she had some redeeming qualities. After all, you had children with her."

"I was young and stupid when I married her, and none of those kids are mine. I told you that. We weren't together most of the time."

"Don't make any more mistakes, Jerry. I've been forgiving, but I can only be pushed so far. I would like to put you in charge of that part of my operations again, but I just don't know if I can trust you."

"Mark, how many times do I have to tell you I'm not a junky? I *never* stole any drugs; Bobbi did that and then lied about it. You know I'm not stupid, and I know what would happen to me."

Both men turned toward the bedroom when the door creaked open. "Jerry, I'm ready to go home now." Estelle staggered out of the bedroom with her shoes in her hand.

On Sunday morning, Jerry thought it best to let Estelle sleep in. He tiptoed out of the room and gently pulled the door shut. He wasn't thrilled about cooking his own breakfast, but he wasn't ready to face her just yet.

A little after noon, there was a soft knock on the door. "Who's there?" Jerry asked.

"It's Rose and Jake."

Jerry opened the door and smiled. "Thanks for watching Jake. Estelle has a headache so she's taking a nap. Come on Jake, I'll make a sandwich for your lunch."

"Do you want me to take him upstairs until Estelle is feeling better?" Rose asked.

"Ah, no, that's okay. He can eat and then play until his mom gets up. Thanks anyway." Jerry shut the door as soon as Jake was inside.

"What kind of sandwich do you want?"

"Where's my mommy?" Jake asked.

"She's a little sick. Her head hurts, so we need to be quiet until she wakes up, okay?" Jerry opened the icebox. "How does grape jam sound?"

"Okay." Jake climbed onto a kitchen chair.

"Here you go. Your mom can fix you something else when she gets up."

"Can I have some milk, please?"

"Oh, yeah, I guess you need something to drink."

When Jake finished the sandwich and milk, he jumped down from the table and said, "I'm done."

"Great. Why don't you go in your room and play with your army men? Don't make a lot of noise; your mom needs to sleep."

"I'll be quiet. Thank you, Jerry." Jake went to his room and shut the door.

Jerry was bored and needed to get out of the apartment. He tapped on Jake's door and went in. "Jake, I have to do some work, but I won't be gone too long. Until your mom wakes up, stay in your room, and don't answer the door. I'll lock it when I leave, so no one can get in."

"Okay, Jerry. I'll be quiet and take care of Mommy."

"That's a good boy. See ya!" Jerry grabbed his jacket and went out the door.

A little over an hour later, Estelle began to stir. Slowly, she opened her eyes and looked around the room. The apartment was quiet—too quiet. Suddenly, her thoughts were flooded with the horrible events of the night before. "*Oh my God, what did I do?*" She pulled on her robe, walked over to the chest of drawers, hoping Jerry's little white pills might help. "I need these today."

There was a soft knock on her bedroom door. "Mommy, are you up?'

Estelle opened the door and scooped Jake into her arms. "Yes, baby, I'm up. When did you get here?"

"Rose brought me home after church. Jerry said your head hurt and you were asleep. He gave me a jelly sandwich and some milk and told me to play very quietly in my room. Was I quiet enough?"

"Yes, you were very good. I didn't hear a peep. Is Jerry in the bathroom?"

"Nope, he's gone. He had to work."

Estelle's anger threatened to boil over. "He left you here alone while I was sleeping?"

"He locked the door and told me not to answer it. No one knocked on the door. I told him I'd take care of you. I'm a big boy, Mommy!"

"Yes, Jake, you are a big boy. I love you." Estelle pulled Jake close. Tears rolled down her cheeks.

"Mommy, why are you crying?"

"Oh, Mommy's head hurts."

Estelle made lunch for Jake and straightened the apartment.

Later that evening, after Jake was in bed, she turned on the radio and listened to soothing music. It was hours before Jerry finally came home.

"Where have you been? I assume you didn't want to face me. Or maybe you were out peddling your other whores? Are there others?" Her voice dripped with hatred.

"I don't have a problem facing you. I had things to do."

"Oh, did you sell some *diamonds* today? That's what you sell, right?"

"Yeah, I sell diamonds. You know that. Mark and Mr. Anderson buy diamonds too."

"Really? I've never seen any diamonds, except the ones you bring home for me to wear. Where do you keep your inventory, Jerry? How many other whores do you have?"

"I don't have any other whores. What are you talking about?"

"So you admit it. I'm your whore."

"I didn't say that. You put it that way; I didn't. I just tried to answer your question."

"You make your money by selling sex to rich old men. You're a pimp!"

Jerry had heard enough. He grabbed the collar of Estelle's robe and pushed her down on the couch. "Get one thing straight. No matter what we have to do, you belong to me. I love you. No one else will ever love you like I do. No one else will ever know you the way I do. You're mine, and don't ever forget it."

"You're hurting me. Get off of me!" Estelle pushed and tried to get Jerry off of her.

He jerked her up by her arm and dragged her to their room, locking the door. "I said you're mine. I call the shots. Now take off your robe."

"No. You make me sick! How could you, after what you made me do last night? I'm leaving you. I can get my job back, and then I'm taking my son and leaving!"

"You really don't understand do you? Mark Lawrence is not simply going to let you walk away now that you know what he really is. I'm the only one who can protect you from him. He's a very dangerous man, sweetheart. He doesn't care who he hurts or uses to get what he wants, and he knows about Jake now. Think about *that*."

Estelle closed her eyes and swallowed the lump in her throat. She was terrified, and her heart pounded as she realized she was trapped. Would Mark Lawrence really harm her child if she tried to leave? She couldn't take that chance.

Jerry continued, "When the time is right, I can get us out of here. And one more thing, little girl, I didn't make you do anything. I explained the deal, and you came out drinking. *You* were giggling and hanging all over that old creep when he led you to the bedroom, so don't tell me I made you do anything." He continued, "Now, as I said, you're mine, so take off your robe."

Slowly, Estelle loosened her robe and let it fall to the floor.

She still took his breath away. Jerry groaned, and his tone softened. "Now that's my girl. You are so beautiful. Oh, baby, I love you so much." As Jerry pulled her close, his hands caressed her shoulders and slowly moved down her back. Estelle refused to tremble; she willed herself to feel absolutely nothing but hatred for Jerry.

Later, he stroked her hair as he held her close. "It's okay, baby. You'll learn that we do what we have to do, and none of it has anything to do with our love. You will always be mine." Jerry picked up a pill bottle. "You look tired, so here, take these so you can sleep."

Obediently, she took the red pills and washed them down with water. She wanted to sleep and never wake up.

16

Once or twice a month, Mark came to town and arranged cocktail parties for his wealthy, affluent customers. The men were from other cities, and occasionally a European gentleman attended. Jerry and Estelle were always invited. Estelle became the most sought after young woman at Mark's soirees. It wasn't long before the parties were a weekly event.

"Jerry, what is going on? With all of these parties, we should have plenty of money now. Even though you don't bother to let me know what these guys pay for me, I know it has to be plenty."

"It takes time. There are expenses, you know. You can't wear rags, and I can't save every penny we make." Jerry hated it when Estelle questioned him about money.

"You still sell diamonds too. At least that's what you say you're doing at night."

"Estelle, shut up. I get sick of you nagging about money. I am putting some away, and it won't be long before we can get out of here."

"Nagging? You are pathetic. I practically have a nervous breakdown every time I have to go to one of those parties. Do you know how many pills I have to take to calm down? You said we would save the money and get away from Mark. You said I could stop doing this. I know those guys pay plenty to be with me, and you accuse me of nagging because I don't know where the money goes? What else is going on that I don't know about? I have a right to know!" Estelle's voice grew louder with every word.

Suddenly, Jerry grabbed her face and shoved her back on the bed. "You have a right to know what? I take the chances arranging everything with these guys. If anything goes wrong, I'm the one Mark will hold responsible. You don't have to do anything but look good and do what comes naturally."

"Jerry, you're hurting me! Stop it; you're going to bruise my face."

"Then shut up! Do you hear me? I'm sick of it!" Jerry let go of Estelle, went into the bathroom, and locked the door.

Estelle sat up on the bed, rubbing her face. "I hate him," she whispered. "One of these days I'm going to find out what he does when he locks himself in that bathroom for so long."

A while later, Jerry came out of the bathroom cool and calm, picked up his jacket, and went out the door.

Estelle went to the window and watched his car pull out of the parking lot. Jake was sleeping, and Estelle decided it was time to do a little searching. If she could find some money, maybe she and Jake could get to the bus station one night while Jerry slept. He was a sound sleeper after all. She would have to leave practically everything they owned behind; but, if they could escape, it would be worth it.

She started in their bedroom, going through every drawer and all of the shelves in the closet. Next, she searched every drawer and cabinet in the kitchen. Again, she found no hidden money. There weren't a lot of places to look in the living room, but she pulled the cushions off of the sofa and chair. Still nothing. Then, she checked every shelf in the linen closet.

Finally she made her way to the bathroom and locked the door behind her. She looked around the room. There didn't seem to be many hiding places, but Jerry spent a lot of time locked in this room. The medicine cabinet yielded nothing, so she took the lid off of the commode and looked under it. Nothing. As she leaned over to replace the lid, she noticed a loose tile under the sink. Getting on her hands and knees, she removed the tile easily.

"You couldn't hide much money in here," she whispered to herself. "Now, what's this?" A small package fell out of the hole in the wall. Just then, she heard the front door open. "Oh, God help me!" She put the package back in the wall without looking inside and then replaced the tile.

Standing up, she flushed the toilet and turned on the faucet for a moment. Faking a yawn, Estelle walked out of the bathroom and headed for the bedroom.

Jerry turned and watched her walk into the bedroom. "What are you doing?"

"I just got up to go to the bathroom." Estelle rubbed her eyes.

"You're still in your dress and shoes, and every light in the place is on." Jerry squinted as he watched her face.

Estelle fought hard to control her voice and not stammer. "I fell asleep on the couch. You know how I am when I take those pills."

"Yeah, okay. Go on to bed. I'll be there in a few minutes." He headed for the bathroom.

The next morning, Jerry and Estelle had breakfast together. Neither mentioned the night before.

"I have a few things to take care of today, but I'll probably be home early tonight." Jerry kissed her on the forehead, grabbed his keys, and went out the door.

Estelle didn't have time to resume her search. She had to get Jake up and get him ready for school. He was so sleepy that morning that everything took longer than usual. Finally, they were out the door and on the way to school. Estelle watched her son walk into the school building. Just before he disappeared through the huge door, he turned, smiled, and waved. He was so innocent. He trusted her, and for a moment, she felt a twinge of guilt. "How did I get into this mess?" Estelle whispered to herself. It was Jerry's fault, and now they were stuck in this situation until they could get away.

The walk back to the apartment seemed longer than usual. Estelle didn't notice Jerry's car in the parking lot as she walked up the sidewalk to the apartment building. She was thinking about that little package behind the loose tile in the bathroom as she unlocked the door and walked into the living room. "Oh my God!" she shrieked. Jerry stood in the middle of the room.

"What's the matter? Are you nervous about something?" Jerry scowled.

"No, I just didn't expect you to be here. You startled me!"

"Yeah, sure."

"Jerry, once you leave in the morning, I never see you until who knows when. Seeing a man standing in the middle of the room scared the wits out of me." Estelle dropped her door key in her handbag and started to clean the kitchen. "Why are you here? I thought you had things to take care of today."

"Well, I thought I would spend a little time with you and take care of business later. I'm a little tired though, so I think I'll just take a little nap for now."

"Sure, go ahead. I'll try not to make too much noise cleaning." Estelle didn't know what he was up to, but she felt uneasy.

"Oh come on, take a nap with me." Jerry grabbed her by the arm and led her to their room.

It seemed like an eternity before Jerry left the apartment for the second time that day. Estelle stood by the window and watched him get in his car and pull away. She decided to put the little chain lock on the door so he couldn't sneak up on her. Then she headed for the bathroom. She bent down and pulled on the loose tile...but it didn't budge. She tried to remove the tile again. "Maybe it was this one." She tried another tile, then another. All of the tiles under the sink were secure. Not one of them was loose at all. "Oh God, he knows I was in here snooping around." Whatever had been there was gone now.

She ran back to the living room and took the chain off of the door, afraid that Jerry might sneak back to check up on her again. Estelle was a bundle of nerves for the rest of the day.

For the next few weeks, Jerry's schedule was more sporadic than usual. Sometimes he stayed home half the day, and other times he came home early at night. Estelle never knew when he would walk in the door. Neither said a word about the tile in the bathroom or the little package Estelle had discovered.

"Jerry, I can't do this anymore. I feel like I'm losing my mind. I take pills to sleep and pills to wake up, and I'm still a nervous wreck. The last time Mark was here, he asked a lot of questions. He asked if you were giving me anything to relax me."

Jerry spun around in a panic. "What the hell did you tell him?" He practically screamed at her.

"Nothing. I said I had to have a few drinks before I could relax and entertain the gentlemen at his parties. He smiled and told me he liked my innocence."

"Good. Don't tell him anything else—especially not about the pills. He doesn't know about the nightmares. What we do is none of his business. You let me know if he asks you any more questions."

"Okay, I won't tell him anything. But that doesn't help my nerves. Sometimes, I think I'm going to throw up when one of those men start pawing on me."

Jerry watched her pace the floor as she continued to complain. He wondered if she was ready for his secret. He knew he could help her calm down and get through this, but he wasn't sure if she was ready just yet. Jerry trembled with excitement. It would be the one thing they could share that no one else could touch. She would belong to him completely, and he would be in total control.

"Did you hear anything I just said? I feel like I'm going to have a nervous breakdown! I have to take more pills to sleep and more pills to wake up. Rose constantly tells me she's worried about me. Pauline calls more often than usual, so I know Rose said something to her."

"So what do you want me to do? I'll do anything to help you feel better. Come here, and tell Daddy what you need."

"I don't know what I need. I only know I'm losing control, and it scares me. I have a child to take care of. I'm all Jake has in this world."

Jerry pulled Estelle onto his lap. "Estelle, do you trust me? Do you understand that everything I do is for us—for our future?"

"I—I try to understand," she lied.

"You know how much I love you. Do you trust me?" Jerry kissed her face and neck as he spoke softly to her.

"Yes, I trust you," she lied again, saying what he wanted to hear.

Jerry carried her to their bedroom. Later, as he stroked her hair, he told her his secret. "Have you ever noticed that when I get really wound up, I take some time alone, and later I'm calm and collected?"

"Yes. I have to admit, I've wondered what you do when you lock yourself in the bathroom sometimes."

"You even snooped around once, didn't you?"

"Well, yes. Yes I did. I was worried about you." Lying had become second nature to her.

"Estelle, why would you worry when I come out and I've calmed down?"

"I don't know. I just felt like you were hiding something from me."

"Did you ever find what I was hiding?"

"No, I didn't. But you knew I had been snooping, didn't you?"

"I did, but I love you so much that I let it go and didn't say anything."

Jerry sat quietly and waited for Estelle to continue. "Jerry, what are you hiding from me?"

Jerry smiled. He thought she'd never ask. "I'm not hiding anything. But my friend, who's a doctor, helps me out by giving me something other than pills."

"Yes?" Estelle held her breath in anticipation. She didn't know what he was about to tell her, but she was trembling. "What is it?"

"Well, it's really a pain killer, but it calms you down also."

"I'm not in pain."

"No, but you need something stronger than you've been taking to help you relax." Estelle didn't say anything and Jerry continued. "It's different than those little pills. It comes in a powder," here goes, Jerry thought, "and you have to take it in a shot."

Estelle jumped up. "A shot? Oh my God! I hate needles. I almost pass out when I get a shot!"

"Estelle, settle down. You barely feel it. I've been taking it so long, that I give myself the shot now, and I can do it for you. I could be a doctor," he bragged.

"I don't know."

"Come on. I didn't steer you wrong on the pills, did I? Have they hurt you?"

"Well, no."

"Have they helped you with the nightmares?"

"Yes. I haven't had a nightmare in months."

"This is a little stronger and will help you more. If I didn't take it myself, I would never give it to you. It hasn't hurt me. You see me every day. Am I ever sick?"

"No, I just don't know. I'm afraid."

"Afraid of what? Are you afraid of me? Listen, Jake's in bed. Let me give you just a little. Mark won't be here this weekend so we can experiment and see how much you need to relax." Before she could answer, Jerry walked out of the room and came back a few minutes later with the little package Estelle found the day she was searching.

"Jerry, can't we wait? I really don't know if I want to do this."

Jerry was oblivious to Estelle's pleading. His back was turned to her so she couldn't see his hands trembling or the drops of perspiration trickling down his face. But she did see him light a match. "What are you doing?"

"It's a powder. It has to be liquid to draw it up. That takes a little water and some heat."

"I've never seen a doctor do that."

"Of course you haven't. They have special equipment. Okay, it's ready. Here, let me tie this around the upper part of your arm."

"Ouch, that's tight!"

"It will just be for a minute. Make a fist and squeeze hard. Turn and look the other way. You'll just feel a little prick."

Estelle's eyes were shut tight, and she turned her head away. She did feel a tiny prick, and it stung a little. "How will it make me feel?"

"Relax your hand now. Let me take this off." Suddenly, warmth moved up her arm. Then it shot straight to her head. Jerry gently slid the needle out of her arm.

"Oh my God, my head! Am I okay?" She jumped up and stumbled against Jerry.

"You're fine. Just relax and let it go."

Her head felt like it could explode, but she tried not to panic. "Jerry, I feel sick. Help me to the bathroom."

Jerry slid his arm around her shoulders and guided her to the bathroom. She threw up in the toilet and then slid to the floor. "That's better. My head was throbbing and I felt so sick. But my stomach is better now."

Jerry laughed. "I've heard it said that if you don't throw up, you didn't get off."

"What?"

"You know, you didn't get enough."

She sat on the floor for a few minutes. "I really just want to lie down. My eyes feel so heavy."

"Come on, let me help you up. That's my girl." Jerry led a wobbly Estelle back to the bedroom.

"I'm so sleepy. I need to lie down."

"Let's stay awake for a while. Come on, sit up and talk to me. I want to see how you do with this stuff before you go to sleep."

"Okay, what do you want to talk about?" Estelle rested her head on Jerry's shoulder and nodded off. Her breathing was deep and steady, so Jerry let her lie back on the bed and sleep.

"You don't need much. We need to be careful, baby. We can't have any marks or bruises," he whispered as he stroked her hair and face.

17

erry, there aren't any marks. And yes, I put makeup on the one little bruise. Settle down. Mark isn't going to strip me down and examine me for God's sake." Estelle had lost a few pounds over the last several weeks, but she was still as beautiful as ever.

"Damn, I should have been more careful. I can't believe I left a bruise! It's none of his business, but he'll make a big deal about it if he finds out." Jerry straightened his tie and picked up the diamond cuff links. "Tonight will be different—very important people. I don't want any problems so I need you to shine, baby. These guys can take us where we want to go. Then Mark can go to hell. He's nobody in their world."

"Who are they?"

"Baby, you don't even want to know their names. Just look beautiful and be friendly; I'll take care of the rest. Now listen close: I don't know for sure who will be there. Mark acted like it was a big secret. There's this big guy who's got really dark eyes and a little grey hair, you know, around the temples. I want you to get his attention and treat him right. He's the one to impress."

"Is he the *only* one with grey hair?"

"You'll know him when you see him. He's at least 6' 2" and always has a suntan. Everyone caters to him. He's the boss."

"Okay, but I'm a little nervous. What if he doesn't like me? He may prefer a redhead or blonde."

"Don't worry, baby, he'll want you. He always wants the best, and those other broads don't hold a candle to you. That sexy dress makes you look like a movie star; and with your hair all down and beautiful, you'll get his attention for sure."

"Okay. Why did you say I don't even want to know their names? Are they dangerous?"

"Dangerous?" His laugh was a little high pitched and nervous. "Do you think I would put you in danger?"

She hesitated. "You seem really excited and nervous."

"This is our chance to get out of this dump and make some real money. If I can get in with these guys, there's no limit. You'll have anything you want—clothes, house, cars, and private school for Jake. Don't worry; just look beautiful and do what you do. I'll handle everything else. Do you have your diaphragm?"

"Of course. It's in my bag."

When a limo picked them up, instead of the usual taxi, she looked at Jerry and didn't say a word.

Estelle was quiet during most of the ride. "Jerry, where are we going? This isn't the way we usually go. And why are we in a limo, not a taxi?"

"We're not going to a hotel this time. We're going to a house—hell, it's a mansion! You won't believe how big it is!"

"I thought Mark always got a suite at the hotel."

Jerry whispered, "Well, these guys are not like anyone you've met before. Mark has to go to them because they're very careful. They have their own security; they don't trust strangers to watch their backs."

"My God, Jerry, who *are* these people?" Estelle felt sick.

He whispered. "Big, baby, they are *big*. They're just what we need to get what we want. You're going to get in with the boss and gain his trust. Then we'll see where we go from there." For a moment, Jerry forgot about the driver and laughed like a maniac, which frightened her even more.

"Jerry, what are you planning? You're scaring me," Estelle whispered.

"Don't worry, baby, we are going to get ours one way or another. Trust me."

When the limo pulled into the driveway, Estelle couldn't believe her eyes. It really was a mansion—three stories, and with the surrounding property, it covered the entire block. The driver pulled to a stop and an attendant slowly opened a huge, ornate gate. They drove toward the house down a long, tree-lined lane.

The grounds were immaculate. There was a beautiful rose garden in the center of the circle drive, directly in front of the house. The car stopped, and the driver came around and opened the car door. Jerry got out and took Estelle's hand, helping her out of the car.

Her backless evening gown fit like a glove, accentuating every curve, and Jerry had insisted she wear almost nothing under it. The long slit exposed much of her thigh as she turned and stepped out of the car. She didn't see the tall man watching from a second floor window, staring at her long, lovely legs. She looked wide-eyed and innocent as she stared at the huge house. The man turned from the window and walked toward the stairway.

"Jerry, this is beautiful. My God, how many rooms are there?"

"Who knows? More than enough for the fat cats who own it, that's for sure." Jerry took Estelle's arm, walked to the door, and took hold of the large brass doorknocker.

The door opened before Jerry could knock. The butler, a small older man with silver hair, dark piercing eyes, and an olive complexion, stood straight as a rod and expressionless. He nodded as he asked their names. "Please step inside and I will announce you. You may wait right here."

Estelle and Jerry stepped into the foyer. Estelle looked like a little girl as she gazed up at the huge crystal chandelier that sparkled overhead like a million diamonds. Mirrors and oil paintings hung in ornate gold frames. There was a sitting area with two overstuffed, wing-backed chairs on the right side of the foyer. Fragrant red roses, in a crystal vase, sat on a beautifully carved, dark-cherry table in the center of the foyer.

"Jerry, they have a butler—with white gloves and everything."

"Baby, they have cooks and maids too."

After a moment or two, the butler was back. "May I take your wrap?" He spoke with a heavy accent.

"Oh, yes. Please." Estelle let the mink stole slide off of her shoulders.

"Please follow me to the library."

The butler led them through the foyer, down the hallway, and through large, cherry-wood doors into the library. Built-in bookshelves covered all four walls, floor to ceiling, and flames danced in the fireplace, giving the large room a cozy feel. Mark was already seated in one of the overstuffed chairs in the center of the room. He looked quite relaxed and at home. Two tall, muscular men stood in opposite corners of the room facing the door. With hands clasped in front of them, they didn't smile or even acknowledge the new arrivals.

"Miss Estelle Shannon and Mr. Jerry Bradley, sir," the butler announced them.

That's when she saw him. He stood at least 6'2", with thick, jet-black hair and the darkest brown eyes she'd ever seen. Just a touch of grey at each temple gave him a distinguished look. He was unbelievably handsome with strong, perfect features.

For a moment, Estelle couldn't move; her eyes locked on his full, sensual lips. He smiled and walked toward her. It was impossible to ignore his powerful body under linen trousers and a soft, cream-colored silk shirt. A gold chain and crucifix flashed around his neck, and a huge diamond sparkled from the thick gold ring on the little finger of his right hand. Estelle was so enamored she almost forgot to breathe. She and her host stared deep into each other's eyes.

"Miss Shannon, Mark did not do you justice. You are far more beautiful than he described." His English was perfect, with only a slight accent. He took her hand, and she caught her breath at the touch of his soft, warm lips. Estelle lowered her eyes and fought to hide her reaction as a shock of electricity shot through her. Her knees were weak, and her heart pounded. "Thank you, sir."

"Please call me Frank."

"Jerry Bradley, sir, nice to meet you." Jerry had been completely forgotten and ignored until he introduced himself.

"Mark has talked about you often, Jerry. Welcome, both of you." The butler hadn't moved since he had announced the guests. "Bartola, please let Cook know that we are ready to dine. Miss Shannon, allow me." He took her arm in his and led the way to the dining room.

"Please, call me Estelle." Frank smiled as he felt her tremble. Mark and Jerry followed the couple to the dining room.

The bodyguards followed the group and once again posted themselves in corners that faced the doors.

"Estelle, I would be honored if you sat here beside me." Frank led her to the chair just to the right of his. He pulled out her chair and then seated himself at the head of the long dining table. The butler showed Mark and Jerry to their seats on the opposite side.

The dining table was adorned with a white lace over linen tablecloth and a beautiful centerpiece of fresh-cut roses. Tall white candles, in silver candelabras, gave off soft light on each side of the centerpiece. Linen napkins, fine china, crystal goblets, and real silver flatware completed each place setting.

Cook and her helpers brought in a large chafing dish filled with steaming soup. The fragrant spices were different than those Estelle's mother had used. One of the servants ladled soup into china bowls at each place. Another filled the crystal goblets with wine.

Frank approved the wine served with each course. Estelle barely noticed the meal as it was served, and she ate small portions along with several glasses of wine. She felt relaxed and warm inside. Frank was attentive, and Estelle held onto his every word as the two made small-talk about the weather and the beautiful grounds of the estate, especially the roses. Estelle was surprised at Frank's interest in them. She completely forgot about Mark and Jerry until she glanced across the table and noticed Jerry's perturbed look. When she saw Mark jab Jerry in the side, she smiled and turned back to Frank.

"Well, gentlemen, why don't we enjoy cigars and brandy in the library while Miss Shannon freshens up? Bartola, please ask Madelena to show Miss Shannon to the guest room."

The butler left the room, and moments later a lovely middle-aged woman stepped in. Estelle followed Madelena up the elegant, winding staircase leading to the second floor.

Frank asked one of his bodyguards to shut the library doors. "Well, Mark, you couldn't have chosen a lovelier young lady. This time I am very pleased. I've almost forgotten that I am paying for her time. She seems rather innocent."

"She has only been with a few of my very select clientele—older gentlemen. And yes, she is special." Mark smiled, pleased with himself.

"She is quite different from the other two women you chose."

Mark's smile was forced; he hated being reminded that Frank hadn't even let the other two women stay for dinner. "Yes, she is. Once we completely understood each other, I realized Estelle would be the perfect evening companion for you, Frank."

"There is a slight change of plan. I would like to spend more time with her than we discussed—the entire weekend actually. You can come back for her on Sunday evening, say around 8:00 p.m."

Jerry jumped up. "That's not what we agreed on, Mark! Why all weekend?" He was frantic.

"Jerry, settle down. This is business. If Frank wants her company for the weekend, I'm sure he will make it worth our while."

Jerry ran his hand through his hair and become more agitated.

"I will pay four times the rate we discussed, half in advance," Frank said.

Jerry looked at Mark who shook his head in agreement.

"I'll make sure she has everything she needs. Let's settle up, and then my driver will take you home. Gentlemen, I'll be right back." One bodyguard stayed with Mark and Jerry and the other followed Frank.

Ten minutes later, Frank and his bodyguard returned. "This should do it." Frank handed a stack of cash to Mark.

"Ah, can I talk to her before we go?" Jerry asked.

"What on earth for?" Mark replied.

"What the hell am I supposed to do about Jake?"

Frank frowned at Jerry. "Who is Jake?"

Mark was livid as Jerry kept talking. "Jake is her son, and I have to deal with the babysitter."

"I'm sure you can handle it, Jerry. Is the babysitter a trustworthy person and good to the child?" Frank asked.

"Yes, she's great. She loves the kid like a grandson."

"Then I don't see the need for you to speak to Estelle. If the boy can stay with the babysitter for the weekend, Estelle won't need to worry."

"Sure, okay." Beads of perspiration formed on Jerry's forehead. He knew by the next day Estelle would be sick, suffering from early withdrawals.

"Is there anything else?" Frank asked.

"No, Frank, there is nothing else." Mark glared at Jerry.

"Bartola, please ask Tony to get the car and show them out. Gentlemen, I'll see you on Sunday." Frank turned and headed for the stairway.

Mark waited until they were in the car before he lit into Jerry. "What on earth is wrong with you? You acted like a jealous schoolboy in there!"

"What the hell does he need the whole weekend for?"

"Jerry, he is paying more than enough for the weekend. This is business, and you had better not forget it again."

"Estelle was all starry-eyed over him. Didn't you watch her?"

"For God's sake, Jerry, she's doing exactly what she is supposed to do! I think you have completely lost your perspective here. This is business, and you are being well paid." Mark practically yelled.

"Yeah, well, you don't have to face Rose and make up some story. She's just like Pauline; she looks right through me. Sometimes it's like she can read my mind. I know she damn well hates me."

"Think, Jerry. Don't go home. I'll get a room for you at the hotel since she was planning to keep Jake tonight anyway. Call her in the morning. Tell her that you ran into some old friends and are making a weekend of it."

"What if she asks to speak to Estelle?"

"Tell her that Estelle is out having brunch with the ladies. Or tell her that she is shopping. My God, use your brain."

"Okay, I'll take care of it." Jerry hoped Estelle could think on her feet when she started to get sick. On second thought, she probably wouldn't even know why—so maybe there was nothing to worry about after all.

Estelle watched through the window as Mark and Jerry climbed into the limo and drove off. She couldn't believe they were leaving her alone with a complete stranger! This was such a different arrangement than Mark's usual parties at the hotel. At least there, if anything went wrong, Jerry and Mark were nearby. Just then, there was a knock at the door. "Yes?" she answered.

"May I come in?" Frank asked.

"Yes, of course." She hurried to the door just as Frank stepped inside the room. They stood mere inches apart. Estelle trembled, completely undone by his nearness. She had an uncontrollable urge to touch his lips and feel his muscular arms around her, but she took a step back.

"I hope you don't mind, but I asked for your company for the entire weekend," Frank smiled.

"The entire weekend? I have a—I have responsibilities to attend to. I can't believe Jerry didn't consult me!"

Frank spoke to her softly. "Estelle, Jerry told me about your son and the woman who looks after him when you're away. I made him promise to speak with her and make sure your little one remains with her for the weekend."

Estelle blushed and looked down.

"Please forgive me for not asking you how you felt about all of this. You are, how can I say … you are fascinating, and I wanted to spend more time with you than we had originally planned."

"Frank, you know what I am. You don't have to consult me." Tears filled her eyes, and she turned away.

Frank gently took hold of her shoulders and turned her to face him. "I know that you are beautiful; and in spite of Mark and Jerry's business dealings, I sense something almost innocent about you. I do not know why you are involved in their business, but I am pleased that you are here with me now." Something about this young woman made him completely forget how she came to be with him. She was breathtakingly beautiful, and the look in her eyes was one of tender, childlike dependence.

Frank tasted salty tears when he lowered his head and kissed her face. "Come sit on the balcony with me for a while. It is a beautiful night." As she followed him, for the first time she noticed the gold band on his left hand. Her heart sank; he had a wife. It didn't matter, and she didn't care. Maybe, even if just for a few days, she could forget the ugly, painful things that had led her to him.

Estelle squeezed her eyes shut—willing herself not to wake from this extraordinary dream. She felt warm and safe in the strong arms that held her. "Mmmmm," she snuggled deeper into the luxurious satin sheets and the thick, hand-embroidered spread that was pulled up to her chin. The room was filled with the fragrance of roses. Smiling, she remembered the rose petals on the bed the night before.

"Bella," Frank's husky voice made her tremble. "Did you sleep well?"

She knew she had no right to be upset that he didn't remember her name, but it hurt nonetheless. "Frank, my name is Estelle."

"I didn't forget your name. Bella means beautiful, and your beauty takes my breath away."

Estelle blushed and didn't quite know what to say. "Thank you."

Frank climbed out of bed and put on a silk robe. He pulled a cord over the bed that rang a bell. Almost immediately, there was a soft knock at the door. Frank opened the door just a crack, keeping Estelle out of view. "Bartola, please tell Cook we will have our breakfast on the terrace in an hour and a half."

"Yes sir."

Later, after Frank left the room to bathe and dress, Madelena came in to help Estelle get ready for the day. "I didn't bring anything with me for the weekend."

"We took the liberty of purchasing some things for you, Miss Estelle."

"Where on earth did you find anything open early enough to get all of these?" Estelle said when Madelena put several bags and boxes on the bed.

"Mr. Moretti has many friends." Madelena held up a lovely soft yellow cashmere sweater and silk floral skirt, and delicate undergarments were laid out on the bed. Soft leather shoes had been placed on the floor next to the bed. "Will these do?"

"Oh my! They're beautiful!"

"I'll draw a bath for you. There are lotions and perfumes in the dressing room."

"Madelena, you don't have to do that."

"It is nothing, Miss Estelle. After your bath, would you like help with your hair?"

"You've done too much already. I can do my hair. Thank you so much."

"Mr. Moretti will be here in less than 30 minutes to escort you to the terrace for breakfast." Madelena headed for the bathroom.

Within minutes, Estelle climbed into the steaming tub of fragrant, luxurious bubbles. A soft, thick towel lay on a chair next to the tub. She hated to rush such a relaxing bath, but she washed and reluctantly climbed out of the tub. She smoothed scented lotion over her entire body before getting dressed. Everything fit perfectly.

Looking at the time, she gave in and let Madelena brush her hair and smooth it into a chic twist. Just as they finished her hair and she dabbed on perfume, there was a knock at the door. Madelena opened the door to Frank. He smiled and walked over to Estelle. "You look lovely, Bella."

"Frank, everything is perfect. It was very kind of you to buy these things for me to wear this weekend." She blushed and looked down.

"You deserve beautiful things. And they are not just for the weekend; they are yours." Taking her delicate chin in his hand, he kissed her softly and then offered his arm. "Breakfast is waiting."

Estelle felt like royalty as they descended the marble staircase. Servants and the ever-present bodyguards stood at attention. Frank guided Estelle to a terrace that offered a spectacular view of the gardens. She gasped when she saw the swimming pool just off the terrace. "What a beautiful pool!"

"It's still a little cool for swimming; but when the weather gets warmer, we can enjoy the pool."

A small, intimate setting awaited the couple. Fresh-cut flowers in a crystal vase sat in the center of the small table. There were pastries, fruit, cheese, and even a dish with some sort of pasta. Estelle was hungry; but as she started to eat, her stomach felt queasy.

"Where is your appetite, Bella?"

"I don't know. Everything looks delicious, but I feel a little queasy right now. I'm sorry; I know your cook worked very hard to prepare all of this food."

"Are you sure you're okay? You look a little pale."

"I don't know. I'm not feeling well right now. I'm so sorry."

"There is nothing to be sorry for, Bella. It is not your fault. We will walk in the garden; maybe the fresh air will help you feel better."

After finishing his meal, Frank took Estelle by the hand and led her down a stone path that wound through the garden. Typically Estelle loved fragrant flowers; but as they walked, she became increasingly nauseated. "Frank, I really don't feel well. Do you mind if I go lie down for just a little while? I am so sorry." Tears welled up in her eyes and spilled onto her cheeks.

Frank wiped away her tears, and they headed back to the house. "Madelena, Miss Estelle is not feeling well and needs to rest. Please prepare her bed." He turned to Estelle, "Rest and I will check on you later. I have some business to attend to, but it won't take long. You may not be accustomed to our spices and sauces. Sicilian foods are very rich and spicy, and last night's dinner may not have agreed with you."

Estelle was tired but couldn't sleep. After about an hour, she ran to the bathroom and threw up. Her stomach continued to churn, and her body ached a bit.

Frank came to check on her later in the afternoon. "Bella, you are shivering." He rang the bell next to the bed, and within minutes there was a soft knock on the door. "Madelena, please get another blanket; she has the chills."

Frank and Madelena covered Estelle with another warm, thick blanket. "Please sit with her, Madelena. I will be back shortly."

About an hour later, Frank returned with a small, balding man who wore thick glasses and carried a black bag. "I took the liberty of asking my physician to stop by and check on you."

"Oh Frank, you didn't have to do that. I am making so much trouble for you. I should just go home and let you enjoy the rest of your weekend. Please call Mark or Jerry. I don't want to be any more of a nuisance." Suddenly, Estelle threw off the covers and ran to the bathroom. There was an uncomfortable silence in the room as the three heard her getting sick to her stomach.

"Doctor, Madelena, please take care of her. I need to make a phone call." Frank turned and walked out of the room.

Estelle finally came out of the bathroom and climbed back into bed. "Your symptoms are very much like influenza or a very bad cold. Let's hope it's not serious. I will give you something to settle your stomach. You are chilling, but you don't seem to have fever yet. I'll give you some aspirin for fever anyway. Madelena, can you please get a glass of water?" The doctor gave Estelle aspirin and some powder in a glass of water to settle her stomach. "Young lady, you get some sleep now and Frank will let me know if I need to check on you again."

"Thank you, Doctor."

By evening, Estelle was worse. Her stomach cramped, yet it was so empty she didn't know how she could throw up anymore. The chills wouldn't stop. To make matters worse, she was sniffling and had a runny nose. Her entire body ached.

Frank slipped into the room quietly. "It's okay, Frank; I'm not sleeping. I feel horrible and I can't sleep."

"Bella, I am sorry that you are so ill. I have called Mark as you asked. If you think you would be more comfortable at home, I will have my driver take you there. But I don't want to simply send you home. I am worried that you may need to go to the hospital."

"Oh, Frank, please. I don't want to go to the hospital. I think I should go home." She started to cry. "I am so sorry. I was supposed to entertain you for the weekend. And I've been such a burden. I don't know what is wrong with me. I never get sick!"

"It is not your fault. I promise we will plan another weekend when I return. I will not forget last night." He smiled and kissed her forehead.

"You're leaving the city?"

"I'm going out of the country. My business requires me to be in Sicily at times."

"Is your family there?"

"Yes. My parents, brothers, sisters, cousins … lots of family."

"And your wife?" She could have bitten her tongue for asking such a question.

"Yes, my wife." He was silent for a moment, "But, I have family here also. My uncle has businesses here. His only son died almost two years ago, so it is my responsibility to step in and help. I divide my time between my home in Sicily and here."

"Oh. Do you have children?"

"We had a son, but he died shortly after birth."

"Frank, I'm so sorry. I had no right to ask about your family. Please forgive me."

"There is no need to be sorry. Now, I will have Tony take you home. You will get better, and we will arrange a weekend when I return."

"I would like that."

"Madelena will help you gather your things."

"Frank?"

"Yes?"

"I, ah—I enjoyed last night also."

"Yes, I know you did, Bella." His smile was dazzling. "There will be other nights; I promise."

When Estelle was ready to go, Frank escorted her to the limo and kissed the top of her head.

Estelle somehow managed to make it home without throwing up in the limo. As she unlocked the door and stepped inside the small apartment, she found Jerry pacing the floor like a madman. "You're back! Mark called and grilled me like a cop. He said you were really sick."

"I am sick, Jerry. I don't remember ever being this sick in my life." Just then, her stomach churned and she ran for the bathroom. When she came out, Jerry was waiting.

"Here, let me give you a little bit of this and you'll start to feel better."

"Will it really help? My entire body hurts. I have chills and a runny nose; I thought that was just to relax me."

"Estelle, just be quiet and let me do this." After Jerry gave her a shot, she went in the bedroom to lie down. She slept for a short time, and she was amazed at how quickly she started feeling better.

"Have you talked to Rose? Is Jake doing okay? He must really be upset that I didn't come home this morning."

"Jake is fine. I told Rose that we ran into some friends and decided to make a weekend of it, and she was okay with keeping Jake for the weekend. He's going to Sunday school with her in the morning; you know that made her happy. Now that you're feeling better, how about a little welcome home?" Jerry pulled her into his arms.

Without thinking, Estelle pushed him away. "Jerry, I've been sick all day and I'm exhausted. I'm going to bed."

"You weren't exhausted last night with that dago jerk. You were smiling and hanging all over him."

"He was paying for my time, remember? I thought being friendly and attentive was the point. Isn't that what I was *supposed* to do?"

"Yeah, that's what you're supposed to do. But you didn't have to enjoy it so much. You couldn't take your eyes off that guy."

"I'm not going to listen to this; I'm going to bed."

Jerry grabbed her by the arm and pushed her down on the bed. "You'll sleep when I tell you to sleep; now come here. Don't ever forget that you belong to me."

"Jerry, stop it. What's wrong with you?" She tried to push him away.

"What do you think you're doing? I said you belong to me!" She was too weak to fight him, so she gave in.

Later, Jerry sat on the side of the bed, and Estelle turned over to go to sleep. "Well, that was exciting." Jerry's sarcasm wasn't lost on Estelle.

"What did you expect? I've been sick all day." Estelle thought for a moment. "Or at least I *was*. Magically, I'm better after you gave me a shot. Jerry, what is that stuff you give me?" She sat up and leaned against the headboard.

"What do mean what is it? I told you it is something to relax you."

"Oh come on, Jerry; it does more than relax me, and Mark questions me continuously. I take it every day, at least until today, and I was sick until I took it again. What is it?" Her voice was shrill and angry.

"You know something, Estelle? I'm really sick of walking on eggshells with you. You want to know what it is? It's heroin." Estelle gasped, but she couldn't speak. "Since you are so fragile and can't handle your responsibilities, I have to do *something* to help you along."

Estelle put her face in her hands and started to cry. "Heroin, oh my God! I'm not just a whore; you've turned me into drug addict!"

"Shut up, Estelle. You *had* to know you weren't taking medicine. No one could be that stupid."

"Stupid? I'm not stupid. But before I was with you, I would never have dreamed of doing any of these things. I was never around people who did the things you do." Suddenly it all made sense. Estelle gasped and stood up. "She was telling the truth!"

"What the hell are you talking about? Who was telling the truth?"

"Bobbi! She said that your son was in prison; that he liked drugs just like his daddy. That *was* your little girl, and you just let her go to the state when her mother overdosed and died. She's probably in an orphanage. Oh my God!"

Jerry grabbed her and shoved her against the wall. "Shut up! You don't know what you're talking about. Did you tell anyone about her?"

"No—No, I didn't tell anyone. Jerry, you're hurting me!"

"Don't *ever* mention her name again! I told you I didn't know her, and I don't have any kids." He pushed her toward the bed and left the room. Then, she heard him slam the door as he left the apartment.

Estelle was terrified and exhausted; she eventually cried herself to sleep.

18

The next morning, Estelle crawled out of bed and took a bath. Jerry hadn't come home after their fight, but it didn't matter. She knew where he kept his stash. After all, she couldn't stand to be sick again. Having watched Jerry so many times, she was confident she could inject herself. It took several tries, but she finally managed to hit a vein between her toes. Jerry said it was important that she didn't mar her beautiful skin, so he often gave her a shot there.

Now she realized why Jerry was so careful and why Mark questioned her constantly. He at least knew that Jerry had a problem in the past and didn't want any complications. The most terrifying realization was that she was a drug addict—a prostitute *and* a drug addict—trapped in a nightmare with no way of escape.

Estelle had to pull herself together before Rose brought Jake home after church. Makeup didn't help; she was still pale and had dark circles under her eyes. Later, when Rose knocked on the door, Estelle conjured up a smile. "Mommy!" Jake jumped into Estelle's arms. She hadn't realized how weak she was and almost fell backwards.

Rose reached out to steady her. "Estelle, are you okay? You're so pale! Jake, sit on the couch with your mother." Jake got down and ran to the couch. Estelle sat down beside him.

"I'm fine; I was just sick this weekend. I don't know if it was something I ate or a really bad cold, but it cut our weekend short. We actually came home last night." Estelle couldn't look at Rose. "Rose, I'm so sorry I didn't call you."

"Don't worry about it; Jake and I were fine. We baked cookies and went to the park. Well, I'd better get home. If you need anything, please let me know."

"Oh, I'm fine now. Thank you so much for keeping Jake."

"You're welcome, Estelle."

Rose went to her apartment and immediately called Pauline. She was worried about Estelle. Something was going on, and she knew Jerry was behind it. She was so frustrated that Estelle didn't see through Jerry's façade. Rose and Pauline talked and then prayed for Estelle and Jake before saying goodbye.

Estelle didn't see Frank for over a month. She thought it was strange that Mark didn't host any parties during that time. Regardless, she welcomed the break from entertaining Mark's "associates."

When Mark called to arrange another weekend with Frank, Jerry didn't like it; but he agreed. After all, the money was too good to turn down. "You're spending another weekend with that fat cat dago. You know, old lover boy."

Estelle tried to act nonchalant, "Oh really? The weekend or one night?"

"I said the weekend, didn't I? You need to talk to Rose about keeping Jake. This time, I'll make sure you have what you need for the weekend. We don't want any problems." Jerry cursed under his breath and left the apartment without saying goodbye.

The next few days dragged by. Estelle made arrangements with Rose to keep Jake, telling both Rose and Jake that she was going out of town with Jerry on one of his business trips. She carefully packed the clothes Frank bought for her during their first weekend. Her "medicine" and special equipment were hidden in the lining of her handbag.

This time, Mark and Jerry would not accompany her. Frank's driver would meet Jerry and Estelle at the hotel where Jerry would stay for the weekend.

Jerry had been quiet and angry since Mark called about the weekend with Frank. Estelle struggled to hide her excitement; she felt giddy and exhilarated.

"I want you to keep your eyes open this weekend," Jerry enunciated each word.

"What are you talking about?"

"That first night, Frank went down the hall and came back with a wad of bills big enough to choke a horse. Just keep your eyes open; if you see anything that resembles a safe, just remember where it is."

"Jerry, have you lost your mind? He has bodyguards all over the place! Two of them practically never leave his side. My God, isn't the money you're making off of me enough?"

"Just keep your mouth shut and do what you're told."

When the limo pulled up, Estelle barely waited for the driver to open the door. She couldn't wait to get away from Jerry.

Frank was there to greet her when she arrived at the mansion. A surge of emotion washed over her as she watched him approach the limo. His looks were no less breathtaking than the first time she saw him. There was almost a princely air about him. He exuded power and authority; his entire being demanded respect—yet she knew his gentle touch. She had witnessed his kindness to those around him; Frank's bodyguards, driver, and household staff were completely devoted to him.

Friday night, the couple shared an intimate dinner on the balcony that opened from Estelle's room. The weather was perfect. They enjoyed breakfast each morning on the terrace and took long walks in the garden. A few times on Saturday, Frank left Estelle's room to attend to business; and that night, he surprised her with a romantic midnight swim. Early Sunday morning, Estelle awakened to find Frank gone. She heard voices downstairs in the foyer, and someone went out the front door. Estelle hurried to her window and watched as a priest left in the limo. Within minutes, there was a knock at her door; the priest was forgotten, and once again, Estelle was safe in Frank's arms. Estelle managed to slip away and lock the bathroom door each time she needed to take her "medicine."

Frank was like no other man she'd ever been with—certainly not like any other "customer." He laughed and talked with her, telling her stories of his childhood in a beautiful village in Sicily. He loved his parents dearly. He had two brothers, one younger and one older. Three of his four sisters were married with children, but his oldest sister had never married. And there was a multitude of aunts, uncles, and cousins.

Estelle laughed at the stories about his 97-year-old grandmother who still ruled the household staff. Frank declared his Nonna's pasta and sauces were the best in the village. The entire family loved this matriarch, and they treated her with the utmost respect. Frank said she would take a switch to anyone who was disrespectful—children and grownups alike. And God help the person who hurt one of her family members! In Sicily, family is everything; and family members were fiercely loyal to one another.

Estelle had always been thankful to be an only child, but Frank's stories made her a little envious. She'd felt so alone since she'd lost Momma and Poppa.

Frank wanted to know about Estelle, but he was very careful not to push her for details. She felt safe with him—trusted him. As they talked, she opened up and told him about her parents and Ricky.

"Jake is the most important thing in my life. I don't know what I would do without him. He's the only thing that kept me going after I lost Momma and Poppa. I love him so much." Estelle blushed, wondering if Frank believed a prostitute could love her child.

Frank smiled. "I'm sure he is a wonderful little boy."

"I—I never planned to do what I do." Estelle sighed and then continued. "I didn't know what to do or where to go after Ricky left and I lost my parents; I made a huge mistake. I went to live with Ricky's mother, and she was a prostitute. I didn't work for her; we actually hated each other. When I made plans to move out, she paid one of her flunkies to rape me." Her words came faster until they were practically unintelligible. "I got pregnant by that animal, and I couldn't stand it; I couldn't have his baby. I had an abortion—oh my God, I had an abortion." Deep-wrenching sobs shook her body. Frank pulled her close and rocked her while she cried.

Finally, Estelle felt as if she had no tears left. "Jerry came along at a very difficult time in my life, and he basically kept us from starving. I didn't know his real business then." She purposefully left out the nightmares, pills, and her heroin addiction. She poured out her heart as Frank held her, and she realized no one had ever listened to her the way he did.

Sunday evening came all too soon. Estelle slowly packed her things and prepared for the limo to take her back to the hotel and to Jerry.

"Bella, you look so sad. I promise we will have much more time together. I would like to talk with Mark about an arrangement."

"An arrangement?" she whispered.

"I know you didn't choose this life for yourself. Tell me: do you want to continue going to Mark's parties?"

"I *hate* the parties. Those men make me sick." She blushed and looked down at her feet.

"I want to take care of you and Jake. This house is perfect for you both. I will be here with you as often as possible."

"Do you mean that Jake and I would *live* here?"

"Yes; you will be safe and want for nothing."

"Frank, Jerry will never agree. At one time, I thought I loved him, and I believed he loved me. But now I realize I'm nothing more than his property—something he uses to get what he wants. He won't simply let me go."

"What do *you* want, Bella?"

"Being here with you is like a dream—a fairytale. I feel safe with you. Do you know that you are the first man who has ever really listened to me?" She hesitated. "But, Jerry won't let me go."

"Let me worry about Jerry. You say nothing to him about our plan. I will handle everything."

Frank walked with her to the limo, and Estelle prepared herself to return to the real world—the one she had come to hate.

Frank and Estelle spent a few more weekends together between his trips out of the country. He didn't mention talking to Mark, so Estelle didn't ask. He treated her like a princess, and she cherished every moment she spent with him.

Rose continued to care for Jake when Estelle was gone, but she became more and more suspicious about the young woman's weekend trips. She was drawn to Estelle and Jake, and she had grown to love them both. Estelle had kept Rose at a distance, but Rose knew the young woman was in trouble. She needed someone who truly cared about her and her son—someone who understood bad decisions and difficult times. Rose was disappointed that she hadn't been able to break through the barrier Estelle built around herself.

Rose and Pauline prayed together for Jake and Estelle during their weekly phone calls. Pauline's sister had improved and her prognosis was more positive, but she still needed constant care. Pauline just couldn't leave her.

Jerry didn't hide his jealousy and anger each time Estelle spent time with Frank. When he did speak to Estelle, he was sarcastic and crude.

He hated Frank. Each time she came home from a weekend with Frank, he questioned her about Frank's safe and valuables. Estelle didn't know where Frank kept his cash and valuables and told Jerry as much. She had no idea if Mark had talked to Jerry about her seeing Frank exclusively, but thankfully she was no longer invited to Mark's get-togethers.

Estelle was terrified that Jerry would take his anger out on her if Mark spoke to him about Frank's proposed arrangement. Late one night, her fears became reality. Jerry practically broke down the door as he rushed headlong into the apartment in a complete rage. The room shook when he slammed the door behind him. Estelle heard whimpering from Jake's room and realized he was awake. Jerry paced around the living room, cursing under his breath. Estelle stood frozen with fear, "Jerry, what's wrong?"

"What's wrong? You sneaking, conniving whore! What do you think is wrong?" He crossed the room and shoved her against the wall. "I've put all of my time and money into you. I have plans for us—for our future. I've taken Mark's crap to get us where we need to be. Those old guys paid a small fortune to be with you. Do you think you could have done that on your own? No! I made you! Do you hear me? I made you what you are!"

Estelle exploded with a fury that overshadowed her fear. "You made me what I am all right—a whore and a drug addict! I'm supposed to thank you for that? You bast—"

Before she could stop him, Jerry had both hands around her neck, his fingers pressing against her throat. "That dago thinks he's going to take you away from me? I'll kill you first!"

Estelle tried to scream, but she couldn't get any air. For a moment, she couldn't move a muscle. Suddenly, she realized if she didn't fight, she was going to die. With every ounce of strength she could muster, she braced her back against the wall and brought her knee up hard, right between Jerry's legs. Jerry groaned and fell to the ground. The moment he hit the floor, the apartment door burst opened, and Frank and two of his bodyguards rushed in. Jerry struggled to his feet, but Frank landed a punch right on Jerry's chin and knocked him out.

"Are you okay?" Frank wrapped his arms around Estelle.

"Yes; I think so." Estelle trembled as she rubbed her throat where Jerry's hands had been just moments before.

"Bella, we need to gather what you need and get your son. Tony, Bartola, and Madelena are on the way up."

"My God, what happened?" Estelle was in shock.

"I asked Mark to speak to Jerry about our arrangement, but I asked him to wait until you were with me on the weekend. Mark didn't wait, and Jerry completely lost control. Mark did one thing right: he called me. He knew you might be in danger. Please hurry; we only need to pack what you don't want to leave behind. You will have everything you need."

Just then, Tony, Bartola, and Madelena rushed into the apartment carrying several boxes. Estelle was stunned and stood motionless in the middle of the room. "Miss Estelle, please hurry. What should we pack?" Madelena was the first to speak.

"I—I don't know."

"Miss Estelle, you must hurry!" Madelena's tone was sharp.

"Okay. Um … Tony and Bartola, in my room, on the shelf in my closet, there is a hatbox, a small metal box with important papers, and my books. My jewelry box is on the dresser. Please grab my clothes and shoes from the closet and dresser. Madelena, come with me to Jake's room. He needs his toys and clothes." Estelle's heart raced, and she broke out in a sweat.

Estelle and Madelena found Jake shaking and hiding under his covers. Frank had followed them into Jake's room. "Please, let me take him. It's okay, Jake, no one will hurt you or your mommy anymore." Estelle was touched as Frank gently carried her son from the room.

After packing Jake's things, Estelle grabbed her handbag, ran to the bathroom, and locked the door. She took Jerry's stash; she was going to need it. She had no idea what she would do when it ran out; but she grabbed the stash, stuck it in her handbag, and went back to the living room.

In a matter of minutes, everything that was important to her was packed and ready to go.

"Okay—I guess that's it. We're ready." Estelle glanced around the apartment, both relieved and a little sad. "Where's Jerry?"

"Tony is going to convince to him to let this go. Mark will encourage him to handle his dealings in another city. Please don't worry; he won't bother us anymore."

"I should tell Rose we're leaving. She won't know what's happened."

"It's best that you don't tell anyone about this right now; you can contact her later. We need to go now." The boxes had already been taken to the limo, so Estelle hurried out the door and followed Frank to the car. Jake was still frightened and hadn't spoken a word.

Rose was unable to sleep and walked to her window just as the small group made their way to the limo. "Oh my God! Where are they going?" She saw a strange man carrying Jake with Estelle following behind. Two men and a woman put several boxes in the back of a limo, and Jerry was nowhere to be seen. Rose tried to open the window to call to Estelle, but she couldn't make it budge.

Throwing on her robe, she ran barefoot into the hallway and down the stairs. Just as she ran outside, the limo pulled out into the street. "Estelle! Jake!" The driver sped down the street, and she knew no one in the car could hear her. "Oh God, what is happening? Where are they taking them?"

Rose ran back in the building to Estelle's apartment. The door was slightly ajar, so she opened it slowly. "Jerry? Are you here?" There was no answer. When she walked in, the bedroom doors were open. Rushing into Jake's room first, she noticed open dresser drawers and Jake's unmade bed. His clothes were gone from the dresser and closet. All of Estelle's belongings were missing too, but Jerry's things were still there. "What on earth?"

She hurried back to her apartment. It was late, but she *had* to call Pauline. As she waited for Pauline to answer, tears spilled down her cheeks. "Hello?"

"Pauline, I'm sorry to call you this late, but something is wrong!"

"Rose, honey, please slow down. Tell me what happened." Rose told Pauline everything she had seen that night.

"Rose, was Estelle being forced or did it appear that she went willingly?"

Rose hesitated. "It didn't look like she was being forced."

"I have a feeling these people may be helping Estelle get away from Jerry. We both know something has been going on, and Jerry is right in the middle of it. There is nothing to tell the police; it appears that she simply moved out tonight. Hopefully she will contact one of us and let us know that she and Jake are okay. Call me immediately if you hear anything, and I will do the same. Now try to get some sleep."

After they prayed together and said their goodbyes, Rose went to bed; but she lay awake for what seemed like hours. Her heart ached for this young woman and little boy who had come to mean so much to her. Finally, Rose succumbed to sleep.

Estelle was quiet when they pulled up in front of Frank's home—now her and Jake's home. She wondered what she would tell Jake in the morning.

As they stepped out of the limo, the realization of what could have happened hit Estelle full force. "Frank, he tried to kill me. If you hadn't …" She fell against Frank and wept.

He held her and kissed her face. "He can't hurt you now, Bella. I will never let him come near you again."

Jake had fallen asleep, and Tony gently took him from the car and carried him into the house. Frank and Estelle followed. "Boss, which room is Jake's?"

"He should be with his mother tonight, so take him to Estelle's room. We will be right behind you." He turned to Estelle, "Come, Bella, you need to rest. We can talk tomorrow, but rest assured you are safe now."

When Estelle and Jake were settled in, Frank kissed her and said goodnight. She didn't think she could sleep, but she had underestimated how exhausting the night had been. She fell into a sound sleep within minutes.

19

Mommy, where are we? Mommy, wake up!" Sunlight streamed into the room. Estelle slowly opened her eyes and squinted at the light. Jake was standing at the window. "Are we in a castle? There's a park outside with lots of trees and flowers. And there's a swimming pool!" He wasn't at all frightened. Jake was on an adventure.

"Jake, honey, come here." Jake ran over and jumped on the edge of the bed. Estelle sat up and leaned against big, fluffy pillows. She didn't quite know where to begin. "Jake, I know you heard Jerry and I arguing last night. The man who helped us is a friend of mine, and he owns this house; he's going to let us stay here. We're not going back to our apartment, and we're not going back to Jerry."

"We don't have to see Jerry anymore? I don't like Jerry. He's mean and he lies. He takes you away all the time, and he makes you cry. I'm glad he's gone!"

"Jake, did Jerry ever hurt you?"

"Yes. He yelled at me sometimes when you were sleeping late. One time, I asked him about that lady and little girl. He grabbed my arm, and he told me to never tell anyone about her, or he would hit me."

"Oh my God, why didn't you tell me?"

"He said if I told he would hurt you. I couldn't tell anyone."

"Sweetheart, come here. Let me hold you." Jake climbed on the bed and Estelle hugged him tight. "I love you so much. I'm sorry. I will never let anyone hurt you again. We're safe here."

"Will we still see Miss Rose and talk to Miss Pauline?"

Before she could answer, there was a knock at the door. "Come in."

"Good morning! Is anyone here hungry?" Frank smiled at Jake as he walked in.

"I'm starving! Do you have a park outside? Is this a castle?" Jake jumped off the bed and ran to the window again.

"Well, we have gardens. We can go exploring later."

"Yes, yes! I want to go exploring!" Jake was beside himself with excitement.

Estelle cleared her throat. "Jake, this is my friend Frank. Frank, this is my son Jake."

"It's nice to meet you, Jake." Frank extended his hand.

Jake ran across the room and shook Frank's hand. "It's nice to meet you, sir."

Frank smiled down at the boy. "Cook is preparing breakfast. Can you two be ready in 30 minutes or so?"

"Yes, I'll run a bath for Jake, and then one for myself. It won't take us long."

"I'll send Madelena to help. Just come to the terrace when you're ready."

Madelena knocked at the door minutes after Frank left. "Let me draw a bath for your little one. After the two of you go down for breakfast, I can put your things away. Jake will have the room right next to yours. There is an adjoining door that you can leave open at night if you wish." Madelena headed for the bathroom.

"Madelena, thank you so much."

"You are welcome, Miss Estelle."

Jake and Estelle were ready in record time. She managed to give herself a shot of heroin while she was in the bathroom with the door locked. How would she tell Frank about her problem? It would have to be soon; there was only enough for a few days, and she had no idea how to slip away to get more. A chill ran through her. Would Frank put them out on the street when he knew the whole truth about her?

Frank was waiting on the terrace when Jake and Estelle came outside. It was a beautiful, sunny morning, and the temperature was perfect. A few butterflies and honey bees flitted around the garden.

Jake dug into his breakfast with gusto. There were fresh-baked pastries, cheese, fruit, sliced tomatoes, and a steaming plate of fluffy eggs. Cook placed a glass of cold milk in front of Jake. Estelle was suddenly famished and enjoyed a cup of hot coffee with her breakfast. She loved the strong, flavorful coffee that Frank's cook brewed, laced with heavy cream and a little sugar.

"Are we really going to *live* here? Can we go exploring when I'm done?" Jake looked at Frank, talking as fast as he could. In spite of all he'd been through, he was a pretty typical six-year-old.

"Jake, slow down; and please don't talk with food in your mouth," Estelle said.

Frank laughed. "Yes, young man, we will go exploring as soon as you finish your breakfast. And later, you can see your room. It's right next door to your mother's room."

Estelle smiled at the man she had fallen head over heels in love with. She was thrilled. Frank had a way with children, and Jake liked him.

After breakfast, the trio walked through the gardens. Jake explored and found great hiding places. He climbed on the low rock wall that bordered the garden. "This is fun. I love it here!" He swung on a low branch of a tree.

"We've lived in an apartment since Jake was small, and it was a treat to go to the park. This is wonderful, Frank. He's happier than I've seen him in a long time."

Jake ran and played while Frank and Estelle sat on a stone bench in the garden.

"Frank, I feel so stupid for letting Jerry use me. I convinced myself that I somehow sheltered Jake, but I didn't. I was desperate and just let it all happen."

"It's over, and I will never allow anyone to hurt either of you again. Let's enjoy this beautiful day. I will send Tony to purchase some things for Jake to play on when he's outside, and we need to discuss schools before the summer is over. There are some private schools that would benefit Jake. If you agree, I can make all of the arrangements."

"This is a dream. Oh please, don't let me wake up." As they sat on the bench, she suddenly remembered her secret that just might end this perfect dream. "Frank, I need to talk to you tonight," she hesitated and swallowed the lump in her throat, "about something that I haven't told you."

"You look so serious, Bella. We can talk tonight, but we must be careful to protect Jake. I won't come to your room anymore. You can come to mine. Madelena can stay in Jake's room when you are with me, in case he wakes up and finds you gone." He took her hand. "Now let's enjoy our day."

The afternoon was warm, and they went for a swim. Jake played in the pool until he was completely worn out.

After dinner, Estelle ran a warm bath for Jake. As he climbed in bed, he yawned and rubbed his eyes. He was completely exhausted from playing and exploring all day long. She tucked her little man in and went to her room. She needed to think about how she would tell Frank her repulsive secret.

Estelle closed her eyes as she soaked in a warm bubble bath. She was terrified at the possible outcome of the evening. Finally, she climbed out of the tub and wrapped herself in a thick, fluffy towel. The steamy bathroom filled with the fragrance of lotion and sensual, earthy perfume. Taking special care with her appearance, she brushed her hair to a silky sheen. She glanced in the mirror, took a deep breath, and opened her door. The silk negligee brushed lightly against her skin; her satin slippers were silent on the thick plush rug as she made her way down the hallway.

Estelle was overwhelmed with a feeling of worthlessness as she neared Frank's room. It was a lifetime ago, but she'd never forgotten that dreadful night she and her parents walked silently to Lucille Shannon's apartment. Her heart pounded now as it did then. Perspiration formed on her forehead and upper lip, and her hands were clammy. It was hard to breathe. She dreaded the moment Frank would look at her, knowing that she was a drug addict. Finally she stood in front of his door. Wanting to turn and run back to her room, she took a deep breath and knocked softly. Frank smiled as he opened the door.

Estelle caught her breath as he pulled her to him and kissed her. "Bella, you are a vision, too beautiful to be real."

Determined not to be distracted, she stepped away from him. "I hope you still feel that way, when I've told you everything. Please sit down before I lose my courage." She started with the first time she met Mark and her suspicion that Jerry had drugged her. Then she told him about the terrible nightmares—pills to sleep and others to wake up. Finally, she told him about the heroin Jerry gave her to calm her when she had to entertain Mark and Jerry's clients.

"Frank, remember my first weekend with you? Jerry didn't count on my being away the entire weekend. I didn't have any heroin with me." The words tumbled out as she became more and more frantic. "That's why I was so sick. I was so stupid I didn't even know why I was sick until after I went home. He gave me more, and I started feeling better. I started asking questions, so he finally told me the truth. Frank, I have enough for a day or so, and that's it. When I run out, I'm going to get sick—really sick. I don't know what to do, but I can't hide this from you anymore. I don't *want* to do heroin anymore." Frank's face contorted, but he remained silent. Estelle knew it was over. "We will leave if you want. I can have our things packed and ready in the morning."

"*Bastardo!* Lying, filthy scum!" Frank's fury shook the room.

"Frank, I'm so sorry. I'll go." Estelle's voice was a ragged whisper. She turned to leave.

"No, Bella, not you." He lowered his voice and pulled her to him. "How could he do this to you, knowing you trusted him? He knew you had a child to care for. I'm sorry I frightened you; please stay here. I'll be right back." He kissed her on the forehead before he left the room.

Estelle collapsed on the bed and sobbed with relief.

Minutes later, Frank returned. "I called my physician, and he will be here tomorrow evening. This will not be easy, but I want to help you stop taking this poison. We will tell Jake that you are ill. Madelena will care for him, and you will stay in the other wing of the house. You are going to be very ill, but I will not let you go through this alone. I must go to Sicily at the end of the month, so we need to start your recovery in the morning."

"Oh God, Frank, I'm so frightened. I thought I would die before."

"I won't lie to you; it will be worse this time. You may beg for it, but no one will give it to you. I know you want to do this for yourself and your son."

Early the next morning, Estelle slipped back to her room. Within moments, Frank knocked on her door. "We will have breakfast together this morning. Then you can tell Jake that you aren't feeling well. Later, the doctor will arrive. I will explain to Jake that because we don't want him to get sick, you'll be staying in the other wing of the house until you recover. Bella, where is the heroin that you brought with you?"

She hesitated, then walked to the chest and got her handbag. She stood still for a moment. "Frank, I'm terrified." When she turned with a small bag in her hand, there was perspiration on her upper lip and her hand trembled. "Here; this is it."

"Do you have any pills?"

"Yes," she sighed, "let me get them." She dug in her handbag and handed him a small bottle.

"So, this is all you have? If there is anything else, you must give it to me now."

"There is nothing else." She hung her head like a child.

"Before the week is over, you may hate me; but, this is for your own good and for Jake. Do you believe me?"

"Yes, I know it's what's best for Jake and for me. But, it doesn't make it any easier. I'm so scared."

At breakfast, Estelle already felt queasy and could barely eat. She told Jake she wasn't feeling well and went to lie down. Madelena watched over Jake as he played in the yard.

That evening, Frank moved Estelle to a room in the other wing of the house. He explained to Jake that she was ill and they didn't want him to get sick too. He said it might take several days for her to get better, but she would be fine. Jake was concerned about his mother, but Madelena promised that she would stay with him while his mother recovered.

When the doctor arrived, Estelle was sick; but she had no idea how bad it would get. By the end of the second day, she felt as if she had been beaten; every part of her body hurt. She was drenched in sweat, and her body chilled and shook. Her legs were weak, her stomach churned, and she was unable to get out of bed. There was no other choice than to use a pail and a bedpan. What did it matter? She felt like she was dying.

When she wasn't screaming and cursing Jerry, she cried and begged Frank to give her what her body so violently craved.

Frank only left her side for short periods of time to eat, bathe, and take care of business. The doctor was with her when Frank was out, so she was never alone.

When Madelena came in to help the doctor change the bed linens and Estelle's gown, Frank spent time with Jake. Each day, he assured the boy that his mother was getting better.

Days later, the withdrawal symptoms started to subside. Estelle was weak and pale, and she had lost weight. She felt as though she had been to hell and back, and she could hardly believe that she had lived through it.

"Bella, can you try to eat some soup? Maybe just some broth? It will help you begin to get your strength back."

"Actually, I feel just a little bit hungry. Yes, I'd like to try some broth." She took tiny sips of the tasty broth and finished only a small portion. But, it stayed down.

"That's better. I've tried to give you sips, but it always came back up."

"Frank, I thought I would die, but I think it's almost over." She managed to smile.

"You are still weak, but the worst is over."

"When can I go back to my room and see Jake?"

"The doctor said you should be able to go back to your room by tomorrow. But, you must remember you are still very weak, and you will need to be careful for a while."

"I promise I'll rest and do whatever I need to do to get my strength back." She hesitated for just a moment. "You rarely left my side."

"I told you I would stay with you."

It had been so ugly, and now Estelle was embarrassed and humiliated. Her face was pale, but she blushed as she remembered the pail and bedpan. Frank hugged her and kissed her forehead.

By the time Frank was ready to leave for Sicily, Estelle had regained her appetite and much of her strength. She was sleeping well at night, and she spent her days outside in the fresh air and sunshine with Jake and Frank.

The night before Frank left, he and Estelle sat on the balcony just off his room. "Bella, I will leave early in the morning. Now that you live here, I need to talk to you about something very important."

"Frank, you sound so serious. Is anything wrong?" Estelle felt a knot forming in the pit of her stomach.

"No, nothing is wrong. My business dealings are very private, and there are people who are who are envious of my success. That is why I take such care with our safety. You see my bodyguards every day. The grounds are completely fenced, and the gate is locked at all times. There are other security measures that you don't see, but they are important."

"I feel very safe here."

"And you are safe. I will be away for two weeks, and I don't anticipate any problems. Bella, do you realize that successful people, powerful people, have enemies?"

"Well, yes, I suppose I do." She tried to maintain some composure, but fear gripped her.

"Come with me. I want to show you something." She followed him to the large armoire that was near his bed. "This is something that you are not to speak about to anyone. Not my bodyguards, not Madelena, not Jake—no one. Do you understand?"

Her voice was barely a whisper. "Yes, Frank, I understand."

Frank opened the armoire door and shoved all of the clothes to one side. He stepped inside the armoire and motioned for Estelle to follow. She stepped in as Frank moved to the back. He pulled the door closed behind them and locked it. It was pitch dark inside. Suddenly, a door creaked slightly, there was a click, and soft light trickled in from the back of the armoire. Frank opened the second door completely and stepped out of the back of the armoire, pulling Estelle with him and bolting the door after them. She couldn't speak as she looked around. They were in a hallway of sorts. She could see other light bulbs hanging from the ceiling with chains to switch them on. About 20 feet in front of them, a stairway led down into darkness.

"My God, Frank! What on earth is this?"

"Down those stairs is a tunnel. It leads to the house that is just across from the back of our grounds."

"Oh sweet Mother of God." He held her to stop her shaking.

"You must listen to me. See the adjoining passageway over there?"

"Yes." She could barely breathe.

"That one comes from the armoire in your room which opens exactly the same way as mine. The chain for the light is just to the right of the door. There are lights placed all the way through the passageway, and you will need to turn them on. You will find a lantern hanging to the right of the door. Take the lantern with you in case there are problems with the lights."

"Frank, why is this necessary?" Estelle's face was pale with fear.

"It may never be necessary, sweet Bella. As I told you, my uncle's and my businesses are very successful. We must protect those who depend on us as well as our assets. If there is ever a problem with anyone, even if they say they are the police, and I'm not here to protect you, you and Jake are to come here. Make your way to the other house. It's a decoy; no one lives there. I have staff come and go to give the appearance of the house being occupied. You will come out of the tunnel into the basement, and there are stairs that lead outside. Do *not* go upstairs into the house. There is a garage behind the house, and there are shrubs and bushes to provide cover for you to get to there. There is a car in the garage. When it is safe, take the car and get far away as fast as you can. Tell no one you lived here, and trust no one. Now listen carefully: there is a small chest here on the shelf." Estelle looked over and saw a shelf built into the wall of the tunnel. "The key to the chest is hidden in this compartment. If it is ever necessary to escape, open the chest. You will find cash and a set of car keys inside."

Frank took the key from a hidden compartment in the wall and opened the chest. Estelle gasped. She had never seen so much money! "There is enough here for you to get what you need until I can find you." Estelle's face was as white as a sheet. There was also a gun in the chest. "Estelle, are you listening to me?" He never called her Estelle.

"Yes, Frank. Why is there a gun?" she whispered.

"Have you ever handled a gun before?"

"No, why on earth would I?"

"We must protect ourselves. Some people would kill for what we have, so these precautions are necessary. Now, there is also a bag with clothes for you and Jake, and another for me. If I am home, we will meet here. If I am not here, take all of the money, the gun, and the clothes. Do you understand?"

"Yes, I understand. But Frank, why would I need a gun? I don't even know how to use one!"

"You will have your first lesson tomorrow. I will ask Tony to work with you while I'm gone."

"Frank, I'm afraid. I don't want to use a gun."

"Bella, you may never have to use a gun. But, you should know how to protect yourself and Jake if necessary. Promise that you will do as I ask?"

A sob escaped as she answered, "I promise, Frank. I will do as you ask." It all came rushing back—the things Jerry said during the limo ride when she met Frank. He said she didn't want to know anything about these people, not even their names. She hesitated and then whispered the question that she had been afraid to ask, "Frank, are you in the Mafia?"

He silenced her with a kiss. "Shhh, never say such things. Come, let me show you how the door and locks work, and then we can relax."

20

stelle felt so safe when she was with Frank and was completely lost without him. He had been gone a week before her nerves finally started to settle. Everything at the house was calm, and no one burst through the door in the middle of the night. Just as Frank promised, Tony gave Estelle lessons on handling and firing a gun that was identical to the one she had seen in the chest. Each afternoon, Tony and Estelle left the house and drove out to the country. Tony taught her to load and unload the gun, and he set up a target for practice.

The first time Estelle fired the gun; she closed her eyes, squealed, and dropped it. Tony calmly explained how dangerous it was to drop the firearm. He was such a patient teacher. Each day, Estelle became more comfortable with the weapon and was surprised at how quickly she learned.

By the time Frank returned, she had become quite an accomplished shot. Not only could she clean the weapon, but she could load, unload, and fire it with accuracy.

"Well it seems that you are a very bright student! Tony tells me that you are quite the marksman." Frank pulled her into his arms and kissed the top of her head.

Estelle was thrilled that Frank was proud of her. She rested her head on his chest. "I was so frightened at first. Did he tell you that I dropped the gun the first time I fired it?"

"He said there were some challenges, but you learned quickly. Do you feel comfortable now? Do you think you could use the weapon if necessary?"

"I hope I never have to, but I believe I could."

"Good. Now I have missed you terribly my sweet Bella. Is Jake in bed?"

"Yes. Oh Frank, I missed you too. I hate it when you're gone." He pulled her closer and kissed her tenderly.

As the days and weeks passed, Estelle felt more like a newlywed than a mistress. When the weather was nice, breakfast and lunch were served on the terrace. Sometimes, the little family had dinner in the huge dining room. Other evenings, Jake ate in the kitchen while Frank and Estelle shared late romantic suppers on the balcony off of Frank's room.

Frank made arrangements for Jake to attend one of the best parochial schools in Kansas City. He enrolled Jake as his widowed sister's son who had come to live with him. Estelle was thrilled for Jake to attend such an excellent school, especially since Jerry had refused to pay for private school. Tony took him to and from school in the limo. Jake was well-behaved and excelled in his studies.

The estate was absolutely beautiful in the fall. Temperatures cooled, and the trees began to change. Green leaves turned brilliant orange, yellow, and red. The garden boasted marigolds and colorful mums.

Frank spent part of each day tending to business, but his spare time belonged to Estelle and Jake. He treated Estelle like his queen and Jake like his own son. Estelle often wondered how a man so kind and gentle could be a crook. He was nothing like Jerry and Mark; it just didn't make sense. It didn't matter because she loved him; and whether he said it or not, she knew he loved her and Jake too.

One afternoon, Estelle finished talking with Cook about dinner and walked toward Jake's room. She stopped short, stood quiet as a mouse, and smiled at the touching scene. Frank and Jake were both on the floor, racing cars across the room. It appeared Frank hesitated at the beginning of each race, so Jake's car always won. Suddenly, Frank got on all fours and Jake jumped up and rode on his back. "Come on horsey, let's go fast!"

"If I go too fast, you'll fall off. Plus, this horsey is getting tired." Frank lay flat on his stomach; Jake jumped up and ran around the room, pretending to ride a horse. Frank sat up and laughed at the little guy's antics. Then he and Jake noticed Estelle standing in the doorway.

"Let's wrestle—all of us!" Jake tumbled to the floor and grabbed Frank's arm. "Come on, Mom, play with us!"

Estelle hesitated for a moment; Frank never ceased to amaze her. He was the father Jake never had, and he was her knight in shining armor.

She had already lost her heart to him, but with each passing day, she loved him more.

"Mom, come on!" Jake begged. In a flash, she piled on top of Frank. The three wrestled, tickled, and laughed until they were completely out of breath.

As winter approached, Frank told Estelle they would celebrate Christmas together, but it would be two weeks early. Then he would leave for Sicily and be gone for a month. She tried not to show her disappointment.

Deciding not to let the circumstances ruin the holidays, Estelle and Jake helped the staff decorate the house. There were huge, elaborately decorated Christmas trees in five different rooms. Garland and red bows adorned the elegant staircase and doorways. More garland, candles, and small nativity scenes sat on each fireplace mantle. A gorgeous wreath hung on the front door, and a much larger matching wreath hung on the front gate. There was a life-size nativity scene arranged in the yard in front of the house and big red bows about every ten feet on the fence all around the property. Each night, the staff lit candles in the windows of each room. Estelle loved the fragrance of pine that permeated the house.

When Cook started the holiday baking, mouth-watering aromas filled every room. Estelle and Jake made frequent trips to the kitchen, taste-testing Cook's delicious creations.

On the eve of their Christmas celebration, Frank was very secretive. Right before dinner, he headed for the front door, and practically bumped into Estelle and Jake as they walked into the foyer. "I have a surprise for the two of you, so please stay out of the foyer, and don't go near the front door."

"Jake, I'll meet you in the kitchen in a few minutes." As Jake left, Estelle smiled her sweetest smile. "Frank, you can tell me, can't you?"

"No, Bella, you'll have to wait until morning also." He chuckled as she pouted and went back to the kitchen. The next morning, Frank led Estelle and Jake to the front door and told them to close their eyes. Smiling from ear to ear, Frank opened the door and said, "Open your eyes!"

Estelle and Jake peeked out and saw three pairs of old shoes just outside the door, filled with small bags of goodies. Tears streamed down Estelle's face. "Bella, I didn't mean to upset you." Frank pulled her close.

"Oh Frank, you didn't upset me. I just miss Momma and Poppa."

"I remembered your stories about your family's traditions, and I hoped this would make you happy." Frank explained.

"This was so thoughtful, and it does make me happy."

Jake grabbed his shoes filled with treats and ran into the sitting room. He didn't even notice the mountain of gifts at first. An electric train chugged on a track all around the tree. A replica of a train station and a little town sat inside the tracks. "Oh boy, look at that train!" Jake skidded across the polished hardwood floor stopping just short of the train tracks.

"There are more cars and another engine too. We will get it all set up in your room later today." Frank was pleased that Jake loved the train set. "Now, let's open some of these packages."

Frank passed out the gifts. Jake jumped up and tore into his presents—a cowboy hat, chaps, spurs, holsters, and toy guns. Toy cars and trucks filled several other boxes. Jake thanked Frank for the new clothes, even though he was much more excited about the toys.

"Bella, open this first." He handed her a small, rectangular package. Her hands trembled as she opened the black velvet box inside the wrapping paper. "Oh Frank, it's beautiful!" A full carat diamond dangled from a delicate gold chain.

"Here, let me help you with the clasp."

Estelle opened box after box. There were diamond earrings, pearls, cashmere sweaters, skirts, dresses, shoes, handbags, and delicate lingerie. "Frank, this is too much."

"No, sweet Bella, you deserve beautiful things."

Estelle walked to the tree and pulled out a small box. She had saved money that Frank had given her for spending. Frank smiled and slowly opened the box. Inside were matching diamond cuff links and a diamond tie tack. Tony had taken her to the jewelers when Frank was gone. "Bella, these are perfect. Thank you." He pulled her close and kissed her.

Cook served brunch in the sitting room. Throughout the day, they snacked on Cook's Christmas goodies and eggnog. That evening, they feasted on a sumptuous Christmas dinner with all the trimmings.

The next day, Frank spent practically every minute with Estelle and Jake. They were even surprised by the first winter snow. Huge snowflakes made quick work of covering the ground, and the snow was perfect for making a snowman.

Frank knocked on Estelle's door. When she answered, he bounded into the room like a small child. "Get your coats! Oh and boots and gloves. We're going to make a snowman!"

Jake ran from his room and leaped into Frank's arms. "A snowman? Come on, Mom! Hurry!"

There was a flurry of activity as the three donned warm clothing and headed out the front door. Frank carried a few pieces of chocolate and a carrot, provided by Cook. Jake found an extra scarf, and Estelle carried an old hat. Frank taught Jake to make a big snowball and then roll it until it was the right size for the bottom of the snowman. Finally, a grand snowman stood right in the middle of the yard next to the circle drive. "He needs arms." Jake crossed his arms and stared at the snowman.

Frank hurried to a bush and broke off a couple of branches; he stuck a branch on both sides of the snowman. "There we go; now he has arms."

While Frank and Jake admired their creation, Estelle quietly made several snowballs. Wham! The first one hit Frank in the shoulder.

He whirled around and laughed. "This is war!" Soon all three had a cache of snowballs, and the battle was on. After an all-out snowball war, a tired, cold, wet, but happy little group finally went inside for some of Cook's hot chocolate.

Early that evening, Frank and Estelle retired to his room. Madalena entertained Jake and later got him off to bed.

His next trip would be the longest since they had been together. Estelle dreaded not being able to see him for an entire month. As she lay with her head on his chest, just before dawn, tears trickled down her cheeks.

"Bella, why are you crying? I will be back."

"I know, but you've never been gone this long. I'll miss you so much. I feel lost when you're not here."

"In the spring, we will make some changes in the house. I will ask Madalena to make arrangements for you to look at fabric samples while I'm gone. Think about your room and Jake's. When I return, we will look at furnishings, and you can change whatever you wish."

"That will keep me busy for a while, but it won't make me miss you any less." She sniffed and wiped her eyes.

"I will miss you too."

She hesitated and then said what had been in her heart for months. "Frank, I love you."

"I love you too, my sweet Bella." Estelle thought her heart would burst when she heard those words.

"Frank?"

"Yes?"

"I, ah …" It had been about a week since Estelle realized she was pregnant. She wanted to tell Frank, but not right before a month-long trip. She would wait until he returned. "I'll miss you more than ever."

Estelle was on edge and emotional; Frank would be gone for an entire month, and she regretted not telling him about the baby.

The reality of Frank being gone for such a long time conjured up her old fear of abandonment and betrayal; she simply wanted him home again. One minute, she missed him horribly; and the next, she was angry with him for leaving her. In her heart she trusted him, but old memories planted seeds of doubt. At night, alone in her room, she cried and counted the days until his return. During the day, she half-heartedly looked at fabric swatches, pretending to be excited about re-decorating. All she really wanted was for Frank to hold her again.

As Frank's return drew nearer, Estelle was nervous, yet excited, about sharing her news with him. She knew he couldn't marry her, but she also knew he loved her. He would take care of her, Jake, and the baby. With him, it would be okay—finally everything would be okay. She would feel better once she broke the news to him.

It was the day before Frank's return. Estelle fidgeted and paced all day and couldn't sleep that night. Morning came much too soon. She awoke to sunlight streaming in through the drapes and Jake bounding on her bed. "Momma, Frank is coming home today! He can play cowboys and Indians with me!"

"Yes, he should be here this afternoon. He may be a little tired from traveling, so we need to let him rest first. Okay?"

"Sure." Jake's smile faded.

"Come on, let's get ready for breakfast. Later, we can play with your train; and before you know it, he'll be here."

The day crawled by. Estelle tried not to worry when Frank wasn't home by dinner. She saw the priest come to the door and then leave immediately. At one point, Tony left and was gone for about an hour. Estelle stopped him in the hallway. "Tony, why isn't Frank home? He should have been here hours ago."

Tony's face was expressionless. "Miss Estelle, his flight was delayed. I will keep you informed. He may not be here until tomorrow, but please don't worry." Tony quickly turned to leave.

"But Tony, he didn't call me. I haven't heard the phone ring at all. What is going on?"

"I'm sorry. I just know that he's been delayed." With that, Tony walked away.

Estelle was frantic. If he was just running late, why hadn't Frank called her? Her thoughts turned to the passageway and everything Frank told her to do if something went wrong. She went upstairs to get Jake headed for his bath. Every nerve in her body was on edge. Something was wrong; she just knew it. After Jake was in bed, she pulled out her mother's hatbox and the small box with important papers and put them next to her bed. As she lay in bed, she trembled with fear knowing something was horribly wrong. Finally, she drifted off to sleep.

Estelle was suddenly awakened by voices at the bottom of the stairs. It was Tony and another man's voice she didn't recognize, and they sounded agitated. She tiptoed across the room and put her ear to the door. She heard Tony say something about a hit. Estelle gasped and covered her mouth. A hit? Were they talking about Frank? She couldn't stand it another minute. Throwing on her robe, she opened the door and practically ran down the stairs. Tony and the priest, whom she had seen at the house before, were in the entryway. Both men jumped as Estelle rushed down the stairs.

"Tony, what is going on?" Tears streamed down her face.

"Miss Estelle, we didn't mean to wake you. You should go back upstairs."

"And just go back to bed? Tony, I heard part of what you were saying. Frank should have been home yesterday afternoon. Tell me what is going on!" Her voice grew louder with each word.

Tony looked down at the floor. "There is a lot that I don't know right now, but we may be leaving before morning. There has been an incident, and we aren't completely sure what has happened." The phone rang and Tony answered it. He listened for a couple minutes. His face turned almost white. Then he hung up.

"Father, we need to finish getting the house in order and leave here tonight. The staff has already taken care of most of the downstairs and their quarters."

The color drained from the priest's face and he whispered, "I will take care of things on my end." He turned to Estelle. "Miss Estelle, please get your son and do as Frank instructed you. May God be with you." With that, he turned and walked out the front door.

Estelle shook her head and hoped to wake from the nightmare. It was as though time stopped. She felt disconnected from her body, and she couldn't speak or move from where she stood. She could barely breathe. "Miss Estelle, there are things the staff and I must finish, and you must hurry. Please get Jake and go."

"Tony, is Frank dead?" Her voice was shrill, and she could hardly believe she had spoken the words.

"We don't know yet, but there has been an attempt on his life. We have our orders and must get moving. There are things that must be done. Please go, now!" Estelle saw tears in Tony's eyes before he turned away.

"Tony, how will you find me? I must know if Frank is alive."

Tony stopped but didn't turn to face her. "If Frank is alive, he will find you. If he is not, I will find you. You don't want anyone to know of any connection to him. He would want safety for you and Jake above all else." Tony walked away.

Suddenly the need to survive took over. Estelle turned and ran back up the stairs to her room, locking the door after her. Frank had told her there would be clothes in the tunnel. Tearing the sheet from her bed, she gathered as many of Jake's toys as she thought she could carry and put them in a pillowcase. They wouldn't be coming back here, of that she was sure. The train set and most of the toys were too big and too heavy to carry. She packed Jake's cowboy outfit and a few cars and trucks. She opened the armoire door and then the door that led to the passageway. Quickly she turned on the light and put everything she had gathered in the passageway. She almost forgot her mother's hatbox and the small box of papers. There was nothing left in either room that could identify them.

The door to Jake's room squeaked slightly as she opened it. Quickly, she ran over and locked the door that lead to the hallway. She heard voices downstairs, Tony, Madalena, Bartola, and Cook. No one tried to be quiet at this point. The women sobbed as they went about the house.

"Jake, sweetheart, wake up!" Jake stirred and turned over. "Jake, you have to wake up. We need to leave right now!" Her voice was louder. Jake sat up startled and confused. "Come on. We have to go!" She dragged him out of bed, through the door, and to the armoire.

"Momma, what are we doing? I'm tired," Jake whined.

"I said come on. Please Jake, we must hurry." She pulled him inside the armoire and locked the door behind them. The realization that their lives were at stake hit Estelle full force.

As they stepped out into the passageway, Jake's eyes looked huge. "Momma, where are we?"

"Here, put these on; it's cold outside." There were boots, coats, and a few changes of warm clothes waiting for them; Frank missed nothing. "We are going to play a game, okay? We will walk through the tunnel to a car and take a ride. Let's see who can be the quietest." Jake seemed a little unsure, but he said okay and got dressed. "Now, you carry these and I'll get the rest. Follow me."

A short distance down the passageway, Estelle stopped outside the door from Frank's room. She took the key from the hidden compartment and opened the chest. Putting the car keys in her pocket, she moved in front of the chest to block Jake's view and dumped the money, gun, and bullets into a bag. She grabbed the lantern and bag of Frank's clothes. "Okay, let's go."

"I don't want to play this game. I'm scared."

"Jake, you have to do what I say; pick up the bag and follow me, now!" Jake didn't say another word; he simply did as Estelle said. They moved through the passageway, silently turning on lights as they went, and carefully descended the stairs. Estelle was numb. She knew only one thing: she had to protect Jake and the baby she carried. Those thoughts were all that kept her moving.

Finally, they made it to the basement door of the other house. Estelle heard noises from the floors above and whispered to her son, "Jake, put that down for now. Sit here and be very quiet. We're going to stay right here for a little while." As she joined her son on the floor, she realized how anxious she was. Every muscle in her body had been tense since the moment she ran back upstairs to get Jake. She felt completely drained and was grateful for the chance to rest.

After what seemed like an eternity, there were no more footsteps or voices from upstairs. She carefully turned the doorknob and tried to open the door. "Jake, help me. The door is stuck." Jake and Estelle pushed against the door with all their strength, and it finally opened just enough for them to squeeze through with their belongings.

Once inside the basement, Estelle saw shelves on the other side of the door, which made it quite heavy. A full moon helped them to see well enough to make their way across the basement. Silently, she opened the door that led outside. "Jake, stay here for just a minute; I want to look around."

"Momma, please don't leave me. I'm scared," Jake whimpered.

"I'm not leaving you. I'm just going to step outside and look around. Stay here and be very quiet." Jake was petrified and didn't move a muscle or make a sound. A moment later, Estelle was back. "Okay, let's get our bags. We are going to the garage in back. There is a car there for us. Stay close to me and don't make a sound."

They carefully made their way along the hedge across the back-yard. Estelle was gripped with terror when the garage door creaked as she opened it. "Oh God, please help us." The car was there just as Frank had promised. She piled most of their things in the trunk and put a few things in the backseat. "Jake, get down in the backseat for now." Jake obeyed without a word. He was too frightened to disobey.

The car started on the first try, and the gas tank was full. Estelle had learned to drive when she was with Jerry, but she hadn't driven often. She backed out slowly and made her way down the long drive toward the street. As she pulled onto the street, she heard sirens. Looking behind her at the mansion that had been her home, she saw flashing red lights. Several police cars turned down the long lane that led to Frank's house. The blood drained from her face. "Oh sweet Mother of God, we barely made it. I hope the others got out!" she whispered to herself.

Back at the house, Tony and the rest of the staff quickly finished each task to wipe away every trace of the residents of the mansion. Unknown to Estelle, there were other passageways in the house. Each member of the loyal staff made it out before the police broke down the massive front door, only to find what appeared to be a beautifully decorated, yet unoccupied mansion.

Officers swarmed through every room and finally reported back to their superior. "There's no one here, sir. There's no clothing or food in the refrigerator. There are a few canned goods in the cabinets, but that's it. No bills, no papers of any kind in the desks. Either this was a bum tip, or they only use the house during the summer. Look, the furniture is all covered and none of the beds look slept in. They may have been here, but they're gone now."

But the walls had secrets. In the passageways, behind the walls, and under the house, there were piles of clothing, toys, and food. While the officers searched the house, the staff buried everything they couldn't take with them in the passageways. The holes that were dug months ago were covered with flooring for quick, easy access. Tony had gathered every document in the house and all of Frank's personal effects and packed them with his own things. The safe was empty, and the money was dispersed as Frank had instructed. Bartola, Madalena, Cook, and the rest of the staff had emptied the kitchen, the dressers, and all of the closets. They even took all of Jake's toys. The furniture was covered with sheets. Literally everything that made the house look lived in, or could in any way identify the residents, had been removed. Each staff member had instructions and took a different passageway. Each had preplanned destinations and cars stashed at various locations. Every detail for escape had been planned far in advance. Tony was the only one who knew all of the plans.

"Damn it! We don't even know what this character looks like! This is the first time we've even been close, and now we have nothing. He's like a ghost." Agent Barnes ran his hand through his hair. "There was supposed to be a woman and a kid living here! People don't just vanish into thin air. I really thought we had something this time. Okay, let's pull out, but we're coming back tomorrow. If we have to tear this place down piece by piece, we are going to find something. Lock it up! Set a guard at every door until we come back." The agent's voice was full of anger and disappointment. Tracing the home's owner would also lead the authorities to a dead end.

Having been chauffeured while she lived with Frank, Estelle didn't know the upscale neighborhood very well; but she remembered the route they took to get there. With no idea where to go or what to do, she drove toward her old neighborhood. There was a small motel not far from where she had lived. It was risky, but she didn't know where else to go. She just hoped they wouldn't ask too many questions. Her hands shook less, and her breathing finally slowed to somewhat normal. Jake hadn't made a sound since he climbed in the car. "Jake, are you awake?" she whispered.

"I'm awake," his voice sounded small and frightened.

"You can sit up now if you want. We are going to stay at a motel tonight. We should be there in just a few minutes." There was no reply. "Jake, did you hear me sweetheart?"

"Yes, I'm trying to be quiet," he whispered.

"It's okay, sweetheart. You can talk now."

"Okay."

A few minutes later, Estelle pulled in front of the small motel. "Sit here for just a minute while I check in."

She got out of the car and rang the night bell. She had to ring it a few more times before a sleepy, elderly man answered. He wasn't very friendly, but he took her information and cash. "We're not too busy right now, Miss Prebi…"

"Prebilica." Afraid to use Shannon, she had checked in as Estelle Prebilica.

"Okay, here's the key. You can have the room down on the end. It's quiet."

"Thank you."

"Checkout is at noon."

"We may be staying a few days. I'll let you know in the morning. Thank you."

The old man turned off the light and headed back to bed. Estelle climbed in the driver's seat and pulled the car in front of the unit the man had pointed out. She and Jake unloaded their things from the car and carried everything to their room. "Well, it isn't fancy, but it's clean. Let's get to bed." She hugged her frightened son. Jake still had his pajamas on under his clothes. Estelle pulled down the spread and blankets, and they climbed into bed. Within minutes, she could hear Jake's deep, even breathing. At least he was sleeping.

Estelle's body was weary, but her mind raced. Reality hit her full force: Frank was probably dead. The only man who had ever truly loved her was gone. He had treated her like a princess, and he treated Jake like his own son. It was hard to believe that Mark and Jerry arranged their first meeting—a prostitute and a client. She'd settled into the role of a beloved wife, not a mistress. Regret tore at her heart; she hadn't told Frank she carried his child. Tears spilled down her cheeks and soaked her pillow. She stifled her sobs and tried not to disturb Jake. Finally, mercifully, she slept.

21

Estelle snuggled close, warm and safe in Frank's arms. His lips trailed across her forehead; he whispered, "I love you, sweet Bella." Then his voice faded. Suddenly, terror gripped her, and her mind screamed. She thrashed about, grasping at nothing but air. Reality slammed her into the present. Estelle moaned and squeezed her eyes shut tight.

"Momma, are you awake?"

Sunlight poured in through the thin, worn drapes. She covered her head for a moment, wanting sleep to take her once again. "Momma, I'm hungry. Are you awake?"

"Yes, I'm awake." Her voice was monotone. She slowly uncovered her head and sat up. A single tear slid down her cheek as she looked around the shabby room and sighed. "Okay, Jake, we need to bathe, find a diner, and get some breakfast."

"Momma, what happened last night? Why are we here?"

"Let's get cleaned up, and we'll talk later." She didn't know how to tell Jake that Frank might be dead. She had to think. Telling him too much too soon wasn't a good idea.

When she and Jake were both ready to go, Estelle went to the office and paid the old man for a full week. She needed time to devise a plan. Maybe Frank was alive, and he would find them. If not, she had to have a plan for her, Jake, and the baby. They had to survive. Frank had gone to great lengths to make sure that she and Jake were taken care of.

Estelle and Jake had breakfast at a diner on the other side of town. Thankfully, she didn't know anyone there. The food was tasty, and the service was friendly. They ate in silence.

When they were back in their room, Estelle struggled to explain the events of the last several hours in a way that wouldn't make things worse than they already were. "I know last night was frightening." She stopped, not sure what to say next. Jake stared at his mom, waiting for her to continue. "You know how Frank takes care of us? Well, Frank has a lot of money, and there are people who are very jealous of him. There were some problems, and he can't come home right now. He has to stay in Sicily for a while."

"Is he okay?" Jake whispered.

"Yes." It was hard to look into Jake's eyes and lie. "But he just can't come home right now. He left money for us, so we'll be okay until he comes back and finds us." She choked back a sob. Her heart ached, and her stomach was in knots. She wanted to believe her own words. "It may be a while, so I'll have to get a job and find a place for us to live."

"Where will I go to school? I love my school!"

"We can't afford private school right now. You will have to go to school where we live."

"Momma, he'll find us someday, right?"

"It may be a while, Jake. It won't happen tomorrow. Now, why don't you get some of your toys out of the bag and play for a bit, okay?"

Jake knelt down by the pillowcase his mother pointed to and began to look for toys. He pulled everything out, searching frantically. When the pillowcase was empty, he started to cry.

"Jake, what's wrong?" Estelle knelt down beside him.

"My train! It's not here! You left it, didn't you?"

"It was too heavy for us to carry. I *had* to leave it."

"It was my favorite thing in the whole world, and you left it! I hate you!" He flung himself on the bed and sobbed uncontrollably.

For the first time, Estelle realized she had forgotten all of her jewelry, including her mother's wedding ring and pearls. All the lovely clothes Frank gave her for Christmas were left behind. She sighed as she walked over and sat down on the edge of the bed. "Jake, I'm sorry; we couldn't bring all of our things. I left things of mine too. We just couldn't carry everything. The most important thing was for us to get out of the house before the bad people came."

He sat up, eyes wide, "Bad people were coming to the house?"

"Yes, at some point. I don't know when. Frank told me that if anything happened, and he couldn't come home, we were to get out of the house as fast as possible so we would be safe."

"I'm scared. I'm scared he won't come back. I want him to be my dad. I want him to come back!"

Estelle hit her breaking point. She collapsed on the bed and burst into tears. "I want him to come back too. Oh, God, please, please bring him back to us!"

It didn't seem possible that a week had passed since Estelle and Jake had made their escape. Deciding to stay clear of the neighborhood where they had lived with Jerry, Estelle found a small, furnished, two-bedroom apartment not far from Lucille's old house. Thankfully, she had nothing to fear from Lucille and Johnny Moran anymore. The location was convenient, and Jake's school was within walking distance. The apartment was small, but the rent was low.

Fear of her past compelled her to stick with her maiden name, but she enrolled Jake in school under his real name. He had enough to deal with already.

With some of the money Frank left her, Estelle bought an inexpensive gold wedding band to avoid uncomfortable questions when her pregnancy started to show. After paying her first month's rent, there was still a tidy sum of money left; but it wouldn't last forever. She and Jake both needed clothes. They had escaped with only the few outfits that had been hidden in the passageway. She would have to start from scratch for baby clothes.

By the next week, Estelle had a job at a restaurant not far from the apartment. She didn't know anyone who worked there, and it was larger and nicer than the small diners where she'd worked before. The owner, Mr. Davidson, agreed to let her work during Jake's school hours, so there was no need for a babysitter.

She told her boss she had lost her husband in a tragic accident. Mr. Davidson and the other waitresses hovered over her, making sure she ate right and didn't work too hard. She felt guilty lying to them; but if she told them the truth, she'd lose her job.

Sooner or later, Estelle would have to tell Jake she was going to have a baby. Each time she thought about how to tell him, she decided to wait a little longer. But Jake was more observant than his mother realized.

One evening, as they cleared the dinner dishes, he asked his mother why her tummy was getting fat. Estelle dropped the plate she was scraping and it shattered on the kitchen floor. "Damn!"

"Momma, are you okay?"

"Oh, Jake, I need to talk to you. Let me clean up this glass first." She swept the floor and dumped pieces of glass in the trash. "Come to the living room with me." Jake followed his mother and sat down on the sofa.

She fidgeted as she struggled to break the news to him, "I, ah, I'm going to have a baby." She was so nervous that she felt faint.

Jake leapt off the sofa. "A baby? I'm going to have a brother or sister!" He jumped all around the room.

"You're happy?" Estelle breathed a sigh of relief.

"Yes, I'm happy! I've always wanted a brother or sister!"

"You have?"

"Yes!"

Estelle took a deep breath. "Well, that went better than I expected!"

"When, Momma? When will the baby be here?"

"Sometime in late July. That's what the doctor says."

Jake's smile faded. "Momma, do you think Frank will find us before the baby gets here?"

Estelle dissolved in tears. "I don't know, Jake. I just don't know."

Over time, Estelle and Jake adjusted to their new routine. She worked Monday through Friday while Jake was in school. But, the school year was coming to a close, and Jake would need a sitter. She knew it was too dangerous to try to contact Rose; Jerry or Mark Lawrence might find her. She decided to ask around at the restaurant.

As long as Estelle pushed thoughts of Frank to the back of her mind, her days were tolerable. She was actually thankful for her uneventful, mundane existence. But, one morning, about two months before the baby was due, everything changed.

The breakfast rush was over, and she prepared for the next round of customers. She hummed a popular tune as she wiped down tables and arranged clean silverware and napkins. Suddenly, chills ran down her spine; someone was staring at her. She turned slightly, just enough to glance behind her. Silverware hit the floor as she grabbed the table. Mark Lawrence was standing about fifteen feet away, smiling at her. He sauntered over. "We would like to be seated in this section, please."

Wave after wave of nausea washed over her. Terror gripped her as she fought for control. Everything went black, and she slid to the floor. "Estelle!" Her boss and another waitress ran over. "Get a wet cloth. Hurry! She's fainted!"

Was it a dream—a nightmare? She tried to escape from Mark as she moved through a long, dark tunnel. Mr. Davidson called to her in the distance. Gradually, the sound of his voice was closer and closer. Her eyes fluttered opened. "Estelle, just lie here for a moment. You fainted. Peggy, get a chair." Mr. Davidson turned to Mark Lawrence and his associates. "Gentlemen, please give us a moment, and we can seat you."

"Please, don't be concerned with us. Is the young lady hurt?" Mark sounded so sincere. "Oh my, Miss Estelle, is that you?"

Mr. Davidson turned to Mark, "You know her?"

"I met her through a mutual friend some time ago. I would be happy to give her a ride home. She probably shouldn't try to finish her shift."

Estelle tried to protest, but Mark insisted. Mr. Davidson agreed that she should go home and rest. "We can cover things here. Now get some rest before your son gets out of school."

Peggy went in the back room and got Estelle's bag. "You take care."

"I'll be fine. I'll see you tomorrow," Estelle tried to smile.

"Gentlemen, please start without me. I'll be back as soon as possible." Mark took Estelle by the arm and led her out of the restaurant to his car. "Where do you live?" She was terrified but finally gave him the address. Mark ordered the driver to take them to her apartment.

Estelle didn't say a word during the ride. When they pulled to a stop in front of her apartment building, she said thank you without so much as a glance at Mark. "Driver, wait here. I'll be right back."

"Mark, this really isn't necessary. I can get upstairs by myself." He climbed out of the car and followed her into the building and to her apartment. She stopped at the door. "I'm not at all comfortable with you coming in. Thank you for bringing me home."

"Open the door," he ordered. Once inside, Mark taunted her. "Well now, aren't you going to ask me about Jerry? Weren't you madly in love with him before Frank came along?"

"You know as well as I do that Jerry used me. He tried to kill me, for God's sake."

"Yes, and he got you addicted to narcotics, didn't he?"

"What?" she turned and feigned shock. "How dare you!"

"Oh, for Christ's sake, Estelle; I'm not stupid. That idiot told me himself and tried to put the blame on you. I know what he did. He did the same thing to his wife. The difference was she had no class to begin with."

The color drained from Estelle's face. She felt faint again and sat down on the couch. "You mean Bobbi?"

"You knew about her? Well, he had to take care of the whore when she threatened me. What a messy situation."

"Oh my God, he killed her?"

"You know, Estelle, for someone so smart, you act quite stupid. She became a liability." Mark's smile was sickening. "I would venture to say that you think you and Jerry met by happenstance." Her eyes betrayed her surprise. Mark laughed. "Oh my God, you *do* think that. Well, my sweet, your precious husband worked for us. But, of course, he was a sniveling little snitch."

"Ricky worked for you?" Her voice was barely a whisper.

"Yes. He was an asset for a while, but he got careless and greedy. When he agreed to talk to that detective, we had to cut our losses."

"What did you do to Ricky?" Her voice quivered.

"Please, Estelle, I'm tiring of this innocent act. What do you think happened? He was a damned snitch." Estelle sucked in her breath. Mark smiled.

Ricky was dead—murdered. She covered her face with her hands and wept for the boy she fell in love with so long ago, the boy who never had a chance in life, and for Jake who would never know his daddy. She was overwhelmed with regret, remembering her hesitance to introduce Ricky to her parents or friends. She'd wanted him, but she'd been ashamed of him; he wasn't good enough.

"Oh for God's sake, save the theatrics. It's a bit boring. Again, don't you want to know where your beloved Jerry is?" His smile frightened her.

She hesitated, her voice barely a whisper, "I'm afraid to ask."

"Well, I'll tell you anyway. It seems information leaked out about his contact with a Mafioso. Poor fool; he really didn't know a thing, but his reputation preceded him. No one wanted someone like Jerry running his mouth over his lost meal ticket, so he was eliminated."

She flinched, reminded that she had been Jerry's meal ticket. "Who—who eliminated him?" she whispered.

"Frank didn't actually eliminate anyone; he just gave the orders. But either way, Jerry is no longer a concern." He waved his hand as though he were swishing a fly.

For a moment, she felt brave. "Why would you tell me these things? I could send you to prison."

"Oh, I don't think so. Who knows? Maybe *you* wanted Jerry's wife out of the picture. Who would they believe? Think about how it looks—poor Bobbi, the old worn out wife replaced by the beautiful young mistress. And, you might have to answer some pretty tough questions about dear, long-lost Frank. It looks like Frank cleaned you up and got you pregnant. And yes, I heard. The old boy may be dead. It's quite the mystery you know. What a shame. He paid so well, which is the only reason I made sure he rescued you from Jerry. You were quite the investment."

"Is money all that's important to you?"

"What else is there, my dear?"

She cautiously eyed the heartless maniac who stood in front of her. Then she asked the question she had avoided. "You said that I thought Jerry and I met by happenstance. What did you mean?"

"You know, he hid all of that from me for a while. I knew he had a young married kid working for him who turned out to be a snitch. Of course, I didn't always bother myself with details about the little people. I didn't know who Ricky was for some time and didn't make the con-nection to you. He didn't actually tell me the truth about who you were until Frank wanted to play house with you. Then he spilled the beans. That Jerry! He did have an eye for beauty. He told me the first time he saw you with Ricky, you were just a kid and pregnant—but so beautiful. After he took care of your husband, he couldn't let go. So, he kept tabs on you, until the time was right." He laughed again. "Huh, he even told me he was completely livid when you moved in with that cow, Lucille."

"He knew Lucille?" Her voice was barely audible and chills ran down her spine.

"Yes, and he hated her."

Estelle shivered as realization crept in; Lucille and Johnny Moran's deaths were most likely not the result of a botched robbery. She never really knew Jerry. He had watched her, waited like an animal, and then moved in for the kill. Murdering another human being was beyond her comprehension. Her stomach churned; she had been in love with a monster.

With a wave of his hand, Mark continued, "Now, enough of all this. Frank is obviously not coming back. Jerry cost me a lot of money with his little problem, and now he's gone. I plan to recoup some of my losses, so you're going to work for me again."

Estelle stood up and faced Mark. "No, I'm not going to work for you. I can make it working as a waitress. It may not be all the money in the world, but I can sleep at night."

"You, my dear, are not in a position to tell me what you are or are not going to do. I'm sure the authorities would be interested in a young woman who has been involved with so many men of such questionable character," his voice dripped with sarcasm. "Wait tables for now, but when that baby gets here and you get your figure back, you are going to work for me."

He pointed his finger at her. "Keep one thing in mind: I know what you are. Frank may have let you pretend to be something you weren't, but you're just a whore. Don't *ever* forget it. Now I'm going to rejoin my associates. Don't try anything stupid; I will be watching your every move." Without another word, Mark turned and went out the door.

Estelle sat back down on the couch and stared into space for half an hour or so. Finally, tears streamed down her face. Covering her face with her hands, she cried until her stomach lurched and she ran to the bathroom to throw up. Her thoughts raced. There had to be a way to get away from Mark Lawrence.

It was almost time to get Jake from school, and she didn't want him to see her with red, swollen eyes. She dabbed at her eyes with a cool, wet cloth.

That night, after Jake was sleeping, Estelle schemed and planned her escape from Mark. She almost never drove the car, but the paperwork in the glove box showed the car was registered in her name. She would sell the car, keep working as long as possible, and add to what remained of the money Frank left for her. Then when the baby was born, she would take her children and get as far as possible from Kansas City.

The next morning, Estelle walked Jake to school and headed for work. She was embarrassed about her fainting spell from the day before. Hopefully, she could convince Mr. Davidson that she was fine and could continue working. As soon as she walked in to the restaurant, Peggy met her at the door. "The boss wants to talk to you. He's in the back office."

"Oh, Peggy, I'm fine. I don't want anyone fussing over me." Estelle headed for the back office and knocked on the door.

"Come in." Mr. Davidson sat at his desk going over paperwork. His glasses were perched on the tip of his nose. A cloud of cigar smoke hung over his head. "Here, I'll put this out. Estelle, please sit down." He took off his glasses and put the cigar out in the ashtray.

Estelle seated herself in a chair on the other side of the desk. She felt uneasy when she noticed the frown on Mr. Davidson's face. He cleared his throat a couple of times and then looked her directly in the eyes. "Estelle, I don't exactly know how to ask you this, so I'm just going to say it. How do you know Mark Lawrence?"

Completely taken by surprise, she gasped. Perspiration popped out on her forehead, and her hands were clammy. As her face turned bright red, she looked at the floor. "That's all the answer I need," Mr. Davidson stood up.

"No, please, you don't understand. I met him through a friend. I barely know him. That's why I was so uncomfortable letting him take me home." She was frantic.

"I'm sorry; I would really like to believe you since you've been such a good employee. You see, I know a lot of influential people, Estelle—good and bad. Mark Lawrence puts on a good front, and he fraternizes with important people. But, I'm afraid I'm aware of the services he provides for those people." He stopped for a moment and sighed.

"I run a legitimate business, and Mark doesn't usually entertain his associates in my restaurant. I would venture to say that someone recognized you and told him you worked here. Estelle, people bring their children to my restaurant. Families come here after church on Sundays. I'm not a saint, but I run a good, clean business. I can't have men coming in and recognizing a woman they, ah, you know what I mean, that they've paid to be with. I just can't risk my business."

"Mr. Davidson, please. I need this job."

"I'm sorry, Estelle. You can pick up your check on Friday." He looked genuinely sorry as he wiped his brow. "Please, just go on home now."

She was completely numb as she stood up and walked out of his office, through the restaurant, and out the front door. Peggy tried to get her attention, but Estelle kept walking. There were no tears. She felt nothing as she made her way back to the apartment. Once inside, she lay on her bed and cried. Finally, she calmed herself enough to think.

It no longer mattered if Mark knew where she worked. He had found her. Tomorrow, she would go to the other two diners where she'd worked before. They knew her and would surely give her a job. She absolutely *had* to work until the baby was born.

She intended to find a job the very next day. Maybe she would run into Vivian. They had been friends, and that might help. She couldn't hide her pregnancy, but she was healthy and would convince them that she could work.

22

Estelle decided to drive to the diner where she'd met Johnny Moran. It was Thursday, and she thought Vivian might be there.

Taking a deep breath, she entered the diner. Vivian was behind the counter, smiling and talking to customers. When she looked up and saw Estelle, Vivian's big grin faded. Quickly, she glanced around and asked the other waitress to cover for her. She practically ran to Estelle. "Come outside, sugar, and we can talk."

"Why can't we talk in here?"

"Trust me; come on." Vivian took Estelle by the arm and led her outside and down the sidewalk. "Look at you; you're going to have a baby! Jerry?"

"Well, ah, no. Jerry left. I met the most wonderful man, but . . . ," her voice trailed off.

"But what honey?"

"He's dead. He was in an accident." Tears rolled down her cheeks. It was no act.

Vivian pulled Estelle close and hugged her. "Oh, sugar. I'm so sorry. Are you okay? Are you working? How is little Jake?"

"I'm okay, and Jake's in school. You know, he's seven now. I was working, but that's why I'm here. I need a job, and I thought since I used to work here and everyone knows me . . ."

"Estelle, I brought you outside because I didn't want the boss to see you and cause a scene. After you left, there was a lot of talk—rumors."

"Talk about what?"

"About you and Jerry; some folks say he didn't sell diamonds at all. Estelle, there was talk that you were some kind of high-priced call girl, a prostitute."

"Oh my God," Estelle felt dizzy and leaned back against the building.

"Here, let's sit down." Vivian led Estelle over to a low brick wall, and they sat down. "Honey, I hate to tell you this, but no one around here is going to hire you. Rumors were flying. I don't know who started them, but evidently, there are people who think they just might be true."

Estelle stood up. "Vivian, I'm sorry I have to go. It was good to see you. I hope I didn't get you in trouble." She walked to the car.

"Estelle, wait. Do you need help?" Vivian followed her.

"No, I'm fine. You better get back inside, before the boss comes looking for you." Estelle climbed in the car and shut the door. Her tires squealed as she pulled out in front of an oncoming car and barely avoided an accident.

It seemed like a lifetime ago, but she'd felt this way before—lost and alone, not good enough, trapped. She had made the decision then to move in with Lucille, a life-changing decision.

This time, she had nowhere to go—no choices. Frank wanted to take care of her, but his plan was short-sighted. He obviously thought if a problem arose, it would be taken care of quickly, but that wasn't the case. The money he left wouldn't last much longer. By the time she paid expenses for the next few months and the hospital bill, she would be almost penniless. She could only bide her time and look for a way of escape.

Tears slid down her cheeks. Frank must be dead. If he were alive, he would have found them by now. The baby kicked, and Estelle stifled a sob. She missed him so much.

Surprisingly, she missed Pauline and Rose too. She didn't even know if Pauline had ever come back from California. She squinted and rubbed her temples. What was it Pauline said about what she might go through, something about forgiveness and bitterness? Estelle wondered if Pauline could have been right or if it really mattered anymore. If she contacted Pauline or Rose and they tried to interfere with Mark's plans, they could get her, or even themselves, killed.

The last few days had completely exhausted Estelle, both physically and emotionally. This was worse than the haunting nightmares; this was real. A chill shot through her body. Jerry had been a cold-blooded killer, but Mark was worse. He had found her and was successfully blackmailing her. She had no doubt he would watch her every move.

She still didn't want to believe what Mark had said. It was too difficult to think of Frank as a criminal, and it was impossible to imagine that he had ordered Jerry's murder. She couldn't think anymore; it was overwhelming. She closed her eyes and slept.

True to his word, Mark watched Estelle's every move. When she walked to the market or to Jake's school, Mark's driver followed her. At night, when Estelle peeked out her window, she saw the dark car parked on the corner where the driver had a clear view of both the front and back of the apartment building—it was Mark's driver.

The weeks flew by, and the baby was due at any time; nothing could change that. Thankfully, Vivian agreed to take a few days off, when the baby was born, to care for Jake.

The day came much too soon. Estelle's labor was every bit as difficult as it had been with Jake. Finally, it was over, and a nurse placed the baby girl in her arms. Estelle searched her daughter's face and nuzzled her soft, black hair. "Your name is Genevieve Francesca. Your daddy would like that," Estelle sighed. "For now, it's Prebilica."

Ginny opened her eyes; they were so very dark, like Frank's eyes. Ginny whimpered. Estelle shrugged her gown from one shoulder and pulled the baby close. "What a smart little girl." As Ginny suckled at her mother's breast, Estelle's tears dropped onto the baby's tiny face. "Your daddy would have loved you so much, his little princess."

Estelle had just finished feeding and burping Ginny when her nurse walked in. "Mrs. Prebilica, I'll leave these papers with you. You'll need to complete them for the baby's birth certificate. When your husband gets here, please ask him to sign them also. I'll take her back to the nursery if you think she's finished eating, and you should try to get some rest."

"Yes, she's finished. Thank you." The nurse left the papers and a pen on the nightstand and gently took the baby from her mother. Estelle grabbed the forms and glanced over them. "I might as well do this now." She picked up the pen. After "mother's maiden name," she wrote Estelle Anna Prebilica. When she saw "father's name," she hesitated and then remembered Tony's warning; she wrote "unknown." After completing all of the information, she placed the papers and pen on the table.

She was tired and missed her son. Three days away from Jake seemed like an eternity, but she and Ginny would be home soon. Turning on her side, she closed her eyes and slept.

In the wee hours of the morning, the nurse woke Estelle and brought Ginny in for her feeding. Estelle turned to her and said, "I finished the forms. You can take them now."

"Your husband needs to sign them also. I haven't seen anyone come in."

"Please take the forms."

The nurse frowned, picked up the forms, and started to leave the room. Suddenly, she stopped, "Ah, is this correct?"

"Is what correct?" Estelle asked.

"You're not married, and you don't know who the baby's father is?" Her icy tone was almost unrecognizable as the nurse turned to face Estelle.

"That's correct."

"Well, are you keeping this poor child or should we call an agency?"

Estelle sat straight up and faced the nurse. "She's my daughter, and she's going home with me. Is there anything else?"

"You aren't even ashamed, are you?" she sputtered. "I'll be back when the baby is finished. What is this world coming to?" She stomped out, muttering as she went.

Estelle sighed as the baby nursed. "Well, Ginny, I guess we'll have to get used to that."

From that point, until Estelle and Ginny were released from the hospital, the night nurse barely spoke to Estelle. The day nurse, however, was kind and attentive.

On the final day in the hospital, a matronly woman walked into Estelle's room and refused to look at her. "*Miss* Prebilica, I am from the business office. How do you plan to take care of your bill? I understand you don't have a husband to handle these matters."

Estelle took a deep breath and tried to smile. "I can handle it quite well myself. I'll pay with cash, Miss …"

"*Mrs.* Franklin."

"Mrs. Franklin, as I said, I'll pay with cash. If you will direct me, I can stop by the business office before I leave the hospital."

"Make sure you do. We don't have time to track you down trying to get this bill paid."

Estelle slammed her fist into the mattress and leaned toward the lady. "I told you I would stop by the office before I left. I have every intention of paying my bill. Now please get out of my room."

The woman practically ran from the room.

Later that morning, Estelle signed the documents necessary for the hospital to release her and the baby. She packed their things, and a nurse wheeled her and Ginny to the business office. Mrs. Franklin refused to come out of her office, so a gentleman handled Estelle's payment.

Vivian and Jake were waiting downstairs in the lobby. When she saw Jake, Estelle smiled and forgot the humiliation and anger of the last few days. Jake bounded across the lobby to his mother and threw his arms around her neck. "Be careful, sugar; we have to be gentle with your little sister," Estelle said.

"Momma, I missed you so much. Let me see her!" Estelle pulled back the receiving blanket.

"Hi, I'm your big brother! I love you." He touched Ginny's soft little face and looked at his mother with a huge smile. "She's beautiful."

"Estelle, she's a little doll." Estelle had almost forgotten about Vivian.

"Thank you, Vivian. Now, Jake, let's go home. I've missed you so much!"

Six weeks went by far too quickly. Estelle hadn't heard from Mark and dreaded the day when she would. Time was running out; summer was over, and Jake was back in school.

It was a pleasant fall day, and Estelle had just put the baby down for a nap. A loud knock at the door startled her and woke Ginny. She picked Ginny up and hurried to the door. As she looked out the peephole, she saw Mark's driver standing in the hall. Her heart pounded, and waves of nausea threatened to overwhelm her. The driver banged on the door again. Estelle opened the door slowly. The man handed her a note and left without saying a word.

Seemingly suspended in time, Estelle stood motionless in the doorway. She felt disconnected from her own body. Footsteps echoed as the driver descended the stairway. The ticking clock in the living room was loud and exaggerated, almost taunting her. Finally, she closed the door, walked over to the rocking chair, and placed the note, unopened, on the lamp table.

"Rock-a-bye baby, on the treetop ..." Her voice broke, and tears streamed down her face. Finally, she put Ginny back in her crib. Estelle's hands shook as she opened Mark's note. Holding her breath, she read her orders.

> Estelle, there will be a gathering on Saturday evening. My driver will pick you up at 7:00 p.m. sharp. Find someone to care for your brood for the night, as I will not tolerate any problems or interruptions. Buy something that makes the most of that gorgeous body, and wear your hair down. The gentlemen certainly have missed you. We'll discuss compensation when you arrive.
>
> Mark

A lump formed in her throat, and her stomach churned again. Then the dam broke; deep, wrenching sobs shook her body. When she was with Frank, she had believed this part of her life was over. She had believed she was safe from her past, and she would never be with another man.

What on earth would she do with Jake and Ginny? She had procrastinated and failed to make any arrangements for the children. Vivian worked on Saturday nights, and Estelle kept to herself and didn't know a soul in the apartment building. She didn't have many options. When Jake was out of school that afternoon, they would go to her old apartment building and see if Rose still lived there. She had no other choice.

Estelle fidgeted and paced as the day crawled by. Ginny sensed her mother's mood and was unusually fussy, but the baby quieted as she lay in her pram on the way to Jake's school. Estelle couldn't relax; her muscles ached, and her nerves were shot. Jake was oblivious to his mother's mood as they walked from his school. He skipped and talked continuously as they walked. "Where are we going? We passed our apartment."

"Well, we're taking a little walk. I thought we could see if Rose still lives in our old building."

Jake jumped up and down. "I can't wait! Do you think Miss Pauline is back? Miss Rose will be so happy to see us!"

"I hope so," Estelle whispered.

"What?"

"Nothing." Moments later, they arrived at their old apartment building. Estelle left the pram in front and carried Ginny up the stairs as Jake tried to run ahead. "Jake, stay with me. We don't even know if she lives here anymore."

Estelle stood in front of the door, hoping it was still Rose's apartment. "Momma, are you going to knock?"

Estelle didn't answer, but she knocked lightly on the door. She knocked louder the second time and heard the lock click. The door opened, and Rose stood in the doorway. Rose blinked her eyes and then cried as she pulled Jake close. "Where have you been? I've prayed day and night for you to be safe and come back!"

"We lived in a castle, and I had a train. But Frank hasn't found us yet, so we live in an apartment again," Jake chattered and bounded through the door.

"Estelle, I've been so worried, I saw you the night you—who is this?" She reached out to hug Estelle and, for the first time, noticed the bundle in her arms.

"This is Ginny." Estelle pulled back the blanket; Ginny was awake.

"Look at this sweet girl; oh, she's beautiful!" Tears spilled down Rose's cheeks, and she stifled a sob.

"Rose, are you okay?" Estelle touched her shoulder.

Rose took a hankie from her apron pocket and dabbed at her eyes. "I'm fine, Estelle. It's just that she reminds me of my little girl."

"I didn't know you had a daughter. Pauline said you didn't have any family."

"I had a beautiful baby girl, but I lost her and my parents." Rose turned away for just a moment.

"Rose, I'm so sorry. Do you want us to go? I don't want to upset you."

"Oh no, I thought I had lost both of you! Please don't go; please, sit down. Jake, would you like some milk and cookies?"

"Yes, please. Is Miss Pauline here?"

"No, Jake, she is still in California. Hopefully, she will come home soon though. Her sister has improved."

Rose led him to the kitchen, set out fresh-baked cookies, and poured a glass of milk. She wasn't quite sure what to say when she walked back in the living room. "I don't know what to ask. I'm just happy you're here."

"Rose, I don't where to begin. Jerry wasn't the man I thought he was, and I had to get away from him. I had a friend." She blushed as she looked down at her feet. "Well, he helped us and gave us a place to stay. We were quite happy there." Tears formed in her eyes. Rose waited for Estelle to continue. "I loved him. He loved us and took care of us. But something happened. There was an incident, and he was killed."

"Oh Estelle, I'm so sorry." She went to Estelle and put her arms around her. "And little Ginny—this man was her father?"

Estelle couldn't hold back the tears. "Yes, he died before she was born." Rose held the young woman as she cried. "Rose, Jake doesn't know he's dead. I kept thinking that it was a mistake, and he would find us. But he's not coming back, and I don't know how to tell Jake."

Just then, Jake walked back in the room, "Momma, what's wrong?"

"I'm fine, Jake. I'm just happy to see Miss Rose too."

"Jake, you know I kept your toys; they're in the spare bedroom. Why don't you go play for a bit while your mother and I talk?" Jake bounded to the bedroom and started going through toys.

"Rose, I need help. Frank left money for us, but it won't last forever. I tried to get a job, but there were some rumors about Jerry. I couldn't get a job at any of the diners." She took a deep breath and continued, "I do have a job offer, but it would be nights, mainly on the weekends. I need someone to take care of Jake and Ginny, and you're the only person I trust." She couldn't look at Rose.

"Estelle, you know I'll be happy to take care of the children. But what kind of job is this?"

Estelle panicked. Her mouth went dry, "Well, I'll be a kind of a hostess. A gentleman I know hosts dinner parties for his business associates. He is older and not married, so he needs a hostess." She took another breath and looked away.

"Estelle, that doesn't sound quite right. What will you do as a hostess?"

"I'll be his dinner partner. Please, I don't have a choice. If you aren't comfortable with this, I'll find someone in my building to watch the kids."

"No, please don't do that. I will be happy to watch the children," Rose hesitated. "When I was a young woman, I felt that I had few choices. I had no family—no one. I was angry, bitter, and afraid. I made some very unwise decisions—decisions I regret. I thought I would never get out of my circumstances; but someone prayed for me, and God made a way of escape, so to speak."

Estelle bristled, "Well, I'm glad that He helped you, but so far, He's done nothing but take the people I love away from me." She quickly changed the subject. "I have a dinner party Saturday evening. If it's okay, I'll bring the kids over around 5:00 and then go home to get ready. Can you keep them for the night? I don't want to drag them out late at night." Estelle looked away.

"Yes, that will be fine." Rose knew reasoning with Estelle was not going to work. She would call Pauline later.

23

Saturday evening, Estelle soaked in a hot bubble bath. A tear slid down her cheek as she thought about Jake and Ginny. Finally, she climbed out of the tub and wrapped herself in a towel. A slinky black evening gown lay on her bed. It cost far more than she could afford, but Mark would be furious if she wore anything cheap. By the time she bought the gown, jewelry, shoes, a bag, makeup, and expensive perfume, she had spent too much of her precious savings.

At 7:00 p.m. sharp, Mark's driver pulled up in front of Estelle's building. She took one more look in the mirror, grabbed her evening bag, and hurried down the stairs. The driver opened the door for her, but he didn't speak. When the car pulled up in front of the hotel, Estelle felt bile rising in her throat. Her heart pounded, and her hands were clammy. She took a deep breath and climbed out of the car. The driver spoke to her for the first time, "Mr. Lawrence said to tell you same floor, same suite."

"Thank you."

The hotel doorman smiled and held the door for her. She looked straight ahead as she crossed the lobby and rang for the elevator.

"What floor please?" the elevator attendant asked.

"The penthouse." She refused to look at the attendant. He smirked and closed the elevator door.

"Have a nice evening, Miss." Estelle didn't answer; she swallowed the lump in her throat as she stepped off the elevator and headed for the penthouse door. The door opened before she knocked, and Mark took a moment to give her the once over. Pleased with what he saw, he motioned for her to enter.

"You follow orders well, my dear. I like that. And, you look rather bewitching tonight. I'm quite tempted to keep you for myself, but poor Mr. Anderson has been awaiting your return." He leaned closer. "He's practically foaming at the mouth. Hopefully, he can demonstrate some control and not drag you off the minute he lays eyes on you." He laughed, quite pleased with himself. "Smile, Estelle, it is part of what's required of you."

She pasted on the best smile she could conjure up and walked into the sumptuous suite. All of the conversations stopped. The men did little to conceal their lust and devoured her with their eyes, each one jealous that Mr. Anderson would have her tonight. She almost laughed as she thought about telling Rose it was a dinner party.

Mr. Anderson indeed rushed to her side. "Estelle, my dear, I have missed you terribly. Mark told me you were back in town and would be here tonight. I immediately flew back from Paris." Mr. Anderson kissed her hand and gave her a knowing look. Then he whispered. "Let me introduce you to the others. We'll make conversation for 15 minutes or so and then retire to the larger bedroom. I've missed you my dear; I've dreamed of you night after night."

Estelle fought for control. She felt lightheaded, and her stomach churned. "Please excuse me; I'll be right back." Heading for the powder room, tears stung her eyes. She locked the door behind her and took slow deep breaths.

There was a knock on the powder room door. "Estelle, is anything wrong?" It was Mark. "You have a guest to entertain. He's waiting."

It was the first time since she had gone through the hell of withdrawals that she wished she had some heroin. She wanted to feel nothing. "I'm coming, Mark." She walked out and glared at her employer. "I'm fine, thank you. Please step aside, and I will join Mr. Anderson."

"Good. I hoped we wouldn't have any problems. I'd almost forgotten that you are a professional. Oh my, that is a nasty look," Mark laughed and rejoined his guests.

In the wee hours of the morning, Estelle and Mr. Anderson emerged from their room. Mark sat in a comfy overstuffed chair, smoking a cigar. "I wondered when you two love birds were coming out." He smiled, got up, and shook Mr. Anderson's hand. "I trust you are not disappointed."

"Oh no; I will be back next weekend and would like to see Estelle again."

"Certainly, we can arrange that." The two men talked about her as though she wasn't there. "We will see you next week then." Mark escorted Mr. Anderson to the door. "I will get my driver to take you home, Estelle. Here you are. This is more than you'd make in weeks at one of those diners."

Estelle sneered and snatched the money from his hand. "Yes, and I'm sure it is a pittance compared to what you made off of me tonight."

"I have expenses, my dear. Smile and act like you enjoy what you're doing. Maybe your cut will increase a bit. After all, you merely have to do what you do best." His smile was sickening.

"I hate you, Mark Lawrence. If Frank were here, he would kill you for what you're making me do."

"I suppose he would; but alas, he isn't here. Neither is Jerry. Poor Estelle, you have no one to protect you but me. Be careful; I might make you spend an evening with me. That may just be a good idea—I think you need a little discipline." He picked up the phone and called for his driver.

Estelle rode home in complete silence. At four o'clock in the morning, she ran a tub of hot water and to no avail tried to soak away the dirty feeling. There were no pills, no heroin—nothing to take away the pain. She had to pull herself together and handle this.

What other choice did she have? Mark would watch her even closer now that she was making money for him again. He would never let her go. Mark Lawrence was a monster capable of just about anything, and Estelle couldn't risk the safety of her children. She went to bed and cried herself to sleep.

Estelle entertained Mark's clientele on a regular basis. Mr. Anderson managed to attend the soirees at least a couple of times a month; but when he wasn't in town, there were other men who vied for Estelle's services. Her earnings increased, and she suspected that each week she went to the highest bidder. Mark forced her to spend a few evenings with him, and he made good on the discipline he had threatened. She despised him more and more.

Rose stopped questioning Estelle about her job. She had no intention of pushing the young woman away and losing contact again. Whatever was going on, the children were safe with Rose when their mother worked. Rose and Pauline prayed for Estelle every day.

Estelle was miserable and became more and more withdrawn. She had difficulty sleeping, and her appetite suffered. On the nights she worked, she dropped the kids off with Rose and hurried out the door, avoiding any conversation.

Mark mentioned that she had dark circles under eyes and had lost a little weight. Of course, he questioned her about drug use—he even examined her arms. For Mark, it was all business. He was as cold as ice and completely incapable of real emotion. Estelle was terrified of her employer. She knew he could kill her and leave her children orphaned without so much as batting an eye.

In spite of her earnings, Estelle had little savings. Mark insisted she buy expensive new gowns and jewelry each week. And he demanded she purchase furs—a stole and a full-length coat. Those items were a huge expense. Paying rent, household expenses, and caring for two children took more than she realized. Estelle's plan to take the kids and disappear seemed more out of reach with each passing day.

Pauline was still in California. Her sister had improved, but she still could not be left alone. Estelle knew Pauline would help if she and the kids could just get away. It wouldn't be possible to tell anyone until they actually arrived in California, but Pauline could contact Rose once they were safe. It was the only plan she had—one that was complicated by Mark's constant surveillance.

One morning, as Estelle walked home from Jake's school, she saw someone familiar just down the block. On a couple of occasions, Estelle had gone with Jerry to buy drugs from Stan. Her heart pounded when Stan recognized her and headed her way. He smiled as he approached her. "Hey Estelle, where you been? I haven't seen you in a long time."

"I've been around." She slowed, but she kept walking.

"Man, Jerry's been gone forever. Is he ever coming back to town?"

"No, I don't think so. We broke up, and I don't hear from him." Estelle willed herself not to react, but her body betrayed her. Her stomach churned, her hands shook, and her mouth felt dry.

Stan fell into step with her. "Whose kid?" Stan looked at the toddler riding in the pram.

"Mine."

"Jerry's?"

"No."

"Okay, so how you doin? You look a little uptight. Anything I can help you with?" He smiled, showing uneven, nicotine-stained teeth.

"No Stan, I'm fine; I have to go." She quickened her step.

Stan smiled as he watched her hurry down the street. "She'll be back."

That night, Estelle couldn't sleep. She lay awake for hours thinking about the upcoming weekend. She had to work Friday night as well as Saturday night. It wasn't enough that Mark had added a mid-week soiree a month or so ago. There was no end to the man's greed. Finally, she got up and paced back and forth in the living room. "I can't take much more of this, and I can't get away yet," she whispered to herself. "I just need a little help getting through this." She licked her lips and tried to steady her hands.

The next day, she ran into Stan again. She greeted him, "Hi Stan."

He smiled and turned to face her, "Hey Estelle."

"I, uh, I thought maybe I might get a few of those pills that Jerry used to get from you." She fidgeted and couldn't look him in the eyes. "You know the ones that calmed him down and helped him sleep."

"Are you sure they'll be strong enough. You know I …"

"Yes, that's all I need," she responded quickly.

"Sure. Why don't I throw in a few of these so you can wake up in the morning? You know, just until you get used to them again."

"Okay; that's great." Estelle waited as Stan slipped a small package to her. He took her money and walked away.

With each passing day, Estelle's thoughts constantly turned to Stan. She trembled and perspired when he crossed her mind. Why? She didn't even like the man. Something stirred deep within her. Denying its existence, Estelle refused to recognize the ravenous beast that awakened inside.

At night, she dreamed of warmth spreading through every part of her body—fear and anxiety faded, replaced by liquid calm and heat rushing through her veins.

Pills to sleep and pills to wake up were no longer enough. She needed more—just for a while. She needed that numb, nothingness to survive.

Between Stan's urging and her growing obsession to dull the pain, it took a total of three weeks for Estelle to convince herself she could take small amounts of heroin, just until she could save enough money to get away. It would help her cope and do what she had to do, and then she would quit. Believing her own lie, she walked back into the nightmare she had escaped. As the old addiction took hold and her need grew, her savings dwindled even more. Jake and Ginny continued to stay with Rose when Estelle worked. At home, she paid less and less attention to her children. The beast was hungry and would soon consume her entire world.

When Estelle had been with Jerry, he made sure that she ate regularly, and he limited how much heroin she took. He was only protecting his investment, but there had been some boundaries.

For some time, Estelle succeeded at limiting herself and managed to eat at least once or twice a day. But, Jerry was gone, and eventually she spiraled out of control. Practically every waking moment was consumed by thoughts of her next fix. Escape became a fairytale, always just out of reach.

She went to great lengths to hide her addiction from Mark, knowing the consequences could be deadly.

As Estelle became more and more consumed by her love affair with heroin, Jake easily fell into the role of Ginny's caregiver at home. Jake was ten, and Ginny had just turned three when Estelle left them alone for the first time to meet Stan. "Now, I'm just going to be gone for a few minutes. Don't answer the door, and make sure Ginny doesn't get into anything."

"Why can't we stay with Miss Rose?"

"Jake, I told you; I'll only be gone for a few minutes. You'll be fine; just do as I say." She rushed out the door without as much as a hug for her kids. Jake walked over and locked the door.

The first few times she left them alone, Jake was frightened. But, he adjusted to his mother's daily outings. Each time he thought about telling Miss Rose that he and Ginny were being left alone, his loyalty and love for his mother stopped him.

Rose became frantic as she witnessed Estelle's decline. Pauline encouraged her to continue praying and never give up. "Rose, we must never give up hope. The Lord sent Estelle and these children into our lives for a reason." Pauline's voice was calming as they talked on the phone.

"Pauline, we can't pretend that we don't know she is a prostitute. I'm worried about Jake and Ginny."

"I am too, but we must trust that the Lord will protect them. For now, she is not working from home and the children are with you when she's gone. Our only other option is to take measures to have the children taken from her."

"I can't, Pauline. I cannot do that to her. You know I can't."

"Rose, what about the children?"

"You said it yourself, Pauline; they're safe when she works. They're with me."

Pauline sighed. She wanted to go home desperately, but her sister was still unable to care for herself. "Let's keep praying. That is the best thing we can do."

24

Jake sulked all the way home. When Rose unlocked the apartment door, he stomped in and threw his books on the floor. "Ginny, why don't you play with your dolls?" After Ginny was settled with her dolls, Rose went back to the living room. Jake sat on the sofa with his arms crossed, pouting. "Jake, what's wrong?" She sat next to him.

"Nothing."

"Sweetheart, I know something is wrong. You didn't say a word all the way home from school, and you literally threw your books down when we came in. You're upset about something; it's all over your face."

His eyes were moist, but he struggled not to cry. "This kid at school said I didn't have a dad. He said me and Ginny are bas ..." His voice trailed away as he looked down at the floor. "He called our mom a tramp, so I punched him, and now I'm in trouble. The teacher sent a note home for my mom." He pulled a crumpled piece of paper from his pocket.

"Oh, Jake, I'm so sorry; but what that boy said is just not true. Your mother was married to your daddy when she had you. And she was still technically married to Jerry when Ginny was born." She took the note that Jake handed her, but she didn't look at it. "Do you know that people said those kinds of things about Jesus?"

Jake sat up straighter. "They did?"

"Yes, they did. Mary was pregnant before she and Joseph were married. People thought Mary had done something wrong, but she didn't. God was her baby's father, but the people at the time didn't believe it; they called Jesus a bastard." Jake gasped when Rose said that word. "The word is used to refer to children who were born to mothers who had them before being married. It has become a pretty bad word. Circumstances may not be the best, but God loves and has a plan and purpose for every baby that is born."

"He does?"

"Yes, he does. Now, let's see what this note says, and I will talk to your mom. Okay?"

"Okay."

Rose opened the crumpled note and started to read. "Dear Mrs. Preb—" She gasped and dropped the note. The color drained from her face.

"Miss Rose, what's wrong?"

Rose took a deep breath and quickly sat down. "I'm fine. Jake, I thought your mother's last name was Shannon."

"It is, but ..." He hesitated. "Well, I'm not supposed to tell anyone."

"Tell anyone what?"

"I can trust you, right?" he paused. "After we left Frank's house, Mom was really scared. She didn't want the people who were after Frank to find us, so she decided to use the name she had before she got married, Prebilica. It was my grandma and grandpa's last name."

"Do you know your grandparents' first names?" Time stood still as she waited for the answer.

"They died when I was a baby, but Mom used to tell me stories about them. My grandpa's name was Nick, Nikola, or something like that. And my grandma's name was Mary. She said they loved us a lot."

Rose struggled to control her emotions. Prebilica. It was *her* maiden name—Rosalie Elizabeth Prebilica. *Her* parents were Nikola and Mary Prebilica.

It all came flooding back. She had been so young—barely fifteen. Her strict, overprotective parents had reluctantly allowed her to go to a carnival with several other girls. A handsome carnival worker struck up a conversation with her and flirted outrageously. At the end of the day, he asked her out. Her friends dared her to accept, and she did. He was at least ten years older than Rosalie. She knew her parents would never approve, so she lied to them and sneaked out to meet him.

The carnival was in town for two weeks, and Rosalie climbed out her bedroom window almost every night to see the man she had fallen head over heels in love with. When the carnival pulled out of town, Timothy Baker was gone without so much as a goodbye to Rosalie.

Two months later, Rosalie had realized she was pregnant. Her parents were completely devastated, and planned to hide Rose away and pretend the baby belonged to them, but she refused. Mere days after turning sixteen, she gave birth to a beautiful baby girl and named her Anna Emilija Prebilica.

The following year, when the carnival returned to her neighborhood in Chicago, Rose went in search of Timothy. Much to her misfortune, she found him. She was thrilled that he was happy to be with her again—until she told him about the baby. Rose knew it would take time for him to get used to having a baby, but she couldn't imagine the plans he had for both her and Anna—plans that would benefit him financially. The two slipped away the week before the carnival was scheduled to pull out of town. Rose lied about her age to the Justice of the Peace, and they were married.

Rose remembered the hurt on her parents' faces when she brought her new husband home and announced that she and little Anna would travel with him. They had begrudgingly allowed Timothy to stay in their home.

In a matter of days, Rose's life became a nightmare. Her new husband had no intention of being tied down with a baby. Her thoughts drifted back to the night her parents overheard an argument. Timothy said he planned to sell Anna to a wealthy couple and then kidnap her back after taking the couple's money.

Rosalie was hysterical when her parents burst into the room and confronted Timothy. He laughed, telling them it was a joke; and Rosalie believed him. She wouldn't listen when they begged her to leave him, and the next morning she awakened to find her parents and little Anna gone. Having lost one of his "assets," as he referred to them, Timothy didn't plan to lose the other. He forced her to leave with him and took a job with a different carnival to keep Rosalie's family from finding them.

Timothy was cruel, and he controlled Rosalie's every move, often flying into rages and beating her over nothing. Rose came to know the depravity of the human soul when Timothy sold her for sex to men in the towns on the carnival's circuit.

Timothy kept a constant watch over her; there was no escape. She ached for her child and her parents. Only once did she manage to sneak a letter to her parents through a sympathetic older woman who promised not to tell Timothy. She did not know if they received it.

Almost a year after taking Rosalie away from her family, Timothy was killed in a barroom brawl. Rosalie's hatred for him was so intense that her only regret was not having killed him herself. She tore their trailer apart until she found the money he had hidden; she'd earned it. There was no funeral, no graveside service. Rosalie fled, leaving the owner of the carnival to bury him in an unmarked pauper's grave. She returned to Chicago to find her parents and her little girl gone. Broken, bitter, and angry, she searched for years, never finding a trace of them.

"Miss Rose." She continued to stare into space, so Jake spoke louder. "Miss Rose!" Rose jumped.

"Oh. I'm sorry. Jake, I actually need to do some cleaning in my room. Do you have any homework?"

"Yes."

"Why don't you get that done? Can you keep an eye on Ginny for a few minutes?"

"Sure," Jake answered.

Rose went into her room and shut the door. She lay on her bed and muffled her sobs with a pillow. Finally, she sat up and called Pauline.

"Hello?"

"Pauline—" The words caught in her throat. She swallowed and went on. "Oh my God!" She sobbed. "I can't believe it!"

"Rose, what is it? Are you okay?"

"Pauline, it's her. I found her!"

After calming down enough to speak, Rose told Pauline what had happened to Jake at school and about the note. "Pauline, how could I not have known my own child? She even looks like me! And Ginny! My God, she looks just like Anna when she was a baby. I should have known my own daughter!" She cried.

"Rose, sweetheart, don't torture yourself. How could you have known?"

"I don't know," Rose sniffled. "What should I do?"

"I don't know for sure, but I do know that God has orchestrated this. We have prayed for this day since I met you at the revival in Chicago and led you to Christ, but you must be careful. Estelle is very fragile right now, so I don't know how she will handle such a revelation. We will pray and ask God what to do. You must let Him lead you—and you must be prepared for her not to react the way that you want her to."

"It's Friday, and she works tonight, so the children will be with me. I won't see her until she comes to get them tomorrow."

"That's good. Take that time to calm down and pray. Ask God to direct you. Please don't jump the gun." Pauline paused for a moment.

"Now let me pray with you before we hang up." The two prayed together for a few minutes before ending the call.

Rose got very little sleep that night. She prayed and read her Bible for hours; but as hard as she tried, she couldn't control her emotions. Finally, she cried herself into a fitful sleep.

The next morning, Rose woke to a kiss on the cheek from Ginny. "Oh, sweetheart; I overslept. Where's Jake?"

"There." Ginny pointed to the living room where Jake was looking at comic books.

Pulling on her robe, Rose walked to the living room. "Well, I guess I'm lazy today. Now, what would you two like for breakfast?"

"Pancakes and sausages!" Jake seemed to have recovered from the incident at school.

"Panycakes!" Ginny squealed.

"Then pancakes and sausages it is. Jake, would you please set the table while I get started?"

"Yes, ma'am."

Later, as they finished breakfast, Jake thanked Rose. "Miss Rose, I love your pancakes and sausages. My mom used to make them for me all the time, but she doesn't anymore." His voice trailed off. "We eat cornflakes all the time now."

Rose didn't quite know what to say. "You know, Jake, it takes a lot of work to care for a little one, keep things clean, and cook, and your mom is doing it all by herself."

Jake's eyes flashed with anger. "*I* take care of Ginny! Mom hardly ever pays any attention to her. She even leaves—" Jake stopped, realizing he had crossed a boundary.

"Jake, what were you about to say?"

"Nothing. May I be excused please?" He wouldn't look at her.

"Yes, Jake, you may." Rose was more worried than ever. She just knew Jake was about to tell her that Estelle left them alone, but how often and for how long? She cleared the table and washed the dishes. She couldn't wait any longer to tell Estelle—she had to know she had family. Estelle obviously needed more help, and she needed it now.

Just after lunch, Estelle came to get the kids. She tried to rush them out the door, but Rose stopped her. "Estelle, please. I need to talk to you. It's very important."

"Look, if you want to lecture me about my job again, please don't bother. It won't change anything."

"I'm not going to lecture you about your job, I promise. Please stay a moment."

"Only for a few minutes; I'm tired."

"Jake, why don't you take Ginny and help her play with her blocks in the other room?" Jake sensed something was wrong, but he led Ginny to the other room and shut the door.

Rose relayed the story that Jake had told her.

"That little brat, and his mother, what a b—"

"Estelle, stop it. There's more to this than what happened at school." Her hands shook as she pulled the note from her pocket. "This is the note from Jake's teacher. It is addressed to Mrs. Prebilica." She stopped and took a deep breath. "I knew your name was Estelle Shannon, but I didn't know your maiden name."

"Okay. So I'm using my maiden name right now. Is that a crime?"

"No, Estelle, it isn't." Rose stopped, cleared her throat and continued. "My maiden name is also Prebilica."

"So?" Estelle was irritated. Then it hit her. Rose Prebilica, Rosalie? She gasped. "Who are you?" her voice barely a whisper.

"I believe I'm your mother," Rose's voice broke.

Estelle jumped up. "No, you are not my mother—my mother is dead. Her name was Mary. Why are you telling me this?"

"I named my baby girl Anna Emilija Prebilica. My parents were Nikola and Mary Prebilica. We lived in Chicago. My married name is Baker, but my maiden name is Rosalie Elizabeth Prebilica." Rose couldn't look at Estelle; she wrung her hands and paced the floor.

Horrified, Estelle continued, her voice barely a whisper. "But my name is Estelle—Estelle Anna Prebilica."

"They must have changed your name when they left Chicago."

"But why would they take me from you?"

Rose looked into her daughter's eyes. "Because I was married to a monster, and they were afraid for you. At the time, I was too young and stupid to see what kind of man he was."

"If I am your daughter, then that means you left me. How could you leave me?" Estelle's voice got louder with every word.

"I didn't leave you. He took me away and wouldn't let me come back." Rose was losing control.

"How old was I when you left?"

"Almost three months." Tears streamed down her face.

"We didn't move from Chicago until after I was a year old. You didn't come back for me. You abandoned me!" Estelle yelled.

Just then, Jake opened the door. "What's going on? What's wrong?"

Rose wiped her eyes. "Jake, we're talking; please close the door."

"No. Jake, get your sister. Where are your things? We're leaving."

"Estelle, please. It wasn't the way you think. He wouldn't let me come back! He died about a year after we were married; but when I went back to Chicago, you were gone. There wasn't even a trace! I searched for you for years."

"I don't believe you. You left me." Estelle's eyes burned with tears. Jake brought Ginny in the room as his mother had asked. "Jake, get your books and bag, now!" She grabbed Ginny by the arm, and Jake followed her out of the apartment.

"Estelle, please come back. Let me explain!" Rose pleaded and followed them down the hall.

"No. Stay away from me, and stay away from my kids. We don't need you! Jake, come on." Estelle picked Ginny up and hurried down the stairs.

Rose stood helplessly in the hallway and watched them leave. She stumbled back in the apartment and collapsed in a heap on the living room floor. Deep-wrenching sobs shook her to her very core.

Jake practically ran to keep up with his mother. "Why are you mad at Miss Rose?"

"It's nothing for you to be concerned with."

"Who will watch us?"

"You'll be fine. We don't need her."

"Yes, we do; she loves us!"

"I said we'll be fine! Now stop questioning me!" When they got home, Estelle went to her room and locked the door. She needed a fix, and she needed to sleep.

That afternoon, Jake played with Ginny and put her down for a nap while his mother rested. He didn't understand why she was so angry, but he was afraid of losing someone else he loved. Pauline left them, Frank never came back, and now his mom said Miss Rose had to stay away from them. He and Ginny loved Miss Rose, and she loved them too. Tears formed in his eyes, but he wiped them away, determined not to cry. At ten years old, Jake sensed that life was about to change drastically for him and for Ginny.

That evening, Estelle came out of her room calmer than she had been earlier. "Jake, I have to get ready to go to work. We're going to do something different tonight—you're going to stay here and watch Ginny. It'll be close to her bedtime when I leave, so you don't have to worry."

"We have to stay here alone at night?" he whispered.

"Oh for God's sake, you're not a baby anymore. We have neighbors right down the hall, and we have a phone. There is no reason in the world why I have to find someone else to watch you!" She swore under her breath as she walked away.

It was hours before Rose was coherent enough to call Pauline.

When she heard Pauline's voice on the other end of the phone line, she burst into tears. "Pauline, I've lost her again. I can't stand it! I've lost them all!"

Tears streamed down Pauline's own face as she listened to her dear friend. She waited silently for a few minutes. "Rose, I know your heart is aching right now, but it's not time to give up. We talked about being prepared for her not to react the way we wanted her to, and that's what happened. Do you believe God is in control in this situation?"

Rose sniffled. "Yes, but Pauline, she's hurt and angry and so stubborn!"

"That may be true; but if you think back, you'll remember another young woman who was broken, angry, and stubborn. God never took his eyes off of you, Rose, and He sent you my way. It didn't happen overnight, and you know that."

"I know. It's just so hard! I finally found her, I have two beautiful grandchildren, and now she hates me!" she cried.

"We won't give up, and we'll continue to pray for Estelle and those children. Do you hear me?"

"Yes. Yes, we will, but I suspect my emotions are going to get in the way."

"I'm sure they will. But remember this: God made you a survivor. You will get through this, and I believe you'll have a relationship with your daughter and grandchildren someday."

Rose cried again. "I believe it too. I love you; you always encourage me and give me hope."

"I love you too, Rose. You've encouraged me many times. Let's pray." The two women prayed and then said goodbye. Rose still ached for her daughter and grandchildren, but she was calmer after talking to her friend.

That first night alone in the apartment, Jake tried to be brave for Ginny. He read to his little sister and put her to bed. Later, as he sat in the living room, sounds he hadn't noticed before were exaggerated by his fear. The stairs creaked, and he heard footsteps in the hallway. Faceless enemies lurked just outside the apartment door. Two cats fought, with monster-like snarls, in the alley behind the building. Jake cringed in the corner of the sofa with a blanket pulled up to his chin.

He heard the door handle turn; someone was coming in! The hair stood up on his arms. Small beads of perspiration formed on his forehead, and his heart pounded. He sat still and didn't make a sound, afraid to breathe. Seconds later, when the neighbor's door opened and closed, he let out a huge sigh. Just then, the windows rattled as a blast of wind hit them, and images of hideous creatures reflected on the glass.

He tried to stay up and protect Ginny, but his eyes were heavy and he could no longer stay awake. Estelle found him sleeping on the sofa when she staggered in. "What the hell? Why isn't he in bed?" She felt a momentary twinge of guilt before she pushed it aside. She covered her son with his blanket and went to bed.

Over time, Jake adjusted. He chased away the monsters that lurked in the hallway and just outside the windows. He conquered his fears and cared for Ginny when his mother worked or went out. Occasionally, he was tempted to call Miss Rose; but he knew he was forbidden to speak to her—he couldn't betray his mother.

25

Estelle hurried down the street after meeting Stan—her only focus was to get home and get high. She didn't pay attention when a car pulled up and stopped right next to her; she just kept walking. "Estelle, get in the car." Frozen in her tracks, she felt stark terror as Mark Lawrence grabbed her arm and dragged her to the car. "I said get in."

"Mark, what are you doing? I'm not working tonight." Unsuccessfully, she tried to appear calm and collected.

"The question, my dear, is what are *you* doing? Haven't I warned you about drug use?"

"I don't know what you're talking about. I was just going to the market."

"Well the market is the other direction. You were heading home, and you don't have any bags. By the way, Stan works for someone who works for me. I just saw you talking to him, and he slipped you a bag."

"I don't know him. The guy just talked to me when I walked by." Her heart pounded.

"Stop lying to me. You've been using for some time now, I suspect. At first I thought you were just distraught over losing Frank and having to go back to work. But, over time, I realized you were using and I followed you. I thought we might as well let you work until it started to show."

"I'm not, Mark. I swear I'm not using!" She was terrified.

He slapped her hard across the face. "Shut up! Do you think I'm an idiot? Even your beloved Mr. Anderson has had some complaints of late. Look at you; it *is* starting to show. You look like hell."

Estelle wiped the blood from her lip. "Mark, please, I'm sorry. I can kick this. I did before."

"I don't give a damn if you kick it. You can put yourself in the grave with it for all I care."

"Good, then I won't have to work for you anymore." She felt brave for just a moment. "After all, you can't have a *junkie* servicing your gentlemen."

"Oh, on the contrary while you still breathe, you will work for me. You'll just deal with a different level of my clientele. You certainly won't come to our parties anymore. Mr. Anderson will recover and find love again." Mark laughed. "I'll send the clients to you. I don't waste money on their level."

"What? I can't do this in my apartment. I have kids!"

"Take them to a babysitter. Lock them in their room. I don't care. They're not my concern. Consider yourself lucky I don't put you on a street corner. Now get out of my car."

Estelle stumbled and fell on the sidewalk in her rush to get away from Mark.

"Mom, why do I have to stay in our room? Ginny is sleeping. Don't you go to work tonight?"

"Just do what I say. I'm not going to work. I have company coming over, and you need to stay out of the way. Now go on. Go to the bathroom first, and then go to your room. Shut the door and don't come out. If Ginny wakes up, don't let her come out."

Jake stormed into the bathroom and slammed the door. A few minutes later, Estelle heard the kids' bedroom door slam. She was nervous and shaking, as this was completely new. She had no idea who this guy was. Mark insisted on some level of discretion and said the man would be at her back door at 9:30 tonight; it was 9:15, and time was crawling.

At 9:30 sharp, there was a knock at the kitchen door. Estelle took a deep breath and opened the door.

"Hi, I'm Mr. Smith."

"Sure you are," she whispered, "and I'm Susie Jones." She closed the door, and "Mr. Smith" followed her to the bedroom.

"Mark, how am I supposed to live on this pittance you give me? I have kids to feed!"

"Yes, and you have a habit to support. I suppose you just may have to entertain a few more gentlemen each week, my dear. I can arrange it."

"You love this, don't you? How can you be so uncaring? What about my kids?"

"Me? Uncaring? Look at you—a mother. Most of what you make goes straight in your veins. I'd bet you buy heroin before you buy food for those kids. No one twisted your arm to start using again. You had a good thing going, and you destroyed it, Estelle."

Tears streamed down her face as she walked away. She had to find Stan. He wasn't on the street, but she knew where he lived.

Estelle knocked several times before Stan asked who was there. "It's Estelle. I need to talk to you."

He opened the door. "You need more so soon?"

"Yes, but I won't have any money until tomorrow. Can you just give me enough to make it through the day?"

He leaned against the doorframe and stared at her. She was still very attractive—thinner, but attractive nonetheless. He smiled. "Sure, come on in. I think we can work something out."

The apartment building Estelle lived in was sold, and maintenance was obviously not a priority for the new owner. The building fell into disrepair, and many of the old tenants moved out. Some of the units remained empty, and the new tenants didn't much care that men knocked on Estelle's kitchen door at all hours of the day and night.

It didn't take long for Jake to figure out that his mother didn't just have a lot of boyfriends. He kept Ginny out of the way of his mother and her men, fuming when guys came over before he and Ginny went to bed. He did everything he could to keep the apartment neat and clean, spending most of his time caring for his sister while Estelle practically ignored them. He had no other choice than to leave Ginny with his mom when he had to go to school.

Most of the neighborhood families knew what his mother did for a living, and he was ashamed and embarrassed. He despised what she did, but he wouldn't tolerate the crude remarks other kids made about her. His anger boiled over often, and fighting became second nature. Jake was smart and did well in every subject at school, but his frequent fights landed him in the principal's office at least once a week. Principal Watkins knew Jake was intelligent and was basically a good kid, and that was the only thing that saved him from being suspended. Hoping to turn the boy's focus in a more positive direction, he tried to encourage Jake to take part in after school activities, but Jake was always in a hurry to get home.

"Jake, we need some milk and bread. Go down to Polanski's, and take Ginny with you. There's money on the counter in the kitchen. Don't spend anything on candy or any silly crap. I may be gone when you get back, but I won't be long."

Jake didn't answer her. He counted out the money from the kitchen, took Ginny by the hand, and went out the door. "We're going to the store, and I'm going to get you some candy. What do you think about that?"

"Candy!" Ginny jumped up and down. He didn't care what his mother said; sometimes he bought little treats for his sister. The two walked several blocks to the market.

"Will that be it, Jake?" Mr. Polanski smiled at the children as Jake set a bottle of milk and a loaf of bread on the counter.

"One of those peppermint sticks for Ginny, please," Jake said as he counted his coins.

"You know what? The peppermint sticks are on the house today." Mr. Polanski handed one to Ginny and one to Jake.

"Thank you, Mr. Polanski."

"You're welcome. You two come in and see us more often, okay?"

"Okay, we will. Come on Ginny, we need to get home."

Margaret Polanski walked out of the back room just as the children went out the front door. "Joe, those children are so precious. I worry about them."

"So do I, Margaret."

"Estelle used to come in herself, but I haven't seen her for the longest time. You know Rose from our church? She knows them. I believe she used to watch the children, but something happened and she doesn't see them anymore. She never fails to pray for them at our women's Bible studies. We should let her know we are praying for them too."

"Why don't you talk to her at your next meeting? Maybe the two of you can get together and pray for Estelle and the children. We should do everything we can to help them."

"Joe, I've been thinking, maybe we could offer Jake an after school job. He could do simple things to earn a little money, and it would be an opportunity for us to offer real help to Jake and his family."

"I'll talk to him the next time he comes in." He hugged his wife and kissed her on the cheek.

Kansas City, Missouri
1961

part three

26

July of 1961 was a sizzler. Day in and day out, it was hot and sticky. Morning didn't bring much relief. Once in a great while, rain moved in, dropping the temperature just a bit. Even if it was short lived, the cooler air masked the alley's stench of garbage cans, cheap wine, and urine.

Jake loved the peaceful quiet of early morning. No upstairs neighbors fighting, no crying babies, and no moms smacking their kids. No noises from his mother's bedroom. It was the one time of day he could let his mind wander, delude himself a little, and temporarily escape what life had dealt him.

At 12 years old, Jake should have spent his summer vacation riding bikes, exploring nearby creeks and woods with his buddies, and day-dreaming about his first crush. But he didn't have time to play. He had traded childhood for the adult responsibilities his mother had abandoned. Like a grown man, each morning he headed for work. It was 6:15 a.m., and other kids in the neighborhood were still sleeping. Jake knew sleeping late was a waste of time, and time was money.

His dark, wavy hair was clean and neatly combed; being poor was no excuse for being dirty. He loved clean, and he loved order. His jeans were neatly creased. Each night, he took time to fold them just right and slide them under his mattress on the floor. It was as good as ironing any day. As he headed to work that morning, he didn't realize the waistband of his second pair of jeans peeked out in the back.

Jake's dark brown eyes were incredible—eyes that had seen far too much, far too soon. The intense, almost hypnotic gaze seemed out of place in his childlike face. His smooth, unblemished skin was bronzed from the summer sun.

He knew he was lucky when Mr. Polanski gave him a job at the market. Joe and Margaret Polanski were well-liked and respected by those in their community. They had built their business on honesty, hard work, and compassion. Everyone knew Joe Polanski would extend credit to a family in need longer than any other grocer in town. He often hired men who were out of work to sweep up around the store and work on the house and the yard.

On Fridays, when most of the families made payments on their grocery bills, Margaret made sure all of the children left with a bag of candy—on the house. Joe and Margaret never had children of their own, but they loved the neighborhood kids. Over the years, they watched, worried, and prayed for the children who frequented their market.

Jake walked a little faster. Polanski's Market was only one more block away. Old man Bertz waved from his rocker on the porch. "Good morning, Jake! It's going to be a scorcher today."

"Yeah, it sure is, Mr. Bertz," The old man was having his morning cigarette. His wife had a hissy if he smoked in the house.

Mrs. Bertz came out of the front door screeching. "John, your breakfast is getting cold. I'm going to have to put it in the garbage if you don't come in and eat right now!" As she watched Jake walk past the house, she shook her head. "That poor little boy, his mother should be ashamed. God bless his heart. John, come inside and eat." With that, she went back in the house, and the screen door slammed behind her.

At 6:30 a.m. sharp, Jake met Joe Polanski at the front door of Polanski's Market. It was Jake's job to set up the carts in front of the market and fill them with fresh fruit and vegetables. He took pride in the way he arranged the produce. He polished apples with a soft cloth and washed plump strawberries, heads of lettuce, and juicy tomatoes. Fresh garlic and a variety of onions were stacked neatly on a separate cart.

Mrs. Polanski was inside the market making sure everything was neat and clean. Every morning, she served coffee and breakfast in the back room. Jake loved the smell of freshly brewed coffee. "Good morning, Jake! Take a minute and have something to eat." Margaret Polanski made sure Jake's coffee had plenty of milk and sugar. She knew youngsters didn't really need to drink coffee, but she also knew Jake loved it. "The biscuits are still warm from the oven. Make sure you get plenty of preserves. There's some ham left also, dear."

Jake downed a large piece of ham and two biscuits with strawberry preserves—all washed down with the milky-sweet coffee. He loved coffee, even in the summer. "Thank you, Mrs. Polanski; that was delicious."

"You are so welcome, Jake. I have a bag with some biscuits, ham, and fruit for you to take home to Ginny. There's also some coffee cake left from yesterday. It's in a bag in the icebox. Don't forget it when you break for lunch."

Jake felt guilty as Mrs. Polanski smiled at him. Lately, he'd been taking a little food here and there and hiding it around back until after hours. Then he would stash it in the pockets of the second pair of jeans and take it home to his mom and Ginny. It made him feel like a jerk, but the Polanskis had no idea how bad things were at home.

His mom was always short on the rent. He didn't like thinking about it; he just had to take care of it. Ginny couldn't live on the street, so stealing what he could and selling it was the only way he could make up the difference. Selling cigarettes he stole from the larger supermarket and booze he copped from the neighborhood liquor store was easy and profitable, but it wasn't always enough. Jake didn't know what else to do. He couldn't steal from his mom's customers anymore. All hell broke loose when the last guy caught Jake going through his pockets. That was the night he discovered his mom had a gun, and it was the end of Jake's rolling Estelle's customers. It was too dangerous for Ginny, so he had to resort to other means of adding to his wages to help make ends meet—like stealing from the Polanskis. He respected them, which made him feel miserable when he took food from the market. A couple of times, he even let himself think about what it would have been like to have Joe and Margaret for parents. He treasured them just as much as Pauline, Rose, and Frank. He didn't want to think about any of that; those thoughts made him ache, and tears welled up in his eyes.

It didn't matter anyway; daydreaming got you nowhere. The Polanskis weren't his parents. He was Jake Shannon. He had never known his dad. His mother was Estelle Shannon, a first generation American and a prostitute. They were poor, but Jake had no intention of staying that way. He made $1.65 an hour at the market—it was fair, but he needed more.

Jake shook himself and focused on work. Everything was ready by the time the first early morning shoppers arrived. The neighborhood ladies picked over all of the produce, squeezing and smelling the fruit and vegetables, examining each purchase carefully. He heard the things they said about his mom. They pitied him—he didn't want their pity, and he hated it when they talked about him like he wasn't there.

When lunch break rolled around, Jake headed home to check on Ginny. It was getting warmer, and the humidity was climbing. Jake hated smelling like sweat, but he walked faster as he thought about Ginny and home. Estelle's last customer, Bob, had stayed the night. Jake hated it when those creeps were still there in the morning. Bob had a wife and three kids. He was a salesman. He was flashy, cheap, and thought he was a real tough guy. Jake heard his mom crying a couple of times when Bob roughed her up. His old lady probably ruled the roost, and Bob had to push someone else around to feel like a man. Jake despised him.

As he opened the apartment door, Jake heard Ginny crying. The second floor apartment was stifling, and keeping the windows open didn't help much. The smell of stale sweat and whiskey almost made him gag. The curtains were still closed, and his eyes had to adjust to the dingy room. Ginny's muffled cry came from the direction of the sofa.

Finally Jake's eyes adjusted to the dim light. Bob's shirt was open, and he was in his underwear. Ginny struggled and whimpered on his lap, dressed in nothing but her panties. Bob hugged her and tried to kiss her.

Blinded with rage, Jake lunged across the room. He screamed profanities at Ginny's attacker. "I'll kill you!" Without thinking, Jake grabbed a lamp from the rickety table near the sofa. Bob, startled and still drunk, reacted slowly. The faded lampshade fell on the floor as Jake raised the lamp high in the air and in one motion brought the thin metal base down on the back of Bob's head. There was a thud, and blood splattered on the wall. Jake was nauseated for just a second, but he swallowed the hot, bitter liquid that rose in his throat. Bob roared and fell over on his side. Jake thought he had killed him until Bob moaned and started to get up.

Ready for a fight, Jake grabbed Ginny and dragged her to the kitchen. He shoved her behind the curtain under the counter. "Ginny, you stay put, no matter what happens. Don't come out unless I tell you to!" His eyes darted around the tiny kitchen until they focused on a dirty butcher knife in the sink. Snatching it up, he ran back into the living room just in time to see Bob run out the door and down the stairway, holding his pants up as he ran.

Jake screamed out the window as Bob sprinted towards his car. "Creep, I'll kill you if I ever see you on this block again! Go back to your own neighborhood, you stinkin' pervert!"

Suddenly, a string of curses shook the room. "Jake, what the hell are you doing?" Estelle staggered in from the bedroom. She looked awful. Her hair was dirty and tangled with oil and sweat. Her makeup was smeared, and her eyes were puffy and bloodshot. Jake didn't want to get close enough to smell her breath.

"Your *boyfriend* tried to hurt Ginny!"

Estelle pulled her bathrobe together. "Jake, you're crazy. He's one of my best customers. Look, he left me extra money." Bob was one of the customers that Estelle dealt with directly on occasion, cutting Mark out. She had to be careful, but at least sometimes the money was all hers.

"Yeah, he left it for *Ginny*. He was half-naked and hugging and kissing on her. He hurt her!"

Just then, Jake remembered Ginny huddled under the counter in the kitchen. "Oh God, Ginny!" He ran to the kitchen and gently pulled his sister from her hiding place. She put her little arms around his neck and buried her soft face against his shoulder. "It's okay. I'm here, and no one is going to hurt you again. I'll take care of you." Sobs shook her tiny body.

He found the bag of treats that Margaret had sent for Ginny. "Look, I brought you some biscuits and jam." He tasted salty tears as he kissed her cheek. "Oh man, look at her face! The jerk bruised her!" Jake spun around to face his mother. "Why didn't you hear her? Why'd you let him hurt her?" Jake screamed.

With Ginny on his hip, Jake stormed into his mom's room. He looked past the rumpled bed, empty booze bottles, and dirty clothes scattered on the floor. He knew exactly what he was looking for; he'd suspected it for a long time. Jake sat Ginny down on the bed and pulled a box of his mom's lingerie from under the bed. Estelle followed him screaming. "Get out of there! Nothing in this room is your business. Jake, stop it right now!" Suddenly Estelle stopped shouting and stood in the doorway with her hands covering her face.

"Here it is. I knew it! Damn your soul to hell, you junkie!" He pulled out the small cloth bag and dumped its contents on the floor: matches, a spoon, cotton, a make-shift tourniquet, and the hypodermic needle. Now he knew why his mom worked more but brought home less money.

He walked over to his mom. "Let me see your arms!" Like an obedient child, she held out her arms. Jake pushed up the sleeves of her robe, and his stomach churned at the sight of the scars and bruises up and down her arms. In an instant, the tough guy faded away, and Jake started to cry. "Why, Mom? Why this? Aren't things bad enough without you spending everything you make on dope? I've been stealing from the Polanskis so Ginny can eat—yeah, the people who try to help us. Do you know how much I hate that? I steal cigarettes and booze from across town so we can pay the rent. I do all that, just so you can put your money in your stinkin' veins?"

Estelle crumpled in a heap on the floor and rambled. "Baby, I didn't mean for it to get this bad. After we got away from Jerry, I never wanted to do this again. I thought it was over when I met Frank, but Mark found me and made me go back to work for him. It was driving me crazy! I thought I could just calm myself down until we could get away and then I could stop. But I can't get away from Mark, and I can't stop."

Jake paced the floor. "What do you mean you can't get away from Mark? Who's Mark?"

"He's my boss."

"Just tell him you're not working for him anymore!"

"It's complicated, Jake. If I try to stop working for him, he'll kill me. He's a very dangerous man, and I know too much about him. He'll never let me stop. I swear he'd kill me first." She wondered if someday she would be able to tell Jake that this man had ordered his father's murder.

The silence was thick and heavy, and the room seemed darker than it was moments before. As Jake flopped down on the bed next to Ginny, Estelle turned and then knelt on the rough hardwood floor in front of her kids. It had been so long since she'd hugged Jake. He had been more of a parent to Ginny than she had been. Shame and remorse gripped her as she looked into the faces of her children. She put her arms around them and began to gently rock them from side to side.

She regretted so many things, but most of all she hated what she had done to her children. Sooner or later, she'd be dead or in prison, and they would be completely on their own. "God, how did it come to this?" With tears streaming down her face, she closed her eyes and tried to remember how things had gone so wrong.

Estelle held her children and cried. Jake dried his eyes and stood up. "I'm not leaving Ginny here with you. She's going to work with me. I'll make up some excuse."

"Jake, please leave her here. I can take care of her."

"No, you can't. I'm taking her with me." Jake took Ginny to the bathroom, washed her up, and got her dressed. "We'll be back when I'm finished." He gathered a few old toys, took Ginny's hand, and opened the door.

"Jake," she hesitated, "I love you, both of you." Estelle hadn't said those words for a very long time.

Jake stood in the doorway and looked at his mom. No matter what she did, he loved her. He remembered how things used to be. She was a good mom before she met Jerry. "I love you too, Mom." He closed the door and headed back to work with Ginny in tow.

Ginny was excited about going with her big brother—her hero. She always felt safe with Jake. She skipped along and stayed right by his side. When they arrived at the market, Jake was anxious and worried that the Polanskis might not let Ginny stay.

"Ginny, look at you! You are getting prettier every time I see you," Margaret Polanski greeted them as they walked in the door. "Oh sweetheart, what happened to your face?"

Jake answered too quickly. "She fell down. Uh, Mrs. Polanski, I'm sorry but my mom is sick, and I had to bring Ginny back with me. She has some toys. She won't be any trouble, I promise."

Margaret heard the desperation in Jake's voice. "Jake, that's fine. I was just about to go upstairs for a while. Ginny, would you like to come with me?" They had an unoccupied apartment upstairs that was convenient for cooking daytime meals. When things were slow in the afternoon, Joe and Margaret would sometimes take turns resting upstairs.

Ginny looked at Jake for approval. "You can go. You'll have fun. I'll be right down here okay?"

"Okay," Ginny smiled and took Mrs. Polanski's hand. The two headed to the stairway in the back of the store.

"Uh, Mrs. Polanski, I don't know how long my mom will be sick. I may have to bring Ginny with me for a while. Is that okay?"

"Of course, Jake. Don't worry about it."

Jake sighed. He had plenty to worry about and no idea what to do.

Jake and the Polanskis fell into a routine with Ginny. The Polanskis didn't ask questions; they simply did what they could to help the children who had been sent their way. Ginny absolutely loved Joe and Margaret. She spent a good part of each day upstairs with Mrs. Polanski. Jake continued to help Joe with the store and no longer went home for lunch. Margaret fed the children every day and sent food home with them for supper.

Ginny was never again alone in the apartment with Estelle and her customers. Estelle wanted to stop, but she couldn't; she couldn't stop turning tricks or doing drugs. Her addiction had completely taken over her life. Though she no longer dealt with Mark's elite clientele, he still would not let her go. In spite of the circumstances, something had been sparked inside her the day Bob attacked Ginny and Jake found her stash. She wanted to stop. She didn't know how, but she desperately wanted to stop. Her kids deserved a normal life, not this nightmare she had dragged them into. She just didn't have the strength to change things.

27

Jake held Ginny by the hand as they walked into the supermarket. He didn't want to bring her with him to steal cigarettes, but he couldn't leave her with his mom. A couple of times he'd made an excuse and left her with the Polanskis, but today was Wednesday, and they had gone home to get ready for church.

As the two of them walked through the store, Jake was nervous and not his usual nonchalant self. Ginny, oblivious to the task at hand, smiled and chatted.

"Can I have some candy?"

"Not this time, Ginny. We need bread and milk." He was anxious as they walked to the section with the cigarettes.

"Why are you getting cig'rettes, Jake?"

"Ginny, just be quiet." He held a loaf of bread under one arm as he looked around and stuffed packs of cigarettes in his jeans.

"Jake, what are you doing?"

"Ginny, I said be quiet!"

"Young man, may I help you with something?" The store manager said as he came around the corner.

Jake quickly turned to face him. "No thank you. I just need to get some milk."

"Well, the milk is that way."

"Thanks Mister; my little sister tried to wander off."

"Jake, I—"

"Come on, Ginny, let's get our milk." As Jake dragged her with him, he didn't realize that a pack of cigarettes poked out of the waistband of his second pair of jeans.

"Hey kid, come back here! What are you doing with those cigarettes?"

Jake picked Ginny up and made a run for the front door, but he couldn't run fast and carry her too. The store manager caught up to him, grabbed him by the arm, and jerked him to a stop. "I said stop!"

"Get your hands off me! You're scaring my little sister!" Ginny started to cry as Jake struggled to get away.

"Tom, call the police," the manager yelled. "This kid is stealing cigarettes. Now come with me—both of you." He practically dragged Jake by the arm. Jake held tight to Ginny.

Joe and Margaret were getting ready to walk out the front door when the phone rang. Margaret hesitated for a moment, deciding whether or not to answer it. She quickly picked up the receiver. Her face turned white as she listened to the caller. Joe hurried to her side. "Margaret, what's wrong?"

She put her hand over the receiver. "It's the police. It's Jake and little Ginny."

"My God, are they hurt?"

"No, but they are at the police station."

"The police station?"

"Yes, Jake was caught stealing cigarettes. He refused to give the police his mother's number." She spoke to the officer again. "Yes, officer, we'll be there right away."

When Margaret ended the call, she dialed another number. "Hello, Rose? It's Margaret. Jake is in trouble; he and Ginny are both at the police station. We are going to get them. In light of what you've shared with me, I think you should come too." She listened for a moment. "Yes, we'll pick you up in 10 minutes."

Margaret turned to her husband. "We need to pick Rose up on the way. It's a long story, but you'll find out soon enough. Rose is Jake and Ginny's grandmother. Estelle doesn't want her to see the children, but I think it's time for her to get involved."

Joe didn't say a word. He just grabbed his jacket and the keys to the car.

The ride to the police station was quiet. Rose, Margaret, and Joe, each lost in their own thoughts, whispered prayers for the children. None of the three quite knew what they would say or do once they arrived.

Joe broke the silence as he pulled into the parking lot. "Well, we're here." He got out and opened the car doors for Margaret and Rose. They all walked toward front door of the police station.

Joe approached the officer at the desk. "Excuse me, my name is Joseph Polanski. We received a phone call regarding two children who are here: Jake Shannon and his little sister Ginny."

The officer looked over the reading glasses perched on his nose. "Yes, please have a seat. The officer who is handling the situation would like to speak with you."

A few minutes later, an officer walked over to the group. "I'm Officer Dean. If you'll follow me, we can talk." He led them down the hall and into an office. "Let me get one more chair."

Once the group was seated, Joe made the introductions. "I am Joseph Polanski, this is my wife Margaret Polanski, and the children's grandmother, Rose Baker. Margaret and I own a small market where Jake works part-time."

The officer looked surprised. "I've talked to Jake, and I wasn't aware that he had a grandmother."

Rose spoke up. "My daughter has not allowed me to see the children for some time. There are some problems."

"There are definitely some problems. We are somewhat familiar with Estelle Shannon. We suspect that she is engaged in prostitution, but she doesn't solicit on the street. She's been seen with someone who is involved in the sale of narcotics. Regardless, none of this is a good situation for these kids."

"Yes, officer, we also have those same suspicions. We want to help in any way that we can. The children must be our first priority," Joe sighed as he spoke.

"First of all, the storeowner has decided not to file charges against Jake. He talked to the boy while he waited for an officer to arrive and found out that Jake is stealing to help support the family. He is trying to take care of his little sister, as I understand it."

Rose stifled a sob as the officer spoke.

"I'm sorry; I know this must be difficult for you. What I can tell you is that I *can* release the children to a family member." He looked at Rose.

"Oh yes," Rose wiped her eyes. "I brought a copy of my birth certificate in case you need proof. Please, when can we see them?"

"In just a few minutes; but first, let's go over some things. Now, if you take the children back to their mother, I can guarantee you that this boy will be back in here in no time at all. Sooner or later, he'll wind up in jail. I suggest that you either convince his mother to sign papers giving you guardianship of the children or go to court and try to get custody. Jake has to understand the stealing must stop. I'm sure the supermarket is not his only spot. I hope he can be turned around; he seems like a good kid."

"He is a wonderful boy. He's responsible, trustworthy, and has been such a help to us at the store. Jake is like a parent to Ginny," Margaret added.

Rose looked at Joe and Margaret. "I think we should take the children to my apartment and talk to them. Joe, would you mind staying with the children while Margaret and I talk to Estelle? They don't need to be in the middle of an argument."

"I'm a little concerned about you two ladies going to her apartment alone. Why don't we ask Pastor if he and his wife would keep the children company for a bit, and I'll go too?"

Margaret looked at Rose, who nodded in agreement. "If you don't mind Rose, we can go to our house first. It's closer to Pastor's house."

"That's fine."

"Okay, it sounds like the three of you have at least the beginning of a plan. If you'll wait here, I'll go get the kids." Officer Dean left the room.

About ten minutes later, Officer Dean opened the door, and Jake walked in slowly, looking at the floor. The officer carried Ginny, who was sleeping soundly, and handed her to Mr. Polanski. "I'm sorry, Mr. and Mrs. Polanski. Please don't be mad at—" Just then, Jake looked up. "Miss Rose!" He ran across the room and into her arms.

"Oh Jake, I've missed you so!" Rose held him and cried.

Jake looked up. "I'm glad you're here, but I don't want my mom to get mad at you again."

"Jake, we need to talk." Rose turned to the officer. "May we leave now?"

"If you'll sign these papers, you can take the children and be on your way."

Everyone was quiet on the ride to the Polanskis' home. A solemn group walked into the house. "Ladies, I'll put Ginny to bed in the guest room, and then we can talk to Jake." Joe headed down the hallway.

Margaret turned to Jake. "Jake, have you had supper?"

"Yes, ma'am; the officer made sure we got something to eat."

"Jake, there are some things I need to tell you, and they're going to be a little confusing. I hope you won't hate me when I'm finished." Rose tried to keep her voice steady.

"I love you, Miss Rose. I won't hate you!" Jake waited for Rose to continue.

"Jake, do you remember the last day your mother and I spoke? The day she left with you and Ginny?"

"Yes."

"I don't know where to start," Rose stopped for a moment. "When I was a teenager, I was very rebellious and I had a baby before I was married—a baby girl." She stifled a sob. "Later, I married my baby's father, and I thought everything would be fine. I was wrong; he turned out to be a very bad man. He took me away from my family and from my baby girl. He did many horrible things." She paused as she collected her thoughts.

"About a year after we were married, he died, and I went back home to find my parents and my baby; but they were gone. My parents took her away to protect her from my husband. I searched for years and could never find a trace of them." She looked Jake directly in the eyes. "Jake, my baby girl is your mother. I am your grandmother."

Jake sucked in his breath. Tears welled up in his eyes and spilled down his cheeks. "You're my grandmother?" He gulped and tried not to cry.

"Yes. I didn't know until the day you brought the note home from school." The dam burst, and Jake ran into his grandmother's arms. He was safe, something he hadn't felt for a long time. She held him until his sobbing subsided. Finally, Jake sat up, wiped his eyes, and smiled. Rose hated to tell him what they had to do. "Jake, our pastor and his wife are going to stay with you and Ginny for a bit this evening, while we go talk to your mother." Rose hesitated for a moment. "I can no longer allow you and Ginny to live the way that you have been living. And, I want to help my daughter, if she will let me."

His smile faded. "She'll be *really* mad. Maybe you should just take us home. I promise not to steal anymore."

"We know why you were stealing; and if we simply take you back, those circumstances are not going to change. We know that she leaves the two of you alone and that there are people who come to the apartment who could be dangerous to you and Ginny. I hope your mom will listen to reason and we can help her. But, regardless, you and Ginny are not living this way anymore."

Jake almost whispered. "If she won't let you help her, who will take care of her if I'm not there?"

"Sweetheart, you are so responsible, but you're a child. You can't take care of your mother with the problems she has." A tear slid down his grandmother's cheek. "Sometimes, a person has to completely hit bottom before they will let anyone help them. We have to pray and ask God to take care of her, Jake." Jake was somewhat relieved, but he was frightened for his mother.

"I owe you and Ginny an apology. I should have done this when I first realized who you were." She looked down. "But, I didn't want to hurt your mother. I kept thinking maybe things would change. You and Ginny suffered because I didn't have the courage to do the right thing." Rose burst into tears again.

"Grand—Miss Rose, it's not your fault." He was too afraid to tell them what had almost happened to Ginny. "What do you want us to call you?"

Rose regained her composure. "Well, what do you want to call me, Jake?"

"Grandma Rose." Jake managed to smile.

"Grandma Rose it is. Jake, I want you to know that I will *never* abandon your mother. She is my daughter, and I love her too much."

"Thank you, Miss—Grandma Rose."

Just then, there was a knock at the door. Joe opened it and greeted their pastor and his wife. It had been a while, but Jake had been to the church and was acquainted with the pastor.

There was a flurry of hugging and instructions for Jake to get some rest. Finally Joe, Margaret, and Rose walked out the door.

Joe pulled into the parking lot, and the three made their way into the building and up the stairs. Rose paused in front of the apartment door, whispered a prayer, and then knocked. No one answered. She knocked several more times before she heard voices and footsteps inside the apartment. "Who's there?" Estelle demanded.

"Estelle, it's Rose and the Polanskis." Rose tried to keep her voice steady.

"Get away from here! I told you I don't want anything to do with you!"

"Please, open the door. We need to talk to you about the children."

"I told you to stay away from them too. Now get the hell out of here!"

"Estelle, it's dark outside. Don't you realize that Jake and Ginny haven't come home?" They heard swearing. A door opened and then shut, and Estelle told someone to get out. A man protested, but finally another door opened and closed.

After what seemed like an eternity, Estelle opened the door. She was thin and unkempt. Rose burst into tears, and Joe had to take over. "Estelle, please let us come in."

"Where the hell are my kids?" She glared at Rose.

"That's what we need to talk to you about. The children are okay, but they were picked up by the police earlier this evening," Joe answered.

"The police? What for?"

"Jake was caught stealing cigarettes from the supermarket. Ginny was with him."

"You're not serious! You're making a big deal about a kid taking a pack of smokes? Come on. Where are my kids?"

Rose managed to calm herself down. "Estelle, he wasn't just taking a pack of cigarettes. He told the storeowner *why* he was stealing. He's trying to help pay the rent and make sure that Ginny has food to eat."

"Oh my God," she laughed nervously, "he's lying. I take care of the bills around here." She couldn't look any of them in the face.

"No Estelle, you don't. We know what you do for a living, and we know that you have a drug problem. Jake has been taking Ginny to work with him for weeks. I suspect he is afraid to leave her here. Please let us help you and the children," Rose pleaded.

"What I do for a living is none of your damned business! And who are you to accuse me of not taking care of my children? You abandoned me when I was a baby!" Estelle shouted.

Rose felt strangely calm. "I didn't abandon you, but we've been over that already. I love you Estelle, and I want to help you. But if you won't accept that help, I can't force you."

"I don't want your help. Now where are my kids?"

"They are safe, and they're not coming back here to live. Until you will allow someone to help you, the children are going to stay with me. You—"

Estelle raged out of control and lunged at Rose. Joe grabbed her and held her arms at her side as she screamed. "I hate you. Do you hear me? I hate you! You are not taking my kids away from me!"

"No, I'm not taking them away from you; but I am going to care for them until you can. We can either draw up guardianship papers for you to sign, or I will go to court and get custody—the choice is yours. If things continue as they are, Jake may end up in jail, and God only knows what could happen to Ginny." Rose shivered thinking about Ginny being in the apartment with Estelle's customers.

"Get out! I'm not signing anything. Now get out!" Estelle screamed and struggled against Joe.

Margaret gently took Rose by the arm, and they walked down the hall. Joe finally let Estelle go. She backed away from him. "Miss Estelle, please let us help you."

"Get out," Estelle hissed at Joe.

By the time Joe turned and left the apartment, Rose and Margaret were already in the car. Rose held her face in her hands and cried all the way back to the Polanskis' home. Joe and Margaret were quiet.

The three walked into the house, making as little noise as possible since Jake and Ginny were both sleeping. They relayed an account of what happened to Pastor Williams and his wife, and they asked for prayer. The small group gathered in a circle and prayed for Estelle, Jake, Ginny, and Rose.

"Rose, why don't you spend the night here? We have plenty of room, and you won't have to wake the children or leave them for the night." Margaret asked. Joe shook his head in agreement.

"Thank you, Margaret. They've been through so much today."

"Let me get the other guest room ready. Come with me; I have a gown for you." Rose followed Margaret down the hall.

Joe and Margaret were quiet the next morning, hoping their three guests could rest as long as possible. Joe left for the market, and Margaret stayed home.

Around 8:00 a.m., Rose walked into the Polanskis' kitchen. "I never sleep this late!"

"You were completely exhausted last night. I'm glad you were able to sleep. Are the children still sleeping?"

"Yes, but Ginny is stirring; I'm sure they'll be up soon. Oh, Margaret, I dread telling Jake that his mother refused our help. You know this is going to be a fight. She is not going to just let me keep the kids."

"Joe and I talked this morning. He is going to call our attorney today and talk to him about the situation. He should be able to help or at least give us some direction."

"Thank you. I honestly have no idea how to handle any of this."

"Rose, it won't be easy. If it goes to court, you are going to have to reveal some very unpleasant things about your daughter. It will be very painful for both of you, but we can no longer turn a deaf ear to the circumstances."

"I know. I called Pauline last night while I waited for you and Joe to pick me up. She said practically the same thing: we have to protect Jake and Ginny." Rose knew what she was doing was right, but it didn't ease the pain she felt for her daughter.

Just then, Jake and Ginny walked into the room. Ginny rubbed her eyes and smiled at Rose. "Grandma Rose!" She ran to her grandmother.

"When she woke up, I told her that you're our grandma. I hope that was okay." Jake looked a little uncertain.

"Jake, that's fine; Ginny looks up to you. The news should have come from you." Rose held Ginny on her lap.

"Well, we have eggs, bacon, and hot biscuits this morning. Is anyone hungry?" Margaret smiled at Rose and the kids.

"I'm starving! Are you hungry Ginny?" Jake smiled at his little sister.

"Yes." Ginny giggled and looked at Rose.

Rose started to put Ginny in a chair. "Let me help you."

"No, you sit there; I can handle this." Jake took his little sister and gently placed her on the chair. Rose smiled. It would take some time for Jake to learn to be a child again. Jake and Ginny had only each other for so long; she would have to be very careful. Caring for them without making Jake feel threatened would be a challenge.

Later that morning, Margaret took Rose and the children downtown to get some things they needed. She had toys for them at the apartment, but both of them had grown, so none of the clothes she'd kept would fit them anymore.

As they opened the door to her apartment, all carrying bags, Rose turned to Margaret. "I just want to thank you and Joe for everything."

"You're welcome. Oh, I can watch over Jake and Ginny when you work. Just let me know what your schedule will be.

"I work in the church office three days a week, but I may need to find a second job. I want to make sure the kids have what they need."

"Before you look for anything else, let me talk to Joe; we may have a solution. I'll call you this evening to see how things are going." Margaret gave all three a quick hug and walked out the door.

Rose turned and looked at Jake and Ginny. "Jake, you can have the spare bedroom and we can move the other twin bed to my room for Ginny. I want you to have a room of your own."

"But Ginny might be scared if I'm not in her room. She's always been with me," Jake frowned.

Rose stood still and thought for a moment. Jake had been Ginny's caretaker and protector for some time. Change wouldn't be easy. "Why don't we let you and Ginny share a room for now?" She walked over to him and put her arm around his shoulder. "I love you both so much. I'm proud of you; you've taken such good care of Ginny. I'm not taking her away from you; I just want you to be able to be a child and have fun. I want you to feel safe and cared for."

Jake was quiet for a minute. "Do you think my mom is okay?"

"Oh Jake, I pray that she is." She didn't know how to say what she needed to say. "You know she may come here and try to take you and Ginny. I love her, Jake, but if she tries to take you, I must stop her." Rose let out a huge sigh. "If I have to, I'll threaten to call the police."

Jake shook off her arm and faced her. "You can't have our mom arrested. You can't do that Miss Rose, I mean Grandma Rose."

"Jake, I really believe that all I will have to do is threaten to call and she will leave. She doesn't want to deal with the police." Jake looked at Rose. He wanted to trust her; he really *needed* to trust her. "Come on, let's get your things put away, and then we can have some lunch. Ginny will probably be ready for a nap after we eat." Rose made sure that the door was locked and the chain was latched.

28

Just as Rose expected, Estelle came that very evening. Jake, wide-eyed and frightened, grabbed Ginny and backed against the wall when Estelle pounded on the apartment door.

"Jake, please take Ginny to your room and shut the door." Rose tried to remain as calm as possible.

"Open this door now! I want my kids!" Estelle screamed and kicked the door.

Rose pressed her face to the door but didn't unlock it. "Estelle, please don't do this. The children aren't going home with you. They are staying here. Please stop beating on the door; you're frightening them." Her hearted pounded.

Estelle let out a stream of profanity that made Rose cringe. She called her mother every filthy name she could think of. Rose swallowed and took a deep breath. "Estelle, if you don't leave right now, I'm going to call the police."

"Go ahead—you have my kids."

"Yes I do, and I'm their grandmother. The police know about the prostitution, and they're also looking into your drug use. They've been watching you. Estelle, please leave. If they come, you'll be arrested." Rose wiped the tears that streamed down her face. Her heart ached for her daughter. She wanted nothing more than to open the door and take her in her arms, but she knew that would be a horrendous mistake.

Estelle uttered a final filthy name at her mother and ran down the stairs.

Rose calmed herself and then opened the bedroom door. "You can come out now. It's okay."

Ginny held Jake's neck in a death grip and hid her face against his chest. She was terrified, and Jake was white as a ghost. "Come here. Let me hold you for a minute." Jake carried Ginny to the couch. They sat down, and Rose held them in her arms for the longest time.

When it was bedtime, Rose knew both children were still upset. "Why don't we all sleep in one room tonight? Jake, you can sleep in your bed, and I can sleep with Ginny. Is that okay?"

"Yes, Ginny would probably like that," he said quietly. He didn't want anyone to know that he was afraid. He wasn't afraid of his mother, but he didn't want her to go jail, and he didn't want her to hurt Grandma Rose.

After they were ready for bed, Rose tucked them in and crawled in bed next to Ginny. Every time Jake closed his eyes, he could hear his mother beating on the door and screaming at Grandma Rose. He lay awake and worried about his mother. He was so afraid that something would happen to her. Finally, he drifted off to sleep.

After leaving Rose's apartment building, Estelle screamed and yelled as she made her way home. She bruised her foot when she kicked a trashcan. Back in her apartment, she fluctuated between rage and crying her heart out. What would she do? If she had an opportunity to grab the kids, Rose and the Polanskis would just call the cops. Cops—that's all she needed. They'd find drugs in her apartment, and she would go to jail.

She paced and threw brushes and combs across the room. That stinking Mark Lawrence—all of this was his fault. She hated him. Now she was going to lose her kids. She sobbed until her breath came in short hiccups.

Estelle knew she didn't take care of the kids. Jake took care of Ginny, and she left them alone all the time. She bought heroin instead of food, and she couldn't come up with the rent half the time. Jake had been caught stealing while trying to take care of her and Ginny. And the men—they came and went at all hours. That damned Bob had tried to hurt Ginny. How could she have known he was that kind of pervert? He had kids!

"No more customers tonight," she whispered as she headed for her bedroom. She needed a fix, and she needed it bad.

The next morning, Rose got out of bed carefully, trying not to wake Ginny. Jake's breathing was deep and steady. She left the door ajar just a crack and went to the kitchen to make coffee. Sitting at the kitchen table, she enjoyed her coffee, read some scripture, and prayed.

The kids slept a little later than usual, probably because they were physically and emotionally exhausted. The phone rang, and she grabbed the receiver before the noise woke them. "Hello?"

"Hi Rose, it's Margaret. Joe and I would like to talk to you about some things. Can you and the children drop by the market around noon so we can talk and have lunch? We'll close the market for an hour or so." Margaret sounded excited and barely took a breath.

"Certainly; I'm sure the kids would like that. Margaret, I want to tell you this before the children wake up. Estelle came to the door last night, and it was horrible. She beat and kicked the door. I was afraid a neighbor would call the police when she screamed and cursed at me. Fortunately, they didn't. I finally had to threaten to call them to get her to leave."

"Oh Rose, I think we all knew that would happen. And she may come back, so you need to be very careful. I don't want you to walk over here; I'll have Joe pick you up just before noon."

"Thank you. We'll see you at noon." Rose hung up the receiver.

When the kids woke up around 9:00 a.m., Rose had breakfast ready, and they each took a bath and got dressed for the day.

"Mrs. Polanski called and invited us to lunch today. Mr. Polanski is going to pick us up!"

"Okay." Jake had been quiet all morning.

"Jake, I know this is horrible for you. Are you okay?"

"Sure, I'm okay." But he wasn't. All he could think about was his mom.

Just before noon, Rose and the kids went downstairs to watch for Joe. He drove up just as they walked out the front door. The very first thing he noticed was the look on Jake's face. The young man couldn't hide the worry or sadness that gripped his heart.

"Oh come in! Joe, would you put the 'Closed for Lunch' sign out and lock the door, please?" Margaret hugged Rose, Jake, and Ginny. "Let's go upstairs. Lunch is ready!"

The adults chatted as they enjoyed fried chicken, potato salad, baked beans, and chocolate cake for dessert. Ginny ate every bite on her plate, but Jake was distracted and picked at his food.

"Jake, sweetheart, aren't you hungry?" Rose worried.

"No. I guess I'm still full from breakfast." Jake mumbled and looked down.

"Well, I'll just pack up the leftovers and send them home with you. You can eat later when you're hungry. Jake, would you mind taking Ginny to the playroom for a bit?" Margaret had transformed one of the bedrooms into a playroom when Ginny started coming to work with Jake.

"Sure." Jake got up and took Ginny's hand. "Let's go. We can build something with your blocks." Ginny skipped alongside her brother as they went to play.

Joe and Margaret looked at each other, then at Rose. "We talked and prayed for quite some time last night, and there are some things that we would like to discuss with you," Margaret paused. "First of all, we really need someone else to help here at the market a few days a week. Would you be interested?"

"Oh, I would. I want to make sure that I have enough money to take care of the children."

"Well, the second thing is the apartment." Rose looked a little puzzled. "The couple who owned the market before we did had a family, so the apartment here has three bedrooms plus a room that could be used as a sitting room or another bedroom. We would like to offer to rent it to you. The utilities would be included in the rent, and the rent would be fair and affordable."

"I don't know what to say! This apartment is so much bigger than mine. And with the balcony and little yard in the back, it would be perfect for Jake and Ginny! I'll need to talk to Pauline though. She's been in California for so long, but I did sublet the apartment from her. We are on a month-to-month lease, so if she agrees, I'd be thrilled to rent the apartment!"

"You can bring whatever furnishings you want, and we can put what you don't need in storage in the basement," Joe added.

Joe stood up. "Rose, there's one more thing. You know Margaret and I were never blessed with children of our own. Jake has been so special to us, and little Ginny too. We know that he has had some problems at school." He hesitated for a moment, "Margaret and I would like to pay tuition for Jake and Ginny both to go to a private school in the fall. It would be a fresh start for them."

Rose gulped as tears streamed down her face. "I don't know how to thank you!"

"Knowing that those two children are being taken care of is all the thanks we need." Margaret put her arm around her friend.

"We don't have long before school starts. I need to have guardianship or custody by then."

"Joe already spoke to our attorney, and he's drawing up papers now. If Estelle won't sign the papers, he is prepared to go to court. We will take care of his fee."

Rose broke down and cried. "This will be so hard. I don't want to take the children from her; I just want them to be safe and cared for."

"We'll be here by your side through it all." Margaret hugged her. "The attorney is going to her apartment to try to discuss the situation with her tomorrow."

"Oh God! She is going to be so angry!" Rose cried.

"We know. Why don't you talk to Pauline this evening? We can wait until the attorney talks to Estelle before we tell Jake about any of this." Margaret's voice was soothing.

Mr. Shelton, the Polanskis' attorney, pulled into a parking space in front of Estelle's building and took a deep breath. The building was certainly shabby—those poor kids. He didn't look forward to meeting with their mother. He whispered a prayer, as it was sure to be difficult.

Estelle crawled out of bed when the persistent knocking wouldn't stop. She wasn't expecting anyone; it was too early. "Who is it?" she snarled.

"I need to discuss a matter with you regarding your children."

Shelton was startled when Estelle flung the door open and slammed it against the wall. "What the hell do you want?"

He cleared his throat. "Ben Shelton. I'm an attorney, Mrs.—is it Shannon or Bradley?"

"Shannon," Estelle hissed.

"Mrs. Shannon, I represent your mother, Rose Baker. Are you aware that your children were held at the police station the other day when Jake was caught stealing, and they are now with your mother?"

At the mention of her mother, Estelle screamed a string of threats and filthy names that made Mr. Shelton blush. He lost patience and interrupted her tirade. "Look, I'm not going to dance around with you. I'm sorry things have come to this point in your life, but the children are the first priority. I am preparing paperwork to petition the court to appoint Rose Baker as guardian for the children until such time as you are able to care for them. You can sign guardianship over to Rose, or we can go to court."

"Get the hell out of here!" Estelle shrieked as she tried to close the door.

Mr. Shelton put his weight against the door and held it open. "Mrs. Shannon, please make it easy on yourself and the children; here's my card. The paperwork will be ready on Tuesday of next week. Come in at 2:00 p.m., and we can take care of it quickly. If we go to court, you won't win, and you may lose custody of your children permanently. Think about it." He stepped back and walked away.

Estelle stood in the open doorway staring at the business card. She knew she would never win in court. First of all, she couldn't afford an attorney. Second, she didn't even have a real job; it wouldn't be hard to prove that she was a prostitute. And the drugs? They could probably prove that too.

She had no choice; she would have to sign the papers. Deep inside, she knew it was the right thing to do for Jake and Ginny. As much as she wanted to hate Rose, she knew the woman loved the children and would take good care of them, but she couldn't think about it anymore. The only things she could think about right now were to get high and get ready for tonight.

By the weekend, Jake's mood had not improved. He wasn't sleeping well, and he thought about his mom constantly. He knew she couldn't take care of herself right now. What if one of those jerks hurt her? What if she overdosed and no one was there? He hated just about everything she did, but he still loved his mom. He was more fortunate than Ginny; he had good memories of his mom. She had been a great mom—a good person. It was hard to understand how all of this happened.

He had to know if she was okay. Earlier, he had told Grandma Rose that Ginny wanted to stay with her that night. Rose was a little surprised in light of Jake being so protective of his little sister, and it was strange that he would relinquish her into anyone's care so soon. But, she took it as a positive step.

Jake waited until he was sure Grandma Rose and Ginny were sleeping soundly. He'd managed to pry the bedroom window that afternoon and loosened it up to sneak out later. He'd also made sure the fire escape stairs were down. The stairs were squeaky, and he prayed no one would hear. Listening one more time for any sound from his grandmother's room, he carefully opened the window and climbed out onto the fire escape.

Finally, he jumped the few feet to the ground and took off running in the direction of his mom's apartment building. He sprinted just about all the way there and was out of breath when he reached the front door of the building. Stopping just inside the door, he took a couple of minutes to catch his breath.

He knew his mom probably had company, but he didn't care. He had to know she was okay. Finally he gathered his courage and started up the stairway.

He stopped in front of the apartment door. She was going to be mad at him for getting caught copping smokes. He knocked and knocked, trying not to wake the other tenants. Finally, he heard footsteps. "Who is it?" Her voice was gruff.

"Mom, it's Jake."

The door seemed to fly open. He saw the brief smile, and then she grabbed his arm and dragged him inside. "What are you doing here? Does Rose know you're gone?" She cursed. "Of course she doesn't; it's the middle of the night." Her words stung.

"I missed you. I wanted to know if you were okay."

She pulled him to her and hugged him. He thought he felt tears on her face. "Jake, you can't stay. You have to go back."

"Mom, I love Grandma Rose, but you need me. I want to be here with you."

She turned away for a moment and wiped her face. Just then a man called to her from the bedroom. "I'll be there in a minute!" she yelled.

"Look, you need to go back. You can't stay here right now." She tried to calm her voice.

"You're our mom; we want to be with you." She could see tears in Jake's eyes.

"Damn it, you can't right now! Now go back to Rose." She choked back tears.

"No, I'm staying here!" he yelled.

"No, you're not. I'm signing papers next week to let Rose have you guys for a while—you know, until I can get back on my feet."

"You can't get back on your feet if you won't let anyone help you. You don't want us. Just admit it—you don't want us!" he screamed in her face.

It took everything in her, but she did it—she slapped him across the face. "I said get out of here and go back to Rose!"

He sucked in his breath and stared at her for a moment. "I hate you!" He turned and ran down the hallway.

For a moment, Estelle stood in the doorway and watched him go. Then, she collapsed onto the floor and began to wail and sob. Her customer came out of the bedroom. "You're nuts; I'm outta here. You think you're gettin' paid? You can forget it." He stepped over her and left.

Estelle didn't know how long she lay in a heap on the floor and cried. Jake and Ginny didn't deserve to be dragged through her nightmare anymore. She knew what she had done was best for them, but her heart was shattered. She finally shut the door and went to her room, pulling her stash from under the bed. She needed to sleep—to sleep and never wake up. She wanted to die.

Jake's pain was more intense than anything he'd ever experienced. He ran out of his mom's apartment building sobbing. By the time he made it to the street, he forced himself to stop crying. No one would ever make him cry again. His tears were replaced by a blinding rage, and he took it out on the first storefront he came to. He didn't remember picking up the brick; but the next thing he knew, he was standing, dazed, in front of a broken window, and there were sirens in the distance.

He shook his head. Run—he knew he had to run. He took off at full speed down the alley until a cop car pulled into the other end of the alley. Jake turned on a dime and ran back the direction he'd come from, but it was too late. Another cop blocked that end of the alley. The officers stepped out of their cars. "Come on son, take it easy. We don't want to hurt you." It was the same cop who had arrested Jake at the supermarket. He had his hand on his holster. "Do you have a weapon?"

Jake gave up—there was nowhere to run. "No, sir; I don't have a weapon."

"Put your hands up." The cop was by his side in an instant, pulling first one arm and then other behind him. He felt the cold metal handcuffs snap into place.

29

Less than an hour after Jake climbed out of his bedroom window, Rose sat straight up in bed. She was wide awake, and she knew something was wrong. Careful not to wake Ginny, she got out of bed, put on her robe, and went to Jake's room. The door creaked as she opened it. Whispering a prayer that this feeling had nothing to do with him, she walked over to Jake's bed. He was turned away from her, so she went to the other side. "Oh God, no!" There were only pillows under his blanket.

Running barefoot down the hall to the living room, she grabbed the phone and called Joe and Margaret. She heard a sleepy hello when Joe answered.

"Joe, I'm sorry to call you so late, but Jake is gone!" she cried.

"Gone?"

"I woke up and went in to check on him, but he's not in his bed. He's nowhere in the apartment. I know he's gone to see his mother!" she cried. "What should I do?"

She could hear Margaret in the background as Joe answered. "Rose, call the police and tell them what's happened. We're getting up right now, and we'll be on our way in just a few minutes."

Rose said goodbye and immediately called the police. The dispatcher assured her they would be on the lookout for Jake. If they found him, they would take him to the station and call her.

Rose made coffee as she waited for Joe and Margaret. Within minutes, there was a soft knock at the door. She opened the door and collapsed in Margaret's arms. They stood in the doorway for several minutes while Rose cried.

"I'm sorry." Rose said as she wiped her eyes.

"You have nothing to apologize for." Margaret kissed her friend on the cheek.

"If I don't hear from the police soon," Rose replied, "I would like to go to Estelle's apartment and see if he's there." Just then, the phone rang.

Rose ran to answer it. "Hello?" She listened. "Oh thank God. Is he okay?" The color drained from her face as she listened to the officer. "He did what? Yes, I'll be right there."

She turned to Joe and Margaret. "Jake's not hurt, at least not physically. Someone reported a burglary near Estelle's building, and the police found Jake standing on the sidewalk in front of a shattered store window. He ran from the police, but they caught him. He's at the police station right now."

"Margaret will stay with Ginny. Rose, I'll take you to get Jake." Joe leaned over and kissed his wife on the cheek.

Rose quickly grabbed her bag, and they rushed out the door.

"Joe, do you really believe Jake tried to break into a store?"

"Rose, I can't imagine it, but let's wait and see what the officer has to say."

They were silent for the remainder of the ride. Rose didn't wait for Joe to open her door after he parked the car. She jumped out and practically ran into the police station, straight to the front desk. "My name is Rose Baker. Jake Shannon is my grandson. I understand you are holding him."

"Yes. If you'll have a seat, an officer will be with you in a few minutes." The officer looked down at his paperwork again.

"Thank you." Rose and Joe went over to a row of chairs against the wall.

Almost an hour later, with her patience waning, Rose went back to the desk. "How much longer do we have to wait before someone tells us anything? I want to see my grandson. He is a child for heaven's sake," she sniffled.

"Rose," Joe walked over, "why don't you have a seat and let me talk to the officer."

Joe spoke quietly. "Officer, can you tell us anything? As she said, Jake is just a boy, and he's been through some really tough times lately."

The officer glanced at Rose and then whispered to Joe.

"Thank you," Joe replied before walking back to Rose. "I think they are trying to work something out with the store owner. My guess is they are trying to convince him not to file charges."

"Charges? Oh my God, they might put him in jail?" She covered her face and cried.

Joe felt a little awkward and whispered a prayer.

About fifteen minutes later, Officer Dean walked out. "Mrs. Baker, Mr. Polanski? I wish I could say it's nice to see you. Come on back and we can talk."

Rose couldn't speak. She and Joe followed Officer Dean down the hall to an office.

"Mrs. Baker, can you tell me how this all started?"

"Jake has been so worried about his mother. I'm sure he sneaked out to check on her. When I woke up and found him gone, I called the police," Rose answered.

"Well, that's what I suspected." He sighed and then continued. "I've been talking to the arresting officer, who is also familiar with Jake's situation, and I've talked to the storeowner. When the arresting officer first spotted Jake, he wasn't trying to go in through the broken window; he was just standing there. When they caught up to him, it was obvious that he'd been crying, and he seemed a little dazed. I can tell you, the owner is extremely angry, but we gave him a little background on Jake."

Tears streamed down Rose's cheeks. What on earth happened when Jake found his mother?

The officer continued. "What we've managed to do is this: the storeowner will not file any charges if the damages are paid for."

"Oh thank God," Rose whispered.

"Officer, please ask him to contact me, and I will take care of the damages."

"Joe, you can't do that. I'll manage. You and Margaret have done too much already."

"Rose, there's no discussion. We will take care of it."

"Thank you."

"Mr. Polanski, then why don't you come with me? You and the owner can talk and make arrangements. I'm sure he'll have some costs in a day or so." He turned to Rose. "Mrs. Baker, I'll go get Jake."

About ten minutes later, the door opened slowly, and Jake walked in. Officer Dean nodded to Rose, closed the door, and left them alone.

Jake wouldn't look at her. He clenched his jaw and struggled not to cry.

Rose held her emotions in check and was careful not to move quickly. "Jake, I'm so happy to see you."

He stood just inside the room and didn't answer her.

"Jake, are you okay?" Her voice was quiet and calm.

"Okay?" he whispered as he glared at her. That's when she saw the red handprint on the other side of his face. "Mom doesn't want us anymore." He choked back a sob, refusing to cry.

"Jake, you know that isn't true. She's not herself right now. She loves you and Ginny—you know she does."

His voice was louder with each word. "She told me to get out and go back to you! She's going to sign some papers and give us to you." He glared at Rose. "She doesn't want us! I hate her!" Jake said, enunciating each word.

Shaken by the cold, hard look in his eyes, Rose fought to maintain her composure.

As Joe walked back into the room, Rose gave him a warning look. He noticed the handprint on Jake's face, but thought it best not to ask what happened. "We're finished here. Are we ready to go?"

"Yes, we're ready," Rose answered quietly.

They all walked to the car and drove home without so much as a word. Joe walked in first when they got back to the apartment. When Margaret saw Jake, Joe shook his head and whispered, asking her not to question the boy.

She gasped when she saw Jake's face. The handprint was fading but still visible. The boy couldn't hide his pain and anger. "Jake, I'm so glad you're here," Margaret said quietly.

"Thanks, me too," he mumbled and then turned to Rose. "May I go to bed now?"

"Yes, Jake, you may."

He went to his room and closed the door behind him.

Rose quietly told Joe and Margaret what happened when she first talked to Jake.

"His heart is broken, and he's covering it up with anger," Margaret whispered.

"I really believe that Estelle is trying to do what's best for Jake and Ginny. She knows she can't take care of them right now." A tear slid down Rose's face.

"She shouldn't have slapped him, Rose." Joe couldn't hide his anger.

"I realize that, but we have to remember that she is a drug addict, and her life is in complete shambles right now. I believe she took drastic measures to make Jake come back to me." Rose continued, "She knows she can't take care of the children in her condition."

"You may be right, but he is hurt beyond words, and he's angry. That's not a good combination for anyone, especially a boy his age. Rose, you heard that officer; he broke that window in a fit of rage and seemed dazed when they caught him," Joe replied.

"For longer than I care to think about, Jake has taken on the responsibility of caring not only for Ginny, but for his mother. Pauline talked about Estelle all the time; and when I first met Estelle, she was nothing like she is now. Pauline has shared some things with me in confidence. Estelle has been through hell." Rose hesitated, "You and Margaret can't imagine."

"I'm sorry, Rose." Joe looked sheepish. "I have to remember that not only are these your grandchildren, but Estelle is also your daughter."

"Yes, and I have no intention of losing her. I know God is faithful. I don't know how He will take care of this, but I know He will—somehow, He will."

As the weeks passed, it seemed that Jake recovered from the confrontation with his mother; but Rose knew better. He was obedient and pleasant, but he was much quieter than he'd ever been before. He also stopped asking about his mother.

The children attended the mid-week service, Sunday school, and Sunday service with Rose every week. Ginny absolutely loved it! Jake had always enjoyed going to church with her; but while he never complained, he didn't seem quite as enthusiastic as he'd been before.

It was almost time for school to start. Rose and Estelle had signed the guardianship papers at separate times, as the attorney put it, to avoid an uncomfortable situation.

Pauline thought it was a wonderful idea for Rose and the children to move into the apartment over Polanski's Market. Jake agreed, without an argument, that Ginny should have a room of her own.

The move went well, and Margaret helped Rose get everything put away. They hung pictures and new drapes. Rose was thrilled with all the space. The bathroom was larger, and the kitchen was huge compared to the one in the old apartment. A small table and chairs fit in one corner of the kitchen. There was a formal dining room that was already furnished with a pretty cherry-wood table, china cabinet, and buffet. There were cabinets galore and plenty of closet space.

Everything in Ginny's room was frilly and pink. Several baby dolls and teddy bears shared her bed. Joe paid a man in the neighborhood to build a toy box and a dollhouse for her.

Jake's room was done in blue. He had a desk, chair, and bookcase that matched his bed. There was a bin in his closet with two footballs, baseballs, gloves, a couple of bats, and army men. The most excitement anyone had seen from him in weeks was the morning he found the shiny new bicycle that Joe bought for him.

There was also an extra bedroom that was used as a sitting room. Rose stood in the doorway every single day and prayed that one day her daughter would occupy that room.

Rose adjusted her schedule, working at the church two days a week and at the market the other three. She had Saturdays off, and the market was closed on Sundays.

Margaret enjoyed caring for Ginny while Rose worked. She told everyone she had retired. To keep Jake occupied, he still worked a few hours at the market.

Jake and Ginny were enrolled in parochial school, and as promised, Joe and Margaret paid their tuition. Jake met a couple of boys who lived near the market and went to the same school that he and Ginny would attend.

Joe, Margaret, and Rose took time every day to pray for Estelle and the children, and Rose and Pauline prayed together on the phone at least once a week.

They hadn't heard a word from Estelle—no visits or phone calls to check on the children.

Estelle existed day to day, in a drug-induced stupor, servicing Mark's lower echelon customers. When she wasn't working or trying to score, she slept. It was easier to sleep than to think; thinking was dangerous at this point.

Stan grew tired of her offering herself in exchange for heroin when she was short on money. He sent her away empty handed if she didn't have cash. Her apartment wasn't far from the West Bottoms, one of Kansas City's industrial areas, that was no stranger to prostitution. Turning a few tricks in the alleys with guys who frequented the neighboring bars helped support her daily habit. She had to be careful not to infringe on anyone's territory; and as always, she had to make sure Mark didn't catch her.

Estelle lost more weight and no longer bathed every day. Her hair was often dirty and tangled, and wearing the same clothes for days became par. It was a vicious cycle. She needed more money every day, but she had lost customers because of her appearance. There were a few, however, who didn't care how she looked or smelled.

She was spiraling downward and couldn't stop the fall.

30

Jake seemed to like his new school and did well in every subject. He made friends who didn't know about his mother. As a matter of fact, he told his new friends that he and Ginny's parents were dead, and that's why they lived with their grandmother.

Late one afternoon, while he and his buddies were riding bikes, Jake realized they had ventured too close to his mom's apartment. He was nervous and told the guys he needed to head back home. Just then, he saw her. His stomach churned, and he gasped. His mom walked into an alley with a man, looking worse than he'd ever seen her.

"Guys, look at the hooker going in the alley with that guy. He must be desperate. Hey man, put a bag over her head!" Jimmy shouted and laughed. Tommy joined in.

"Shut up." Jake fought to control his rage.

"What's your problem?" Jimmy asked.

"You don't know her. Why do you want to say stuff like that about someone you don't even know?" Jake yelled in his face.

"That your momma or something?" Jimmy laughed louder.

Jake snapped. His head roared, and his mind went blank. The next thing he was consciously aware of was two of his friends pulling him off Jimmy. He tasted blood, but he didn't know if it was his or not. His adrenaline was pumping, and he didn't feel any pain. Jimmy was on the ground crying, as blood spurted from his nose. The kid's lip was bleeding, and there was a cut on his head.

"Jake, what's wrong with you? You trying to kill him?" Tommy shouted.

"Stay away from me!" Jake shouted as he jumped on his bike.

"Stay away from you? You stay away from us! You're crazy!" Tommy yelled as Jake took off down the street.

Mike jumped on his bike. "Where are you going?" Tommy demanded.

"Jake's my friend; something must be wrong for him to act like that."

"I thought Jimmy was your friend too."

"Yeah, well Jimmy has a smart mouth." Mike took off after Jake.

When he had almost caught up to Jake, he yelled, "Hey man, wait up!"

"I said stay away from me!" Jake kept going.

"Jake, come on, I wasn't laughing. Jimmy is a jerk."

Jake finally stopped and stood, straddling his bike.

"Look, I don't know what's going on, but I'm your friend. You can talk to me if you need to." Mike could see tears forming in Jake's eyes, but his friend refused to cry.

"I can't talk to anyone."

Mike was a year older than Jake. He was a good kid and was more level-headed than the other guys they hung around with. "If you need to, you can. You know, we all have secrets. You want to know mine?"

"I can guarantee you it's nothing compared to mine," Jake answered.

"I want to be a priest," Mike said quietly.

"A priest? You're kidding!" Jake stared at his friend.

"Nope, I'm not. I haven't said anything to the other guys. They'll just laugh and make jokes, but it's true. I want to give my whole life to God and help people."

The conversation had a calming effect on Jake. His breathing gradually returned to normal, and the pounding in his head was gone. "Wow, that's, well, I guess that's kind of cool. My great-grandparents were Catholic. They died when I was a baby, so I don't remember them. My mom said they were good people, and they loved us."

"Come on, I'll race you back to Polanski's." Mike jumped on his bike and took off. Jake was right behind him.

The bikes kicked up dust as the boys skidded to a stop in front of the market. "Jake, listen, you should probably talk to your grandmother about what happened today."

"Tell Grandma Rose?"

"Jimmy's mom will call her before the night's over. It'll be better if you tell her first. Trust me; Jimmy's mom *will* call."

"Man. I guess you're right. I better tell her first."

"Hey, I'll see you tomorrow." Mike turned his bike around and headed home.

Jake took his time as he headed to put his bike away. "Jake, is that you?" Rose heard the bell when the door opened.

"Yeah, it's me. I'm just putting my bike away."

"Can you help me close things up?"

"Sure, I'll be right there." Jake's stomach was in knots. He hurried to the storeroom and then went to face his grandmother.

Jake pulled the carts inside, put the produce in the cooler, and swept up. Rose straightened the store, completed the bookkeeping for the day, and put the money from the cash register in the small office safe. "Okay, that does it. Are you ready for dinner?"

"Yeah. I'm starving."

"Let's go!"

"Actually, uh, Grandma Rose, I need to talk to you about something."

"Can we talk upstairs? I'm sure Margaret is ready to head home."

"Sure." He was relieved.

They locked up and headed upstairs to their apartment. Margaret said her goodbyes and left for home. Rose pulled a meatloaf from the refrigerator and started washing potatoes for baking. "Jake, do you want to talk now while I'm getting dinner ready? Ginny's playing in her room."

"Okay." He put his hands in his pockets, looked down, and shuffled his feet.

"Are you okay?"

"Yeah, well, I don't know." He let his breath out in a huge sigh.

Rose stopped working on dinner and washed her hands. "Let's sit down."

Jake's feet felt as if they were glued to the floor, but he managed to walk over and sit down at the kitchen table.

"Jake, honey, what's bothering you?"

"Well, this afternoon the guys and I were riding our bikes. We wound up in my old neighborhood." He stopped.

Rose held her breath.

"I, uh, we saw a woman going into an alley with a guy from one of the bars. It was, uh ..." It sounded like he choked, but he didn't cry.

She waited, her heart pounding. She knew what he was about to say.

Jake took a deep breath and continued. "It was my mom. Jimmy said something really nasty about her and laughed. At first, I just told him to shut up." Jake looked at the floor. "But he kept on. He laughed and asked why I cared; he said, '*Is that your mom or something?*'"

"Oh Jake, people can be so cruel."

"I don't know what happened. I don't remember punching him, but the next thing I knew, Tommy and Mike were pulling me off of him. He was bleeding. His mom will probably call you." He hung his head.

"He shouldn't have said those things about your mother." Rose tried to control the anger in her voice.

"He didn't know it really *was* my mom. I told the kids at my new school that my parents are both dead. That's why we live with you." He looked at the floor again.

"Oh Jake, I had no idea," Rose whispered.

"I'll understand if you take away privileges."

Rose walked over and put her arms around Jake. "Right now, I don't know how we will deal with this." She took his face in her hands and looked directly in his eyes. "I want you to know that sticking up for your mother was not wrong. I wish you hadn't hit the boy, but telling him not to say those things was right. You are holding a lot of pain inside; and I think today, it boiled over. Believe me, I understand that."

"You do?"

"It may be hard for you to imagine, but I used to be a very angry young woman. My husband was a cruel, vicious man. You know I told you that when he died and I was finally free to go home, I found that my parents and my baby were gone. I searched and couldn't find a trace of them. I became very bitter and angry, and I hated just about everything and everyone. My temper was often out of control."

"Did you fight?"

"Actually I did once, but I'm not proud of it. My anger usually came out in words."

"But you're so nice now! What happened?"

"Let me put the meatloaf and potatoes in the oven, and I'll tell you." Rose hurried to finish dinner and quickly checked on Ginny.

Just as she sat back down to talk to Jake, the telephone rang. "Hello? Yes, this is Jake's grandmother. My name is Rose Baker." She paused and listened. Jake watched her clinch her jaw. "Yes, Jake told me exactly what happened." Again she listened, and her face turned red. "Are his injuries serious? Okay. Well thank you for the advice, but I suggest that you teach your son not to say cruel things about people who are less fortunate." Rose was quiet again. She pursed her lips. "That suits me just fine. I prefer that my grandson not associate with young men who hurl insults and make fun of people they know nothing about." Her voice was louder with each word; then she took a deep breath. "I'm glad your son is okay. Thank you for calling. Goodbye!" She slammed the receiver down.

"Is Jimmy okay?"

"Yes. He had a bloody nose and lip and a scrape on his head. I'm sure his pride suffered a little too." Jake watched as she worked to calm herself. "It seems we keep getting interrupted. Why don't you check on Ginny, and I'll finish dinner. We can finish our conversation after Ginny is in bed, okay?"

"Okay."

After dinner, Rose gave Ginny a bath and got her ready for bed. They read scriptures and stories as they did every night. Rose read to Ginny until her little eyes were heavy. "Okay, little princess, it's time to tuck you in and let you go to sleep." Ginny smiled as her grandmother kissed her on the cheek. She was asleep before Rose left the room.

Rose knocked on Jake's door. "Are you ready to finish our conversation?"

Jake opened his door. "Sure."

"Let's go in the kitchen, and I'll make a cup of tea. Would you like some milk and cookies?"

"Yes, thank you." Jake was subdued. He wasn't certain if and how he would be punished for fighting.

Rose hurried around the kitchen. Once she had her tea, she poured a glass of cold milk for Jake and grabbed the cookie jar. She ate an oatmeal cookie and sipped her tea. "Well, I guess I'll start at the beginning." She told him about lying to her parents, sneaking out, and having her baby girl, making sure she only told the details that were appropriate for her grandson to hear. Jake held on to every word as his grandmother spoke.

"He refused to let me go home to get my baby girl. I wasn't even allowed to write to my parents. They had no idea what happened to me. I did sneak a letter to them once, but they may have already left Chicago by then. I don't know. They were so frightened that my husband would actually try to sell the baby—I know that's why they finally moved away with her."

She stopped for a minute and took a breath. "Losing your mother was the worst thing that ever happened to me. My husband forced me into a life very similar to the one that Jerry pushed your mother into."

Jake's eyes were huge. "You were a prostitute?"

"Against my will, but yes—I was." She stopped for a minute. "Even that was nothing compared to losing your mother. My heart was broken—nothing else mattered." She sighed before continuing. "Every day I didn't find a trace of my parents or my baby, I became more angry and bitter."

A tear slid down her cheek. "There was a time when I blamed my parents, and I hated them—at least I tried to. I was so angry with them, but they only tried to protect little Anna—that's what I named your mother."

"So, they changed her name to Estelle?"

"Yes."

"What happened when you couldn't find them?"

"I was seventeen and didn't really know what to do. I talked to a couple of my parents' friends, but they knew nothing. If they did, they wouldn't tell me. I'm sure they knew all about Timothy Baker."

"Was that your husband's name?"

"Yes. Anyway, I had taken all of the money that we had after Timothy was killed, so I got a small apartment and kept searching. Finally, I ran out of money. I went to work at a diner and met a man who seemed to be so nice and caring." Tears welled up in her eyes again. "He wasn't; I guess he was like Jerry. He gained my trust, and he told me that I was beautiful and could be a model for a department store. I believed him and quit my job. When it was too late, I realized what he was. I thought I would never get away from him."

"How *did* you get away?"

"Well, it was about fifteen years ago, and I was so desperate. One night, when I was working, I walked past this huge tent. There were a lot of people going in, and they all looked so happy. I asked one lady what was going on, and she told me it was a revival meeting. She was so kind and genuine. She even asked me to come inside with her." Tears began to stream down her face.

"I don't know why, but I did. I felt so out of place, dressed the way I was, but she didn't seem to notice. We found a seat, and the preacher started his message. It was wonderful. Like a lot of kids, I hadn't paid much attention to Bible stories when I was growing up. That night, the minister preached about the woman taken in adultery. Do you know that story?"

"Yes, Jesus didn't want them to stone her. He forgave her."

"That's right. As I listened, tears ran down my face. I sobbed and couldn't stop. For the first time since I had married Timothy and my nightmare started, I felt hope. Somehow, inside, I knew that if Jesus him-self didn't judge her and forgave her, there was hope for me too."

Jake leaned forward with his chin in his hands.

"When the preacher gave the altar call, the lady who had invited me in asked if I wanted to receive Jesus. She said she would go forward with me if I wanted to. Before I could even think, I said yes. She took my hand and led me to the front." Rose cried softly for a moment.

"She and another lady led me in a prayer of salvation. I repented and accepted Jesus as my Lord and Savior that night."

"What happened next? Did you have to go back to the streets?"

"No. As we talked at the altar, I told her my story. She asked me if I wanted to go to Kansas City and stay with her until I could get on my feet. She said that I needed time to heal in a safe place. I felt so clean and new; I couldn't stand the thought of going back on the streets, so I said yes. I stayed in her hotel room that night, and we took a train to Kansas City the next morning."

"Who was she?" Jake asked.

"It was Miss Pauline, Jake."

"Miss Pauline?" Jake whispered.

"Yes, and she had her work cut out for her; I didn't change over-night. While I never wanted to go back to the streets, I still held so much anger and bitterness inside. She was a very patient teacher. She taught me scriptures and prayed with me daily. If I had questions that she couldn't answer, she found the answer." Rose watched his face. "Jake, it took time for me to let go of the pain that made me so angry and bitter, and I had to learn to control my temper. It wasn't easy, but it was worth it. After finishing high school, I finally got my own place and the job at the church office."

"So you don't get angry anymore?"

"Oh, I get angry. I'm not perfect, and I still make mistakes. But I've learned to control my actions and my words."

"So that's why you and Miss Pauline are such good friends?"

"We're more than friends; she's like a mother to me."

"Yeah, she was like a grandmother to me before she had to leave. I miss her."

"I miss her too." They were both quiet for several minutes. "Jake, I'm sorry about what happened today. Seeing your mother that way had to be very painful, and I know it hurts to lose friends too."

Jake didn't want to think about his mother. "Well, I didn't lose all my friends. Mike came after me. He's still my friend. He's the one who told me to tell you about what happened today."

"He did?"

"He wants to be a priest so he can help people. The other guys don't know yet. They'd just laugh and make jokes."

"That's wonderful, Jake. Mike sounds like a good friend." Rose smiled, realizing that God was bringing key people into Jake's life. "One reason I wanted to share my story with you was to let you know there is always hope. I'll never give up on your mother, and I hope you won't either."

Jake quickly changed the subject. "So what's my punishment for fighting?"

"I'm not so sure that's what you need in light of the circumstances. But I do have an idea. I'll write down some scripture passages for you, and you can read about a couple of men in the Bible—Paul for one, before and after his encounter with Jesus. And then there was Peter, who had a bit of a temper problem. I think you'll be quite surprised at what they went through. How does that sound?"

"Okay. I can do that. Should I start tonight?"

"No, it's getting late; you can start tomorrow. Why don't you brush your teeth and get ready for bed?" Jake headed for the bathroom as Rose rinsed their snack dishes.

She felt she had made some progress with Jake, but she knew there were still more battles ahead. He still avoided talking about his mother.

The revelation that Estelle was actually turning tricks made Rose worry more than ever. She had to check on her daughter, whether she was welcome or not.

Jake said goodnight as he went to his room. Since it wasn't too late in California, Rose picked up the phone and called Pauline. They talked and prayed together for some time. Rose prayed her daughter would find the same forgiveness she had found.

31

The weekend had been uneventful, but Rose had taken the time to tell Joe and Margaret about Jake's fight.

Monday afternoon, she asked if she could take an hour or so to run an errand. The store wasn't busy, so Joe told her to go ahead. She went upstairs and told Margaret that she was leaving for a short time, and then she headed for Estelle's apartment.

It was a beautiful day, but the closer she came to Estelle's apartment building, the more her nerves were on edge. Not sure what she would face, she whispered a prayer as she walked.

About a block before she reached Estelle's place, Rose saw Estelle standing on the corner outside a bar. Rose felt sick to her stomach as she watched her daughter pace. Estelle's clothes were rumpled and hung on her stick-thin body. Her hair was dull and messy. Terrifying memories flooded Rose's consciousness, and fear for her daughter threatened to overwhelm her.

"God, please help me." She took a deep breath and started across the street.

Rose was just about ten feet away when Estelle looked up and saw her mother. Estelle threw her cigarette on the ground and ran.

"Estelle, stop, please! I just want to talk to you!" But Estelle just kept running. Rose hurried after her as Estelle disappeared inside her apartment building and sprinted up the stairs.

Rose ran inside after her. By the time Rose reached the apartment, Estelle was inside with the door locked. She knocked.

"Go away!" Estelle shouted.

"Estelle, I just want to talk to you."

"We have nothing to talk about!"

"Please, let me help you."

She heard laughter from inside the apartment. "Help me what?"

"You're killing yourself with drugs, and you put yourself in danger every time you are with one of those men. Jake and Ginny need you."

"They're better off without me, and you know it!"

"No, Estelle; they're not. They love you, and I know you love them."

"Go away. There's no help for me."

"Yes, there is. Please open the door." Rose stayed at the door and cried for almost an hour. Estelle refused to let her in and finally quit talking to her.

"Estelle, I know you can hear me. I'm not giving up on you—do you understand? I am not giving up!" She turned and slowly walked down the stairs and out of the building.

Week after week, Rose took every opportunity to check on her daughter. A few times, she almost caught her on the street. Other times, she knocked on the apartment door. Estelle refused to answer, but Rose didn't give up. She chased after Estelle, not willing to let her go.

When Jake read and studied the passages that his grandmother asked him to read, he was completely enthralled. Paul and Peter were real men—manly men. Paul's story especially got his interest. Paul was so completely changed after meeting Jesus, and Peter still had some problems with his temper, even after he followed Jesus. But Jesus loved him, and he was still one of the disciples.

Periodically, Rose asked Jake about his reading. They discussed the stories, and Rose answered his questions.

Jake talked to Mike about what he read almost every day.

"Did you know that Paul ran with people who killed Christians?" Jake asked.

"Yes he did." Mike smiled at his friend's new-found interest in the Bible.

Jake paused for a moment. "Mike, you remember that day Jimmy made the comments about the woman going in the alley with that guy?"

"Yeah?"

"Well, I lied to you when we first met. I told you that my folks were dead, and that's why we live with Grandma Rose." Jake stopped and sighed.

"You lied?"

"I don't know where my dad is, but my mom lives not far from here. She, uh, she's got some problems." His voice was barely a whisper. "The lady we saw that day *was* my mom." He quickly looked at Mike to see his reaction.

Mike took a big breath. "Jake, I'm sorry. That's got to be tough, but I know you still love your mom—otherwise you wouldn't have defended her when the guys said those things."

Jake turned away. "I'm so mad at her that I can't feel it anymore."

"Jake, you need to let your anger go and try to forgive her. She's your mom."

"I want to, but I can't. She doesn't want us anymore, and she gave us to Grandma Rose."

"Maybe she's just trying to protect you and Ginny from what she does." Mike was wise beyond his years.

"That's what Grandma Rose believes." He was quiet for a minute. "She used to be such a good mom."

"Something really bad must have happened for her to do the things she does now. You need to pray for her, Jake."

Jake didn't answer.

Estelle grew accustomed to frequent visits from Rose. She never let her mother in, but she found herself waiting for Rose to show up.

Things had gone from bad to worse. Estelle had to moonlight on the street more often to support her habit, and she barely kept the rent paid with the earnings from her regulars. She was so thin that sometimes she didn't even recognize herself when she passed a mirror, since she didn't waste much money on food. Why should she? She wasn't hungry most of the time anyway.

The days were getting cooler, so Estelle grabbed a sweater as she headed out for the corner bar. She'd made a sad attempt at brushing her teeth, wiped her face with a wet rag, and dabbed on some cheap perfume. Some of the guys from the West Bottoms who got off early would be showing up soon; she needed to be on the corner when they arrived.

Her mind was focused on one thing: getting enough money to score. Hurrying out the door and down the stairs, she didn't notice the dark car parked down the street.

The cool breeze blew right through her thin sweater as she stood against the building near the alley. She hoped someone would want her services soon. Just then, a burly guy she'd never seen before approached her. They talked and then ducked into the alley.

Rose couldn't shake the sense of urgency to check on her daughter. She hadn't slept well the night before and kept dreaming about Estelle, so she made arrangements for Margaret to look after Ginny. Jake was working in the store with Joe. By this time, Joe and Margaret knew that her frequent errands were actually attempts to talk to Estelle. They helped with the kids and prayed for the mother and daughter.

Rose grabbed her bag and sweater and headed for Estelle's apartment, feeling more anxious and afraid with each step. Something was wrong, and the walk seemed to take longer than usual. She quickened her step.

Estelle's customer came out of the alley and went into the bar. She walked out of the alley a couple of minutes later, stuffing money into her bra. She needed to score and get home in time for one of her regulars. As she hurried up the street, the dark car pulled out and followed her. Suddenly, it sped up and then screeched to a halt right next to her. She jumped and let out a startled scream.

The scream froze in her throat when she saw Mark Lawrence step out of the car. "Get in."

She didn't argue—she didn't speak at all. Obediently, she climbed in the back seat of the car and cringed in the corner. Mark got in the front seat next to the driver. "Take us to her apartment building and park around the corner—out of sight."

The driver let them out at the front door and pulled around the corner.

"Get upstairs. I'm not going to touch you; you're disgusting," Mark growled.

Estelle practically ran up the stairs. Her hands shook, and she dropped the key as she tried to open the door.

"Hurry up, you idiot," he hissed, looking around.

She finally opened the door, and they stepped inside. Mark locked the door after them. "So, you decided to go around me, huh? Yes, I know about your little street business. I also know that you have cut into my profits with some of our regulars." He clucked his tongue as though he was talking to a disobedient child.

She backed away from him, completely terrified. "I couldn't make it on what you paid me. I didn't do it a lot. I'll pay you back, Mark. I promise." Her eyes were wide with fear.

"Pay me back?" he laughed. "You're a junkie! You're not going to pay me back. I knew this day would come. You are no longer at all useful to me, Estelle," he smiled at her, "and you know far too much about me to simply let you go."

"Mark, I can still work."

"Oh shut up. You are pathetic. Even most of my lowest-level clients are no longer interested in you."

"Please, give me one more chance. Think of my kids!"

"You should have thought about your kids long ago. They aren't even with you anymore; they're with Rose. I do keep tabs, you know. There is a positive side of this: it looks like your son may be following in his father's footsteps. I'll have to keep an eye on him after you're gone."

"No, please leave my kids alone!" she cried.

"Face it, Estelle—you are a burnt-out, used-up whore and of no use to anyone. How sad. Another junky whore OD's." He pulled a package out of his pocket.

As she watched him mix and draw up a dose of heroin that was sure to kill her, she stood paralyzed and couldn't move to escape.

He turned and started toward her. "Now, this won't hurt. You'll just go to sleep. Come on, don't bother fighting. Let's just get this over with. I have guests coming soon, and I have to get back to my suite." He was as cold as ice.

She managed to back away a few more steps.

"Stop. I really don't care to touch you, but I'm sure I can hold you down if necessary. Of course then I'll have to bathe and change my clothes, so just take it. What do you have to live for anyway?" He moved closer.

Suddenly, all Estelle could see were the faces of Jake and Ginny. With her adrenaline pumping, she sidestepped Mark and then sprinted to her bedroom, locking the door behind her.

"Estelle, this isn't going to work. I'll just break down this flimsy door. Now open the door!" Mark yelled.

She slid across the floor and pulled a box from under the bed. Her hands shook as she loaded the gun that Frank had left for her.

Just as she rolled back and stood up, Mark broke through the door. His face was almost purple with rage as he burst into the room. "I'll strangle you with my bare hands if I have to!"

Estelle tripped and fell to the floor. Mark saw the gun and was on top of her in mere seconds. As they struggled for the gun, they rolled and knocked over the lamp table. The lamp crashed to the floor next to Estelle's head, and she felt glass cutting into her scalp and shoulder. They grappled until Mark snatched the gun from her hand. She struggled against him as he turned the barrel toward her chest. With strength she didn't know she had, Estelle fought for her life.

Finally, Rose made her way up the walk to Estelle's building. Just as she opened the front door, she heard bloodcurdling screams and then two shots rang out. She knew it was Estelle.

"Jesus, help us!" Rose cried as she stumbled through the door and ran up the stairs. Estelle's apartment door was locked. Rose rammed against it to no avail. The door wouldn't budge. She screamed her daughter's name. There were no more sounds from inside.

Just then, a man in a neighboring apartment came out into the hallway. "Were those gunshots?" he asked.

"Yes! Please help me with the door. My daughter's in there!" Rose cried and kept trying to break down the door.

The man approached the door cautiously. "Hello? Hello? Do you need help in there?"

There was no answer—not even a sound.

"Please," Rose begged. "Kick the door in! The shots came from inside."

He looked around and then rammed his shoulder into the door. The doorframe splintered as the door flung open.

Rose ran into the living room, but no one was there. Then she hurried to the bedroom. "No, no, nooooooo!" she screamed.

The only thing the neighbor heard was screaming and moaning from inside the apartment before he ran back to his apartment and called the police.

When the police and the ambulance arrived, the neighbor pointed the way to the apartment.

The officers found Rose on the floor, covered in blood, holding her daughter in her arms.

"Please, Miss. You need to let her go."

"I can't let her go. I won't!" Rose sobbed.

"Please, you have to let her go." The young police officer pried her arms away from Estelle's limp body and helped Rose to the other side of the room.

The ambulance attendants rushed in.

"Don't waste your time; this one's dead," one officer whispered.

"Get over here! This one has a weak pulse—lost a lot of blood though." There was a flurry of activity as they worked to stop the bleeding.

Moments later, they loaded one victim onto a gurney and rushed to the hospital. But there was no rush for the other victim; the coroner was on his way.

Rose was in shock and could barely speak. An officer finally managed to find something in her purse that identified her, and they found the number to Polanski's Market.

32

Joe was locking up just as the phone behind the counter rang. He walked around and picked up the receiver. "Hello?" he paused, "Yes, this is Joe Polanski." He listened. "Yes officer, Rose Baker works for us. What is this about?" Cold chills ran up and down his spine as he waited for the answer.

"Oh my God," he choked out the words. "Yes, we'll be there." He hung up the phone and slid down in the chair behind the counter. Tears stung his eyes. "Oh God, oh God, what will we tell the children?" He put his head in his hands and cried.

When Joe calmed down enough to speak, he picked up the phone and dialed Rose's number. He had to break the news to Margaret, and he knew he couldn't keep his emotions in check enough to tell her with the children around.

"Hello?" Margaret answered the phone.

"Margaret, where are the children?" Joe's voice was a ragged whisper.

"Jake is in his room doing homework, and Ginny is playing in her room. Joe, what's wrong?" Hearing the pain in his voice, she listened and then sank into a kitchen chair, with her hand to her chest. Soft sobs shook her body. "How will we tell the children?"

After a long pause, Margaret spoke again. "Yes, you should call Pastor Williams. Maybe Mrs. Williams can sit with the children and Pastor can go with us. We need to get to Rose as soon as possible. I should call Pauline, but I'll wait and call from downstairs.

Margaret fought to control her emotions. She went in to tell Jake that they had to take care of some business; but since Grandma Rose wasn't back yet, Mrs. Williams would sit with them until they returned. Jake didn't know what was wrong, but he'd never seen Mrs. Polanski so upset. When Mrs. Williams arrived, Margaret kissed the kids and went downstairs to call Pauline.

Pauline wasn't sure what was going on, but she hadn't slept well the night before and couldn't get her mind off of Rose, Estelle, and the children. When the phone rang, she was walking back and forth in her room, praying.

After Margaret gave her the news, she whispered goodbye and fell to her knees, sobbing and praying. Finally, Pauline pulled herself together and went to tell her sister that she had to go home immediately.

The doctor shook his head and stared at the poor soul who lay before him, barely alive. They had done everything they could; now it was a waiting game. It would take a miracle for this one to make it through another night. They had almost lost their shooting victim the night before; since then, it had been touch and go. The blood loss alone was bad enough, but there were other complications. He whispered a prayer, hoping they could save this life. He called to let his wife know that he couldn't leave and would be at the hospital until his patient either improved or died.

"Nurse, I'm going to lie down for a bit. If there is even the slightest change, send someone for me immediately," Dr. Michael Stanovich instructed and left the room. He walked to the nurses' station. "If Kate calls, tell her I will call her after I take a nap. I'm dead on my feet right now."

The phone at the nurses' station rang seconds after Dr. Stanovich walked through the double doors. It was Kate, and she was upset. "Mrs. Stanovich, I'm sorry, but he's been up all night with this patient, and he gave strict orders to let him sleep unless there was change in the patient's condition." She listened to the doctor's wife. "The newspaper? He's resting, ma'am. I'm not going to interrupt him with something from the newspaper."

The young nurse rolled her eyes as the doctor's wife ranted in near hysteria on the other end of the phone. "Please, I don't want to get in trouble." She paused. "Okay; if he wakes up before you get here, I'll let him know that you're on your way." After hanging up the phone, she huffed and went back to her charts. "That woman needs to calm down. We've had non-stop emergencies all night, and now *she's* on her way."

Rose let Margaret hold her. Ginny slept in Joe's arms, and Jake was on the other side of his grandmother, his eyes red and swollen, holding her arm in a death grip.

Margaret's voice was calm and soothing. "Pauline will be here tonight. She told me she was already making arrangements to move back. It was going to be a surprise." Margaret stroked the younger woman's hair as she spoke softly.

Rose hiccupped like a child who had cried too long. "Thank God. We need her. I'm so glad her sister is well enough to care of herself for now. "Everyone except Ginny jumped when a strange lady walked in, crying and holding a newspaper.

"Are you friends of Estelle Prebilica—I mean Shannon?" she asked between sobs.

Margaret stood up. "Yes, we are her friends and family."

"Jake?" She walked across the hospital waiting room. "I'm Kate! Your mom and I grew up together. When you were a baby, I watched you when your mom worked at the diner." She wiped her eyes with a hankie.

Jake stared at her, then Rose stood up. "You knew my parents?"

Kate stared at the woman who had just spoken—she looked so much like Mary and Estelle. She gasped—the subject of a lifelong mystery stood right in front of her. "Rosalie? Sweet Mother of God, it's you." Kate crossed herself and took a deep breath. "I'm sorry, but you were quite a mystery for years. And yes, our parents were best friends. My mother finally told me the truth about you before she died." When the shock of meeting Rosalie subsided, Kate held up the newspaper. A sob caught in her throat. "Is she going to make it?"

The door to the waiting room swung open again. "Kate, what on earth are you doing here? Darling, these people are exhausted!" Dr. Stanovich looked at the little group.

"Michael, it's Estelle—Estelle Prebilica."

"Prebilica? My patient's last name is Shannon."

"Estelle's maiden name is Prebilica."

His eyes widened. "Your childhood friend?"

She nodded her head and leaned against her husband's chest. "Michael, is she going to make it?"

He glanced at Jake. "Why don't we all sit down?"

As everyone took a seat, Dr. Stanovich cleared his throat. "She's alive—barely, but she's alive. The bullet missed her vital organs, but there was internal bleeding."

The ladies all broke down. Joe looked completely helpless while Jake was white as a ghost.

"I can't make any promises. She lost a lot of blood." He turned to Rose. "If you hadn't held your sweater against her wound and slowed the bleeding, she most likely wouldn't have made it." He paused. "There are other complications that make her recovery difficult." He looked at Jake and then at Rose.

"He knows about his mother's addiction, doctor."

"I see." He cleared his throat and continued. "Well, her body is in shock, and she's weak from the blood loss. She's also going through withdrawals, making her recovery much more difficult." Kate put her head in her hands and sobbed as her husband spoke. "She was in surgery a good part of the night. The damage has been repaired, and the bleeding has stopped, but we are going to keep her sedated in hopes of minimizing the affects of drug withdrawals. The goal is to help her body get through them with no further damage. She's also had a blood transfusion, and we're giving her fluids, antibiotics, and some other medications." He sighed and ran his hand through his hair. "I'm going to be honest with you; it's going to be touch and go for days. We're going to do everything we can for her; but if she lives, it will be a miracle."

Michael hesitated and then continued. "There's one other thing. I hate to tell you this, but you must be prepared. Police officers are posted outside her door, and a detective spoke to me just a short time ago. If she does recover, she will be questioned and very likely charged with murder."

Rose jumped to her feet. "Murder? I saw that room, and I heard her screams. She was fighting for her life!"

"I'm sorry; I'm just telling you what the detective told me. I guess Mr. Lawrence was a respected businessman from out of town, but he came here frequently on business trips. They think she lured him to her apartment to rob him, and he defended himself. There were no witnesses to the actual shooting."

"Oh my God! What one earth are we going to do?" Rose paced the floor.

"Doctor?" Michael turned as he heard Jake's soft voice.

"Yes son, what is it?"

"Mark Lawrence was not a *respected* businessman." He emphasized the word respected. "He was my mom's boss. She told me that he wouldn't let her go—she said he would kill her first. She was really afraid of him."

Suddenly, the room was silent. The adults all looked at the young boy who had just dropped a bombshell.

Rose cried, "Oh my God, I should have done more to help her. That monster forced her. I can't believe I judged her—my own daughter!" Rose sobbed uncontrollably.

"Rose, we are all guilty of standing by far too long. We can't change what we've done, but now we can do everything in our power to help her." Margaret consoled her friend.

"Margaret, we need to call our attorney today and ask if he can take this case, or if he can recommend someone who can," Joe spoke up.

Dr. Stanovich stood up. "I think that would be a very good idea. I have to get back and check on my other patients. Kate, come by my office before you leave." He kissed his wife on the cheek and left the room.

"Kate, would you mind if we prayed together for Estelle?" Rose asked.

"Certainly not; may I join you?"

The small group gathered close and prayed for a miracle. After they finished praying, Kate sat down across from Rose.

They made small talk for a few minutes while Margaret told Kate about their market and the little church they all attended. Kate told them that she and Michael lived on the Kansas side and attended St. John's.

"Estelle looks so much like you—it's amazing." As inquisitive as always, Kate couldn't hold her questions. "Rose, how did you find her?"

"It's quite a long story."

"I don't think we will be leaving any time soon. I'd love to hear it," Kate smiled.

Rose started at the beginning, and Kate hung on to every word. Rose told her everything; and when she finished, Kate was quiet for a moment, tears streaming down her face.

"Rose, there is something you should know. Momma told me that your parents looked for you for years and were never able to find you. Their hearts were broken. As Estelle grew, they didn't know how to tell her about you—they were afraid of losing her too. They loved you Rose, and they regretted running away with Estelle; but they were terrified of what Estelle's father had planned for her. Both of them prayed for forgiveness and hoped that you would forgive them too."

Rose cried unashamedly. "I forgave them a long time ago, but it hurts that I didn't get to see them again before they died. I loved them with all my heart. Thank you for telling me; it helps to know that they still loved me and tried to find me too."

Joe stood up and carried Ginny to her grandmother. "I want to be at the airport in case Pauline's plane gets in early."

"Kate, are you going to stay here for a while?" Margaret asked.

"Yes."

"Then I think I'll go with Joe to pick up Pauline."

"Okay. Rose, let me take Ginny; you should try to get some rest." Kate gently picked up Ginny.

"I don't know if I can sleep. I haven't seen her yet—not since I found her in the apartment, bleeding and ..." her voice trailed off.

"Please, try to get some rest. Jake, why don't you try to rest too? It may be a little while before any of us can see her. It won't do her any good if the two of you are sick."

Rose turned slightly and rested her head against the back of the couch, and Jake leaned against her shoulder. Kate put Ginny on the other couch, pulled the drapes closed, and turned off the lights, darkening the room as much as possible. Moments later, Rose and Jake were sleeping— maybe not soundly, and maybe not for long, but they were sleeping.

Kate sat on the couch next to Ginny and leaned back. Her thoughts drifted back to her childhood and good times with her best friend, Estelle.

The next thing Kate knew, the Polanskis and another lady walked through the door. It seemed like only minutes had passed, but it had actually been about two hours. Rose and Jake were still sleeping, but Ginny stirred as Margaret introduced Kate to Pauline.

"It is so nice to meet you, Miss Temple." Kate stood up.

"Please, call me Pauline. It's so nice to meet you, dear. Has there been any further news on Estelle's condition?"

"Nothing since Margaret and Joe left. I think I'll track down my husband and see if there is anything new."

"Thank you," Pauline said. Ginny sat up, rubbed her eyes, and smiled. "Is this Ginny? What a beautiful little princess!" Pauline smiled as well.

Kate excused herself and left the room.

"Ginny, this is Miss Pauline. I'm sure you've heard Jake and your grandmother talk about her," Margaret explained.

Suddenly, Jake sat up and yawned. "Miss Pauline!" He ran across the room.

"Jake!" Pauline cried. "You've grown up while I was gone. Look at you—I don't believe it!"

Rose woke up to all the commotion. "Oh Pauline, thank God you're here!"

It looked like a small huddle as Jake, Rose, and Pauline hugged and held onto each other. Finally, they all sat down. Ginny immediately took a liking to Pauline and climbed up on her lap.

About thirty minutes later, Kate walked back into the room with her husband in tow. The doctor looked tired, but he smiled at the little group.

"I wish I had something new for you, but I don't. It's too soon for much improvement. The positive thing is that she has not taken a downward turn; she's holding her own."

"We'll hold on to that. Oh, my name is Pauline Temple. Rose and I have known each other for years, and I used to care for Jake when Estelle and I lived in the same building."

"I'm Dr. Stanovich, Kate's husband. It's nice to meet you. Well, as I told the others earlier, we are keeping her sedated, and we are giving her other medications that should help with the withdrawals. We have to get her through that without putting much more shock on her body, since she needs every bit of strength she has to heal. I promise to let you know if there is any change."

"Doctor, when can we see her?" Rose asked.

"I can arrange for each of you to see her for a few minutes at a time."

"Can I see my mom?" Jake's eyes looked enormous.

"How old are you, son?"

"I'm 12."

"Doctor, please. He needs to see his mother, but I don't think he should go in alone." Pauline spoke up.

"I'll take care of it, but please don't say anything about your age to anyone else, son. One of you can go in with him, but only for a few minutes though—and only a couple of visitors each hour. Okay?"

"Yes, whatever you say. We just need to see her; she needs us." Rose stood up.

"Mrs. Baker, come with me, and I'll get you in first. Then Jake can go in with an adult."

"Pauline, will you go in with Jake?"

"Of course, dear."

Rose followed Dr. Stanovich out of the room. They walked to the nurses' station just outside of Estelle's room. "Nurse, this is Rose Baker, Estelle Shannon's mother. She is going in to see her daughter, and I'm allowing Mrs. Shannon's son to go in after his grandmother. In light of her condition, I'm allowing an adult to accompany him. The family can have two short visits each hour, one at time, other than the boy. Please make sure that the other nurses are aware and relay my orders to the next shift."

"Yes, doctor."

"Mrs. Baker, why don't I go in with you? It may be a shock to see her in this condition. She's very pale, and there are tubes and equipment all around her."

"Thank you, Doctor. I appreciate it."

Rose whispered a prayer and tried to gather herself, but nothing could have prepared her for what she saw. A steady beeping greeted her from one of the machines. Estelle lay in a hospital bed with her head bandaged. She was deathly pale, and her face was swollen and bruised. Her chest rose and fell slightly, as her breathing was shallow. Equipment, tubes, and needles were everywhere, just as Dr. Stanovich had warned. Rose swayed and gasped, quickly covering her mouth with her hand. The doctor steadied her. "Are you sure you're up to this?" he asked.

"Yes. She's my daughter, and she needs me." Rose walked over to the bed. "Estelle, it's Rose, your mother." She took a deep breath and exhaled slowly. "Sweetheart, I'm here. Pauline is here too, and the Polanskis. We're praying, and you're going to be fine." The words caught in her throat. "I love you so much, and I am not going anywhere." She picked up her daughter's frail hand and held it for a moment. She kissed Estelle's hand and gently placed it back on the bed. Then she turned to Dr. Stanovich, "I'll let Jake and Pauline come in now."

Rose held her emotions all the way back to the waiting room and told Pauline and Jake how to get to the nurses' station. Pauline took Jake's hand and walked out of the waiting room. After a moment or two, Rose collapsed on the couch, put her head in her hands, and cried. Kate and Margaret rushed to her side while Joe took Ginny for a walk down the hall.

Pauline and Jake stood just outside Estelle's room. "Jake, this may be very difficult. Your mother is sleeping, and they use a lot of equipment when people have had surgery. I will be right by your side, and so will the Lord. Do you still want to go in?"

"Yes. I have to see my mom. I have to tell her something. I can do it." Jake was pale.

Pauline and Jake heard steady beeping as they opened the door. Jake stopped for a moment when he saw the tubes and needles. "Are you okay?"

"Yes," he whispered.

Slowly, Jake walked to his mother's bed. He took a deep breath. Tears trickled down Pauline's face as she watched him stroke his mother's hand. "Mom, it's me, Jake. I'm here." He gulped and choked back a sob. "I don't hate you. I'm so sorry I said that. I was really mad. I love you. Mom, can you hear me? I love you." Pauline rushed to his side when she saw his shoulders shaking. The dam burst. Tears he held so long spilled down his cheeks.

"Jake, I believe she can hear you." Pauline put a hand on Jake's shoulder, and then she leaned close to Estelle. "Estelle, it's Pauline. I've come home, and I'm not leaving again. We're all praying for you. I love you, Estelle." She led Jake out of the room and back to the waiting room.

Dr. Stanovich found it necessary to temporarily suspend all visits as the withdrawals ravaged Estelle's body. When the ferocious cravings finally subsided, Estelle had survived her wounds and—for the second time—the horror of heroin withdrawals.

Rose only left the hospital for short periods of time to bathe and change clothes. When she was allowed to see Estelle again, she told her daughter the story of how they came to be separated and how the Lord brought them back together. She shared the nightmare she had lived and the rescue she had experienced. In the waiting room, with her Bible on her lap, Rose read and prayed for a miracle every day.

Five-year-old Ginny was shielded from as much information as possible regarding her mother's condition. Margaret took Ginny to school in the mornings, and Pauline stayed at the apartment and cared for Ginny when she wasn't in school. The ladies alternated going to the hospital during the day, and they all went together in the evenings.

No one had the heart to ask Jake to leave his mother and go back to school, so Joe and Margaret managed to get approval from his school for a tutor to come to the hospital.

Mike and his parents also visited several times. Everyone liked Mike, and they were thankful that Jake had such a good friend. It was no surprise that his parents were also kind, compassionate people.

Kate's friendship with Rose, Pauline, and the Polanskis grew. She helped with Ginny and spent every possible moment at the hospital.

Dr. Stanovich confirmed that Estelle's physical condition had improved, so he stopped sedating her. However, Estelle did not wake up. Her color returned, her vital signs were stronger, and she was past the danger of withdrawals. But she continued to sleep.

The district attorney had not yet filed charges; his suspect was in the hospital and in a coma. He questioned Rose and the neighbor who broke down the door the evening of the shooting. With Rose present, he also talked to Jake. The young man swore that Mark Lawrence had been his mother's boss and that she had been terrified of the man. The district attorney did some checking into Mark's background. The more he learned, the more his confidence waned about the future case.

Joe and Margaret's attorney referred them to a criminal attorney who agreed to take the case—if charges were filed.

As the weeks passed, Estelle's body healed. She was moved to a private room, making it easier for her loved ones to visit. Soon, they would have to move her to another facility. Her family waited, but Estelle continued to sleep.

33

Morning Mass was over, and Father Vincent strolled leisurely down the long hallway toward his study. The click of his Italian leather shoes on the polished marble floor and the soft swishing of his robes were the only sounds he heard.

It was nice to be back. He had enjoyed his trip abroad, seeing family and his childhood home, but this is where he belonged now. The six weeks had gone by quickly, and he had much catching up to do.

His jet-black hair, now salt and pepper at the temples, made him look younger than his years. His 6' 2" muscular build, olive skin, dark brown eyes, and handsome features had been a problem on more than one occasion with female parishioners. But his relationship with God and his calling were too important to him.

He smiled as he anticipated the opportunity to relax this morning. A stack of newspapers had been arranged on his desk with the oldest on top. He wanted to at least peruse the headlines to get back in touch with events that had taken place during his absence. After all, this had been his hometown for several years now. He cared for the people here, and he felt it important to keep up on what happened in Kansas City.

As he closed his office door behind him, he was thankful for his quiet time this morning. He hadn't slept well for weeks, waking periodically with an overwhelming sense of foreboding. Each time he awoke in the middle of the night, he prayed and then fell back into a fitful sleep. The last time he'd felt this way, his brother was nearly killed. He'd already been in touch with family members, and it seemed everyone was fine. Hopefully, he would start sleeping better now that he was back where he belonged.

Removing his robes and hanging them neatly in the small closet, he turned and headed for his desk. The aroma of freshly brewed coffee and pastries warm from the oven made his mouth water. His chair creaked as he leaned back slightly and glanced at the front page of the first newspaper in the stack.

He had just started his second cup of coffee and had gone through a few days' worth of newspapers when he saw the article.

Hot liquid splattered on his lap and soaked one corner of the newspaper as he choked and spewed coffee everywhere. He jumped up and grabbed a linen napkin to wipe his trousers. Then he snatched up the newspaper and took a closer look. The headline with two pictures below read, "Deadly Shooting…"

"Sweet Mother of God, it's her!" He crossed himself and dropped to his knees, never letting go of the paper. Managing to get back in his chair, he tried to compose himself. His hands shook as he picked up the phone and dialed.

"She squeezed my hand today, Miss Pauline. I know she did!" Jake's excitement was contagious as he ran across the waiting room to greet Pauline. Ginny and the Polanskis were right behind her.

"It's true; she did—Jake and I were in the room. We were both talking to her. As Jake held her hand, I saw her fingers move. She didn't open her eyes, but she squeezed his hand." Rose laughed and cried at the same time.

"What does the doctor think?" Joe asked.

"Well, he said there is still so much they don't understand about comatose patients, but he feels it is positive."

"She looks so much healthier than when we first saw her. Something good must be going on," Pauline added. "Our prayers are being answered, maybe not as quickly as we'd like—but they are being answered."

Estelle was trapped in a dream and couldn't get out. Sometimes, she simply heard noises, beeping, and such. Sometimes strangers floated in and out of her dream. She saw no one—she only heard the voices. Her eyes wouldn't open, no matter how hard she tried.

She dreamed of Rose and Jake. The Polanskis sometimes entered her dream. And Pauline was there too. But as hard as she tried, she never heard Ginny. Even Kate Molech was there at times. How long had it been since she'd thought of Kate? Her best friend—she missed her so much.

Oddly enough, it was comforting when Estelle dreamed about Rose. Rose said she loved her and told her such wonderful stories—stories of hope. But it was just a dream. There was no hope for her, and there was no way Rose had done the things Estelle had done.

Even in her dreams, Estelle's stomach churned at the thought of the men and drugs. She should have left Jerry the minute his stories didn't add up. But, then again, he forced her; it wasn't her fault. Yeah right; who was she kidding? How could she have been so stupid? She believed his lies—she followed him blindly into his disgusting world. Worst of all, she had dragged Jake along with her.

Why hadn't she gone straight to the police when Mark forced her to go back to work for him? She had been terrified; Mark gave her no choice. If she hadn't run into that stupid Stan, she would never have started using heroin again. Suddenly, she was overwhelmed with guilt; *she* had made those decisions. Surely she could have done something differently. *She* had abandoned her children, even before Rose took them. If only the stories Rose told her in her dreams were true. But they weren't. Was it just a nightmare meant to torment her with hope that didn't exist? This nightmare had no end.

Mark. Even in the dreams, the mention of his name sent chills down her spine. Why did he continue to torment her in her dreams? She couldn't escape him. Oh God, he was in the room. She knew it— she could feel the chill in the air. "Estelle," his cold, sing-song voice cut through her. "Are you trying to hide from me? Remember what I said? You are a burned-out, used-up, junkie whore. No one needs you any- more. Come now, let's end this now. Tsk, tsk, I have so many things to do, and you are such an inconvenience."

She tried to get away from Mark, but her body wouldn't respond. She couldn't move, and her scream froze in her throat. Where was he? She couldn't see him. He must be hiding, waiting to pounce at any moment.

She drifted off into darkness once more. When she dreamt again, Mark was no longer there. This time, Jake was with her. Again and again she tried to open her eyes, but it felt as if they were glued shut. She wanted to talk to him, but her lips wouldn't move and no sound came out. She thought her fingers moved once when he held her hand, but she wasn't sure it was real. After all, she was trapped in this never-ending dream. When Jake left, she was alone again.

Suddenly, her breathing quickened. She was back in her apartment, and Mark was there. He looked like a maniac. With the syringe in his hand, he came closer, trying to back her into a corner. He always came when the others were gone. This time he was here to kill her. She knew she had to fight for her life. He was like something from a horror movie—a crazed lunatic bent on annihilating her very existence. He was going to kill her and then destroy her son just like he'd destroyed Ricky. She couldn't let it happen. They both held onto Frank's gun, rolling, fighting, and struggling for control. Glass cut into her scalp and shoulder as she twisted and rolled over the broken lamp. Then she heard shots and felt fire in her side.

Maybe this wasn't a dream after all. Maybe she was dead and being tormented, never to see her children again. Her mind struggled to come back to reality. She prayed and cried to God for help—nothing. She must be dead.

"Pauline, she cried today! We walked in the room, and there were tears rolling down her face. Later, her eyelids quivered. They didn't open, but Dr. Stanovich thinks she may gradually be coming out of the coma. It's just a matter of time before she wakes up—I know it is!" Rose trembled with excitement.

Pauline laughed and cried on the other end of the phone. "Yes, she'll wake up soon—I feel it. We'll all be there tonight. I'll see you then."

"Grandma Rose, is she really going to wake up?" Jake wanted to believe it, but it had been weeks, and his mother was still in a coma. At this point, he was too afraid to hope.

"Yes Jake, I believe she will, and Dr. Stanovich does too. That may be why she squeezed your hand one time and then cried tears today. We need to be patient and not give up hope."

Jake smiled at his grandmother and sat back down on the waiting room couch. He kept his thoughts to himself. When she did wake up, would she go back to the way she was? Would she do drugs and turn tricks again? He loved her, but he couldn't stand for that to happen. Maybe it would be better if she just slept, at least for now.

"Hello? Yes, I've told you at least ten times we will meet you at the airport. Yes, he's here, and I promise we will be there early. Okay; see you then." Father Vincent laughed as he hung up the phone.

"Is his flight on time?" The younger man's long, muscular frame took up the entire couch as he reclined on the other side of Father Vincent's study.

"As far as I know. Hopefully he doesn't work himself into a complete frenzy before he gets here."

"It's just crazy. We all completely gave up hope of finding her. It's been years. I can't believe I let Mark Lawrence send me on a wild goose chase all over the country and then just gave up. I guess it was easier to believe that she'd taken off with another man than to watch Frank beat himself up with guilt anymore."

"Our focus was on keeping him alive. We were all ready to see him move on—which he obviously never did."

Tony got up and paced the floor. "Vince, it makes me mad as hell. She was here all the time—her *and* Jake. They needed us, and Frank needed them. Mark Lawrence deserved what he got, that rotten bas ..."

"Tony! Mark Lawrence is dead. I hate to admit that I also feel there is justice in that, but we are Frank's brothers. We need to keep him calm, not get him worked up any more than he already is. Come on, let's get some lunch and then head to the airport." Father Vincent grabbed his jacket and put his arm around his kid brother's shoulders as they walked out the door. "Do you really believe we have the same parents?"

Tony laughed and punched his older brother playfully.

After lunch, the brothers were quiet as they drove downtown to Kansas City's Municipal Airport. Tony parked the car, and they walked to the terminal. Once inside, Father Vincent went to the counter and asked about Frank's flight before he went back and sat next to Tony. "His flight left a bit late, so he should be here in an hour or so. We may as well wait here, since there's no point in leaving and coming back."

As they waited for Frank's flight to arrive, Father Vincent tried to put the pieces together, talking more to himself than to Tony. "You know she has visitors at the hospital—friends or family, I guess. I tried to be inconspicuous when I peeked in the waiting room, pretending to look for another family. Yesterday afternoon, I saw Jake, but he didn't see me. He's a young man now. It's hard to think about what that boy has been through. There was a woman there too. She looked a lot like Estelle, only a bit older. But last night I saw a couple of older ladies and a man. They had a little girl with them."

"I thought Frank said she didn't have any family."

Father Vincent ignored his brother and stared into space. "She may belong to the other lady, the one who looks like Estelle."

"Who?"

"She's a beautiful little girl, about four or five years old. Really dark, curly hair, olive complexion, and the darkest brown eyes I've ever seen." Suddenly, he gasped and his eyes were as big as saucers.

"Vince, what is it?"

"Oh my God; that little girl is Frank's child! I should have realized it the minute I saw her."

"What? Okay, don't you think we need to be sure before we drop that bombshell?"

"Don't worry, we're not telling him anything. We'll take it one step at a time. But, if she's there when we go to the hospital, take a look at her and then tell me she's not Frank's child."

"We'll see." Tony shook his head.

The brothers sat quietly lost in their own thoughts.

It was an hour and a half before Frank's flight landed. Father Vincent and Tony stood around waiting for the passengers to disembark. They stretched to their full height, looking for that first glimpse of their middle brother's face.

"Hey, there he is! Frank, over here!" Tony waved and hurried through the group of people coming from the arrival gate. Father Vincent smiled and waited right where he was. Frank and Tony hugged and slapped each other on the back, then headed for their older brother. His limp was barely noticeable these days, the cane no longer necessary.

"Frank." Father Vincent pulled his brother into a bear hug. "Let's get your luggage." Forty-five minutes later, they had Frank's luggage and were headed to the door.

It was difficult to ignore the three handsome men who looked so much alike. One lady blushed when she realized she was ogling a priest.

The three laughed as they walked out of the terminal together.

"Frank, let's go back to my place, and we can talk before we do anything," Tony suggested.

"I want to go straight to the hospital."

"Frank, you can't just barge in. There are people in the waiting room—her family and friends. Think about it—*Jake* is there. We need to go about this carefully. These people have been through enough." His older brother reasoned with him.

"She doesn't have any family, other than Jake."

"Look, I was there twice yesterday after I called you. In the afternoon, Jake was there with a woman who looks enough like Estelle to be her sister, but she's a little older, maybe an aunt or older cousin. Don't worry, I was very discreet. Jake didn't see me. When I went by again last night, I also noticed an older man and two older ladies." When Vince left out the part about the little girl, Tony breathed a sigh of relief.

"Vince, she said she didn't have any family. She was an only child and her parents are both dead. Her husband ran out on her. She had no other family in America. I *know* she was telling the truth."

"Well, it's possible that more of her family immigrated and tracked her down," Tony added.

"Tony, we couldn't track her down, and we had all sorts of resources at our disposal. How could her family from overseas track her down?" Frank was frustrated and confused. "I've waited long enough. You can take me, or I'll just grab a taxi. But I'm going to the hospital *now.*"

"Settle down; we're going with you. God be with us." Father Vincent looked heavenward and whispered a prayer. "Let's at least go by and put your things away. By the time we do that, we can grab some dinner and then go to the hospital." He had a way of calming his younger brother.

"Okay. I guess I need to gather my thoughts. Wait—you saw Jake? He's half grown isn't he?" Frank missed Jake almost as much as he missed Estelle.

"He's a young man now, Frank. He's not the little boy you remember." His older brother thought about the boy and how he might react to Frank after so long, realizing that Jake had no idea why Frank didn't come back for them. This could get messy before there was time to explain.

They dropped Frank's bags off at Tony's house. On the way to the hospital, they stopped for a quick bite at a little Italian restaurant. Frank was antsy and ate very little. "Are you guys about finished?" He had been rushing his brothers since they left the airport.

"Frank, I really prefer not to have indigestion. Please, we don't need to choke our food down. Look at you, eating like a woman, barely touching your food. Where's your appetite?" Tony poked fun at his older brother.

Father Vincent shook his head and added, "Try to relax. You need to be as calm as possible when we get there."

"Well I'm not going to be calm if you two keep going at this pace."

Finally, his brothers finished their meals and were ready to go. Tony stood up and let out a huge sigh. "Okay, let's do this." He knew they had delayed the trip to the hospital as long as possible.

34

Pauline, Joe, Margaret, and Ginny were at the hospital that evening with Jake and Rose. Mike and his family stopped by the hospital and brought a few comic books for Jake.

Ginny played with a baby doll in the corner of the room while Jake and Mike were completely absorbed in their comic books. Rose looked up as a priest walked into the room. She had noticed him a couple other times, but he hadn't come into the room before. Had she just seen him yesterday? His face was ruggedly handsome, but his eyes were gentle. He looked nothing like the priests she remembered from her childhood.

He smiled as he walked over to her and held out his hand. "I'm Father Vincent." She stood and shook his hand.

"Nice to meet you. My name is Rose Baker."

"It's nice to meet you too, Mrs. Baker. I'm sorry to intrude, but I saw you here yesterday."

"Yes, my daughter has been here for quite some time. She was injured and is in a coma." She thought it was odd that he didn't remove the hat that was pulled low, almost covering his eyes.

"What is her name? I've visited with several patients."

"Estelle—Estelle Shannon."

He looked puzzled for a moment, "Mrs. Baker, may I have a word with you, in private?"

"Certainly, we can step down the hall. Pauline, I'll be right back."

The children didn't seem to notice the priest, but the other adults were quite interested. "You go ahead. We'll keep an eye on Ginny," Pauline answered.

Rose and the priest walked down the hall until they were out of earshot of the waiting room. Father Vincent took a deep breath. "I'm not really sure where to start." He hesitated. "My family is from Sicily. Some of our family immigrated to America years ago. One particular uncle became a very successful businessman, and his only son joined him in the business as he prepared to retire." He stopped again, and Rose waited.

"Several years ago, his son—my cousin—was murdered. It was a group of criminals who were trying to force businesses to pay for protection. He refused."

"I don't mean to be rude, but why are you telling me this?"

"I know this is confusing, but you will understand when I finish. We Sicilians are very loyal—sometimes vengeful when it comes to family. My brothers and I had been in America for several years when our cousin was murdered. We worked with the FBI to find his killers and bring them to justice. We were 'undercover' in a sense, or maybe we were bait. One of my brothers posed as a successful yet unscrupulous businessman looking for avenues to launder money."

Rose was clearly getting more agitated by the minute. "This is all very interesting, but I still don't understand why you are telling me."

"My brother was active in New York where our cousin was murdered, but he came to Kansas City when the group he had infiltrated thought he was traveling abroad. It was sort of a haven or hiding place for him." Normally calm, Father Vincent removed his hat and nervously ran his fingers through his hair. "His name is Frank. Estelle and Jake lived with him here in Kansas City."

Rose gasped and almost collapsed against the wall. Father Vincent reached out to steady her. The realization finally hit her. "His name *is* Frank? He's not dead, is he?" She fought to control the anger that suddenly overwhelmed her. "Why did he leave them? Estelle loved him, and he was like a father to Jake."

"He didn't leave them."

"Yes he did. She waited and waited until that monster, Mark Lawrence, forced her back into prostitution," she hissed.

"No, he didn't leave them; his cover was blown. He was ambushed in New York, and he was beaten, shot, and left for dead. We almost lost him. He hovered between life and death for weeks. When he did come out of it, he was weak and those murderers were still on the loose, so we took him back to Sicily to recover. Tony, our younger brother, came back to the States and searched for Estelle and Jake. Mark Lawrence sent him on a wild goose chase all over the country, convincing him that she had run away with another wealthy man."

Rose's eyelids fluttered and her face was flushed. "Oh my God, does he know she had his child?"

"No, but he will soon enough. He's here, but I managed to get him to agree to let me approach you first."

"He's here in the hospital?" The color drained from her face.

"Yes. We had all been abroad and just returned to the States. I saw the article about the shooting in the newspaper yesterday, and I recognized Estelle's picture immediately. I called Frank, and he flew in today."

Rose didn't know what to do. "He can't see her. She thinks he's dead! She's in a coma right now, but I believe she can hear us. The shock might be too much for her, so no one can tell her. She's been making progress and may wake up at any time."

"He's not going anywhere, whether he can see her or not. He wants to see Jake and explain everything to him."

"Oh, I don't know if that is a good idea." Rose panicked.

"I'm sorry, but I don't know how much longer Tony is going to be able to keep him downstairs."

Hearing footsteps, Rose turned and watched two men walk around the corner. There was no question they were the priest's brothers. They all looked so much alike.

"Vince, I've waited long enough." Frank was clearly agitated. When he saw Rose, he stopped short and stared at her. "Who are you? You look so much like Estelle."

"I'm her mother. My name is Rosalie."

"Please forgive me for being so abrupt, but she told me her parents were dead and she had no other family."

"My parents raised Estelle. She thought they *were* her parents, and she knew nothing about me until recently."

He shook his head trying to clear his thoughts. "Is Jake here? I'd like to see him."

"He's in the waiting room at the end of the hall. But it may not be a good—" Without letting her finish, Frank turned and headed down the hall. Tony and Father Vincent hurried after him. Rose practically ran to keep up with their long strides.

Frank stopped in the doorway when he saw Jake sitting on the couch reading comic books. Vince was right; he wasn't a little boy anymore. Suddenly aware of Frank's stare, Jake looked up. His expression was nothing short of shock. He dropped his comic book, jumped up, and smiled—until realization washed over him. It was Frank. He *wasn't* dead; he ran out on them. Where had he been, and why was he here now?

Everyone in the room froze as they watched the transformation. Jake's smile faded, and rage exploded from deep within him. His face contorted, and he clenched and unclenched his fists. Suddenly, he launched himself across the room and roared at the man in the doorway.

Frank braced himself against the doorframe and let Jake run headlong into him. Tony and Mike both moved quickly to grab Jake, intending to pull him off. Frank held up one hand and mouthed the word, "No." Jake was out of control, flailing and punching Frank in his side. It was painful to watch.

Finally, Jake collapsed against Frank and sobbed incoherently. "You left us! You never came back! Why? She waited for you, and she had Ginny all alone. She waited for you, and you didn't come back! He made her go back to work; he *made* her! Now she might die!"

Frank held the young man until the sobbing subsided and his breathing returned to something near normal. "Jake, I didn't leave you. I was attacked and almost died, much like your mother. Tony searched for you and your mother for months," his voice broke.

Frank heard the soft sweet voice before he saw the little girl tugging on Jake's pant leg, "Jake, why are you crying?"

No one else in the room moved as Jake pulled away from Frank and stooped down. Looking at his sister, he wiped his eyes on his sleeve. "Ginny, this is Frank. He's your daddy."

She looked up at Frank, her huge brown eyes sparkling. She reached for his hand as she smiled. "Hi! I didn't know I had a daddy!" Frank's heart pounded. It was *true*. She was beautiful, a perfect blend of Estelle and him. He hit his breaking point and went down on both knees, gathering Jake and Ginny in his arms. There, on the floor of the hospital waiting room, Frank Moretti cried like a baby.

No one was immune to the touching scene that had just unfolded. Mike's parents, who knew less about the situation than anyone in the room, even held each other and cried. Joe, Tony, and Father Vincent pulled handkerchiefs from their pockets and wiped tears from their faces. Rose, Pauline and Margaret wept in each other's arms. Mike smiled through his tears as he watched his best friend.

Several minutes passed before anyone spoke. Finally, Jake stood up and looked at Frank. "Tell me what happened—everything, please. I have to know."

Frank stood up with Ginny still in his arms. He pulled a handkerchief from his pocket and wiped his face. "Let's sit down."

Mike's parents felt awkward. "We should go. We don't want to intrude."

"No, please stay. Mike is my best friend, so I want him to hear too," Jake spoke up.

"Both of you and Mike have been so kind in coming to the hospital and praying for all of us. Please stay," Rose insisted. Frank nodded his head in agreement.

Once everyone had taken a seat, Frank cleared his throat and started at the beginning. The entire group sat completely mesmerized as he spoke. He told them about his uncle and the men who murdered his cousin. He also told them about going undercover to help catch the killers, and he told them how he met Estelle. He continued, "I loved Estelle. I wanted to marry her, but I had to finish what I started before I could do that. I was eaten up with hatred for the men who murdered my cousin."

"Will they try to kill you again?" Jake's voice was quiet.

"No. The two men who killed my cousin, the same ones who ambushed me, were killed when federal agents tried to take them into custody. Their organization was small but very dangerous. And their numbers were increasing. All of the others are in prison for a very long time. None of them knew my real identity."

"So you're not in the Mafia?" Jake asked.

Frank smiled, "Jake, not everyone from Sicily is in the Mafia. I won't lie to you. I do know Mafiosi, and some of them are even relatives. At one point, I was tempted to join forces with them, but that decision would have changed everything—there would have been no turning back. In the end, we saved them the time and trouble of dealing with a renegade organization, and that put us in their good graces.

My family has owned vineyards and wineries in Sicily for generations. I have a vineyard and winery in California. My older brother

Vincent is a priest and lives here in Kansas City. Tony is my younger brother and my partner. He has a home here in Kansas City also. Do you remember Madelena?"

"Yes, she helped take care of me."

"Madelena is a nun. She's my sister, and she lives in our village in Sicily."

Jake smiled for a moment. "Frank, why did we have to sneak away and hide? Why did the police come?"

"For the first few days, no one knew who was responsible for the attempt on my life. To protect my cover, part of the plan was for my home here to be raided. We had to be certain the men who tried to kill me had not discovered my place in Kansas City. And if they had, we hoped to convince them that I was the crook I pretended to be. The federal agent in charge was in on the plan, but the local authorities weren't. I understand he put on quite an act." He continued. "The men who murdered my cousin were out of control and ruthless. My cousin was not their first victim. They had no regard for anyone, including women and children. I couldn't take any chances with you and your mother."

Frank turned to Rose. "There's something I have to tell Estelle."

"Frank, I don't know if you should see her yet. We need to talk to her doctor." Rose worried.

"She thought I was married. It was part of my cover. I was married years ago, but my wife died in childbirth, and our son died a few hours later. I was angry and bitter, and I never remarried." He pulled Ginny closer and kissed the top of her head.

"It was wrong to bring someone else into our vendetta, but I was so caught up in my cover, that a mistress was just part of it. And I wasn't exactly devout at that point in my life. I didn't know she had a child when she first came to me, and falling in love with her wasn't part of my plan. But I did love her—I still love her. I brought Estelle and Jake to live with me to get her out of that life and protect them until it was all over." He stopped for a moment. "Jake, I thought I lost you both."

Pauline stood up. "I think we should take this one step at a time. We all have a lot to mull over." She looked at Frank. "This has been a shock to you and your family as well as to us. And Rose is right; we need to talk to Estelle's doctor. We also need to pray—that's the first thing we should do. Estelle has been through, well, she's been through hell, and we have no idea what her frame of mind will be when she wakes up. We have to put her recovery first. That must be our priority."

Frank's need to see Estelle and his desire to protect her were at war. He wanted nothing more than to see her face, to hold her in his arms once again. He ground his teeth and clenched his fists; every muscle in his body was tense. Frank looked at his older brother and saw the warning in his eyes. He knew he had no choice; he *had* to wait.

Joe Polanski was quiet as Frank and the others talked, but he listened closely and watched. He liked this man. Joe detected no pretense, only sincerity and honesty.

Frank managed to get himself under control. "I'll wait. I'll do whatever is best for Estelle, but I would like to see Jake and Ginny as often as possible—that is, if they *want* to see me. I'll take financial responsibility for them immediately. Whatever they need—whatever you need, Rose—everything." There was no point in arguing with him. He certainly hadn't lost his air of authority. "Now, when will the doctor be in to talk with us?"

"He makes his rounds in the morning and comes in to talk with us after he's checked on Estelle. Frank, it may be necessary to move Estelle soon. We need to be prepared to find a suitable facility," Rose answered.

"Why?"

Rose hesitated. She didn't want to say anything about money, but that was exactly what it was about. "Well, the hospital bill is mounting. Joe and Margaret have helped so much, and I can't expect th—"

Frank interrupted. "There is no need to move her. I will take care of the hospital expenses. She should not be moved until she is well enough to go home. Now, do you mind if we wait with the family for a while?"

"You are all welcome to stay, and I would like to pray together. Father, would you mind leading us?" Rose asked softly.

"I would be honored," Father Vincent replied.

That evening, Frank waited somewhat impatiently while family and friends looked in on Estelle, but no one had anything new to report on her condition. Had it not been for Jake and Ginny, he might have thrown caution to the wind and barged into Estelle's room.

Ginny had no trouble warming up to her daddy. Frank was spellbound as she giggled and chattered about her friends at school and her dollies. She stayed on his lap and finally went to sleep in his arms. Every time he looked at his little girl's face, he was overcome with conflicting emotions. She was his child. He had loved her instantly—the moment he realized she was his and Estelle's. He wanted to protect her and take care of her.

But the remorse was excruciating. He wasn't there when she was born. Estelle went through the pregnancy and delivery alone, waiting for him to find her. She struggled to care for the children, and Frank wasn't there. The money he left wasn't enough. No one was there to protect her and the children from Mark Lawrence. His plan had been less than perfect. Estelle, Jake, and Ginny had suffered because of it.

Jake had been through hell; Frank knew it without being told. The little boy Frank had planned to adopt and acknowledge as his own son was gone.

It was Pauline's turn to stay with Estelle through the night, and Rose would go home with Jake and Ginny. Frank reluctantly handed Ginny to Joe as they gathered their things.

He walked over to the large window and looked out at the city lights sparkling in the darkness. He closed his eyes, lost in memories of Estelle, her long chestnut hair, and her sweet laughter. She was beautiful, but it was her innocent, wide-eyed look that had attracted him at first. She had depended on him—loved him. He loved her more than he ever thought it possible to love anyone. Coma or no coma, it would take every ounce of control he had to stay away from her.

"Frank, it's time to go; are you ready?" Tony put his hand on his brother's shoulder.

"What? Oh, yes I'm ready." He looked at Ginny, sleeping on Joe's lap. "Do you mind if I carry her to your car?"

"Of course not, here you go." Joe gently placed Ginny in her daddy's arms.

"Jake, are you ready?" Frank asked.

Jake gathered his comic books and walked next to Frank all the way to the car. Frank kissed Ginny on the cheek and placed her in Rose's arms. "Jake, I will see you here tomorrow." He patted Jake on the back and then pulled him close and hugged him. Jake didn't pull away.

"See you tomorrow, Frank," Jake answered.

"Jake, I have something for you. It's in Tony's car. Let me get part of it." Frank walked over to Tony's car. Tony opened the trunk. Whatever it was, it was in a box.

"We've kept this for a long time, and I want you to have it again."

Jake took the box and looked inside. He gasped as he saw the engine of the train Frank had given him for Christmas. "My train," he whispered as his breath caught in his throat. Frank hugged him.

"We can bring the rest of the train to your apartment tomorrow." He turned to Rose, "I would like to go over some things with you then, if you don't mind. As I said, I want to take care of the children's financial needs immediately."

Rose was slightly frustrated and embarrassed to share her financial situation with a stranger, but she realized this was an important step for Frank and the children. "That will be fine. We'll see you tomorrow." Her voice softened, "Frank, there are some things I need to share with you about Estelle. You need to know what happened, how bad things were, and what we are facing now. You need to know how she got to this point."

"You're right. I do need to know." Frank closed the car door and watched them drive out of the parking lot and down the street.

"Come on, Frank. You need to get some rest too. You have a lot to deal with in the coming days." His older brother put his arm around his shoulder and guided him to Tony's car.

35

When they arrived back at the apartment, Rose called Kate and told her everything that had happened that day. She wanted Kate to be prepared when she met Frank at the hospital.

Rose lay awake for hours that night. She knew how much Estelle had loved Frank, but she also knew how completely abandoned her daughter felt when he didn't come back for them, devastated that the man she loved was dead. How would Estelle deal with the fact that he *wasn't* dead? Would she understand that Frank had been close to death and unable to search for her? Would she believe that Tony had searched the country for her while Mark lied to him, providing false trails?

And the kids—how would they handle this man being a part of their lives? Ginny would most likely adjust, since it was obvious that she was completely captivated by him. But how would Jake handle it? She could see that he loved Frank and looked up to him, but she also saw a glimmer of anger and mistrust in his eyes. He still blamed Frank to some extent, even after hearing what had really happened.

Frank would have to handle Jake with kid gloves. The boy had been in charge for so long, taking care of Ginny and his mother. It was a major accomplishment for Rose to take the reins and care for Ginny without Jake feeling threatened. Frank would need much prayer and support, regardless of how strong and powerful he was. Before it was over, this could bring him to his knees.

Sleep finally claimed her, and she slept right through the alarm the next morning. She still managed to get Ginny ready on time, and Margaret dropped Ginny off at school and then took Rose and Jake to the hospital.

Frank was already in the waiting room having coffee when Rose and Jake hurried through the door. He smiled and offered Rose a cup also. "Thank you. I slept through my alarm, so I had no time for coffee this morning."

"Jake, I brought some pastries for you."

"Thanks. Oh, I love these!" Jake already had breakfast, but he devoured the pastries anyway.

"The doctor hasn't come in yet, has he?" Rose asked.

"Pauline came in for a few minutes, but I haven't seen anyone else since I arrived."

Just then, Pauline walked through the door. "Good morning everyone, the doctor is with Estelle. After he talks with us, I'll go on home and come back this evening."

The small group waited together silently, not wanting to start an important conversation that would ultimately be interrupted by Estelle's doctor.

Frank stood up as Dr. Stanovich walked in smiling. Rose stood and introduced the two men, and they shook hands. "Frank, Kate told me what she could last night."

"We're all still reeling just a little ourselves." Rose smiled and sat back down.

Dr. Stanovich pulled up a chair facing the group. "Well, she is still improving physically, and I am hopeful that she may be coming out of the coma. The nurses have noticed more eyelid movement."

"Yes, Jake and I have noticed that too!" Rose couldn't hide her excitement.

"That in combination with her tears and squeezing Jake's hand a few times gives us hope," the doctor added.

"Doctor, when do you think I can see her? I must talk to her. She needs to know that I'm alive and I'm here—that I love her." Frank spoke without shame or embarrassment.

"Frank, it is imperative that we wait until Estelle is awake. Then we need to let someone break this to her as gently as possible, at the right time. We want to avoid any additional trauma right away. There's still so much we don't know about comatose patients. Is it purely physical or are there psychological issues also? Please try to understand—we can't risk it right now." Michael hated telling Frank he couldn't see her yet. If

Kate were in this situation, he'd go completely insane if he couldn't be with her.

Frank got up and walked to the window. He turned his back to them and ran his hands through his hair. The situation was maddening, but he knew he had to do what was best for Estelle. "I understand, but I'm going to be here every day, waiting for her to wake up. I'm not going anywhere."

"You may not have to wait much longer. I need to finish my rounds. Do any of you have any questions?" After they all said no, Dr. Stanovich added, "It was a pleasure to meet you, Frank."

"Yes, it was my pleasure also."

Dr. Stanovich excused himself and left the room.

"Frank, Jake's tutor will be here soon, so we'll be able to talk then," Rose cleared her throat and didn't look at Frank.

"I'm going to leave now." Pauline hugged Rose and Jake. "Frank, your heart seems to be in the right place. I want you to know I'm glad you're here." Pauline turned and left the room.

"Jacob, are you ready for your lessons?" Lost in thought, Frank was startled by the nun who stood in the doorway. She looked to be in her sixties with a kind, gentle face. Her green eyes twinkled as Frank stood and nodded his head in respect. Jake grabbed his books and followed her down the hall.

"Well, where would you like to start?" Frank asked Rose.

"Why don't I start? This might take a while. Then we can go over the financial issues, if you wish," Rose answered.

Frank sighed, knowing that he was going to hear things that would hurt and make him angry.

Rose took a deep breath. She didn't hide anything from Frank—not even her story, because it was part of Estelle's story too. He needed to know what Estelle and the children had been through. He had to understand how Estelle wound up involved in prostitution and drugs again. He also had to know that when she woke up, she would most likely face murder charges.

As Frank listened to detail after detail of Estelle's decline, his anger boiled over. Rose paused when he jumped up and paced the floor. Finally, he sat back down and didn't interrupt her again; he let her tell it all.

When she finished, his stomach churned. His knuckles were white as he gripped the arms of the chair. Rose held her breath; the very air was charged with fury. He practically shot out of the chair and paced again. He wanted to throw furniture around the room, to rant and rave; he wanted to bash someone's face in. His words came out in a tortured growl, "I wish that rotten bast—" he struggled to watch his language with Rose in the room, "piece of—of garbage had lived. Then I could have choked the life out of him with my bare hands." Like a caged animal, he continued to pace. Rose didn't say a word.

Frank finally calmed himself enough to think clearly. "She's not going to face any charges. Mark Lawrence and Jerry Bradley brought her to me the first time. Mark was her boss. I'm going to contact a federal agent I know. He can deal with the local authorities. If necessary, I can get the best attorney money can buy, but I don't think it will get that far."

Rose took a ragged breath and choked back a sob. "Oh, thank God. I couldn't stand for her to go to jail after all she's been through. It would be horrible for Jake and Ginny."

Frank sat down and put his head in his hands. "My God, she will hate me. If only we could have found her, none of this would have happened." Rose sat quietly as tears dropped on Frank's pant legs.

Later that day, Frank made the necessary phone calls to clear Estelle of any wrongdoing related to Mark's death. His friend with the FBI called the prosecutor and filled him in on Mark Lawrence and his real activities. There would be no charges filed against Estelle; it was clearly a case of self-defense, so police officers were no longer posted outside her room. Rose called Pauline, Margaret, and Kate with the news. At least part of the nightmare was over.

When Jake's tutoring session was over, he walked back to the waiting room.

Frank stood and greeted him. "Jake, your grandmother and I talked while you were gone. She told me what happened after you and your mother fled my home." Frank stopped for a moment, struggling with his emotions. "I understand why it is hard for you to trust me. I'm sorry we didn't find you—I'm sorry for everything all of you went through. I wish I could change it, but I can't. I'll take care of all of you, and I'll protect you. No matter what happens, I will always love all of you."

"I forgive you, Frank. I just hope Mom will too."

"Thank you, Jake. There's one more thing. We made some phone calls today, and your mother is not going to face any charges. She was protecting herself from Mark. She won't go to jail."

Jake turned away, wiping his eyes on his sleeve.

36

stelle was awake; she wasn't dreaming after all. The voices she had heard were real, and she knew she was in a hospital. The constant beeping was annoying, and she wanted it to go away.

Struggling once again to open her eyes, it was as if she was in a fog. Little by little, light penetrated the haze. Shadows moved around her. A door opened and then closed. She had visitors, and they were whispering. Why were they whispering? It was maddening.

She struggled to open her eyes and tried to move her head closer to the sound of the voices, hoping to hear her visitors clearly.

Suddenly, her eyes opened and bright light flooded the room. Pain shot through her eyes and exploded in her head. She squeezed her eyes shut again and gasped. Her visitors began to sob.

There were shouts and noises like thunder rumbling through her brain. "She opened her eyes! Nurse, she opened her eyes!" Rose teetered on the edge of hysteria.

A flurry of activity surrounded her. "I'll turn the lights off. Get Dr. Stanovich immediately. Estelle, can you hear me? I'm your nurse. You opened your eyes. Can you hear me?"

Her throat felt dry and scratchy. She licked her lips and forced the words out. Her voice cracked. "Yes, I hear you." She kept her eyes closed, afraid to feel the pain again. She heard footsteps as someone ran from the room, crying. "She's awake! Oh thank God, she's awake!"

It was a strange thing to notice, but Estelle was keenly aware of the absence of her insatiable appetite for heroin. She was hungry—starving actually—but she wanted food, not heroin. She took a deep breath, filling her lungs with clean, fresh air. Her mind began to clear.

Kate had joined Frank in the waiting room. They froze when they heard shouting and crying from down the hall. Both of them jumped to their feet at the same time. Rose ran down the hallway and straight into Kate's arms. "She opened her eyes! She answered the nurse! She's awake!" Kate and Frank helped Rose to a chair as her knees gave way.

"Where is Jake?" Frank asked.

"He—uh, I don't know. I think he stayed in the room." Rose could barely think.

"Kate, can you go check on him?" Frank wanted to run full speed ahead to Estelle's room, but he knew he couldn't. Not yet.

Kate hurried down the hall to Estelle's room and met her husband at the door. "Kate, let me check on her first."

"Michael, Jake's still in the room with her."

"Okay, come on." They hurried in together.

The room was dimly lit and the curtains were drawn, shutting out as much sunlight as possible. Jake stood next to his mother's bed, holding her hand, tears streaming down his face. He turned to Dr. Stanovich and Kate. "She's awake! She talked to me! Please don't make me leave," he pleaded.

"I won't make you leave, son. But why don't you step over here with Kate for a moment? I need to check on your mother."

"Mom, I'm not leaving—I'll be right here. The doctor just wants to check on you." He gently released her hand.

"Jake," she pleaded, her voice dry and scratchy. "Don't leave me. Why am I here?"

"Mrs. Shannon, I'm Dr. Stanovich. You have been in the hospital for several weeks. How do you feel? Are you in pain?"

"I don't think so—maybe. It hurt when I opened my eyes—not so bad now." Each word was a struggle.

"Do you know who you are?"

She tried to laugh. "I'm Estelle, Estelle Shannon."

"Do you recognize the young man who was holding your hand?"

"My son, Jake."

"Do you remember what happened to you?"

Suddenly, the nightmare flooded her consciousness. It all came back, and tears spilled down her cheeks. "Mark Lawrence tried to kill me."

"It's okay, Estelle. He can't hurt you anymore." He turned to Kate and Jake. "She doesn't appear to have any amnesia."

"I'm starving."

"Well, that's a good sign." He smiled at Estelle. "Nurse, let's start with some broth and gelatin, just a tiny bit, and then a little more every couple of hours."

"Yes, doctor." The nurse left the room.

Dr. Stanovich checked Estelle's vitals; everything was normal. "Kate, will you stay here with Jake? I'm going to talk to her mother."

"Yes, I'll stay."

Jake went back to his mother's side. "Mom, someone is here to see you. You haven't seen her for a very long time, but she's been here with us, waiting for you to get better."

"Kate? Is it really you?" Estelle really had heard Kate in her dreams.

"Estelle." Kate took her other hand.

"I've missed you so much." Estelle looked at her friend.

"I've missed you too." Kate could barely speak.

The door opened, and the nurse came back in the room with a small dish of gelatin and some chicken broth. "Let's start with a sip of broth first."

The steaming, flavorful broth was heavenly. It soothed her dry throat and warmed her inside, and the gelatin was sweet and delicious. "Not too much this time. We will try again a little later. Maybe tomorrow you can have something a little more substantial." The nurse smiled as she gathered the cup and gelatin dish.

"Kate?" Tears ran down Estelle's cheeks.

"Estelle, what is it? You're safe; it's okay." Kate reassured her friend.

"I'm so sorry for the horrible things I said to you, and I'm sorry for cutting you out of my life. Please forgive me."

"I forgive you, Estelle. You were frightened and confused. I suppose my mother didn't help matters. You know, she was sorry she reacted the way she did. She wished we would have helped you more."

"She did?"

"Yes, she told me many things before she died."

"I'm sure she knew that my mother's heart was broken because of me—and poor Poppa. I was so selfish; I hurt them so much." Estelle sobbed.

"Estelle, if you only knew how much they loved you. They felt guilty because of what they had done—taking you and running away. But they did it to protect you from your father. Rose was young; Timothy Baker had her completely fooled and under his control. They kept in touch with some of their old neighbors in Chicago for years, but there was never any word about Rosalie. If anyone knew anything, they didn't tell. As time went by, they didn't know how to tell you about your mother. They tried to make it up to you, but I guess in the process, they sheltered you and indulged you a little too much."

"It seems we were all carrying a lot of guilt around with us. I wish I could tell them how sorry I am for causing them such pain."

"Estelle, they forgave you. And you know they absolutely adored Jake. They put both of you in God's hands before they died. They just wanted you and Jake to be happy and cared for. They never stopped loving you, and they blamed you for nothing. You know they both had health problems; you had nothing to do with their deaths."

Estelle wept, realizing Kate's words were true. Her parents had always loved her and had never blamed her for anything.

By the time Michael walked to the waiting room, Pauline, Ginny, and the Polanskis had arrived. Joe was typically a safe driver; but after Frank's call, he had made it to Ginny's school and then to the hospital in record time.

"Good, everyone is here. As you already know, Estelle is awake. I've talked with her, and there seems to be no amnesia. She knows who she is; she recognized Jake; and sadly, she remembers what happened to her. But her vitals are good," he smiled, "and she said she was starving."

They all laughed and cried at the same time.

He turned to Frank. "I know this is difficult for you, but we are going to monitor her very closely over the next few days. I would like for you to wait until I feel she can handle seeing you, and then we may have someone else break the news to her first. We must be careful with her."

Difficult? That was an understatement! Frank's insides were twisted in knots. He wanted nothing more than to run down the hall, burst through the door, and hold Estelle in his arms. "I understand, and I want what's best for her. I'll wait."

"Thank you, Frank. Now, the rest of you can take turns visiting with her. Let's keep it short though, since we don't want to wear her out." He looked at Ginny. "She needs reassurance right now—to be surrounded by people who love her. I'm going to break the rules and allow you to slip the little one in for a few minutes. This is not an ordinary situation."

"Pauline, will you take Ginny in? I'll go in after you. I really want to be alone with her if I can." Rose was still a little shaky.

"Of course, Rose."

"Pauline, Ginny, why don't you come with me then?" Dr. Stanovich turned and walked out the door.

Pauline took Ginny by the hand and followed Dr. Stanovich. "We are going to see your mommy. She's been very sick, but we can see her now."

Ginny smiled up at Pauline. "Okay!"

Dr. Stanovich opened the door to Estelle's room. None of the nurses dared say a word as they watched Pauline and Ginny follow him in.

Kate looked up as they walked in. "You have more company, so I'll be back to see you later." She kissed Estelle's hand and left the room.

"Pauline? You really are here!"

"I'm here, and I won't be leaving. But someone else is here to see you. Some strings were pulled for this visit." She lifted Ginny up and sat her on the edge of her mother's hospital bed.

"Oh, Ginny, I've missed you! I love you so much!" Estelle took the small hand in hers.

Ginny was unaccustomed to much attention from her mother, so she looked at Pauline and then answered. "I love you too, Mommy."

Estelle pulled Ginny close and hugged her.

"We are so grateful you're awake. The Polanskis are in the waiting room."

"And Rose—um—is my mother here?"

"She's barely left to bathe and change clothes. Estelle, do you remember that she was the one who found you? She helped stop the bleeding until help arrived."

"I do remember something about it. I was so cold, and I felt like I was floating away. I heard her screaming my name, crying, and praying. It was as if she kept pulling me back."

"The doctor told us that she saved your life. Had she not been there…" Pauline wasn't able to finish.

"I'd like to see her. I need to apologize for the way I've treated her."

"Oh, she'll be in here soon. I don't think anyone could drag her away from here. We have to make our visits short for the time being, so Jake, would you mind coming with Ginny and me? Your mother and grandmother need a little time alone."

"Okay. I promised I wouldn't leave her though."

"Jake, it's okay; you can come back." Estelle smiled. "I'm not going anywhere."

Jake noticed the smile. It was the way his mom used to smile at him, before things got so crazy. He felt hopeful that maybe things might really be okay. "I'll be back later. Mom, I love you."

"I love you too, Jake."

Estelle hugged Ginny one more time before her little girl slid down from the bed. Pauline took Ginny's hand, and Jake followed them out of the room. An anxious group awaited their return.

Rose stood up, calmer than she had been earlier. "How is she?"

Pauline let go of Ginny's hand. "She talked to us. She asked about you, Rose. She wants to see you."

Rose smiled as she walked down the hallway, clutching a letter in her hand. She hadn't told anyone about the letter, but she'd simply waited for the moment she could place it in her daughter's hands, hoping it would ease some of Estelle's pain. A nurse at the desk nodded, motioning for her to go in the room. Slowly, she pushed the door open and stepped inside. For a moment she held her breath and didn't move. Estelle was propped up in the bed, looking out the window. She turned her head and smiled at Rose. It was impossible for either of them to stop the tears. "Ro—Mother?" Rose ran the short distance to the bed, throwing her arms around her daughter.

Estelle's IV had been removed, so she hugged her mother close. She was a little sore, but she didn't really care. Rose pulled the chair close to Estelle's bed.

Both women were quiet until Estelle broke the silence. "I don't know where to start, but I want to apologize for the way I treated you, for keeping Jake and Ginny from you, and for the horrible things I said to you. I'm so sorry. Please forgive me."

"You don't have to apologize for anything. I've already forgiven you."

"Yes, I do. You are my mother, and you saved my life." Estelle hesitated. "How did you know I needed you?"

Rose held her hand. "I had been worried all day, and I couldn't stand it a moment longer. I had to check on you—to make sure you were okay. I prayed and prayed. When I reached the apartment building, I heard you screaming, and then I heard gunshots. Everything is a bit blurry after that. I know I ran upstairs and couldn't get your door open, so a neighbor kicked it down. I found you in the bedroom. You were so still and bleeding—there was so much blood." Her voice trailed off, and she took a deep breath. "I tried to stop the bleeding, and I held you and prayed. Then the police were there. I don't remember much after that, but somehow, I wound up at the hospital with the Polanskis and the kids."

"You held me, prayed, and called my name." Estelle shuddered as she remembered everything. "Oh God! Mark is going after Jake! He'll use him and destroy him, just like he did Ricky and me. Someone has to stop him!" Her face was white with fear.

Rose didn't want to face this situation so soon, but she saw the terror in her daughter's eyes. "Estelle, when the two of you struggled for the gun, he was shot too. He was dead when the police arrived."

"Dead? Oh my God, I'll go to prison!" Estelle wailed.

Rose jumped up and put her arms around her daughter. "No you won't! Fr—some people were aware of what Mark really did, so they came forward. The prosecutor will not file any charges, and they know it was self-defense."

"Who would have done that for me?"

Rose stood up and turned away slightly. "Well, um … they did question Jake. And, ah … some people saw the article in the newspaper. And they, ah, they came forward."

Estelle had no idea what was going on, but she knew Rose was hiding something to protect her. She decided to drop it for now. "I remember you talking to me every time you came in the room, but I thought I was dreaming. You told me a lot of stories, about when I was born and later about you." She hesitated for a moment. "Were you really … ah … were you …" She couldn't finish.

"Was I really a prostitute? Yes—yes I was. And like you, it wasn't my choice."

"My father forced you into that life when you were just a kid, didn't he?"

"Yes, he did. Of course I had to take responsibility for being stubborn and rebellious to begin with," Rose answered quietly. "But I will never regret having you—never. Do you remember the part about when I met Pauline?"

Tears trickled down Estelle's cheeks. "Yes," she almost whispered. "I remember the story of the woman taken in adultery and how it gave you hope." She squeezed her eyes shut for a moment. "Can I feel clean like you did? I never want to live that way again. I want to be a good mom again. Is there hope for me?"

"Oh, yes! Yes there is!" Rose thought her heart would burst. "There are many things you will need to face in the coming days, but you won't have to face them alone. Would you like to pray with me?"

"There is something else I have to tell you first." Tears trickled down Estelle's cheeks.

"Estelle, whatever it is, we can deal with it," Rose answered.

"When I lived with Ricky's mother, I was raped. Later I discovered I was pregnant." Estelle's voice caught in her throat. "I had an abortion; I killed my baby." Remorse overwhelmed her, and tears streamed down her face. "Are you sure there is still hope for me?"

"Yes, sweetheart, there is forgiveness and hope. Let me show you some scriptures and then we can pray." Rose pulled a Bible from the nightstand next to Estelle's bed.

Estelle stopped her mother one more time. "But I can't ask Momma and Poppa to forgive me. They're gone. You have no idea how much I hurt them—well I guess you do know."

"Yes I do, and I also know God doesn't take our loved ones away to punish us. He has so much compassion and mercy. Before we pray, I have something for you. It's a letter to you from Momma. I didn't read it. It was with some of Momma and Poppa's papers we found in your apartment." Rose handed the unopened letter to Estelle.

Estelle held the letter for a moment. She opened the envelope slowly and deliberately. The moment she saw Mary's handwriting, the tears started to flow.

My sweet Estelle,

You will read this letter when I am gone. Leaving this world no longer frightens me, but facing you with the truth does. It makes me sad to leave you, Poppa, and our precious little Jacob, but I am so very tired. I must trust God to take care of each of you. My beloved Nikola will not be far behind me, so my prayers are mostly for you and little Jacob.

I pray someday you can forgive Poppa and me for not telling you the truth. We wanted to tell you about your mother Rosalie for so many years. You are the image of her, our beautiful Rosalie, our daughter.

Rosalie was so naïve, and the man she married was an evil man who took advantage of her innocence. His name was Timothy Baker. Rosalie would not listen to us, and she would not leave him. We were desperate and afraid for you, so we took you and fled in the night. When you were safe, Poppa went back for your mother, but she and Timothy were gone. We knew she did not leave willingly.

Though it was wrong, we changed your birth certificate and moved here. Poppa made several trips back to Chicago to search for Rosalie, but there was no trace of her. We searched for years and could not find her.

I am so sorry—Poppa and I are so sorry. We always thought we would find her. As the years passed, we did not know how to tell you. In my heart, I believe our Rosalie is alive. My prayer is that she will find you.

Estelle, Poppa and I love you so very much. You have brought such joy to our lives. I am sorry for the things I said to you when you told me you were pregnant. We would not trade our little Jacob for anything in this world. He was not a mistake and neither were you.

God has forgiven us for what we have done, and we pray that you can forgive us also. Sweetheart, I am sorry to leave you so soon, but I have been sick for many years. I can only say once more how very much Poppa and I love you and Jacob. You both have made our lives worth living.

Momma

Estelle dropped the letter on her bed and wept. Rose sat in complete silence until her daughter's tears were spent. Finally, Estelle handed the letter to Rose. "Please read it. They loved us both so much."

Tears streamed down Rose's face as she read the letter her mother had written to Estelle. "She wrote a letter to me also. They understood that we all make our own mistakes. We grow and learn from them." Rose wiped her eyes.

"They didn't blame either of us for anything. They carried their own guilt for so many years, and I've wasted so much time running and feeling guilty. I think I'm ready to let go of the guilt and make a new start. I would love to read those scriptures now and pray together." Estelle took a deep breath.

Rose smiled and opened her Bible.

Rose couldn't contain her excitement when she returned to the waiting room. "She remembered everything I told her while she was in the coma." She smiled, and then her forehead wrinkled with worry. "She asked about Mark Lawrence. I didn't want to tell her, but I couldn't lie. She was frantic until I told her Mark was dead. I told her someone came forward, exposing Mark Lawrence for what he was, so she knows she isn't going to jail." Rose looked at Frank. "I almost said your name. She knows I'm hiding something, but she didn't question me further."

Her face lit up again. "She wanted to talk about what I had been through and when I met you, Pauline. She asked me to pray with her!"

Pauline practically flew out of her chair and pulled Rose into her arms. "How wonderful! God is so faithful!"

Frank found it difficult to join in the excitement. To be honest, he could only think about how Estelle would react to him when she discovered he had been alive all this time and hadn't rescued her. He smiled, but he felt sick on the inside. The powerful Frank Moretti was afraid. He was afraid that Estelle would hate him, and she would no longer want him the way he wanted her.

Within a couple of days, Estelle was able to eat solid foods, and she never left anything on her tray. Having not eaten real food for so long, everything tasted good—even if it was hospital food. She grew stronger by the day, and Dr. Stanovich was confident that she would be able to go home soon.

"The children and I moved into the apartment over Joe and Margaret's market. It's so big, and there's an extra bedroom. Will you stay with us when the doctor releases you? I don't want you to go back to your apartment," Rose pleaded.

Estelle sighed, "I don't want to go back there, and I want to be with Jake and Ginny, and with you. You know I'll have to find a job. I can't let you and the Polanskis support all of us, but I don't know who will hire me."

Rose seemed a little uncomfortable. "Estelle, sweetheart, that won't be necessary—at least not yet. Please don't worry about money. We ... ah, we are fine really. There is nothing to be concerned about. We gathered all of your things from the apartment; we didn't want you to go back there. There wasn't much: a hatbox, a small box with some documents, and a few toys and knickknacks. The clothes weren't worth keeping." Rose remembered something important and changed the subject. "When I found the letters, I took the liberty of going through all of Momma and Poppa's papers. I hope you don't mind."

"No, I had never been able to bring myself to look at them."

"I found your birth certificate too. If you use a magnifying glass, you can see that it was altered." Rose paused for a moment, "I really miss them."

"I do too. I wish you would have had a chance to say goodbye to them before they died." She paused. "I heard Poppa call your name at

Momma's graveside and cry. I didn't know who you were then, but I know they loved you."

"They were wonderful parents—to both of us." Rose paused. "I suppose we both need to heal. And in the meantime, there is no reason for you to be concerned with money or finding a job; we will be fine."

Estelle noticed Rose was still nervous and avoided looking at her. Her mother was definitely hiding something. "Ro—Mother, what are you hiding from me?"

Rose stood up. She couldn't look at her daughter. "What makes you think I'm hiding something?" Rose laughed nervously. "Oh, I need to let Pauline come in for a bit." She was a terrible liar. She kissed Estelle on the forehead and left the room.

37

Rose fretted all the way back to the waiting room. Frank had been looking for a house to buy for them. How on earth could they hide that? They couldn't simply move into a house and not tell Estelle how they came to own it. Then there were all the new clothes for the children—not to mention the toys.

When Rose walked into the waiting room, Pauline immediately noticed she was flushed and agitated. "Rose, what's wrong?"

Frank looked up from the newspaper when he heard the concern in Pauline's voice.

"We need to talk to Dr. Stanovich, and we need to do it right away. Estelle is talking about getting a job because she's worried about money. I'm telling you—she *knows* I'm hiding something. Pauline, I think it's time to let her know about Frank. Sooner or later, I'm going to say the wrong thing. I can't just lie to her—and what about when we get home? We can't expect Ginny not to say anything about her *daddy*. It's time. We have to tell her."

Frank could barely think. He had waited for this moment from the time his brother called him with the news about Estelle. Suddenly, he felt like a foolish schoolboy, fearing rejection. His stomach was in knots. What was wrong with him? He gathered his courage and stood up. "You're right. There is no reason to delay any longer. I'm going to ask one of the nurses to call Dr. Stanovich." In no time, he was out of the room.

"Oh, Pauline, I feel like I may get sick or faint. I need to sit down."

"Rose, try to be calm. We knew this day was coming, and it has to be done. We can't hide Frank from her much longer. Sooner or later he is going to lose patience—the man is completely in love with her," Pauline sighed.

"He does love her, and he loves Jake and Ginny too. Oh, I just want her to be happy—to be safe and secure," Rose replied.

"We'll just keep praying, Rose. God has brought her this far."

Frank walked back in the room. "Dr. Stanovich will be here in a while. Vince—ah, Father Vincent, is coming too." He walked to the window and stared at nothing as his mind wandered to another place, another time.

Jake sat in the back of the room listening to the adults, and he watched Frank. The man's face was pallid under his tan, and he couldn't sit or stand still. When Jake saw pure, unadulterated fear in Frank's eyes, he felt sick. What if his mom rejected Frank? Why couldn't things just be simple?

Pauline called the Polanskis, and they all decided it was best to keep Ginny at home for the time being. No one knew what the next few hours might hold.

About an hour later, Dr. Stanovich and Kate arrived with Father Vincent right behind them.

"Well, I understand it is getting more difficult to keep this situation from Estelle." Dr. Stanovich stood in the middle of the room. "Frank, I would prefer that someone else talk with Estelle first. This is going to be a shock to her. Then, she can decide if she wants to see you. Remember, Estelle is still fragile, and we need to be careful."

Frank clenched his jaw, and his lips were pressed in a thin line. He tried to hold the angry response that went through his head. "I'm trying to be patient. You must know that I want what's best for her. Who should talk to her?" He looked at Pauline and Rose.

"Pauline, if you feel comfortable doing it, I would like you to talk with her. Father Vincent may be able to clear some things up," Rose spoke up.

Pauline nodded. "Yes, I'll talk to her."

"I agree; I may be of some help," Father Vincent added.

"This isn't going to be easy. Let's pray together before we go in." Pauline looked around the room, and Father Vincent nodded in agreement.

Frank was nervous and distracted, but he stood with them as they prayed. He knew they needed prayer—*he* needed prayer right now. His future depended on what happened in that hospital room. As beads of perspiration formed on his forehead, he pulled a handkerchief from his pocket and wiped it away.

"Frank, it's going to be okay. Surely you know it was no accident that I saw the article and we're here." Father Vincent rested his hand on his younger brother's shoulder.

"I hope so," Frank whispered.

"Frank, regardless of what happens next you must be patient with Estelle. She is going to need a tremendous amount of love and support as she continues to heal. Even if she is happy to see you, it won't be easy. She has so much to deal with: guilt, rejection—Estelle needs to learn to live like a normal human being again. There will be old habits to break and new habits to form. She will need guidance and assurance—she has to learn how to love herself again. It is going to be a long road, and it may be bumpy along the way. Do you understand?" Pauline looked directly in his eyes.

"Yes, I understand."

Pauline and Father Vincent walked down the hallway. "You should go in first. She may recognize me." Father Vincent put his hat back on.

Pauline tapped on the door and opened it slowly. "Estelle, I'm glad you're awake, darling. Can we talk?"

Estelle smiled. Whatever the secrecy was about, Pauline had been elected to handle it. She didn't notice the priest until Pauline was at her bedside. She thought it was odd that he didn't remove his hat.

"You brought a priest? Am I okay?" Estelle teased.

"Of course you are. I just need to talk to you about something, and Father Vincent may be able to clear up some of the details."

Fear gripped her, and she leaned forward. "Are the kids okay? Ginny hasn't been back since that first day."

"Estelle, everyone is fine. I need to tell you something, and it's going to be quite a shock." Pauline took a deep breath. "It's about Frank."

Estelle gasped. "Frank? Do you know where he's buried? Have you found his family?"

Pauline looked up and whispered a prayer. "I don't know how to tell you this, so I'll just say it. Estelle, Frank is alive."

Alive? The room started spinning, and Estelle couldn't breathe. She felt disconnected from her body, and the color drained from her face.

"Get the doctor!" Pauline shouted to the nurse. "Estelle, try to calm down. I know it's a shock, but please let us explain."

Estelle tried to control her breathing, grabbed the bed rails, and screamed, "Explain what? He's alive? He never came back for us! He just left us!" Her shoulders shook as she sobbed, unable to hold back the tears.

Father Vincent stepped in. "Estelle, please, there are many things to explain. Frank didn't leave you—someone tried to kill him. He was beaten, shot, and left for dead; and he hovered between life and death for weeks. The men who attacked him were still out there, so we took him back to Sicily as soon as he was able to make the trip. It took months for him to recover."

He took a breath and continued, "Tony came back to the States right away and looked for you. He found Mark Lawrence, but Mark lied to him. He told Tony you had taken off with another wealthy man. Tony went from one end of the country to the other looking for you and Jake."

"You're the priest who came to Frank's house." Estelle rubbed her temples as she struggled to put the pieces together.

"I'm Frank's older brother. Tony is our younger brother."

Estelle shook her head. It was all too much. "Brothers? I thought Tony worked for Frank."

Dr. Stanovich interrupted as he hurried into the room. "How is she?"

"I'm sorry for sounding the alarm, Doctor. She's fine. It was just a complete shock for her," Pauline apologized.

Dr. Stanovich looked at his patient. She was distraught, but she wasn't in any serious distress. "I'll be right outside if you need me." He left the room.

"Estelle, there are so many things that need to be explained, and I think it would be best if Frank did that himself," Father Vincent sighed.

She sat straight up, her knuckles white as she gripped the handrails. "He's here?"

"Yes, he's been here every day since I saw the article about the shooting—he was here before you came out of the coma."

"Has he seen the kids? Does he know about Ginny?"

Pauline stroked her hair. "Yes, sweetheart. Jake was upset at first, but he settled down after hearing what happened. He and Frank are now quite close, and Ginny absolutely adores her daddy."

Estelle put her face in her hands and cried. "I don't want to see him. I don't want him to see me like this—too much has happened." She looked up. "Does he know that I went back; does he know about the men and the drugs?" She continued without waiting for an answer. "He'll hate me."

"Estelle, that isn't true. He knows that you were alone and desperate, and he knows that Mark forced you back into that life. He's been waiting day after day to see you." Father Vincent's voice was soft.

"Look at me—I look like a scarecrow! How could he want to see me? I was a junky again—a whore again!" she screamed. "He needs to go home to his wife!"

That did it. Frank was standing just outside the door with Dr. Stanovich, and he'd heard enough. Suddenly, the door flew open and hit the wall with a loud bang, startling everyone in the room. Frank stood in the doorway, his chest rose and fell as he tried to control his emotions—his yearning to be with Estelle. No one moved a muscle—no one made a sound.

He had memorized every detail of her face. She was thinner, but she was still the most beautiful woman he'd ever seen. Her eyes were wide with fear, and her lips parted as she took short quick breaths. "Bella," he whispered.

It was like the first time she saw him. He was more handsome than she remembered, and he still took her breath away. Quickly, she turned her face to the wall. "Go away, Frank. Please—go away." The words were soft and filled with pain.

"I'm not going anywhere."

She wouldn't look at him. "Don't worry I won't keep you from seeing Jake and Ginny. Just go back to your family—your wife. Please don't do this to me."

"Bella, I don't have a wife. I did, years ago, but she died giving birth to our only son. He died a short time later. I never remarried. I'm sorry I lied to you, but please let me explain."

Slowly, she turned to face him, her eyes flaming with rage. "You weren't married? You let me believe you had a wife while I was your mistress? How could you?"

"Estelle, please, this is complicated," Pauline interrupted. "You need to listen to him. Father, why don't we step out and let them talk?" Pauline and Father Vincent walked out and closed the door behind them.

"Pauline, don't leave!" Estelle panicked. Terrified of being alone with him, she trembled uncontrollably.

Frank pulled a chair close to her bed and sat down. "I'm going to tell you what happened. I can't make you forgive me, but I won't leave until I've told you everything."

She knew he wouldn't leave, so she simply nodded her head.

"Do you remember when I told you I came to America to help my uncle run his businesses after his only son died?" When Estelle nodded, Frank continued. "There was much more to the story. My cousin was murdered by a small crime organization. He had written them off as small-time punks when they demanded protection money from him. They really were small-time, but they were also cold-blooded killers. After my cousin was murdered, other businesses paid the 'protection money' and kept their mouths shut." He paused. "Tony and I wanted to hunt them down and kill them, but Vince and Madalena convinced us to let the authorities handle it."

"Madalena?" Estelle whispered.

"Madalena is my sister; she's a nun." Estelle didn't reply.

"My cousin loved America and wanted to be buried here; so while our family was here for the funeral, I spoke with the authorities and we devised a plan. Vince, Tony, Madalena, and I went undercover to help apprehend the men who killed our cousin. We even brought some of our staff from Sicily. When I first met you I was a selfish, vengeful man accustomed to having my way. I had one goal: to make the men who murdered my cousin pay. I never intended to put you and Jake in any danger. A mistress made my cover more believable and helped me look like the big-time crook I was supposed to be. Falling in love with you wasn't part of my plan, but it happened—I fell in love with you."

Frank stopped for a moment, but Estelle didn't say a word. "I had decided to tell you the truth when I returned from my last trip. I wanted to marry you and make Jake my son. Bella, we had them; it was almost over—I had one last meeting with them. The feds were going to break in and make the arrests; but those guys trusted no one, so the meeting location was changed. I had no time to call my contact with the FBI. At that point, I didn't know what to do, but I couldn't just let them walk away. I thought if nothing else, I would set my own trap. But they had plans of their own—plans to get their hands on the money they thought would be in my briefcase. I was ambushed, and I don't remember much after that point. I was told that my contact with the FBI watched me more closely than I realized and probably saved my life."

"When my family took me back to Sicily to protect me, I was in and out of consciousness for days—and at one point, like you, I was in a coma. Later, the men who ambushed me were killed in a shootout with the FBI, and the few followers they had will be old men when they get out of prison."

Frank took hold of Estelle's hand. "Bella, I never dreamed I wouldn't be able to come back to you and Jake. Even if things went wrong, I thought Tony would find you, and you would be taken care of. I was careless in my planning, and all of you suffered. Please forgive me. I never stopped loving you." He finished, but Estelle remained silent.

He stood up and sighed. "I don't know what more to say. You can let Rose or Pauline know if you want to see me again. I'm going to take care of you and the children whether you want to see me or not—and your mother too. You all need her."

She wouldn't look at him, and she still hadn't said a word. There was a lump in his throat as realization set in. The truth of what happened didn't matter; she still hated him. His heart was heavy as he sighed and turned to leave.

Estelle felt as if she was in a dream. She'd had no idea that Frank was living his own personal nightmare when they met. There had always been something about him that hadn't quite fit the "crime boss" image he had portrayed. Of course she hadn't known it was just an image—a role he had played. He was kind, thoughtful, and loving to both her and Jake. She should have known.

Suddenly, it all soaked in. He had planned to tell her the truth, propose to her, and take care of her and Jake. Frank had accepted her just as she was, and he had never judged her. He *was* the man her heart said he was. He *did* love her! She had loved him then, and she loved him now. For a moment, she watched him as he turned and walked toward the door. Maybe it would be easier to just let him go. Maybe. She hesitated. "Frank?" she spoke his name softly. He turned back, afraid he had imagined it. "Please don't leave," she whispered.

He didn't remember crossing the distance between them. He only remembered pulling her into his arms. For years, he'd dreamt of holding her again, protecting her. As she clung to him, he felt her warm breath on his throat. Their tears mingled as he kissed her face.

Estelle finally pulled back and looked directly into Frank's eyes. "Frank, none of this was your fault. Mark made sure no one could find me. He only had one goal—money—no matter who got hurt."

"But I should have protected you and Jake."

"How could you have done that when you were fighting for your life? You didn't know we were in danger. Mark took advantage of what happened, and he hunted me down. He lied—he was a mad man, and we were in his path. I have so many regrets in my life, but what I will never regret is meeting you."

"Bella, I love you, and I will never let anyone hurt you again."

Neither of them knew how long they held each other until the door opened and Pauline, Father Vincent, and Dr. Stanovich walked back in the room.

Frank kissed Estelle on the cheek and stood up. "Doctor, there's something I want to ask Estelle, but I would like her family and friends to be here. Can you arrange that?"

"Yes, just give me a moment." The doctor left the room.

"Pauline, there is a small box with my things in the waiting room. Can you bring it back with you?" Frank asked.

"Yes, I can, and we'll go help round everyone up." Pauline and Father Vincent followed the doctor out.

Estelle hated to break the spell while they waited for their family and friends, but she finally asked the question that had plagued her. "Frank, what really happened to Jerry? Mark said that you had Jerry killed."

She saw the confusion on Frank's face. "I hated him, but I didn't kill him. When my bodyguards took Jerry out of the apartment, they planned to deliver him to Mark. He was going to convince Jerry to take care of his dealings in another city, but Jerry escaped. The boys thought he was still unconscious, and they didn't watch him carefully. We assumed he went to Mark and then left town."

The color drained from Estelle's face. "Mark was one of the few people Jerry was afraid of, so he would never have gone back to him. He knew Mark would have killed him." She closed her eyes and shivered. "Jerry is still alive."

"If he is still alive, he would never chance coming back here and running into Mark."

"Oh, Frank, what if he finds out Mark is dead? Did you know that Ricky worked for Jerry? The police picked Ricky up, and he was going to cooperate so Jerry killed him. He was just a kid." She shivered slightly again. "Mark told me that Jerry started watching me when I was pregnant with Jake. He watched me until he felt the time was right."

"Does Jake know any of this?"

"No."

"At this point, I don't think it would be wise for him to know. Please don't be afraid. I'll never let him get near you again."

"He killed Lucille and Johnny Moran—he even killed his own wife! He's a monster, Frank. He'll come back. I know he will!"

Frank pulled her close and held her. "I'll protect you, Bella."

There was a knock at the door. Dr. Stanovich walked in, followed by Pauline, Rose, Jake, Ginny, Kate, Joe and Margaret Polanski, Father Vincent, and Tony. "I had to pull some strings and make a few threats to staff members, but everyone is here."

Pauline handed Frank the box he asked her to bring.

"Let's talk about happier things," Frank whispered to Estelle. He stood up, moved the chair away from Estelle's bed, and pulled out a small velvet box. Bending down on one knee, he took a deep breath. "Bella—Estelle, I knew the moment I first saw you that I couldn't let you go. I love you, and I'm willing to do whatever you wish. I'll even court you. I know we need time to heal, and I promise not to rush you. I'm willing to wait as long as it takes. I want to love you and protect you for the rest of our lives. Will you be my wife?"

She looked into his eyes. "Frank, I never stopped loving you, even when I thought you were dead; but I don't want wake up tomorrow to find that you can't live with what I've done. I've hurt everyone I ever loved. It is still a struggle for me to understand that I can be forgiven, but there's one thing I do know: I can never again live the way I did in the past. This is all new to me—this commitment I've made ..." Estelle looked down.

Frank smiled. "I made that commitment as I lay between life and death. My big brother helped me along the way. I'm not perfect, but I too am determined to never live the way I did in the past. Look at what I've done. I lied to you, and I didn't protect you. My fear is that you will hate me. In spite of that fear, I love you, and I can't just walk away. We both have so much to learn, and we will make mistakes. But look around us—our friends and family never gave up, and they are still here for us." He hesitated. "Estelle, will you marry me?"

For a moment Estelle couldn't speak. Her heart pounded. She was still afraid this was a dream. "Yes," she whispered as Frank slipped a beautiful diamond ring on her finger.

Family and friends clapped and cried. Rose and Pauline were overjoyed. Jake and Ginny ran to their mother's bedside, and Frank wrapped his arms around them.

A few minutes later, Frank handed Estelle the box he'd taken the ring box from. "I have something else for you. Tony packed everything that you weren't able to take when you and Jake fled the house that night." Estelle was curious as she removed the lid. She gasped and tears streamed down her face. "It's the jewelry you gave me for Christmas! And Momma's pearls and wedding ring!" She looked up at Frank. "You kept these even though you thought I had run away with another man?"

"I told you I never stopped loving you."

Suddenly, Jake ran to the window. "Mom, look! It's the first snow!" He pulled the drapes back farther, unveiling a pristine, almost magical landscape. Snow blanketed the ground and streets, clinging to tree branches and bushes. Huge, wet snowflakes floated to the ground. Leafless trees and drab lawns were transformed, clean and glistening in the glow of the streetlights.

Estelle's thoughts drifted back over the years. She had been trapped in darkness for so long—in a frightening nightmare that was much of her own making. It had taken a terrifying turn when she met Jerry. She had been in a freefall, spiraling out of control and running from God. She didn't understand why God cared about someone like her—someone who had done the things she had done, but she was thankful that He did. Finally, she felt clean and pure—like the first snow.

Epilogue

The healing process took time. It was a long, difficult road for Frank, Estelle, Jake, and Ginny; but their family and friends stood by them, loved them, and prayed for them.

Each one had to learn to trust again. Little by little they healed, and they grew stronger in the process.

Frank and Estelle knew Jerry Bradley was out there somewhere, and it was a haunting secret they kept from their children. They both knew if Jerry ever found them, Estelle would be in grave danger.

Frank and Estelle were married in a lovely ceremony in Pastor Williams' church in Kansas City, Missouri. Joe Polanski was honored to walk Estelle down the aisle. Estelle finally believed her new life was real when Frank placed the ring on her finger and said his vows. Then she heard the words, "I now pronounce you husband and wife."

The next morning, Frank and Estelle left to honeymoon in Venice before traveling on to Frank's village in Sicily.

Frank made arrangements for all of Estelle's family and friends to join them in Sicily, in preparation for a second ceremony. The couple was married for the second time in the village church by the priest who had known Frank for most of his life.

The second wedding was a huge affair. Frank's family was large, and no one missed the event. The church was filled with candles and exquisite floral arrangements. The attendants included Jake, Tony, three of Frank's married sisters, and several of Frank's cousins. Ginny, joined by three of Frank's younger nieces, was once again a flower girl. Two of Frank's nephews were candle lighters. As Madalena sang *Ava Maria* in her lovely soprano voice, many were moved to tears. Father Vincent prayed a beautiful blessing over the couple.

After they returned to Kansas City, Frank, Estelle, and the children attended services at Pastor Williams' church and Mass at Father Vincent's church. When the school year ended, they moved to Frank's property in the beautiful Napa Valley. It was a fresh start for Estelle and the children, away from painful memories and the people who knew Estelle from a different world. Frank insisted that Rose and Pauline move with them, and they weren't hard to convince. They had all spent too much time apart.

The Polanskis retired, hired a manager for their market, and planned to take Frank up on his offer to visit as often as possible.

Michael and Kate Stanovich promised to visit at least once a year.

Happily ever after only exists in fairy tales. Frank and Estelle would grow old together; but along with their children, they would face challenges and heartache along the way. Their faith in God and their love for one another would be tested, but would ultimately sustain them.

Acknowledgements

When my son Jared was just a boy, he offered me a tidbit of wisdom that was far beyond his years: "Mom, just do something you really like to do." Well, I loved to write! Of course I kept my day job, but I started writing. Over the years, my husband Dennis asked the same question repeatedly: "Have you been working on your book?" As I often struggled with confidence issues, the constant questions became irritating; but they worked. Years later, I finally had a rough draft of my first novel.

My Aunt Colleen volunteered her editing skills. She asked great questions and made awesome suggestions—even when she had paying gigs waiting for her expertise. Mom, who spent a lot of time in Strawberry Hill during her childhood, encouraged me and was a great help with historical details. My step-mom, Pauline, helped greatly with the initial editing process. My sisters (and best friends) Jan and Brenda and my daughters Becky and Jessica cheered me on. Each of my children, Rob, Becky, Jared, Jessica, and my daughters of the heart, Ketta, Pam, Adina, and Amanda, helped me believe I could do this. Without my family, I would never have completed *Freefall*.

A multitude of family and friends have encouraged me throughout this journey, including my brother-in-law, Bruce Jonas, who created an awesome cover concept, and my niece, Melody Jonas, who took my photo for the book and website.

Leslie Eden, my friend and a former boss, most likely has no idea how much she helped to rebuild my self-esteem. She encouraged me to believe in myself and taught me to step back and regroup when I was overwhelmed—to take it one step at a time.

I appreciate my co-workers at Stone Manufacturing who also encouraged me along the way.

Charles Fairchild, an attorney and family friend, helped me maneuver my way through contract negotiations. I would have been lost without his guidance.

Thank you to Ted Haub of Haub Photographic Studio & Gallery for the beautiful photo of my youngest daughter used on the cover.

Thankfully, Indigo River Publishing took a chance on me. Donna Melillo, my first contact and editor, also became my cheerleader and my hand-holder. Adam Tillinghast patiently offered his guidance and expertise—I'm sure I didn't always make the "patient" part easy. Dan, Kayte, and the rest of the staff worked hard to help make my book its very best. Their graphic artist must be a saint for putting up with me.

And most of all, I thank God for His guidance every step of the way!

I will be forever grateful.

About the Author

Linda Howell Betz is a descendant of Croatian immigrants who settled in the community of Strawberry Hill in Kansas City, Kansas. As a child, she loved visiting her grandparents' home and listening to stories from the "old country"—her grandparents were captivating storytellers. Linda enjoys spending time with her family and adores her four children, seven grandchildren, and the others she's taken into her heart and claimed as her own. She currently resides in Raytown, Missouri.